Richmond Public Library

3 1511 00048 2470

W9-ACN-669

F

DATE DUE

NOV 1 6 2000		
AUG 1 6 2016		

DEMCO 38-296

Richmond Public Library
35200 Division
Richmond, Michigan 48062

BAKER & TAYLOR

Balancing Act

ALSO BY ANITA RICHMOND BUNKLEY

Starlight Passage
Wild Embers
Black Gold

Balancing
Act

Anita  Richmond Bunkley

A DUTTON BOOK

DUTTON
Published by the Penguin Group
Penguin Books USA Inc., 375 Hudson Street, New York, New York 10014, U.S.A.
Penguin Books Ltd, 27 Wrights Lane, London W8 5TZ, England
Penguin Books Australia Ltd, Ringwood, Victoria, Australia
Penguin Books Canada Ltd, 10 Alcorn Avenue, Toronto, Ontario, Canada M4V 3B2
Penguin Books (N.Z.) Ltd, 182–190 Wairau Road, Auckland 10, New Zealand

Penguin Books Ltd, Registered Offices:
Harmondsworth, Middlesex, England

First published by Dutton, an imprint of Dutton Signet,
a division of Penguin Books USA Inc.
Distributed in Canada by McClelland & Stewart Inc.

First Printing, July, 1997
1 3 5 7 9 10 8 6 4 2

Copyright © Anita Richmond Bunkley, 1997
All rights reserved

REGISTERED TRADEMARK—MARCA REGISTRADA

LIBRARY OF CONGRESS CATALOGING-IN-PUBLICATION DATA
Bunkley, Anita R. (Anita Richmond)
Balancing act / Anita Richmond Bunkley.
p.   cm.
ISBN 0-525-94010-3
I. Title.
PS3552.U4715B3   1997
813'.54—dc21   96-29900
                                                    CIP

Printed in the United States of America
Set in Janson Text
Designed by Jesse Cohen

Without limiting the rights under copyright reserved above, no part of this publication may be
reproduced, stored in or introduced into a retrieval system, or transmitted, in any form, or by
any means (electronic, mechanical, photocopying, recording, or otherwise), without the prior
written permission of both the copyright owner and the above publisher of this book.

PUBLISHER'S NOTE
This is a work of fiction. Names, characters, places, and incidents either are the product of the
author's imagination or are used fictitiously, and any resemblance to actual persons, living or
dead, events, or locales is entirely coincidental.

This book is printed on acid-free paper. ∞

Balancing Act

2/98

$23 95

Baker + Taylor

PROLOGUE

July 9, 1995

The flashing neon sign above Fresca's Icehouse faded into a dim yellow blur. The man in the pickup truck blinked his weary eyes, jerking them from the rearview mirror to concentrate on what lay ahead—a deserted ribbon of asphalt highway as flat and black and warm as a cast iron griddle left out in the sun.

Too much tequila. Too many cigarettes. Too good a poker game to cut short this time, and as the faint urgings of dawn nudged the slim crescent moon from the sky, he knew he'd stayed out far too long.

But he wasn't worried. He had no one waiting for him at home, no one to answer to. He could drink as much whiskey, smoke as many cigarettes, and shuffle as many decks of cards as he wanted, then gamble away the few dollars he had in his pockets without accounting for a dime. He was completely alone, in charge of his life, and it was eating away at his soul.

When the balmy summer breeze off Galveston Bay washed him with a cool velvet touch, he almost smiled. It felt good. It smelled clean and fresh, especially after breathing the foul musty air inside

Guapo's Cantina since four o'clock yesterday afternoon. He filled his lungs with it, angling back his head to pull in long deep breaths, but the damp smell of mondo shrubs, mixed with the fragrance of blooming hibiscus, ignited memories of Rosalía. Frowning, he rolled the window up, cutting off the flow of warm coastal air and the unwanted images that flitted through his mind. He flipped the air-conditioning on high.

For almost twelve hours, he'd been able to forget her, but now her face exploded against the black canvas of his drunken mind, sizzling like a cascade of fireworks. A year had passed since Rosalía's death, yet he remained a broken man, a shattered soul. The terror that had claimed him when she died and the fury that now drove him close to madness weighed him down like a second layer of skin, keeping his heart heavy and his spirit in shreds.

All hope was gone, and he was very, very angry—not only because his life mate was dead but because of the way she had been taken from him. And this dreadful loneliness, fueled by hatred, was what had driven him back across the border today.

Rosalía's angelic face haunted him. The image of her long black hair, entwined with Mexican heather, remained branded in his mind. He felt small tears growing large in his eyes, and started to turn the truck around to go back to the smoky cantina where, for a little while at least, he'd been able to forget the wails, the cries, and the god-awful shrieks that had filled his village over one year ago.

Rosalía had lain on the ground like a toppled marble statue, lips parted, eyes fluttering slightly, so weak so quickly he'd almost missed connecting with her. But she had recognized him and smiled, then opened her rose-petal mouth wider to whisper "I love you" before simply vanishing from his life forever.

The steady stream of frigid air blowing from the dash pulled the man from his somber thoughts, forcing him alert. He squirmed in his seat, sitting more fully erect, then fiddled with the radio until he found a Spanish-language station. Lighting a Marlboro, he inhaled deeply, trying to concentrate on the twang of Moila Mariachis's gringo rendition of "La luna de amor."

The dark road curved, sloping gently away from the bay, coming to an abrupt dead end at a drought-ravished field of corn. The acres of parched stalks were brown and brittle, swaying in the breeze, touching and rustling in chaffed, scratchy whispers. He stopped the truck and blinked, trying to remember where he was. He had to make a decision—go left and enter the wide, smooth interstate to begin the long trip back toward the border, or go right and head north on Old Galveston Road where he believed the evil that had killed his Rosalía lurked among the shadows.

The man rotated the steering wheel under his palms, preparing to turn left, then stopped and looked around, not surprised that he was alone on the lonely back road.

Maybe I ought to go find it, he thought. What harm could there be in that? Impulsively, he dug into the pocket of his dirty Levi's and removed a matchbook, turned on the overhead light, and read what the bartender had scribbled inside the cover. With a deep breath, the man swung his truck to the right.

What the hell, he told himself, increasing his speed. He had to go. He had to try. There was nothing else to do.

His right foot was so heavy with tequila and lack of sleep it was numb, giving him no sense of how hard he was pressing on the accelerator, but he liked the feeling of going fast. It was as if he were flying, soaring, stretching newly found wings to fly over the bay, above the choppy dark Gulf to float forever—maybe into heaven— where he would reclaim his lovely wife.

The black night closed in tightly against the truck's windows, creating a sense of being entombed. It was nice. He felt Rosalía watching, waiting, anxious for him to join her.

At a tall chain-link fence topped with bold floodlights, he saw the blue-and-white sign he'd been looking for hanging on the front gate of a secured warehouse complex. A perverse grin split his haggard face and a gleam of decision flashed his bleary eyes. With a thrust, he smashed the accelerator to the floor and squeezed his eyes tightly closed.

He heard the crash and felt a terrible jolt as the front end of his truck burst through the gates. The metal fencing flew away, striking the roof and scraping the truck bed before clattering to the black surface of the darkened highway. The man screamed when his head slammed down against the dashboard, but he soon lay stunned and quiet, hoping for a black hole to sweep over him and pull him away from his pain.

Please let me die, he prayed, hoping it would soon be over, longing for the pleasure of resting, once again, in Rosalía's perfumed arms. Then, he knew, the dull ache in his chest would finally be gone.

But the pain throbbed viciously, savagely, making it impossible to lie still for long. Slowly, he raised his head, then slumped back against the headrest, disappointed.

The truck had struck a cement wall that surrounded one of the low white buildings behind the metal fence. He cursed aloud, furious to have been thwarted by a simple block of stone. The pain in his head burned like acid and he was prepared to go blank, to sink into that soft dark tunnel where swirling white lights would guide him to Rosalía. But nothing happened, at least not what he both prayed for and feared.

Cautiously, he opened his eyes, then shrank down into his seat, terrified. A huge plume of fire shot out from beneath the hood of the pickup truck and licked the cement wall. The man's mouth fell open in horror, then he screamed, savagely, hoarsely, stricken by the sight of streaks of orange rising higher and higher, turning the building into a tower of flames. With a hiss, the firestorm skyrocketed upward, arching like a ragged comet, then plunged down onto the next sleek building, setting it aflame.

The white-hot ball torched the warehouse, sputtering on the rooftop until the structure exploded. The flames leaped across a narrow driveway and torched the next building, then another, playing tag among the neat square structures that filled the gated complex.

In a panic, the man struggled to unfasten his seat belt while flames licked at him through a hole in the floor, igniting the legs of his pants. Yelling and tugging, he fought the metal clasp, unable to force it open.

Amazement, disappointment, and fear swept through the man as he watched the fire skim its way from one building to another, snaking along like a strip of liquid gold. With a life of its own, the yellow serpent sped through the complex, racing madly, claiming everything in its path. Sparks popped heavenward, then showered the ground as the fire churned and gnashed its way toward the road that separated the complex from a cluster of modest houses huddled in the moonlight on the other side of the fence.

There was a loud hiss, then an explosion as the first house blew apart.

The man screamed, clawing at the window, his plea for help bouncing off the windshield, mocking him with its futile ring. No one was coming. No one could save him. He watched uniformed guards running around, yelling and waving their arms, but heard nothing but a siren ringing in his ears.

The inferno inside the truck raged and roiled, evolving into a ball of fire. Closing his eyes, the man fell limp, embracing death, no longer afraid. Life was not worth living without his beautiful Rosalía.

CHAPTER I

Gray drifts of smoke filled the deserted coastal road, curling in silver wisps around the words SCANTRON SECURITY INTERNATIONAL that were painted in blue on both sides of Elise Jeffries's white Volvo. When her headlights struck the hazy curtain, she immediately slowed down, settling her hips more firmly into her seat, tensing her manicured fingers tightly around the padded steering wheel.

Staring into the murky swirl, Elise tried to stick to the middle of the road, ignoring the sense of foreboding that had descended as soon as she heard the news. The call from John Farren had come at 4:15 A.M. The ScanTron Security complex at the Tide County location had been ripped apart by a massive explosion, and the closer she got to the tall column of black smoke rising in the distance, the more intense her fear became, growing stronger with each pulse of the twin green dots that blinked incessantly in the digital clock on the dashboard of her company car.

Breaking clear of the foggy veil, she searched the blackened pre-dawn sky. Nearly two hours after the initial explosion, the fire was still raging out of control. The sight of an intense orange glow spreading over the horizon, simmering beneath waves of pitch-black smoke frightened her, and she was certain she'd underestimated the extent of the fire. It was clear that the two-hundred-acre site, the heart of ScanTron's creative operation, was now an absolute inferno.

Elise had assured her boss that she could be on the scene by five-thirty, but it was already six o'clock, and she calculated that it might take twenty more minutes to reach the scene of the explosion. Elise pressed hard on the accelerator, speeding forward in the gray half-light, heading south toward the back road that would take her straight to ScanTron's front gates.

In her hurry to get out of the house and on the scene, Elise hadn't had time to speculate on the cause of the explosion, but now that she could see how bad a fire it was, she began to look around. Fires spread quickly in this part of Texas where, in July, the flat coastal plains were covered with bone-dry brush—scorched brown by the triple-digit temperatures and droughtlike conditions that had persisted for the past three weeks. With half of the summer still waiting to unfold, the dune grass and prairie scrub that blanketed two-thirds of Tide County were as dry as well-cured hay, creating dangerous conditions in the low, isolated flats.

Elise focused on the asphalt road that used to be as familiar to her as the suburban Houston street where she now lived. Old Galveston Road had been a regular route between Flatwoods and the big city, and as a teenager, Elise had thundered back and forth over the narrow thoroughfare in her father's Chevy pickup truck many times —when the road had been no more than a ribbon of dust. She'd driven it in the dead of night, during blinding rainstorms, and usually with her best friend, Damita, as they'd set off on their rowdy adventures. Now the road seemed alien, its curves and dips and landmarks no longer appearing as she remembered.

Unfortunately, explosions, chemical spills, and toxic air alerts were an accepted by-product of living in an area thick with heavy refining industry, and so far, Flatwoods had been spared a major disaster. Elise was beginning to believe that her hometown's luck may have finally run out.

The smoke suddenly thinned. Elise sped up, disappointed to see that Global Oil had constructed a new administration building where the old palmetto grove used to be. Hard concrete pathways branched off the road like heavy limbs of a giant live oak, replacing the spiked, fan-shaped trees that had always bordered the sandy dunes. A lot had changed since Elise had driven this back road, and she wasn't happy about the way progress was tampering with the wild, raw landscape that she had roamed and explored as a child.

Perspiration slid between Elise's shoulder blades and dampened the back of her new red suit despite the blast of cold air that whooshed from the air conditioner. She fumbled inside her purse, took out a tissue, and blindly blotted moisture from her face and neck, then stopped the car to tilt the rearview mirror down. She wanted to arrive looking her corporate best—composed, makeup intact, ready to face the barrage of reporters and news cameras that had probably already descended on the devastated complex.

She leaned close to the mirror, one eye on the road as she patted her caramel cheeks, taking care not to smear her rose-petal blush, or the plum-colored Borghese lipstick she'd paid twenty dollars for. As she'd quickly slicked the latest fashion shade over her lips this morning, a pang of guilt had struck. She'd charged it, and her suit, and her new haircut to her Saks account yesterday, despite her promise to Blake that she was going to close it. They had struggled so hard to pay the account off, and now she was secretly using it again.

Well, he'll just have to get used to it, she told herself, fluffing the sides of her walnut-brown hair, enjoying the way her new haircut cupped her jawline. Sometimes it was impossible to scrimp and save and pinch pennies—at least not the way Blake would like her to. He might be a whiz at managing other people's money, she thought, but now that she was working again, she planned to spend whatever was necessary to create her new image—the corporate image John Farren expected.

After repositioning the mirror, Elise drove on, arrived at a yellow sign and rolled down the window, disappointed. A dead-end notice was stuck in the concrete driveway of Global's delivery entrance. How dare those intrusive, greedy industrialists alter the course of Old Galveston Road? Somehow it seemed sacrilegious. She'd have to circle back to the interstate, cut across the northern tip of the county, then double back toward Flatwoods, losing quite a bit of time.

It was six-thirty when Elise finally nosed her company car in at an angle behind a Tide County Fire Department vehicle. She surveyed the scene from the safety of her car, a nervous shiver running over her arms.

A tangle of fire trucks, from Tide County and neighboring counties, were parked parallel to ScanTron's tall chain-link fence and in front of the row of burning houses across the road. Each truck was topped with firemen wearing heavy protective gear, and they stood rigidly upright, training pressured streams of water onto the stubborn fires. Other firefighters scurried back and forth between the hydrants and the trucks, working the pressure gauges, tugging at the tangled hosing.

As water hit the burning warehouses and roofs of houses, it steamed and hissed, propelling charred debris skyward before plunging onto the water-soaked ground to drift into the open drainage ditches that separated Flatwoods from the roaring industrial complex.

Pieces of seared electrical wire, shredded paper, and pulverized concrete littered the ground. Bits of ash and flecks of soot fell from the sky like scorched snowflakes, clouding Elise's windshield. She pushed a button to deliver a spray of cleanser onto the dirty glass, then flicked on the wipers. It did little good—the sticky residue quickly hardened and, she noted glumly, dotted the hood of her car.

A clump of charred wood hit her windshield, and she flinched, an unexpected surge of tears brimming her eyes. Clenching her jaw, she sucked in a long, audible breath, trying to gather enough courage to get out of the car.

It was a nightmare scene. The warehouse complex was turning to ashes before her eyes. The entire northern side of the neighborhood where she had been born was a rolling wave of flames. If the firemen didn't bring the fire under control soon, she knew the southeast side, where her old home had been, would go up next.

With one hand on the door handle, she waited, unable to force herself out.

Why am I hesitating? Why so nervous? What's wrong? she wondered. Hadn't she convinced herself that she was ready to deal with the media again, face her old colleagues, and field questions from the crush of new hotshot reporters who knew nothing about her past?

Now she wasn't so sure. A knot hardened, then settled uncomfortably in the middle of her stomach. Things had to go well. They just had to. But the fact that John Farren had spoken frankly with her, warning her about Al Patterson, still rumbled through her thoughts like a runaway train.

The manager of ScanTron's Tide County complex was a loose cannon, a wild card—a longtime company employee who had neither patience nor interest in change. He was the kind of manager who had no qualms about speaking directly to the press—in violation of company policy. She had to get out of the car and get control of the situation before Al said something damaging—or stupid—that would make her job harder than it looked like it was going to be.

The warning sirens started up again. She flinched to hear the familiar wail that anyone who had grown up in the refining corridors of Tide County immediately recognized and respected. Three shorts followed by a long blast: the signal to stay inside, windows and doors tightly closed.

An exhausted firefighter stumbled past Elise's car toward an open water hydrant. He splashed water on his face, wiped sweat from his neck, then jerked his head up in relief when a seventh fire truck roared onto the scene. The exhausted firefighter raised an arm in greeting as the Tide County fire captain hurried to welcome his much-needed reinforcements, who had arrived from the adjacent county.

Assessing the situation, Elise knew immediately that ScanTron was in deep trouble. This was major. A real disaster. The explosion had ripped through every four-story building behind the gates, searing pipes, wiring, and steel framing that jutted out of the burning mass like blackened skeletal bones. The perpetual coastal wind had whipped the fire into a wall of hungry flames that jumped the road, spreading north and east, searing everything in its path. It had already leveled the first block of bungalows in Flatwoods.

Elise shuddered, remembering when an expanse of green, undeveloped land had encircled the close-knit community. Now refineries and huge petrochemical industries, who had snapped up every bit of available acreage in the county, had built their storage tanks, warehouses, and testing units as close as twenty feet away from the local residents' houses.

Elise saw a fireman leap from the top of his truck and land on a smoldering building at the edge of the property. He scooped up a frightened German shepherd that had been trapped behind the fence. Hoisting the animal up, he handed it over to a man in a bathrobe, who knelt and quieted the quivering animal. A loud cheer erupted from the crowd that had gathered under the trees on the downside of the windy inferno despite the warnings to stay inside.

The sidewalks out of danger were filled with people. Elise searched the crowd for familiar faces but saw none. With the exception of her best friend, Damita, most of the residents of Flatwoods who had been her neighbors when she was a child had either left the county or moved closer to town, as her parents had six years ago.

A thump on the passenger-side window broke into Elise's thoughts. She jerked around. A man wearing a red baseball cap was leaning over, motioning for her to get out.

"Well, somebody from headquarters finally showed," he muttered tightly as soon as Elise met him at the rear of her car. He stood with huge hands anchored on hips that squared off under a wide leather belt that was cinched with a silver Texas lone star buckle. He wore stiff creased denims, a starched white shirt, and a leather-strapped watch with a face as big and round as a silver dollar. He was solidly built, stocky but not fat, with the tightly muscled body of a man who probably never broke a sweat to maintain it. His blue eyes were hard and glinty, focused, like those of a gambler who never lost a bet. The beak of his cap stood straight up, and the wind ruffled a fringe of graying hair that stood out in tufts around its bright red rim.

Elise inhaled, then coughed, nodding her hello as smoke stung the insides of her lungs.

"I'm Al Patterson, manager of the complex," he said. "Farren told me you'd be here by five-thirty. What the hell happened? Where've you been?" His tone was terse, almost accusatory.

"Elise Jeffries," she managed, straining to speak, shaking hands with her new on-site supervisor for the duration of the assignment. "Traffic out of Houston was hell," she said, forcing a lightness into her reply. Her predictions were already coming true. Al Patterson was going to be a pain in the ass, all right. A complication she didn't need.

Al shrugged, curling his lip, making his salt-and-pepper mustache tilt to one side. "Wouldn't be the first time Farren promised me something he couldn't deliver. But . . . let's get it straight from the start, young lady. I'm not one to sit around and wait for the main office to take care of my problems. I can handle things fine. By myself." And with that, he squinted defensively, watching Elise.

She simply stared, gathering her thoughts, observing how the set of vertical lines between Al's eyebrows gradually began to deepen. The little Elise knew about Al Patterson had been gleaned from the gossipy conversations of chatty secretaries and the briefings given her by low-level supervisors at the Houston headquarters during her recent ten-day new-hire orientation.

Patterson had been in charge of the coastal complex since it was built in 1981, and had the reputation of being an independent, free-wheeling manager who skirted company policy whenever possible. John Farren tolerated Al's blustery, hands-off attitude because the Tide County facility, where innovative new security devices were created, tested, manufactured, and warehoused for shipment around the world, never failed to impact the profit margins of the company in a positive way. Al delivered on his word to local and foreign clients, on time and with little complication, whenever a contract was signed. Though he grudgingly followed affirmative action guidelines, building a loyal workforce of several hundred employees, his management team was neither racially nor gender balanced.

Al dressed like a big-city rodeo rider, shunning a coat and tie, and favoring long-sleeved western-cut shirts, leather string ties, and his dry-cleaned jeans over the conservative business suits required of ScanTron managers who worked at headquarters. Today he wore his trademark horsehair vest and lizardskin, pointy-toed cowboy boots.

Anxious for a smooth start, Elise knew better than to challenge Patterson on his own turf, but if he hadn't been the local manager, she'd have told him to go to hell. This assignment might be temporary, but he was still a member of ScanTron management, and she could not afford to take that lightly.

"Being so far from headquarters, it's easy to understand why you might feel somewhat out of the loop," she offered.

"Damn straight," Al agreed, hooking his thumbs over his belt. "That's why I learned early on to go ahead and take care of whatever needs to be done. I don't need you or any head office mouthpiece comin' down here to speak for me."

Elise rested her gaze on Al's face for a moment, forcing him to make eye contact with her. If they were going to work together on this disaster, they'd better find a level playing ground fast. Whether he liked it or not, *she* was the new media spokesperson for ScanTron Security International—well, almost—as soon as her probationary period was completed, but on the company flow charts, she was clearly Patterson's peer.

Elise gave him a knowing look, not so much hurt by his candid remarks as curious. In fact, she was secretly pleased. At least she knew where he stood on the issue of her arrival on the scene, and that would help a lot.

Forcing a hesitant smile, she reminded Al, "I'm here to help you *and* the company get through this crisis. I know it's been a hell of a morning, and there's a lot to sort out, but for now why don't you relax? Let me deal with the press, okay?"

The words had spilled out of her mouth so easily and confidently they frightened her. Relax? Was she so sure about that? What if the situation mushroomed out of control, like the Baby Kitzmiller incident had? Could she handle it this time and not panic? Did her colleagues in the media still respect her? Would they believe her? She tensed at the thought of bungling this assignment. A misstep now could stall her career—and possibly end her marriage.

Al took off his hat, revealing a nearly bald head, and mopped perspiration from his face and neck with a folded handkerchief. "Why's Farren so antsy about me talking to the press all of a sudden?" he sputtered, starting to walk away. "Been doing it for years."

Elise hurried along beside him, sloshing through a puddle of water, trying not to let on how much it hurt to get her new pumps wet. She hadn't even got her first paycheck yet, and she'd already spent it twice over to bring her corporate wardrobe up to date.

Al talked as fast as he walked. "You didn't have to come. Theresa White never set foot in my office, or in this county for that matter, the whole time she had your job."

"That may be true, but things have changed," Elise said, almost running to keep up. "From what I understand, the board of directors is putting pressure on Farren to adhere more strictly to company policy. Something about an impromptu media exchange between unauthorized personnel and a reporter at the Baltimore facility that ended up with us being sued."

"Yeah, yeah, I heard."

"So," Elise continued, "Farren is tightening up every department, starting with public affairs." She stepped over a thick white hose. "He expects all press materials, releases, statements to the media, and any discussions about this situation with anyone to come through me."

"Whatever," Al muttered, lowering his head, striding faster. "Well, missy, you sure got your work cut out for you."

The remark pierced Elise like a dagger. She drew in a short breath, clearly annoyed, but forced herself to ignore Al's condescending tone. "Who's here?" she asked, ready to get down to business.

"Channel Three's been here since four-thirty," Al replied, continuing his breakneck pace. "KKLX Radio is broadcasting live from that helicopter up there." He pointed skyward, then looked down, sidestepping a wandering cat. He added, "And those goddamned environmentalists are already mouthing off. If you want to help me, just give those hell-raisin' fanatics the kinds of answers they want and get them off my back."

"What can you tell me about the hazards? Any threats to the environment? Health?"

"Absolutely not. There was nothing toxic in those warehouses and they need to shut the hell up."

Falling into step beside Al, Elise's mind whirled as she hurried to keep up with his long-legged stride. "What about the fire? How did it start?"

"Don't know much. A pickup with Mexican plates crashed the gates at three-ten. Hit the wall in front of the main building. Blew up like a cannonball; then all hell broke loose. Every damn building in the complex was on fire when I got here."

"I see the fire jumped the fence, burned quite a few houses over there."

Al made a horizontal motion with his hand as if razing the neighborhood. "Not a house over there is worth the land it's built on, but you can bet those people are already calculating just how much they can get out of us."

Elise opened her mouth to defend the residents of Flatwoods, to let Al know that *those people* were her people—this was her hometown. The residents he had so easily criticized were just like her mother and father—hardworking, honest, and deserving of respect. She hesitated, unsure of how to phrase her reply without sounding defensive, too personally involved.

This morning, when Farren had called her, telling her to get down to the Tide County facility and handle the press, she had assured him that her familiarity with the area, her status as a daughter of Flatwoods, would work to her advantage. But she was beginning to rethink that approach. This was major. ScanTron would be in for millions, maybe tens of millions, depending on how many residents filed claims.

"Look at 'em," Patterson continued, nodding toward the cluster of people standing in front of their small brick houses. "Like vultures, ready to pounce. This is gonna cost us plenty. Those—" He stopped in midsentence, nervously eyed Elise, then continued. "Those folks over there are experts at filing claims, pretending like they got all kinds of health problems. And property damages! Jesus! They'll try to break us. Watch."

Resentment burned inside Elise, threatening to force its way into her throat. A sharp retort gathered on her tongue, but she held her peace, busying herself with adjusting the strap of the black attaché case anchored on her shoulder. For the moment, she decided, the less said, the better. There were more pressing matters to tend to than Al Patterson's opinion of his complex's neighbors.

At a side street facing away from the fire, they turned and headed down Thornhill Road, the street farthest from the blaze. They walked toward what appeared to be a press command center that had sprung up on one of the lawns.

"Who was driving the pickup?" Elise asked, steering away from the subject of property damages.

He continued to walk briskly, as if trying to get away from her, and didn't glance back as he answered. "Anybody's guess. Probably an illegal. There's a bunch of 'em working the fields over in Angleton."

"Deliberate? Accident?" Elise rushed to ask, eyeing the TV cameras that were already swinging her way. She had to get as much from Al as she could before facing the reporters, and it didn't sound like he had much to give.

At the beginning of any emergency, things were usually chaotic and few facts were available, but the more details she had that she could rely on, the less chance she had of making a mistake, the kind of slip of the tongue that was impossible to repair. The kind that had nearly destroyed her not too long ago.

"Male? Female?" she prompted.

Al stopped abruptly, turned, and spoke in a low voice, forcing Elise to step nearer. "Can't tell. Whoever it was burned like a cow chip tossed on a campfire."

Elise flinched at Al's vivid description. "Any injuries reported yet?"

"Two kids. Burned pretty bad. They were rushed to League City's burn unit."

"God," Elise groaned, "Let's hope the injuries stay low."

Al continued. "The sheriff's running a check on the plates on the truck. They have a feeling it was stolen. Probably some wetback—" Al broke off, glancing at the throng of reporters approaching on his left. "Here they come. I'm outta here. Farren hired *you* to talk to 'em, so I suggest you get busy and earn your pay." He strode off toward a white van that had the words ScanTron Security painted on its side.

"Wait a minute." Elise stopped him. "What's the setup for claims? Procedures for damage reports?" The media was one thing, but the public deserved assistance. She could use some local backup. Why the devil couldn't he help with that?

Al jogged back and thrust a stack of crumpled papers at her. "Here. Standard instructions for dealing with emergencies down here. Just pass 'em out. Stonewall the hard stuff. Buy us some time 'cause it's gonna get sticky. Real sticky."

"Yeah . . . thanks," Elise murmured vaguely, smoothing the wrinkles from the papers.

Al lifted his hand, index finger pointed at Elise. "Staff briefing at eight-thirty. Be there."

"Where?" she called out over the wail of an ambulance siren.

"Had to set up temporary offices in the old JCPenney catalog store. Corner of Main and—"

"Third. I know," Elise finished, lowering her eyes as the ambulance screeched to a halt at the end of the street.

CHAPTER 2

The reporters turned from Elise and rushed toward the red-and-white emergency vehicle that screeched to a halt at the curb, its flashing blue lights casting an eerie sheen over the frightened people wandering the streets.

Wails of disbelief penetrated the hissing sound of water hitting the roofs of the burning houses, competing with the crash and splinter of wood and concrete tumbling to the ground. Outside their homes, people sobbed like graveside mourners. Others watched the fire totally mute, stunned into silence by the horror of seeing their possessions go up in flames. And others shouted in venomous protest, hurling angry threats at ScanTron.

Billowing black clouds surged upward, staining the pale gray sky, fusing above their heads like huge caps of ebony mushrooms. Elise pressed a hand to her mouth, trying to gain control, more terrified by the pain the people were in than by the destructive claw of the fire, which raged orange-red and hungry, fueling dense waves of smoke.

People forced from their homes stared at the real-life nightmare that had jerked them from their beds, shattering the sense of safety that had followed them into their dreams. Men, women, children, and pets. Neighbors and strangers were milling around in bathrobes, some shirtless, some shoeless, many with blankets clutched around their shoulders. Children in hastily pulled on clothing, unbuttoned and hanging loose, cried and gaped at the conflagration. All seemed unable to believe what had happened to them.

Gulping the strong stench of charred air, Elise tensed the muscles in her stomach, stiffening her spine, unwilling to let her emotions take over. As much as she felt like adding her own shouts of protest to the cries of the people, she knew she couldn't. John Farren had hired her to bring an image of a concerned, sympathetic, and well-run company to those now huddled in fear. As media spokesperson for ScanTron Security, Elise was the public's link to the company and its board of directors. She had to be professional. She wasn't about to let ScanTron down.

Elise looked in the direction that the paramedics had gone, scanning the crowd before pushing herself to the front of a knot of people who were quietly sobbing. With a jolt, she stopped and looked down. An elderly woman was lying on the ground and she looked as if she were dead.

There was barely enough space on the sidewalk for the paramedics to examine the woman. One of them shouted for the crowd to move back, waving his arms, forcing the frightened residents of Flatwoods to reluctantly edge aside. Moving onto their neighbors' grass, they trampled a FOR SALE sign that had been stuck in the lawn.

The two men in white knelt and began checking the woman's vital signs. After securing an oxygen mask over the victim's nose, one attendant told the man holding the lady's hand that she was suffering from smoke inhalation and was in shock. When they lifted the woman onto a litter and started toward the ambulance, the elderly man followed, climbing in to sit beside her.

"What's wrong with her?" someone shouted.

"Probably sick from what's burning in those warehouses," a tearful woman in the crowd replied.

"Where are you taking her?" A *Chronicle* reporter yelled at the ambulance driver.

"The Tide County Clinic," one of the paramedics answered. He slammed the rear doors shut, went to the front of the ambulance, and climbed in.

"Is she gonna die?" a little girl sobbed, pressing close to her mother.

"Shh . . . ," the mother hissed, eyes riveted to the red-and-white double doors. "Nobody's talking about dying. Grandma will be fine."

The little girl broke into a howl.

The siren's scream started up again, intensifying as the blue lights began to flash. The ambulance sped off down the road.

Elise stepped away from the crowd, shaken by what she'd just witnessed, dreading the questions she knew would soon be hurled at her.

"I don't know what's burning, but it's making me sick, too," a man grumbled, holding his stomach.

Elise looked over at the man and was about to say something to him when she noticed three TV cameramen at her side, lenses trained on her face.

A gaggle of reporters advanced closer, microphones in hand, followed by a throng of locals.

"Are you with ScanTron?"

Masking apprehension with a somber expression of confidence, Elise acknowledged the reporters. "Yes. I'm Elise Jeffries, media spokesperson for ScanTron Security International."

"There are a lot of sick people around here. A lady just passed out," a fast-talking newspaper reporter said. "And I understand two children were severely burned."

"Yes," Elise acknowledged. "The more serious cases have been taken to the burn unit at League City Hospital. The county clinic is handling other, less serious, medical problems."

"What can you tell us about this fire and explosion?" a reporter asked.

"I can summarize what I know so far. At approximately three-fifty-five this morning a truck crashed into the entrance gates and exploded. The security guards and all of the night shift personnel at the facility managed to get out unharmed."

A *Chronicle* reporter jumped in and yelled, "Has the identity of the driver who crashed the gates been verified?"

"No. Not yet," Elise said. "That may take some time due to the condition of the body." She paused as reporters scribbled in their notepads. "Our main concern now is that the fire department get the fire extinguished as quickly as possible; then a full-scale investigation can be initiated."

"Any motive yet?"

"No," Elise replied. "The fire department will conduct a full investigation."

"What exactly was stored in those warehouses?" a tall blond woman wearing large glasses and a press tag that said the *Leader* asked bluntly.

"This was our research facility where new security devices and products were developed. But the majority of the buildings at this complex were warehouses, filled with inventory earmarked for our overseas clients. Computerized, high-tech, state-of-the-art systems were stored here. Quite a loss for ScanTron. Also, there were various types of plastics, wires, metals—the materials needed to put the internal components and exteriors together of many ScanTron security systems." Elise spoke with authority, though the looks of skepticism on the faces of the reporters was unnerving. She'd toured the complex as part of her orientation and knew what she was talking about. Resentment flared and she silently challenged the reporters to prove her wrong.

"What kinds of toxins or chemicals were used at this facility?" another reporter asked.

"Nothing toxic on the premises."

"But people have been complaining of nausea, headaches, dizziness. What could cause these symptoms except something terribly harmful?"

Elise gritted her teeth, trying to conceal her irritation. "Let me again assure everyone, especially the residents of Flatwoods, that

ScanTron has never warehoused any chemicals, controlled substances, or hazardous materials at this location."

The reporters began shouting questions, waving their notebooks
and microphones to get her attention. She answered each one quickly,
cleanly, as she'd been trained to do, sticking to three key points:
expressions of regret and concern, assurances that all safety measures
had been followed, and her understanding that all danger in the situation was under control. Careful not to overexplain or attempt to
"prove" her points, Elise gave the reporters exactly what she expected
them to put on the air.

Glancing over their heads, she searched for a friendly face, but
her spirits quickly sagged. Damita was not there to support her, or
at least make her feel less the enemy. Elise looked toward the back
side of the residential area where squat brick bungalows wrapped behind the complex. Because of the northern drift of the coastal winds,
the flames that had jumped the fence and crossed the road had not
claimed the back section of Flatwoods. It looked as if Thornhill Road
would be spared, but Elise still worried that Damita, who lived alone,
might be trapped or stranded, in trouble.

The crowd grew restless, churning in agitation. One man turned
surly and shoved his way to the front of the crowd, demanding Elise
take the blame for everything that had happened.

Beginning to feel nervous, she almost snapped but checked herself
and calmly addressed his concerns. "ScanTron will cooperate with
the local, state, and federal agencies who may become involved in
investigating this regretful accident, but I cannot speculate on culpability."

The pressure increased with each question Elise answered, and
she fielded them as coolly and professionally as she could. But the
residents were demanding hard answers, and she began to think she
might have made a mistake by assuring Farren that she could handle
this assignment. These were people among whom she had thought
she'd feel comfortable—with whom she hoped to have immediate
rapport and support, but she didn't see a hint of sympathy on any of
the faces or feel the least bit welcome.

"That's easy for you to say," a local man spoke up. "I've been living in constant fear since those warehouses were built. It's bad enough with that Global refinery right down the road. But this?" He pointed across the street. "In our faces! It's hell, lady. Half of our neighborhood has gone up in flames. Poof. We're homeless. And God only knows what we're breathing. Probably standing under a cloud of poison right now."

Elise noticed that the cameras were now focused on the man, no longer interested in what she had to say.

"Nobody listened to us," he went on. "We fought the construction of that big Saturn Chemical plant out on Highway Eight, and lost. We picketed ScanTron when those warehouses were proposed sixteen years ago, and lost again. Now look at what's happened."

Elise's heart drummed in her chest, pounding her ribs like the rush of water from the thick fire hoses that was smothering the stubborn flames. The man reminded her very much of her father with his silver hair and chestnut-colored face. Confrontations like this were expected, and she would not dodge responsibility, but the hatred in the man's eyes was threatening.

Hoping she didn't sound patronizing, Elise could only manage, "I understand how you feel."

"Do you suspect arson? Terrorists? And why would anyone target this complex?" A smooth voice with a trace of a Spanish accent rose above the noise.

Elise froze. There was no mistaking that voice. She searched the rapidly growing crowd. There he was. Carlos Rico. Standing at the outer edges of the gathering, his cameraman at his side.

In the smoky morning light his hard green eyes shone like faceted emeralds in his deeply tanned face. Jet-black hair, waving gently from a broad, intelligent forehead, curled slightly behind his ears and feathered the edges of his white shirt collar. He had a glossy, picture-perfect look about him—all gleaming white teeth and sculpted profile, and Elise knew immediately he'd been under the knife—probably to enhance his ratings as much as the chiseled planes of his photogenic face. And his clothes had never been quite so flamboyantly accessorized or expensively tailored, she knew.

When a smirk angled Carlos's full lips, Elise was struck by how polished he'd become. His investigative show, *The Inside Story*, had hit the number one spot in the local ratings last year, and as far as she knew, was still holding firm. A big change since those early days when Carlos Rico had been a longhaired, slightly overweight journalist with an eye for the ladies and a nose for hard news. She remembered the years of discouragment and rejection he'd suffered through while trying to get the pilot for his television show in front of potential sponsors.

They had worked together as peers when he'd been a scuffy street reporter for Channel 3 dogging her for insider news about the celebrities who routinely checked into Trinity Hospital, hoping to stay incognito. Twice they'd labored together over acoustics, lighting, and programming details for the annual Trinity Hospital Ball, carried live on Channel 3. Carlos, who had started out working the crowd to provide color for the broadcast of the fund-raiser, was now billed as the celebrity emcee.

Elise glared at the reporter, seeing a stranger. Unfortunately, it was the same stranger she'd faced two years ago in court.

He was standing with an arrogant, cocksure tilt to his head, the hand holding the microphone pressed against his trim, athletic body. It was the same seductive expression that had mesmerized Elise the last time she saw him, and had influenced every female juror in the courtroom the day he leveled her world.

She drew in a short breath and held it. Pulling back her shoulders, she shifted to face him fully, even managing to give him a professional nod of recognition, despite her urge to slap the smirk off his face.

"The motivation of the driver and the exact cause of the crash, Mr. Rico," she said evenly, "have not been determined. If you want more details, perhaps the sheriff or the county fire chief over there"—she tilted her head toward a nearby fire truck where the chief was standing with a radio reporter, answering questions on a live remote broadcast—"may be willing to talk to you."

"What makes you so sure the people living here are not in any danger? An awful lot of them are sick," Carlos pressed.

Elise burned beneath his deliberate attempt to make things difficult for her. Though it was a valid question, and she'd expected to hear it, it was the way Carlos asked that made her blood run hot. "We deeply regret this accident, and anyone experiencing health-related problems should go immediately to the county emergency clinic."

"Where is Mr. Patterson? Why can't he explain in more detail what's been going on behind those fences?" Carlos insisted.

Before Elise could answer, the mother with the little girl rushed forward, positioning herself in front of Carlos, facing Elise. "I want to talk to the manager, too! My mother is in the hospital . . . maybe dying, and you—you stand here and tell us not to worry! Lady, are you crazy? Who knows what we're breathing? What's killed our gardens and poisoned our water? I want some answers. Now!"

Rico and the other TV reporters stepped back to give the cameramen room to capture the distraught woman's outburst on film. "Our houses are burned. Our vegetable gardens ruined. All of us will end up dead before this day is over!" she shouted.

A murmur of agreement rumbled through the onlookers.

"Please," Elise started, trying to get the woman's attention, alert to the fact that the cameras were rolling. "I regret that your mother was one of those affected, but I beg you to remain calm." She looked into the sea of anxious faces, willing them to trust her. "All damages to health or property that have resulted from this fire will be addressed."

"What are you hiding from us?"

"Nothing. As in all accidents like this, the proper authorities will be conducting extensive tests, and as soon as more detailed information is available, it will be released to you. For now, please follow the emergency procedures on the flyers you've been given, but until more facts are known, I cannot speculate on the cause of the fire or any other issues related to this unfortunate accident."

"Unfortunate accident?" Carlos stated, squinting skeptically at Elise. "In the middle of nowhere a pickup truck runs off a deserted road and blows up a security facility. Please!" With an aggressive step, he moved closer. "Ms. Jeffries . . . does that make sense to you?"

Her distrust of Carlos flared, then settled sourly on the tip of her tongue. She resented his smart-ass remark but wasn't about to let him bait her into a combative discussion. She clamped her lips shut, refusing to answer, relieved when a lady shouted, "What about property damages? Health claims?"

Elise nodded, then added, "Please take one of these flyers. They detail the procedural guidelines for those who need assistance." She held up the batch of crumpled emergency instruction flyers that Al had pressed on her. "Those who've suffered property damage should file claims with their insurance companies first, then submit damage estimates to the local ScanTron office. We will begin accepting claims immediately and do all we can to help things get back to normal."

"Normal?" an elderly man piped up. "Ain't nothin' been normal around here since you people built those warehouses in our front door. What you talkin' 'bout, lady? What you call normal, huh?"

Elise froze as she looked at the wide-eyed man who was nervously tugging his bathrobe belt tighter around his slight frame. The crowd parted to make room for him to move closer.

"I'm Julius Tarrant," he said proudly. "Mr. Tarrant. Don't you remember me? I remember you. Used to call you Leesie. You lived next door."

Elise prayed he recognized her as friend, not foe, in this awful situation.

"You're Fred Camden's little girl, right?" He craned his neck to see her more clearly.

Elise nodded.

Mr. Tarrant sadly shook his head. "So you are. And just what are you doin' takin' up for these devils who've messed up your old neighborhood?"

Resignation dulled the old man's eyes, and his body sagged with disappointment. Elise wanted to place an arm across his shoulders and reassure him that she, too, was hurt and frightened by what had happened. But instead of softening, she laced trembling fingers into a sweaty web, clenched her hands together, inhaled deeply, then said, "I'm not here to take up for anyone, Mr. Tarrant. I'm here as a representative of ScanTron Security . . . and I'm telling you the truth."

"And what *is* the truth?" Carlos inserted, gesturing for his cameraman to zoom in on Elise.

Without batting an eyelash, she faced the round glass lens. "The truth is that ScanTron Security International is a responsible company that cares as much about preserving the environment as about protecting its neighbors. We plan to do everything possible to minimize the discomfort that the residents of Flatwoods are experiencing."

"How?"

"A temporary assistance center will be set up in the area to assist anyone who needs help getting their lives back to normal." Several people pushed forward to hear what she had to say. "And," she went on, "there are Red Cross shelters set up at Union High School and at the First Baptist Church in town. The County Assistance League will help with food and personal items you may need until you can get back in your homes."

"What really happened?" A man shouted, fists anchored at his waist.

"A truck crashed the gates. Why, I can't speculate on, sir," Elise replied. "An in-depth statement will be forthcoming when the findings of our investigation are available. Please understand. ScanTron continually strives to meet all industry safety standards, and our record, so far, has been very good. But, for now, that's all I can say. An update will be released from our office later this afternoon. Thank you."

Several reporters called out more questions, but Elise ignored them, hurrying back to her car.

Slamming the door, she sat rigidly for a moment, then started the engine, looking into the rearview mirror as she backed up. Water from the huge fire hoses had drained from the burning site to darken the sidewalks and slick the asphalt road. People mingled on lawns, hands pressed to lips, unsure about what to do, frowning suspiciously at the back of Elise's car.

The old man's words pricked her mind like the sting of gravel that flew up and struck the sides of her car. She sped away, a painful lump swelling deep in her throat.

Driving toward the center of town, Elise wanted to lay her head on the steering wheel and cry. The suspicious way she'd been received and the terrifying sight of Flatwoods turning to ashes before her eyes had touched her more deeply than she'd expected. Things had changed a lot in the fifteen years since she'd called the community home, but her emotional connection to the old neighborhood was still very much alive.

Growing up in a place where everyone had known her and watched out for her had been comforting, though somewhat claustrophobic. As a young woman, Elise had burned with anticipation to leave, to go were she could be a stranger and do all the crazy things young people did without worrying about being immediately recognized and betrayed to her parents. When she'd gone off to college to experience big-city living in Dallas, she'd reveled in the anonymity found on the sprawling campus of Southern Methodist University.

She bit her lip, worried, longing for the unconditional trust and familial support that she'd thought she would receive from the people who now, it seemed, didn't believe a word she said.

When Elise had lived in Flatwoods, it had been so far from town people had called her neighborhood the boonies, but now it was surrounded by industrial plants, strip shopping centers, and a scattering of small businesses that lined the road to town.

Passing the tall entrance gates of the Global Oil refinery, Elise slowed down. The monstrous plant had been the major employer in Tide County for more than forty years. Elise's father, and the fathers of most of her friends, had worked at Global at one time or another, as had the majority of the men and women of Flatwoods.

But times had been different then, she thought. Flatwoods had been a lively, close-knit all-black community where everyone knew exactly what was going on in every square brick house in the area, and no one worried about fire, pollution, or toxic contamination. It had been a nice place to live, except during the warm summer months when the wind blew off the Gulf in a decidedly northeastern direction, blanketing the area with rotten smells belched into the air by the string of smokestacks along the coast. Sometimes the stench had been so bad that elderly people, especially those with respiratory problems, had been warned to stay indoors.

The smell of industrial progress jolted a memory to mind—a memory she'd thought long buried—the day she and her best friend, Damita, had cut school to take a joy ride into Beaumont.

The trouble they'd gotten into had taken years to forget, and the incident rushed back with burning shame. Elise flushed as she recalled the horror she'd felt when the heavy hand of the security guard at East Shore Variety Store had closed gently, yet firmly, over her shoulder. Stopped outside the five-and-dime with a cheap charm bracelet tucked inside her sweaty palm, she'd wanted to die. Right there. And never go home. But the scary expression on the man's plum-colored face had not been nearly as terrifying as the disappointment on her mother's or the warning from the judge when he turned her and Damita over to their parents, ordering the two to stay out of trouble.

Elise had been twelve years old, foolishly adventurous, and dreadfully naive about her misguided show of courage in taking up Damita's dare. The two girls had been grounded, unable to talk to or see each other for a month. But once the ordeal had faded, the girls had emerged closer than ever, promising to guard the darkest secret of their young lives forever, never speaking of the incident again.

Elise sped up, pushing down the highway, leaving Flatwoods behind. She zipped past the entrance to Jupiter Plastics, where her mother had worked as a file clerk during Elise's senior year in high school to earn money for the college wardrobe she was going to need. They'd gone into Houston to buy it, and she still had the red polka-dot dress with the low scooped neck they'd splurged on at Neiman Marcus.

In those days, work in the refineries and industrial plants had been steady, the pay had been good, and the benefits liberal—everything necessary to make life easier. But at what cost? Elise now wondered, realizing how much the tiny community had suffered. The faces she had left behind were the bewildered faces of strangers: black, white, Asian, Hispanic. And they were angry, frightened, and wary of her.

Leaning her head back against the seat, Elise reviewed her comments to the press, wishing she *could* have given the reporters and the worried residents more details. A tug of guilt pulled deep inside, but she willed it away, comforted by the fact that she had maintained her cool. Experience and training had kept her on target, successfully avoiding speculation on the cause or the solution of the troubles now facing her employer. It would have been dangerous and irresponsible to make promises that ScanTron could not keep, or infer action that she knew the company could never take.

Elise struggled to corral her emotions, not daring to let them surface. She'd let her feelings dictate her course of action once before, and had paid a very high price.

At the main highway, Elise crossed the ancient railroad track that separated the town from the industrial area, and turned left onto Deerpark Road. Arriving at a four-way stop, she looked to her left, saddened by the ghostly appearance of Main Street, the arrow-straight ribbon that anchored the county seat.

Tide County was divided into two distinctly different areas—Flatwoods, smack in the middle of the heavy refining corridor, mainly populated by blue-collar laborers and weary senior citizens—and Tide City, the county seat, which at one time had claimed twenty-five thousand citizens. Now she guessed fewer than a thousand resided in town.

When Elise had been young, the county seat was a hub of activity, its wide flat streets lined with shops and businesses, its enterprising citizens rapidly becoming prosperous. The town had once boasted sixteen restaurants, seven banks, the biggest farmers market in a three-county area, and a stretch of coastal beachfront that had enticed visitors from around the nation, coaxing them to lie in the sand and stare out across the bay.

Moving toward the only red light still in operation, Elise grew somber. The place was a virtual ghost town. It reminded her of an amusement park suddenly emptied of visitors, void of the gaiety and crush of people that provided the energy to make the place alive. Windows and doors of shops and businesses were boarded over, many splashed with colorful gang graffiti, though Elise doubted that Tide

City had enough teenagers to make up anything vaguely resembling a gang. The lone gas station at the end of the street was the only place where she saw any activity.

When oil prices had been good and production high, the refinery owners and plant workers had had lots of cash to spend. The oil company executives had built big colonial-style houses, embellishing them with fancy iron grillwork, lattice-covered gazebos, swimming pools, patios, and profusely blooming flower gardens of roses, azaleas, and vivid crepe myrtles.

But when the bottom fell out of the oil industry in the eighties and the overextended petrochemical barons went bust, they moved on, leaving their monstrous mansions empty, abandoning the sun-splashed coast, and letting the town rot and decay.

Recently, a struggling movement to rejuvenate the town had begun, attracting a few brave souls who could afford to buy and restore the run-down estates. Twenty years ago, the blacks and Hispanics now residing in the houses Elise was driving past would never have dreamed of entering the heavy front doors that faced the empty street. Not so long ago, and Elise could still remember, very few people of color, unless they were domestics, even ventured into town on any day other than Saturday.

At the corner of Main and Third, Elise pulled into a parking space in front of the old JCPenney catalog store, stopping next to Al Patterson's ScanTron van. She sat, engine running, while she checked the time. Forty-five minutes until the staff meeting. She touched her cheek. It was smudged with soot and she knew her clothes and hair must reek of smoke.

Impulsively she backed out, drove west three blocks, then turned onto Valencia Street, stopping in front of a three-story, white-pillared house that was fronted by a splashy tangle of wild yellow roses, vibrant old-fashioned zinnias, and a low garden filled with a variety of herbs. Elise got out and waved at her father, who was sitting on the steps of the wide shady porch.

CHAPTER 3

Myra Camden snapped a sprig of mint from the hanging basket in her sunny kitchen window and stuck it into the glass of iced tea she had fixed for her daughter. Circling the island cooking station in her newly remodeled kitchen, she handed the glass to Elise.

"Think you're going to like this new job?" Myra asked.

"Oh, yes," Elise said in breathy relief. "It's great to be working full-time again—and for such a good company, too." A smile brightened her face, erasing the tension that had settled on it the moment she'd answered her phone that morning. "Finally. Things are looking up."

"I'll bet Blake is happy," Myra ventured, watching her daughter closely.

Elise nodded, thinking. Sure, Blake had been overjoyed when she'd snagged the position at ScanTron after nearly a year of searching for a permanent job, but she wondered if his joy was due to the fact that they could finally get out of debt or because she was getting her career back on track. She moved from the bar and sat down at the kitchen table, which was set with her mother's cheery daisy-patterned dishes.

"Blake's been so good about everything," she told Myra. "It's been a tough year, but the pressure is easing now that I can pull my own weight again."

"You'll do fine. You and Blake. I'm so proud of you, honey." Myra put a slender finger to her copper-hued cheek, admiring her only child. "Setbacks are to be expected in any marriage. It takes faith and time to get through those difficult periods. But they don't last forever, not if you don't let them."

A youthful fifty-seven, Myra was still dressed in the aqua jogging suit she faithfully wore for her early morning walks. Rain or shine, winter and summer, she never wavered from her routine. Tide County had been her home for over forty years and she'd probably walked over every inch of it. Removing the terrycloth headband that held her springy auburn curls off her forehead, she delicately changed the subject.

"That was an awful thing for old man Tarrant to say to you this morning. I saw him. The old devil. He ought to be ashamed. Talking to you like that. And on television, too."

With a shrug, Elise dismissed the encounter. "I didn't take it personally, Mom. In this job, I have to take the heat. That's what I'm paid to do. Anyway, I understand where he was coming from. He was frightened. Angry. Feeling betrayed." Elise sipped the cool amber tea, anxious to banish the taste of smoke from her mouth and the testy encounter from her mind.

Though she'd washed her face and hands, repaired her makeup, and replaced her silk blouse with one of her mother's, a paisley print that matched her new red jacket, she still smelled the stench of the fire and her hair reeked as well.

Pleasant scents were calming to Elise, but bad ones truly unnerved her. Unwinding after a difficult day usually meant puttering around in her backyard, where she grew herbs, flowering hibiscus, and fragrant old-fashioned roses in her tiny, well-plotted garden. Her home was filled with fresh-cut flowers and her bathroom shelves were crowded with scents, oils, perfumed lotions, and delicious-smelling potpourri that she proudly made herself. Elise drank teas brewed from her own plants and surrounded herself with fragrance—an indulgence she never apologized for, but for the past year since she'd been so cautious about spending money, she had not dared to enter her local garden center or visit Regal Bath Shop at the mall. She couldn't wait to get home and take a long hot shower.

Myra put the pitcher of tea back into the refrigerator, picked up her mug of coffee, and studied her daughter. "I feel sorry for Mr. Tarrant . . . for everybody in Flatwoods, for that matter. But there's little they can do. All the open land and green space they used to have is gone. ScanTron took advantage, building right up to those people's front doors. You watch, that entire area will soon belong to ScanTron, or some other company. It'll be fully developed within the next five years. The big boys will squeeze everybody out. Probably wind up in public housing, that's what all this is leading to."

Elise wrapped a paper napkin around the cool, wet glass and set it on the kitchen table. "Not a very pleasant thought, but I guess it could happen." She took another long swallow of tea, then checked the kitchen clock, glad to see that she had a few minutes more to spend with her mother before heading over to the staff meeting.

"Did you see Damita this morning?" her mother asked.

"No. But you know, her house is on the south side, almost behind the warehouse complex where the fire didn't reach. I hope she's okay."

"You know how cautious and alert she is," Myra said. "Damita was probably the first one to sign in at the Red Cross shelter."

"I hope so."

"The TV coverage has been pretty heavy. They've been breaking in and out of programs all morning. The neighborhood looked awful."

"It was a terrible sight, all right. Especially for those on Baymark Road. That fire just swept through that place like a steamroller leveling sand. The roofs were gone. Just shells were left standing by the time I got there. There'll be a lot of claims from this fire."

"Yeah," Myra said. "That means insurance around here will probably go sky-high. Another reason for folks to move out."

Elise didn't answer, glancing out the window, her thoughts still on the only person in Tide County whom she could call a friend. She hoped Damita was safe. She'd call as soon as the staff meeting was over.

The two girls had shared Barbie doll clothes, chalk, and broken crayons on the dusty sidewalks of Flatwoods, and though they had followed very different paths in life as adults, they had managed to keep their friendship intact. They burned up the phone lines on a regular basis but weren't always able to get together, and sometimes a year might pass without a hug or a face-to-face chat, but the Christmas cards, birthday greetings, and phone calls every Sunday morning bridged the distance between them.

Myra fluffed out her thick auburn curls, then tugged the top of her jogging suit down over her slender hips. "Come to think of it, I haven't seen Damita lately. I usually run into her at Price Mart or at the bank, but she hasn't been out much, I guess."

"I'll track her down before I head home tonight," Elise said, unable to admit that she desperately wanted Damita's opinion on the situation facing the residents of Flatwoods. Would she treat her differently because she was the spokesperson for the company that everyone in Flatwoods believed was out to do them harm? Whenever Elise needed a jolt of reality or help in making an important decision, she turned to Damita, and if Elise ever needed an unbiased take on what she'd got herself into, it was now.

Myra interrupted Elise's thoughts, her comment bringing Elise's predicament keenly into focus. "You handled yourself very well this morning."

"Think so? Really, Mom? How'd I come across?" she asked, anxious to know if Carlos Rico had made her look like a fool.

"You came across fine. Very professional and to the point," Myra replied. "Just as I would expect you to do. I'm sure your boss is pleased. It could have gotten out of hand, you know."

Elise sensed her mother dodging the obvious. "You mean Carlos could have pushed me over the edge, don't you?"

"Well, I did notice who was asking the most difficult questions." Myra wiped her hands on a dish towel, then clamped them together at her waist as if Elise's question had caused her pain. "Of course, he's a lowlife, Carlos Rico. I refuse to watch his television program, and if he hadn't been interviewing you, I'd have changed channels immediately. He was his usual arrogant self. God, he must think he's Geraldo or something. All that posturing. Such an aggressive, obnoxious man." Then suddenly Myra grinned. "I'll bet he was shocked to see you representing ScanTron—an international company. Humph. You sure showed him!"

Elise shrugged. "Yeah, he was his usual swell-headed self. I knew I'd run into him sooner or later. It's happened, it's over. And if I keep on seeing him around town, so what?"

"Be careful," Myra warned, lowering her tone as well as the long lashes fringing her deep hazel eyes. "Don't give him the opportunity to hurt you again. People like him don't change."

"I'm not worried. He's already done all the damage he'll ever do to me, and luckily, I survived."

"Yes, you did." Pride shone on Myra's unlined face, and she put a slender hand over her daughter's, squeezing it. "But still, watch out, Elise. Don't be too quick to trust him."

Tilting back her head, Elise watched the ceiling fan whirring above the table, then leveled a determined gaze on her mother. "Oh, you don't have to tell me that. I will be fair, cooperative, even cordial, if I have to, but he'll never get me to talk off the record again."

The suave reporter's image hung in Elise's mind, as darkly vivid and pervasive as the smoldering stench of scorched timber that still lingered in her nose. She wanted to act unaffected by Carlos's callous questioning, but seeing him again had initiated a surge of disparate emotions that she prayed would go away.

He hadn't changed, at least not very much. He looked well-heeled, as he ought to after signing a seven-figure, five-year contract with the local NBC affiliate, and he was much better groomed than he had been while chasing ambulances and local politicians, but his arrogant and narcissistic attitude was definitely still intact.

His custom-made shirt, soft Italian shoes, and designer suit had been regally draped on his male-model frame, accentuating his bold sense of self. His swarthy coloring, chiseled features, and seductive

Latin mannerisms remained the elusive elements that came together to create the charm that oozed from every pore in his body. He never failed to draw attention wherever he showed up, and Elise had once heard a colleague joke that if Carlos Rico was not in the studio in front of a camera, he was probably in the gym in front of a mirror watching himself pump iron. Undoubtedly, Carlos's physical appearance played a major role in the unprecedented success of his consumer-oriented television show, *The Inside Story*, which was watched by everyone Elise knew.

"Myra!" Elise's father's voice, coming from the front porch, boomed into the kitchen. Fred Camden poked his head into the house through the partially opened screen door. His reading glasses were anchored atop his head of thick silver hair and he held the *Galveston Gazette* in one hand. "Vick and Janet are out here," he told his wife. "Bring out two more cups of coffee when you come."

"Okay," Myra called back, reaching up to take two mugs from her kitchen cabinet. "Our newest neighbors," she told Elise. "The Postons. Real nice couple. He has relatives here in town. Retired from NASA to come back and care for his two grandchildren while his daughter is in rehab. Drugs. A real shame, but Vick and Janet are hopeful. They bought the old Allen Bakery over on Prairie Street. Live above it. Fixed it up and opened the place for business a few weeks ago, and they're doing real good. You should see what they've done."

"That's nice," Elise said. "I'm glad to hear that people are starting to return, rebuild. It's encouraging."

"Right. Don't cross Tide City off so quickly. There's plenty of potential here if families can hold on to the properties. American Fuel just bought up that huge tract of deserted land west of Fresca's, and the county is going to grade and clean Southside Beach. We ought to start seeing tourists around here again. Things will pick up." Myra balanced the tray of mugs on one hand as she grabbed two spoons and the sugar bowl. "Come on out. I want you to meet the Postons."

"In a minute," Elise said, watching as her mother finished pouring the coffee, then headed through the high-ceilinged house toward the screened front door.

Sitting quietly, Elise looked around, glad that her father had had the foresight to use his settlement from Global Oil to buy the old colonial. Six years ago when he injured his back on the job, he'd been offered the choice of finishing out his years of service at the company in a less strenuous position or retiring early with a lump-sum disability payment. He'd opted for the generous one-time payment, investing half of it to secure his future, using the remainder to move from Flatwoods. Elise shuddered. Her parents could very easily have been victims of this morning's fire.

Though she had not grown up in the spacious old house, she felt at home. The sofa, chairs, lamps, and pictures on the walls were the same ones that had been in their home in Flatwoods. The only thing her father had splurged on when he moved into the abandoned colonial was a thirty-six-inch color TV, a leather recliner, and a remodeled kitchen for his wife. Other than that, not much had changed.

Elise drained the last of her tea, put the glass in the sink, then picked up her purse. Hopefully, Al's briefing would provide her with added ammunition to face the next barrage of reporters. Her first public information campaign for ScanTron had to be very carefully orchestrated and nothing could be left to chance.

As she headed out of the kitchen, voices from the front porch entered the house, stopping her. Hesitating just inside the front door, she listened to the conversation.

"Just when business is getting steady, this happens," Janet Poston said. "People are so upset and nervous. Vick and I are going over to the Red Cross shelter to see if the volunteers need help with food. We can make up a bunch of sandwiches. A lot of people are homeless; many won't be able to get back into their houses for quite some time."

"Awful, isn't it?" Elise heard her mother say. "This is the third big fire we've had in this county in the past year and a half. I sat straight up in my bed. Thought lightning had struck the house when I heard that explosion."

"I was in the bathroom, getting ready for work," Vick Poston said. "I'm always up before dawn, baking bread and getting the doughnuts on by sunrise. I thought a tornado had hit. The whole place just shook."

"On the news they said a pickup truck crashed the gates and exploded, and that's what caused the fire, but it doesn't make sense," Fred Camden said. "Even if the truck was one of those jobs with double gas tanks, what in the world would feed a fire to make it so big? Something else must be going on."

Janet Poston agreed. "Yeah. Look. Look over there. Smoke is still pouring out of that place."

Elise flinched. Her father sounded angry. "I just paid Zeke Green two thousand dollars to paint this house last month," he said. "All I can say is, it's a good thing the wind's in my favor, 'cause if this paint job had been ruined, somebody would pay. I mean pay! Hey, I can raise Cain along with the best of 'em—if I have to."

His tone shocked Elise. Fred was a mild-mannered man and seldom got riled up about anything. It was his wife who usually did the talking when it came to matters that called for confrontation. Pressing knuckles to her lips, Elise continued to listen.

"Oh, ScanTron's gonna pay. Believe me, they're gonna get hit hard," Janet Poston replied. "Folks are fed up with being burned and smoked and scared out of their homes—terrorized by companies that don't give a damn. Why the devil didn't *they* have tight enough security around that place to prevent something like this from happening?" she grumbled in obvious disgust.

Vick Poston echoed his wife's feelings. "Right. Who was guarding that gate? Sounds like an inside job to me. Something fishy there."

No one spoke for a few seconds, and Elise started to step through the screen door but hung back when Vick spoke again.

"I'm going to the clinic for a checkup as soon as it opens. Taking my grandbabies, too. We feel fine, but who knows? All kinds of complications might show up later. If ScanTron's going to hand out checks, I want my condition on record."

"Probably have to wait in line forever to see the doctor," Elise's mother commented. "You know that place is so understaffed."

"I don't care," Vick replied. "I'm not in a hurry. You watch.

Everybody in the county who can fill out a form is going to claim some kind of problem. ScanTron's got insurance. Let 'em pay."

"I don't want any insurance money," Fred Camden said. "That's not the issue. What I want to know is what we may have been exposed to, and if the government is going to investigate, if they'll give us the results of their tests. Probably gonna have to make a big fuss to get any information."

Unable to listen any longer, Elise pushed the screen door open and stepped out onto the porch.

All conversation stopped while she crossed in front of her mother to sit on the wooden glider next to her father.

"Elise," he said, "these are the Postons. Vick and Janet. They live two streets over. On Prairie."

"Hello. Nice to meet you," Elise said, inclining her head toward them.

"Elise is working on the fire. She's with ScanTron," her mother gently interjected.

Vick frowned. "Oh? What do you do?"

"I'm the company's media spokesperson," Elise replied.

"Didn't you see her on the news? Channel Three this morning," Myra said.

Both Vick and Janet shook their heads, no.

"Well, I'm the one who has to answer those hard questions," Elise said lightly, smiling. No one smiled back. She glanced fearfully at her mother, then opened her purse and took out her car keys. "I've really got to get going. There's an awful lot to sort out."

"Yes," Fred started, "you've got your work cut out for today. All of Tide County is counting on you to tell us the truth. We're sick and tired of being ignored. Nobody tells us a thing. Who knows what might have been stored right in the middle of our town?"

"Dad, nothing toxic was stored at the ScanTron facility," Elise tautly replied.

He lifted his shoulders, opening his hands, palms up. "All I know is what I saw on TV. A lot of people were taken to the clinic and League City Hospital, too. They're saying these people are suffering from more than smoke inhalation."

"Who's *they?*" Elise asked tersely.

"The news reporters."

"Well, better listen to me. I'm telling you the truth."

"Did you ever go inside that place?" her father asked.

Surprised, Elise answered, "Yes, once."

"Well, they probably didn't show you everything. You know how they are. Some things are kept off-limits to us."

"Dad! Please. I work for a reputable, fair company. They'd never jeopardize the community, let alone lie about it."

"Ha!" Vick Poston coughed. "Don't be naive, little lady. Those huge corporations do exactly as they please, so don't be surprised if you've been lied to right along with the rest of us. We know you have to say what they want you to say, and tell us what they want us to believe, but don't buy everything that's handed out."

"Mr. Poston, I don't think you understand," Elise started, leaning past her father, moving to the edge of her seat to get a better view of her parents' neighbor. "I'm not simply a mouthpiece for the company. I've been trained to represent the company and present the facts of a situation as they become available. It's just too early to start drawing conclusions about any of this, and I'd like you to know that I'm as concerned as you are about getting to the truth."

"I'm sure you are, honey," Fred Camden interrupted, attempting to disperse the obvious friction. "And I'm sure ScanTron is as good a company to work for as any in the country. I'm proud that you've got such an important position with them, but you've got to remember where you come from, Elise. Don't compromise your beliefs just to make them look good."

Elise stared at her father, dumbfounded. How dare he speak to her like that in front of his neighbors? She stood, steadying herself by grabbing the porch railing as she distractedly brushed a speck of dust off her suit. Picking up her purse, she said, "You know I'd never say anything I didn't believe in, nor would I ever compromise my values. Trust me, Dad." She hesitated, then leaned over and patted his hand. "I care too much about the people who live here and the future of this town to do otherwise."

In the uncomfortable silence that followed, she walked, head erect, to her car and got in. Pulling away from the curb, she didn't look back. Keeping her chin high and her shoulders rigid, she zoomed down the street, but by the time she entered the parking lot and stopped beside her boss's van, her courageous front had wilted and her stomach had become a quaking mass of flutters.

CHAPTER 4

The columns of figures scrolling across the computer screen blurred as Blake Jeffries yawned. He leaned back in his chair, placing his hands behind his neck to massage the muscles on the tops of his shoulders. The Flexall 454 Elise had rubbed into his aching muscles last night hadn't helped a bit. He felt as stiff and achy as he had last Saturday after sleeping on the ground in a pup tent with Junior when they'd camped out in the backyard.

Blake tilted his body forward, stretching his arms out flat on his desk. Elise was right. He never should have let Paul talk him into adding that extra ten-pound disk to the bench press machine at the gym last night. But he'd thought he could handle it, especially since his brother, who was six years older and fifteen pounds heavier, was pressing two hundred pounds without showing strain.

Blake felt the muscles in his back begin to ease as he toyed with one of the regulation felt-tipped pens the accountants at Century Trust were required to use. He studied the company logo, a small triangle with a C inside stamped in gold on the cap. Momentarily distracted from his work, he sat listening to a confrontational exchange between a coworker and an irritated annuitant as it drifted over the padded divider that separated the two accountants. Irritated, Blake yanked open the center drawer of his desk, tossed the pen inside, then slammed it shut.

After six years in his modular cubicle of an office, constructed of free-standing navy blue panels, he still hated the system that management touted as the most efficient use of space. A thirteen-year veteran at Century Trust, Blake felt he deserved a real office, with walls and a door and enough privacy to allow him to at least speak to his wife without everyone on his floor knowing what he'd said.

The distractions that came with the setup drove him crazy, so he kept a small transistor radio on his bookshelf tuned to a station that played vintage rock and roll twenty-four hours a day. He loved all those songs from the late sixties and seventies that he'd twisted and gyrated to, the tunes he hummed to himself while speeding down the highway, wind on his face, feet high on the pedals, his hands gripping the wide-spaced handlebars of his vintage red Harley.

Some days at the office the music muffled his colleagues' voices, some days it didn't, and today was one of those days when his mind refused to stay focused on the columns of figures flashing across his monitor.

Blake reached up to increase the volume on the radio, his fingers brushing the knotty pine frame of the photo sitting beside it. His favorite picture of Blake Junior, taken two years ago, on his third birthday, with Elise beaming proudly, holding the towering four-layer chocolate cake she had surprisingly managed to concoct.

Blake grinned. Myra Camden was the kind of cook who could put a meal for six people on the table using only three ingredients. Too bad her daughter hadn't inherited any of her mother's culinary skills.

He picked up the wooden framed photo of his wife and examined it closely, studying the expression on Elise's face. She had been happy then, radiant, carefree, and beautiful. Not that she wasn't still beautiful, but Blake had to admit that the Kitzmiller lawsuit had left its scars. Somehow, her free-spirited, go-for-it attitude had softened, gradually dissolving, leaving behind a cautious, less spontaneous person who seemed unable to laugh anymore.

Tracing the outline of her cheek with his finger, Blake felt a surge of desire begin to rise. Her skin was flawless, rich and smooth like melted caramel, and to him she still looked like the twenty-five-year-old girl he'd walked down the aisle with eleven years ago. Elise would always look that way, he knew—never changing, never showing, in his eyes at least, the tiniest shadow of age.

Blake's face fell somber and he let his shoulders go slack, slumping back in his seat, hoping Elise's new job might help her recapture that sparkling energy that had drained away under the unrelenting pressure of bill collectors and their worries over their financial future.

The early phone call, coupled with Elise's abrupt departure, had left Blake wide awake since four o'clock that morning. He was edgy, restless, and exhausted but determined to finish his quarterly report before noon in order to get a jump start on tomorrow's stack of files.

From now on, he'd have to work hard in the mornings in order to leave the office at exactly four-thirty. With Elise back to work full-time, he had to pick up Junior from the day-care center by five o'clock or pay a surcharge of twenty-five dollars an hour.

But there was another reason why Blake planned to leave the office early today; he was going to the bank across the street to pick up the loan application package that was waiting for him. Crossing his fingers, he prayed that the loan officer might be a brother, or a sympathetic sister, someone who would see the potential in his business plan.

With Elise's career suddenly back on track, Blake wanted to move quickly, make up for all the time he'd lost while she had been unemployed. His project had been shelved when Elise was unexpectedly fired from Trinity Hospital, but now that the financial pressure was about to ease up, it was time for him to grasp his dream.

Anticipation swept through Blake. He and Paul were finally going to do it, and after thirteen years of crunching numbers in a cubbyhole of an office, Blake was ready to be his own boss. The day-to-day drudgery of working at Century had taken its toll and Blake could hardly wait until September first, the day Elise's position became permanent. Then he'd hand in his official resignation, toss every goddamn Century felt-tipped pen on his desk into the trash, and assume the title of co-owner of Texas Rider Motorcycles and Bikes.

Jolting upright in his chair, he came out of his reverie, realizing he'd accidentally pressed the page key on his computer keyboard with his elbow.

"Damn," he groaned, watching the last set of numbers in the report whizz past without review. Shaking his head, he paged back to recheck the numbers but found it impossible to concentrate when his mind was filled with images of shiny new Harley cruisers, Suzuki scooters, and Honda ATVs parked under bright florescent lights in his spacious suburban showroom.

A soft tap at his doorway pulled him from the screen. He looked up to see a young lady in a gray pantsuit watching him. Another temp, Blake thought, wondering why his boss couldn't keep a secretary. It seemed as if they changed monthly. He raised his eyebrows in question. "Yes?"

"Sorry to interrupt you, Mr. Jeffries. Mr. Tharp needs your report by noon."

"Really?" Blake replied, ticked off that his three o'clock deadline had been suddenly changed, but feeling smug that he was way ahead of his boss.

"Will that be a problem?" the secretary asked.

"Nope. Not at all. Tell Tharp I'll send it up by Vikki." He checked his watch, then added, "In half an hour."

When the girl didn't leave, Blake reassured her, "Don't worry. It'll be done." He mentally dismissed the perplexed blond, annoyed again at the pressure Tharp was trying to exert.

At the end of every quarter he and his boss went through the same routine, with Blake putting in long hours to deliver the report on time. Spinning around in his chair, he turned back to his work.

With his dream of owning a motorcycle dealership so close, Blake was suddenly no longer intimidated by Tharp's power games. He refused to panic, and liked besting his small-minded boss. Blake knew he had little hope of ever making it into the ranks of management at

Century, and the thought of leaving to start over at some different yet similar accounting firm was not an option at all. Blake's only recourse was to move out as soon as he got his financing together.

It took a few minutes to recheck the last set of figures; then he pushed the print key and sat back, swiveling in his chair as the soft purr of the printer spat out the annuitant dividend statements. He couldn't help smiling at the prospect of turning in his resignation, of telling Tharp and his beleaguered coworkers at Century Trust good-bye. Then he'd be his own boss, and a good one, too, he mused. After the stifling environment at the accounting firm, the thought of walking through his own showroom, of talking bikes all day with customers, of interacting with real people instead of figures on a sheet of paper caused his pulse to race.

"Texas Rider," Blake murmured, trying out the name that he and Paul had chosen. After studying the competition, analyzing the market, and revising their figures many times, Blake knew his projections were on target, and could hardly wait to turn the weed-filled lot north of Houston, which used to be loaded with used Toyotas, into the best showplace for cycles in the state.

Last Sunday, he'd made the fifty-minute drive to Arida Estates alone on his bike, anxious to look over the property he'd discovered two years ago. It was still for sale. Though nut grass and thistles sprouted from cracks in the asphalt and highway trash littered the lot, it still looked good to him.

Driving back, he'd mentally reviewed the blueprints of his venture, unable to think of anything other than the office he planned to design for himself with floor-to-ceiling windows, thick carpet, and walls so thick he could blast his radio as loud and long as he pleased.

His plan was actually moving forward, and he was nervous but excited. Expecting, hoping, wishing, but not about to take anything for granted, he visualized what lay ahead. With his head for numbers and Paul's twelve years as a used-car salesman, not to mention his brother's flair for promotion, they couldn't miss. Blake projected that they could be in business by the first of the year, hopefully before his fortieth birthday, which fell on January 6.

The printer continued to whirr. Blake picked up each page as soon as it rolled out, checked it closely, then inserted it into the red plastic binder. Reaching over the neatly arranged stacks of papers on his desk, he turned up the volume on his radio a little higher when he heard an update on the ScanTron fire.

"Harris County Fire Chief Eddie Corral tells KKLT News that he sent three units to assist the Tide County Fire Department in battling the seven-alarm fire that broke out early this morning at ScanTron Security International's coastal complex," the announcer stated. "At approximately four A.M. this morning, a pickup truck crashed the entrance gates to one of the largest security research and warehouse facilities in the state, causing a massive explosion and fire. According to Elise Jeffries, spokesperson for ScanTron, virtually every building on the two-hundred-acre site has been damaged or destroyed. Luckily, only one fatality has been confirmed, the driver of the pickup, whose identity has not been released. The fire jumped Baymark Road, igniting houses in the community of Flatwoods, which lies directly across the road. Two children, severely burned, were taken to League City Hospital, and many of the residents are suffering from smoke inhalation and complain of burning eyes and skin irritation. Most are being treated at Tide County Clinic. Ms. Jeffries assures the public that the security company did not have any toxic or hazardous materials on the site. However, the locals are taking exception to this and are calling for a thorough investigation, including a disclosure statement from ScanTron about the contents of the warehouses that continue to burn at this time. Stay tuned to this station for more details in the next hour."

Angry residents, people flocking to the clinic. This would surely bring an investigation by the EPA. Blake tensed as he turned the volume down. What if things got complicated? Out of control? As complicated as the Baby Kitzmiller situation? What if Elise broke under the pressure?

Closing his eyes, Blake thought of how far he and Elise had come since those dark days following her firing from Trinity Hospital. It had been a series of unending nightmares. First, Carlos Rico's damaging report. Then the lawsuit. And the financial settlement that had nearly bankrupted them when it had become clear that the libel suit could not be kept out of court. Blake had been forced to sell two-thirds of his Century stock and tap into Junior's college fund in order to pay the high-priced lawyer who represented Elise.

Blake stopped putting his report together long enough to look at the snapshot of Blake Junior again. During those low times, especially when their house had been actually listed for foreclosure auction, the marriage had come close to caving in. Only Blake Junior's innocent, fearful eyes had kept him and Elise from separating. They'd survived the worst. She'd better not falter. Not now. Under the pressure of this new assignment, she'd better not do anything to jeopardize her job.

CHAPTER 5

This is a hell of a mess," Al bellowed, throwing back his head, blowing smoke toward the ceiling. He hurriedly leafed through a folder filled with order forms and contracts, one eye squinted against the curl of smoke that drifted from his cigarette toward the water-stained ceiling. "There's no way we're gonna miss that Netcom deadline, Pete. Get on the phone and find those components—fast. Try Dallas first, then San Diego, and if Johnson insists on a goddamn twenty percent surcharge for overnight delivery, do it. We gotta stay on top of this. After Netcom, start rounding up quarter-inch cable for the Kingston order. That's one account I worked too damn hard on to lose."

Pete Tremont's eyes widened in question, but he said nothing to his boss, lowering his head to make a flurry of entries in his order logbook. Al Patterson's right-hand man for ten years, Pete knew better than to question Al on a good day, let alone at a time of crisis.

"I just got off the phone with the fire department," Al went on. "Looks like things are about under control. Not completely, but getting there."

"What about the admin building?" Pete asked. "Anything left?"

With a hunch of his shoulders, Al leaned forward, placing his elbows on the dusty glass display case that was doubling for a conference table. "We got nothin' left. Nothing. The chief said the only building that still has a roof is the records annex. It's got heavy water damage, but our files ought to be intact."

"That's a relief," Elise said, speaking up for the first time since her introduction to the group.

Once the meeting had begun, all discussion had centered on how the coastal team was going to fulfill outstanding orders and keep from losing too much money. Not a word had been spoken, so far, about the damage control she had to face. Al Patterson was definitely more worried about the interruption the fire had caused in his business than about the talk of lawsuits that swirled outside his door. What the press had to say about the environmental and social ramifications of the fire was clearly not on his mind.

"We should have three more phone lines in here by noon, so everybody can get back to business." Al turned toward Elise, finally addressing her. "Pete will help you get set up. Choose any corner you want."

Elise looked around the large open area that had been haphazardly transformed from a merchandise catalog store into the new ScanTron offices. Amid bins of plastic hangers, spindly clothes racks, and stacks of old catalogs lay the few boxes of current files and account records that Al and Pete had taken home to work on the evening before the fire.

In addition to Pete Tremont, there were three other members of Al's management team seated on folding chairs around the smudged glass case, which still held a few dusty pieces of costume jewelry nestled in blue velvet boxes.

Next to Elise sat Garland Perkins, the head of maintenance and security. Opposite him was Bill Stokes, the director of finance and personnel, and at the end of the makeshift table sat Darrell Grimes, a chemist and technical expert who specialized in the creation of customized security systems, and the only African American on Al Patterson's staff.

"Right, now all I need is access to a phone," Elise told Al, then added, "What about a computer? Any possibility?"

Al shrugged as if he had no idea how to help her, but Darrell lifted his index finger to get her attention. "I've got my laptop already hooked up," he said. "It's yours, if you need it."

"Thanks," Elise replied, giving the chemist a smile.

Elise had heard quite a bit about Darrell Grimes before coming to work for ScanTron. His imaginative and innovative ideas often made the news, leading ScanTron to the cutting edge of the security industry. He had been jokingly tagged as the 007 of the security business and had started his career at ScanTron when the research and warehouse complex had been no more than water pipes jutting out of the ground and a creased blueprint on John Farren's desk.

Darrell had had reservations about leaving his aging parents be-hind in Lansing, Michigan, to come to the middle of what had once been a swampy rice field to work for a company he knew little about. But a 50 percent salary increase, the absence of interference from the head office, and the promise of lucrative stock options had lured him away from his dead-end job with Atlas Security, ScanTron's major competitor. The move had proved fortuitous, especially since he had two sons enrolled in expensive Ivy League schools.

"Let me finish up a report I'm working on. Then it's all yours," Darrell said.

"Great," Elise replied. "I need to get a press release out fast."

Al cleared his throat loudly. Elise glanced his way.

"Run it past me before you release it," Al said in a rapid-fire manner. "This fire is news. Big news. It's gonna be picked up by wire services all over the country, might even make national network to-night. I need to approve what comes out of this office."

Elise stared at Al, praying she'd be able to tolerate him for the duration of the assignment. Domineering and brusque, he was ob-viously going to have things his way no matter how much he might offend her.

"No problem," she told Al in a controlled voice. After seeing him in action with his management team, she understood how to deal with him. Al Patterson wasn't mean, but he was a bully, and he sounded like a general giving orders to his troops. For some reason, those at the table didn't seem to mind. The thought of Al Patterson personally involving himself with every aspect of her job was less than appealing, but if that's what she'd have to do to make a success of this assignment, so be it. She was not going to antagonize him.

Pulling her notepad closer, Elise began writing. "Fill me in," she said. "Where do things stand?"

Al stubbed out his cigarette, much to Elise's relief, and picked up a piece of paper ripped from a yellow legal pad. "The police still haven't identified the body of the man who was driving the pickup." Sweeping everyone with a smug glance, he said, "But he was drinking. Found the remains of a tequila bottle in the cab. Probably one of those quasi-illegals that get ripped every night over at Fresca's and wind up sleeping it off on the beach."

Elise frowned. "Quasi-illegals?"

"Yeah," Al shot back. "Happens all the time. They get in on a temporary work visa, then stay. No ID, no green card. No nothing. All they want to do is drink up their pay and play cards. I see 'em around here all the time." Al chewed his bottom lip for a second, then clenched his jaws tightly, causing the big vein in his neck to pulse.

"Has the fire department ruled out arson, then?" Darrell Grimes asked.

"No *official* statement on that yet. They're still on the scene. Because of the way the roofs collapsed onto the buildings, the chief is worried that hot spots might flare, set the whole thing off again. Might be a day or two before the fire department can get in there and search the rubble."

"What about the EPA?" Elise wanted to know. If she had to promise the public that they had not been exposed to anything deadly, an official statement from the government backing her up would be helpful.

"What about it?" Al replied quickly.

Elise flinched, realizing she'd touched a sore topic with Al. "I assume they'll do tests—water, air, soil. I'm going to need those reports. There are a lot of frightened people out there."

"Hogwash," Al remarked. "Greedy. That's what they are." He smirked at his management team, reflecting his opinion on that topic. "We've already got the Texas Clean Air folks waving signs and screaming down our backs. We'll deal with the government when we have to. They'll be here soon enough."

Elise immediately shot Al a warning glance but decided not to speak.

With a lift of his chin, Al told her, "Wait it out. When they do their thing, you'll be informed. I don't want you calling them, or in any way involved with the EPA. Got that? If they have something to say, they'll say it to me."

"Fine," Elise murmured, her face warming. She lowered her eyes, pretending to make notes on her pad, silently counting to ten, aware that it was neither the time nor the place to lash out at the man she'd be stuck with for the duration of her assignment.

But how dare he treat her like a child! *She* was ScanTron Security's national media spokesperson. Maybe this was her first day on the job, but she had ten years' experience in public affairs and did not consider herself a trainee. He could boss and manipulate those on his staff if he wanted to, but she had been hired by headquarters, and only John Farren could tell her what to do.

"What about property damages?" Bill Stokes asked, his main concern, as always, the bottom line.

"That's what insurance is for," Al snapped. "We pick up after the private insurance pays off, but I doubt many of those people had much coverage. This is gonna cost us, believe it."

"And the medical aspects?" Pete asked.

"We don't do a fuckin' thing until headquarters approves every medical report. This is not gonna turn into a goddamn free-for-all giveaway. If it takes a year to settle their claims, then that's what it's gonna take."

Wide-eyed, Elise could only stare.

Al paced the room. "For God's sake. Folks around here probably breathe more toxic smoke when they barbecue a hamburger on a Saturday afternoon than they got in their lungs this morning." He focused pointedly on Elise. "Don't let those people fool you, you hear? All that crap about being dizzy, itching. A bunch of bullshit! *I'm* not sick." He pointed a finger at each man at the table. "Pete, Garland, Darrell, Bill. They're not sick, and they were all at the site this morning. Crap. That's what this talk about feeling sick is. Pure and simple, crap."

With a shift, Elise sat up straighter, taking a moment to compose her reply. "Okay. Let's say you're right. Some people could be faking it, but the fact remains that two children were seriously burned."

"They'll be taken care of," Al replied.

"Many others were transported by ambulance to the clinic," Elise said. "Are the paramedics faking it, too?"

"Precautions against lawsuits. They gotta take 'em in. That's their job."

Elise reminded Al, "I need hard data to deal with the press *and* the public. Voluntarily disclosing the contents of the warehouses might be our best defense. We're going to be under a lot of pressure and we've got to approach this carefully. A statement detailing what burned this morning could go a long way in calming people down."

"No way! We're gonna stonewall the press. They think they got the right to poke their noses into everybody's business. Play hardball for now, you hear?" He leaned so close to Elise that she could smell the tobacco on his breath. "And don't go making any fuckin' promises to those . . . those," he faltered, glaring at Elise.

"Those *people,*" she finished calmly, finally allowing her anger to surface and her pride to fuel her courage. "Al, you need to know that many of *those* people are *my* people, who used to be my neighbors." Inhaling deeply, Elise swayed back, pressing her spine against the back of the cool metal chair.

Al's face flushed deep purple, the stain of anger rising slowly from his neck. He sniffed suspiciously, puffing up his chest, making his lone star belt buckle rise on his belly until it reflected the sunlight that was streaming through the plate-glass doors. "What's that mean?" he asked tightly.

"It means that I was born and raised in Flatwoods." She paused, absorbing the surprised stares from everyone at the table. "I've been away for years, but my parents still live in Tide County . . . in town. Not too far from here."

Air slipped from Al's lungs in a muted whistle. "Did Farren know that when he sent you here?"

"Of course," Elise replied.

"Jesus! What in God's name did he think he was doing?" He abruptly began to pace again. "Farren oughta have his head examined. How the hell are you going to hold the line for *us* if you're busy sympathizing with *them?*" He threw his pen down on the table and stomped toward his office, which had been set up in the front of the store. At the doorway he turned and bellowed, "Pete, get Farren on the phone. Now."

Pete pushed away from the table, giving Elise a long, dark look before hurrying through the double glass doors toward the only phone in the building, a wall phone in the lobby of the former customer service area. Immediately, Bill and Garland followed, leaving Darrell sitting alone with Elise.

"Well!" Elise remarked, a little dismayed and suddenly very ill at ease. "He's way off base. What a control freak. No one could doubt who's the boss around here!"

Darrell reached across the table, as if to touch Elise's arm, but drew back, resting his hand on the sleeve of his starched white shirt. Elise noticed that he was wearing an unusually attractive gold wedding band.

"Don't feel too bad," Darrell said gently, glancing at the double glass doors. "Al's not the easiest person to work for, true. But I've been with him since the complex opened. Our first six months together were hell. I mean, pure hell. We went round and round like two mad dogs chasing their tails. Every time I'd come up with a new idea or try a different approach to solving a glitch in a system, he'd find something wrong with it. But I was determined to stick it out. I tell you, my laboratory became a battleground. Bill and Garland used to place bets as to when I was going to pack up and leave, but I refused to let Al get to me. When he realized that my ideas were generating interest from the company's high-rolling customers, he simply left me alone to do my thing. Finally he began to respect me and my work, I believe, though he's never really told me so. He can be an irritating jackass sometimes, but I have to give him credit—he's dedicated to the company."

"So I gather," Elise replied, disappointed to think that acting like an ass was a sign of company loyalty. "I appreciate the fact that he's anxious to keep his business on track and is concerned about filling outstanding orders, but don't you think it's strange that he's not concerned about the public? ScanTron owes them. Doesn't he realize what could happen?"

"Probably not. I know how his mind works. If he says nothing toxic was released into the environment, that's it. He's through with that issue."

"There are a lot of people involved who are not about to buy that."

"Well, he'll deal with them if, and when, he's forced to."

"No, *he* won't. I'll have to, and his attitude will only make my job more difficult than it has to be."

The words had slipped out before she could stop them, and she tensed with foreboding. Could that be Al Patterson's plan? To complicate things so much she'd give up and go home?

Leveling her gaze on Darrell's sympathetic face, she connected with him despite the thick, slightly tinted lenses in his wire-rimmed glasses. The flecks of gray in his neatly trimmed hair gave him a fatherly, wise appearance, and she hoped she wasn't misjudging the trust she saw in his eyes.

Darrell smiled knowingly. "Al always has the final say on everything that happens around here. Just try to go along. Hang in." Capping his pen with a loud click, he shoved it into the breast pocket of his stiff shirt, then asked, "So you grew up in these parts?"

Glad that Darrell seemed genuinely interested in her, Elise relaxed a bit, letting the morning's tension drain from her body. "Right in the heart of Flatwoods," she said. "When I was born, it was the only place in Tide County where blacks could buy homes. My father worked for Global Oil back then, and Flatwoods was a real nice community."

"Still is," Darrell defended. "When I first came here, I almost bought a house in Flatwoods, but I found something I liked better closer to the beach." He grinned, shaking his head. "Well, my wife and kids found it, I guess."

Elise chuckled. "Yeah, but Flatwoods's changed a lot. After finishing high school, my parents sent me to Dallas to live with an aunt so I could go to SMU. I graduated with a degree in public affairs, got a job in Houston with a hospital, got married, and never came back here to live."

"You said your parents live in town?"

"Yes. I visit now and then, but they prefer to come into Houston to see me and my family."

"Have children?"

"Yeah. A five-year-old boy—Blake Junior. Named after my husband." She grinned with motherly pride.

"That's nice. Got two boys of my own," Darrell said, gathering up his papers. "Your father still work for Global?"

"Not now. Dad was hurt on the job some years ago. He got a decent lump-sum settlement and decided to buy one of those abandoned colonials over on Valencia Street. It used to belong to Colonel Waters, a vice president at Global. Isn't that ironic?"

Darrell chuckled. "Yep, but I have begun to believe that sooner or later everything makes a circle. Times change. People change. Circumstances arise that make the impossible seem common. You only have to wait it out. Be patient, Elise; your familiarity and connection with the people in this area just might work to the company's advantage."

"Let's hope so," Elise replied as Darrell left the room.

She sat staring at the sketchy notes scribbled on her pad, unable to shake her father's words of warning. She had meant it when she'd promised him not to compromise her values just to make ScanTron look good, but damn it, she had to be realistic.

Though overqualified, she had spent the past eighteen months on and off unemployment while working temporary clerical assignments all over Houston, winding up at ScanTron Security to replace Theresa White, the media spokesperson who had been on maternity leave. Elise was quickly informed that Theresa planned to extend her ten-week maternity leave into permanent status, but had been sworn to secrecy by her coworkers. When John Farren learned that he'd lost Theresa to motherhood, he'd offered Elise the top spot as of September 1—as soon as Theresa's resignation became official and Elise had successfully served out her probationary period.

Until then, Elise was being paid Theresa's high five-figure salary, had use of a company car, and was being subjected to a scrutiny she knew would be microscopic. If she didn't blow it, the interim promotion would be permanent within seven weeks, and this time she *had* to get it right, for herself, for ScanTron, and especially for Blake.

CHAPTER 6

The multicolored *servilletas* hanging from the rafters fluttered gently as the ceiling fan whirred. Like perpetually suspended flakes of confetti, the lace-paper decorations lent an air of festivity to the otherwise dark little room. Only two customers sat at the bar, but loud party music blared from the red plastic radio propped against the cash register, filling the place with a pulsing Latin dance number sung by Selena.

The bartender uncapped another Dos Equis, squeezed a wedge of lime into the neck of the bottle, then slid the cold beer down the polished bar to Carlos Rico, who caught it with a practiced hand and a wink of thanks.

Carlos had been in Fresca's a few times, but not often enough to know much about Guapo, the less than handsome bartender who'd been salting tequila glasses and handing out tortilla chips since the day he opened the Icehouse in 1947.

Stoop-shouldered and showing every bit of his seventy years, Guapo had missed only one day of serving drinks and tacos and chili rellenos from behind the scarred pine bar, and that had been in 1961 when Hurricane Carla pumped twelve feet of water into the white stucco cantina that sat no more than twenty-five yards from the sandy shore.

Carlos studied the old man, who was busy polishing a tray of heavy glass mugs in a mindless, practiced way, waiting for just the right moment to strike up a conversation. As soon as the only other customer in the Icehouse paid his tab and left, Carlos slid three stools over, stopping directly in front of Guapo.

"*Hola,*" he began in a friendly, familiar tone. "I'm Carlos Rico—"

"Oh, I know who you are," Guapo interrupted, grinning expansively, chasing the tiredness from his heavily lined face. "On TV. I see you *every* night."

Carlos gave the man his most dazzling on-air smile, nodding his appreciation. "Terrible explosion this morning, huh?" he began, casually taking a long pull on his beer.

"*Dios mío. ¡Sí!*" With a thump, Guapo set down the mug he had been wiping. "*¡La policía!*" He shook one hand several times, fingers splayed. "All day, they ask questions. But what do I know? I'm just a poor man trying to make a living. I tell them nothing. *Nada.*" He made a gesture as if spitting at the floor.

Carlos nodded sympathetically, easing into Spanish, hoping to put the man in a chatty mood. He'd been there close to an hour and was nursing his second Dos Equis instead of meeting his personal trainer at the gym. But he would rather swig beer in the empty cantina than break sweat on the StairMaster tonight. He was glad he'd thought to come to Fresca's and was hopeful that his hunch would pan out. This was the only place a man could have got drunk within a six-mile radius of the ScanTron complex—at least the only place where a Spanish-speaking illegal would have felt at home.

"Bet you're sick of answering questions, huh?" he prompted.

"Ah," Guapo sighed, neatly folding his towel. "The man was here, all right. He'd been here before, but I don't say nothin' to the police, you know? Legal, illegal. No matter to me. They drink, they play cards, they leave. What they do outside my door is not my worry."

Carlos jumped at the opening, continuing the conversation in the man's native language. "I know it must make you mad as hell. The authorities expecting you to spill your guts about every man who comes in here without a green card in his pocket."

Guapo's eyes glimmered in relief. "Exactly. Why would I know anything? And if I did, why would I tell them? Ruin my business. Nobody would come."

Carlos drained the bottle and ordered another beer, then passed a twenty to the bartender, letting his change lie on the bar after he'd been served. "He was a young man, I heard," Carlos said.

"A sad man," Guapo volunteered. With a glance to his right, then left, as if some invisible customer might be listening, he leaned over and whispered to Carlos. "From Mexico . . . Chiapas, he was. And he was drunk when he left. I was worried about him, so when he asked where the big warehouses were, I wrote down the directions to the ScanTron place. He told me he had a brother who worked somewhere around here as a security guard, and he was trying to find him. Family problems, I guessed. How could I know he would do such a thing?"

"Too bad," Carlos agreed, dramatically lowering his lashes, shadowing his eyes from Guapo's. When he looked up and spoke, his tone fell into a hushed whisper of sympathy. "I'm sorry for his family." Then Carlos brightened. "You know, I have family in Chiapas, too. I miss them terribly."

Carlos watched Guapo closely, hoping he would not ask who those relatives might be because he had no idea who they were. In fact, all he knew about the state where his ancestors had settled was the story of his paternal grandfather's flight from his thousand-acre *finca* in the rich coastal land of Guatemala across the border into Mexico. His grandfather had supported an unsuccessful coup against the ruling Guatemalan military regime and had fled the country to save his life and the lives of his wife and children. Carlos *had* visited Chiapas, once, but he had only been ten years old.

Born in northern Mexico in the border city of Sabinas, Carlos had grown up dreaming of living in the United States. When he was twelve years old, his mother arranged for him to visit a distant cousin in Los Angeles, with whom Carlos eventually lived while going to school after obtaining a green card. At the age of eighteen he'd become a naturalized citizen, and now, fifteen years later, he still felt a surge of pride whenever he repeated the Pledge of Allegiance. America had been good to him and he'd made the most of every opportunity.

Guapo warmed immediately to his new confidant. "Your people are from Chiapas? Really? Maybe you know the man's family. Venustio, the guys called him. Zenoyo Venustio."

Carlos's heart lurched to hear the unusual name that was common to anyone with ties to southern Mexico. Immediately he knew what he had to do. With his jaws locked tightly in an innocent mask, he muttered, "No, doesn't sound familiar." Shaking his head slowly, he finished his beer, forcing himself not to act as impatient as he felt. At last, he got up from the bar stool, noticing that Guapo's attention had turned to the huge tip he left on the bar.

"You come back. Okay?"

"Sure," Carlos said, shaking the bartender's hand.

As his only customer pushed through the heavy oak door, Guapo began humming along with the tune on the radio and resumed wiping the heavy beer glasses.

Carlos headed outside, glad to see that it was still light. Inside his car, he picked up his mobile phone and started pressing buttons.

"Don't worry, Joe," he told his producer, steering with one hand. "I know the roads. I could drive to Refugio with my eyes closed."

"Where's Refugio, Carlos? How far?" Joe asked, leery of his star's compulsion to throw himself into his stories.

"Just south of Victoria, on the road to Corpus. About a hundred sixty miles from Houston."

"Staying over?"

"Yes, I'll probably have to stay overnight, but I'll be back in time for tomorrow night's show." Carlos listened for a second to Joe's worried protests and digs for more information, then cut him off brusquely. "No, I can't say now. Not yet, but if I'm lucky, the man I'm looking for is still alive. If I'm real lucky, he'll be able to remember what he told me a long time ago. This could be hot. Real hot."

"You better call Sherry," Joe added. "She's called here six times tonight looking for you."

"Yeah?" Carlos said, acting surprised. "I wonder what she wants."

After terminating the conversation, Carlos pressed the speed-dial button, holding his breath while his ex-wife's telephone rang. Sherry was going to raise hell and cuss him out—again—he knew, but he also knew he could sweet-talk her into keeping the boys for another day or two.

As soon as I break this story, I'm taking some time off, Carlos vowed, trying to calculate how many weeks of summer vacation were still left. He'd planned to keep the boys all summer this year, giving Sherry a break for the first time since the divorce, but during the past three years he'd been overloaded with work, and something had always come up. Now, as he waited for her to pick up, he wondered whether a trip to Walt Disney World or the Grand Canyon would best appease his eight-year-old twins. Disney World, he decided as Sherry Rico answered the phone.

Elise stood in the shower, letting warm water drum against her back, inhaling the sweet scent of eucalyptus that wafted from the lathering of gel she had slicked over her body. She liked the smell of this new scent, which had come as a sample with her last order of cherry blossom bath oil. She made a mental note to look it up in her latest Herbalist catalog and order some for her mother.

Elise's thoughts swung to Junior and a twinge of guilt immediately struck. She had been dreadfully late getting home and had been so distracted by her own situation, she'd barely paid any attention to his chattering report of his day at the day-care center he attended. Through bites of the spinach lasagna Blake had fixed for dinner, she'd tried to carry on a conversation with her son and disguise her worried state. She wondered how successful she had been.

Thank God I married a man who can cook, she thought. Her new job was going to put his skills to the test.

Poor Junior had fallen asleep before he'd even finished reading the first page of his favorite picture storybook, but not until after she'd reassured him that Grandpa and Grandma were fine.

He'd seen pictures of the fire on the evening news and had begged her to tell him all about it. So she had, in shaded detail, leaving out the part about the woman passing out on the sidewalk and the two children who'd been burned in their beds. He'd believed her when she said the fire had been extinguished and there was nothing at all to worry about.

Junior had listened intently, eyes wide, promising her he was not afraid, and for the few minutes they'd spent together alone in his room, she'd managed to forget just how bone tired she'd been when she'd pulled into the driveway at eight o'clock that evening.

Thick white vapor filled the bathroom now, clouding the mirrors, isolating Elise with her thoughts. Arching her back, she let the stench of the fire and the pressure of her day slip off her shoulders and swirl down the drain.

It had been a tough day, but she'd held her own, and was still surprised that Al had not only approved her press release on the first draft but had told her she'd done a good job. A seed of hope settled at the back of her mind. Maybe they would be able to tolerate each other, or at least not come to blows.

Al had stayed busy rounding up components from supply houses across the country while she was left alone to discuss insurance and environmental matters with John Farren at headquarters, who did not bring up the subject of her personal connection with Flatwoods. The absence of any comment made her believe that he'd most probably told Al to calm down and leave her alone.

Conversations with the beleaguered fire chief, who still couldn't rule out arson, and Dr. Boyd at Tide County Clinic had ended her day. The number of cases of smoke inhalation at the clinic had climbed to thirty, but Dr. Boyd hadn't seemed alarmed, telling Elise that he felt the situation had stabilized.

So far, the news services had run her press releases with few embellishments, and were presenting ScanTron as a fair, responsible company, but she knew better than to relax. The investigation was still in its early stages. Tomorrow morning, a public meeting was going to be held at Flatwoods Community Center, where she, the fire chief, a representative of the county health department, and Justin

Snyder of the EPA would meet the press and answer questions. She did not look forward to going, especially since she'd heard that the well-known activist-lawyer, Yusef Kirk, would be there representing the residents of Flatwoods.

Kirk, the Berkeley-educated environmental attorney who had led a successful protest against the construction of an offshore salt dome for toxic waste storage, was not someone to tangle with. Though his successful demonstration had earned him the status of near folk hero in south Texas, it had also sealed his reputation with many politicians as a stubborn, hard-ass troublemaker.

Elise turned off the water, stepped out of the shower, and pulled on her terrycloth robe. Using one of the monogrammed towels that had been a Christmas present from her mother, she wiped vapor from the large mirror above the twin sinks and stared at her reflection. The two vertical furrows etched between her brows looked deeper than she remembered, and she worried that they might become permanent. As she was running a finger over the delicate skin, the door to the bathroom eased open.

"Feel better?" Blake poked his head into the steamy room.

"Much," Elise replied, toweling her hair.

He came into the fog and set a glass of cognac on the pink marble counter, then moved to stand behind his wife, slipping a muscled arm around her waist. He was wearing jeans, no shirt, and he pressed his warm bare chest against Elise's back as he nuzzled the nape of her neck.

"I'll bet you're exhausted."

Elise arched an eyebrow, nodding.

"Well, you're back in the business of telling people what they want to hear, Elise. Just like old times. You up to it?"

"Mm-hm," Elise murmured, taking a sip of the brandy. "I'm as ready as I'll ever be. But this is not at all like old times, Blake. I had three different bosses during the six years I was at Trinity Hospital and not one of them came close to being the control freak Al Patterson is."

Blake straightened up and began rubbing Elise's shoulders. "Doing PR for an international security company is a whole lot different than working for a private hospital." He eased her around to face him. "Things will fall into place soon enough. Patterson will calm down."

Elise lowered her eyes, running her tongue over her bottom lip. "I hope so. He's something else."

Blake drew her to him, propping his chin on Elise's shoulder, still looking in the spot she'd cleared in the mirror. "Well, you sure smell better," he said, pulling away when Elise playfully swatted at him.

"I would hope so," Elise replied, moving from his arms to set down her glass. She continued toweling her hair. "I must have smelled like a slab of burned barbecued ribs."

"Everyone in the county probably smelled about the same. I'm sure no one noticed."

Elise giggled when Blake kissed her lightly on the shoulder. Turning around, she captured his gaze, recognizing the lazy, seductive look in his light brown eyes that, after eleven years of marriage, still caused somersaults deep in her stomach.

When she'd first met Blake at a fraternity dance during her freshman year at SMU, she'd been drawn to him immediately. From the far side of a room filled with writhing bodies and rowdy partiers entranced by Chaka Khan's husky voice, Elise had spotted Blake and positively dissolved on the spot, longing to know what it would feel like to hold him, to kiss him, to lie with him in bed. From that moment on, the two had been inseparable until Blake, who had been a senior when they met, graduated and moved to Houston to begin his career at Century Trust.

Elise had always loved Blake's ability to lift her spirits. As a small-town girl, she'd been ashamed to admit that her arrival in Dallas was the first time she'd set foot in the big city, and that the hordes of students roaming the sprawling campus intimidated and frightened her.

Blake had only laughed, reassuring her that the majority of the students weren't as sophisticated as they pretended to be, and many came from towns as small as Flatwoods, even smaller.

Blake had been her first love, the dangerously wise senior who had changed Elise from a naive college freshman to a full-fledged woman almost overnight. He had been her first date on campus, and during the two semesters until he graduated and left her behind, he made her days of cramming for finals and waiting for grades much easier to bear.

Now, with the most difficult time in their marriage behind them, Elise felt relieved to be in Blake's arms and was thankful that her family was still intact. Not so very long ago, neither she nor Blake had been sure they would make it this far.

"I'm proud of you, Elise," Blake murmured, placing three fingers under her chin, tilting her face toward his.

Elise smiled, then shrugged, as if embarrassed by his praise.

"I'm serious," Blake insisted. "You've been through a lot, but look at you now—the national spokesperson for ScanTron Security —a more prestigious position than the one you had at Trinity Hospital, not to mention the pay and perks you're going to get. I saw your interview on Channel Three this morning. You did a wonderful job. Held your own against Rico."

"Right!" Elise made a fist, raising it above her head, shaking it twice. "I'd loved to have shoved that microphone right into his smirking face, but I didn't. I acted like a lady and rose above him."

"That was the only way to handle it," Blake agreed, "but please, let's not discuss *him*, okay?"

"Fine," Elise agreed, unwilling to have her time with Blake sullied by a discussion of the man who'd betrayed her. "Let's talk about something else." Tonight all she wanted to do was enjoy being in her husband's embrace.

Blake held her close, moving gently back and forth with his face pressed against her neck. "Well," he started, lifting his head, "we could talk about how nice it's going to be to finally pay off all of our bills and build Junior's bank account back up."

Elise pulled back. "Blake. The pay and the perks of this job are great, but let's not get too far ahead of ourselves. The position isn't final until September first, remember?"

"So?" Blake said.

"So," Elise reminded him, "I may have the paycheck and the car, but the title's still temporary. We'd better be cautious about our spending until everything is finalized." She watched him closely, meaning what she said, unable to admit that the Saks account was already active.

With a squeeze, Blake drew her back to him, kissing the tip of her nose. He fingered a damp curl behind her ear. "You'll get it. If Farren didn't want you to have the job, he wouldn't have made the interim appointment."

Elise picked up the brandy glass, holding it to Blake's lips for him to take a sip. "I hope you're right, but getting used to Al Patterson is going to be tough."

"Consider it a test," Blake said jokingly. "Farren probably wants to see how much heat you can stand. If you pass, the position is yours."

"I don't know about that," Elise replied, setting down the glass to place both hands behind Blake's neck.

Her robe fell open, exposing the silky skin of her still-damp breasts. "Everyone in the office grumbles about Al behind his back, but to his face they treat him as if he's God." With one hand she attempted to close her robe, but Blake stopped her, grazing her skin with his hand as he pulled hers away. Their eyes locked for a second; then he bent and kissed the soft spot between her breasts.

Raising his head, he reassured her, "As long as Patterson is satisfied with your performance, don't worry about anything else. Take it one day at a time. Things will get easier as you get to know him."

"They'd better," Elise said, "because I don't think the situation brewing in Flatwoods is going to remain under control very long. The people are angry, frightened, and they want some answers."

Blake glanced thoughtfully at the ceiling. "Well, stay calm, don't let them rattle you, and be careful about letting down your guard. Whatever you say, even if it's off the record, could come back to haunt you. Remember?"

Elise twitched. *Remember?* How could she forget the depression and pain her lapse of judgment had caused? Inwardly, she resented Blake's insensitive remark but said nothing. They'd argued enough about that.

Elise gently untangled herself from Blake's embrace and reached for the hair conditioner. She rubbed a dot in the center of her hand, then massaged it into her damp curls with a vigorous rub, as if wiping away the sting of Blake's words.

Blake took her hand in his, stopping her. "I'm sorry," he said huskily. Still holding her by the hand, he led her from the bathroom to their king-size bed.

"No more talk about work, okay? Let's celebrate your new position." He sank onto the bed and stretched out on his back, pulling Elise down on top of him. Placing one hand to the side of her face, he guided her lips toward his.

With a shudder, Elise relaxed, allowing the full weight of her body to rest on Blake's while she kissed him, accepting his tongue as it traced sweetly over hers. The kiss deepened, causing a ripple of contractions to lightly tense her body for an exquisite, craving moment before it faded into a warm tingly glow.

Slipping one hand behind Blake's head, she pressed closer, hungrily exploring the taste of him, impatient to forget the day's events and lose herself in their love.

At the darkest times, when their problems had been so large and out of control that neither had felt secure about the future, their ability to put it all behind them while in each other's arms had been their only salvation.

As Blake eased her robe off her shoulders and bent to suckle the taut brown rose-point of one breast, she was filled with love and a sense of gratitude because he believed so strongly in her.

Elise smiled as Blake slipped out of his jeans, then pressed the small of her back until she was flush against him once more, settled warmly over his throbbing shaft, which pulsed against her thigh. Blake knew exactly how to make her forget about everything negative and troublesome. He knew her body, her weak spots, her expectations, and she had nothing to do but melt into the rhythm of his tender caress.

Her mind cleared, her body warmed, and her hands roamed in a practiced way down the length of Blake's now naked form. Nothing mattered but loving Blake, and that was all she intended to do.

Folding his body over hers, Blake swept Elise onto her back in a fluid turn. Nestling in the silky space between her thighs, he parted them with a gentle, familiar nudge.

Elise wrapped both arms around his shoulders, running her widespread fingers across his smooth, bronze back. She rotated her hips, sealing her pelvis against his until he moaned and caught her lips between his. She laughed huskily, her delight muffled by the demanding thrust of his tongue.

When Blake entered her, she shuddered, then melted like slick warm honey, letting her mind spin away from all thoughts of ScanTron, Al Patterson, her promise to her father, and especially Carlos Rico.

CHAPTER 7

Elise turned down the volume on the television in the kitchen, though she had hoped to catch the early morning news. Distracted by the argument Blake was having with Junior about straightening up his room, she listened, leaning against the counter, whipping frothy eggs with a fork. She wished Blake would lower his voice, be a little less demanding and a little more rational. He ought to let her handle what she considered her domain. Shaking some salt and pepper into the yellow swirl, Elise realized that Blake was perfectly within his rights to insist that Junior pick up his clothes and his toys. The boy needed to be disciplined about his increasingly sloppy behavior, but it pained Elise to feel so left out.

She'd seen the mess in his room last night but had chosen to ignore it, too tired to make a fuss. It was summer. He was only five years old. Why couldn't Blake ease up? She knew the housework was slipping, the laundry was piling up, and there was only enough milk in the refrigerator to last through today, but time was at a premium and right now some things would just have to wait. But with Blake taking care of Junior after day care *and* making dinner, she was more determined than ever not to stop fixing breakfast. They needed to eat together as a family at least once a day.

She glanced at the clock. Running late again. But she wasn't about to complain.

"Get over it, girl," she grumbled, admonishing herself as she slipped two pieces of bread into the toaster. A program on *Oprah* she'd seen on single mothers last week came to mind, and Elise knew there were sisters whose situations were a whole lot worse than hers.

Blake and Junior finally came into the kitchen, looking sullen and already mad at the world. Elise reached across the sink and turned up the volume on the TV as Molly Yarboro, the early morning anchorwoman at Channel 3, was finishing the final story in her newscast.

Jerking her head toward the screen, Elise lifted a brow at Blake. "Check this."

He sank down onto a bar stool, sipping his orange juice while listening.

"A hot spot flared overnight in the rubble of the burned-out ScanTron Security research and warehouse complex in Tide County and firefighters are once again on the scene. Forty-eight people have been hospitalized so far. Though a spokesperson for ScanTron Security insists that no hazardous materials were stored in their complex, the residents of nearby Flatwoods are up in arms, demanding to be told what the contents were. They have retained environmental attorney Yusef Kirk to represent them. The EPA is investigating."

Elise snapped off the TV, snatching the crisp bread as it popped up in the toaster. She slapped butter on one piece with an angry stroke, then jammed it atop the eggs on Junior's plate. "Did you hear that? Forty-eight people in the hospital."

Blake calmly sipped his juice, then rose from the bar stool and slipped into his chair at the table opposite his son. "Mmm. I heard. Don't overreact."

Elise crossed the kitchen and plunked down a plate in front of Blake, then Junior, before slipping into her seat to sip her cup of coffee, not nearly as confident as Blake seemed to be that there was no reason to worry.

"That's easy for you to say." She picked up half of Blake's toast and bit off a corner. "The press is going to whip this into a whole lot more than it has to be."

"Are you surprised?" Blake asked, forking a piece of ham. He gulped the last of his juice and was about to say something else when the telephone rang.

Reaching behind her to the wall phone, Elise whispered to Blake as she removed the receiver, "Bet it's Farren." She said hello, then waited, nodding with one hand over the mouthpiece as she listened.

"Yes, I just heard that, Mr. Farren." She rolled her eyes to the ceiling, then at Blake. "Sure. Yes. I'm on my way." She put the phone back into its cradle. "Gotta go. Farren wants me to get in touch with the clinic and get a handle on the kinds of medical complaints the people are making."

Leaving the table, she dashed upstairs, taking them two at a time, grabbed her jacket from the closet and her briefcase from beside the bed, then impulsively went into the bathroom, opened the medicine cabinet, and snatched a bottle of aspirin. With another fire blazing and more people falling ill, she could see a hectic day looming ahead.

Returning to the kitchen, Elise hurriedly kissed Junior good-bye, promising to be home earlier than yesterday.

Blake jumped up from the table, walking with Elise into the garage. "If you can, try to steer clear of Rico," he advised.

Elise glared at him. "How? He's media. He'll be there. No way can I get around dealing with him."

"Well . . . *try*," Blake tossed back sternly. "That man is trouble personified, and this situation sounds like it's about to get pretty complicated. Carlos is looking for dirt, any kind of dirt to sensationalize his show, and you know he can't be trusted."

"Yes, I *do!*" Elise snapped, suddenly feeling cornered. Why did Blake have to talk to her like that, as if he were reprimanding Junior? Why did he have to ruin the beginning of her day by throwing that up in her face?

"Don't get edgy," Blake said, reaching out to take Elise by the arm.

She pulled back defensively. "I'm *not* edgy. When I told Carlos that I suspected Lily Kitzmiller was the one who abducted that baby from the hospital nursery, I was speaking off the record."

"I know you were."

"Can I help it if he put my statement on the air?"

Blake didn't answer.

"I thought Carlos was my friend, at least a professional colleague. Any decent reporter would have respected my confidence."

"Decent ones, yes!" Blake said. "But Carlos Rico isn't decent. And he'll do you in again if you give him half a chance."

"You can rest assured, I won't." Elise's reply was icy. Trembling with indignation, she went on. "How dare you bring this up now, knowing how much it hurts *and* how much I've got on my mind today?" Her voice had grown thin and cold, as frigid as the stream of air whooshing from the air-conditioning unit Blake had installed in the garage so he could tinker with his motorcycles in comfort.

For a moment, the air was still. They stood silent, miserable, until the slam of their neighbor's car door and the sound of an engine turning over broke the awful tension.

"I'm sorry," Blake mumbled. "It was stupid, but I can't help worrying."

"Well, try!" she shot back.

Blake winced. The expression on his face was sincere, but when he touched Elise's cheek, forcing her to look at him, she glanced away, unable to speak. "Please, let's not fight," he urged. "Not about this. I shouldn't have said anything. I know you can handle yourself."

"Yes, I can," Elise said, her words laced with steel.

Blake sighed aloud. "Okay. I admit it. I'm still pissed over all the cash it took to settle that mess Rico created." He reached out and pulled Elise to his chest. "Not to mention the damage he did to you." Smoothing her hair from her face, he murmured, "If Carlos had played it straight, you'd still be at Trinity. We'd have cash in the bank. Security. Paul and I would have our dealership by now and I'd be long gone from Century Trust."

With a jerk, Elise stepped out of his arms. "That's all you care about, isn't it? Those damned motorcycles and leaving Century." She yanked the car door open and got in.

"That's not true, and you know it," Blake denied, coming to stand beside the car. "I care about our future, and I'm willing to take a big risk to make things better."

"Better for you, you mean." Elise slammed the car door, then zapped the remote control, making the garage door groan and squeak as it rolled up above the car.

"You're being childish, Elise."

"Ha!" She spat. "You and Paul are the ones who act like a couple of leftover hippies stuck in a time warp. Bikes, cycles, scooters. That's all you talk about anymore. You'd think you two were Dennis Hopper and Peter Fonda the way you carry on!" Elise sat staring out the windshield, knowing she was way out of line, but too upset to care. Turning, she spoke to Blake through the open window, her voice shaky. "I have a lot facing me today, Blake. Our future isn't riding on what you and Paul do about fulfilling your childhood dreams; it's hanging on how well I handle this assignment. I'm under tremendous pressure. Can't you see that?"

He nodded.

"Well, you might try being a lot less selfish and a little more understanding." Elise gripped the steering wheel, breath trapped in her lungs as she tried to keep her body from shaking.

Blake stepped closer to the car, watching her glumly through the window. "I know. I know. I'm sorry."

Too angry to accept his words of apology, Elise turned the key in the ignition and put the car in reverse.

Blake moved back, a set of worry lines creasing his forehead.

Tears stood glassily in Elise's eyes as she stared into the rearview mirror and backed down the long driveway. She wanted to glance over and wave good-bye as she usually did every morning, but couldn't, so she tore off in a squeal of hot rubber, racing down the middle of her quiet tree-lined street.

The houses along the suburban thoroughfare became a blur of red bricks, white trim, and lush green trees. Out of habit, she slowed at the corner where the school zone was, then sped up as soon as she'd cleared it. The pain of the past two years was threatening to swamp her again, and she bit down hard on her bottom lip, determined not to cry.

Four years ago, after being fired from Trinity Hospital, she'd cried day and night for what seemed like an eternity. She wasn't going to cry anymore. True, she had been stupid to tell Carlos Rico off the record that she suspected the missing baby had probably been abducted by the child's eccentric, shabby aunt. How could she have known that he would air her suspicions, attribute them to her, and launch a major manhunt for Lily Kitzmiller, diverting the police from searching for the guilty party—who turned out to be an embittered hospital orderly who had been under psychiatric care?

How well she remembered the nights she'd spent sobbing in Blake's arms after learning—from an on-air bulletin—that Lily Kitzmiller had filed a million-dollar defamation-of-character lawsuit against her. That had been the start of Elise and Blake's financial and emotional nightmare. They'd survived it, and she'd be damned if she'd give Rico, or any other reporter, an opportunity to trash her again.

When a four-way stop appeared out of nowhere, Elise screeched to a halt. Taking several long breaths to clear her head, she waited as the truck on her right proceeded through the intersection. The shock of the betrayal, the shame of losing her job, and the money problems that had followed had come very close to destroying her—once. There was no way she would allow herself to be so vulnerable again.

Elise zoomed down the street, turned onto the feeder road, and headed toward the interstate, her thoughts focused on Molly Yarboro's morning news report. Forty-eight people hospitalized! What in the world could she possibly say to the residents of Flatwoods to get them to trust her now?

As soon as she was settled at her makeshift desk, she called the county clinic. Dr. Boyd verified the numbers in the morning news report but didn't feel there was cause for alarm. The only cases he considered serious were the two burned children and the woman who had collapsed on the sidewalk early yesterday morning. Her medical history indicated that she had been suffering from chronic emphysema for years and had been hospitalized for respiratory problems three times in the past six months. Her condition was delicate, but he felt hopeful about the prognosis. She had been transferred to League City Hospital and was listed in critical condition, remaining on oxygen in intensive care.

Elise's next call was to Justin Snyder of the EPA, but she was informed that he was at the scene of the fire supervising the collection of soil and air samples. She left a message for him to call her back, then dialed the number to the fire department.

Surprisingly, the fire marshal immediately came on the line, but when he learned she was representing ScanTron Security, he turned wary and clammed up, refusing to answer any questions, recommending that she pose them directly to Assistant Fire Chief Peters at the upcoming community meeting. No attempt would be made to search the rubble for evidence of why the fire burned like it did until the site had completely cooled down, and that might take as long as seventy-two hours.

With little more information than she'd had when she arrived that morning, Elise switched on Darrell Grimes's laptop and drafted a new press release. Then she put her files inside her briefcase and left, heading toward the burned-out site. She wanted to see it for herself by daylight, and she also wanted to check on Damita, hoping she might be back in her home.

Driving toward Flatwoods, Elise saw a thin column of white smoke drifting eastward in the distance. An imperceptible sense of relief crept over her to see smoke that was no longer as thick and black as it had been yesterday. White smoke meant that the second flare-up had been extinguished.

The road she followed took her past the now abandoned elementary school she had attended as a child. Thoughts of Damita filled her again. Truly friends since birth—their mothers had shared a postdelivery room in the League City Hospital maternity ward—Elise and Damita had been inseparable long before entering their kindergarten classroom. Slowing down, Elise pulled over, then stopped in front of the three-story yellow brick structure that held so many memories.

On the eerily quiet school grounds, the rusted monkey bars and swing sets without seats stood as sad reminders of the fun she, Damita, and their long-forgotten classmates had had on the tiny black-topped playground. A scraggly row of top-heavy crepe myrtles lined a broken chain-link fence, their lacy branches sagging under the blazing July sun.

It hurt Elise to see graffiti covering the tall double doors at the front entrance and the empty black holes where shiny panes of glass had been. Smashed by rock-throwing vandals, the remains of the windows lay in mounds of dull gray crystal all around the vacant structure.

The shadowy space next to the doors had been Elise's favorite place to sit while waiting for her friends to arrive at school, and it was where she'd kissed her first boy—Danny Roker, a skinny kid with bushy eyebrows and olive-colored skin, who had gone on to become a world-famous violinist, the first African-American to play with the American Symphony Orchestra. She and Damita could still get a good laugh out of those memories, especially when Elise retold, in exaggerated detail, her disgust and shock when Danny stuck his tongue in her mouth.

Easing the car from the curb, Elise chuckled, driving on, turning left at the next corner to pass Barton's Drugstore, the site of her first real job. At the age of fourteen, Elise had been put in charge of the newsstand, ordering and selling newspapers and magazines. Once, when her cash box had come up short, Mr. Barton had accused Elise of allowing her girlfriends, who were always hanging around, to walk away with the movie magazines without paying for them.

Elise had been hurt, was adamant in her denial, and quickly became embroiled in a nasty argument with her boss. When Mr. Barton made it clear that Elise would be fired if she didn't make restitution, Damita had stepped forward, informing him that she'd taken the magazines when Elise had been busy helping someone else; then she slapped two dollars on the counter. To this day the identity of the thief remained a mystery, but Elise knew Damita never read the glossy publications, and had unselfishly spent her meager allowance to save Elise's job.

It was a disturbing memory, though it brought a thoughtful smile to Elise's lips as she realized how much Damita's actions that day reflected the nature of their friendship. Elise, who was quick to open her mouth and spout off whenever she felt trapped or wronged, was the opposite of Damita, who could hold her tongue and her temper, quietly maneuvering in the background to get things done.

A quick-thinking, studious girl while growing up, Damita had matured into a serious-minded woman who took pride in maintaining their childhood friendship and received a great deal of pleasure from helping others. Damita had often said that if she'd been able to go to college, she would have studied sociology and become an urban social worker, but instead, she'd settled for a clerical position in the human resources department of nearby Saturn Chemical, where she had worked for the past fourteen years.

If I ever needed Damita's take on what I've gotten myself into, it's now, Elise concluded, remembering how her friend's words of advice and support had helped her keep a grip on her sanity during the disastrous Kitzmiller affair. Though Elise's telephone bills had skyrocketed into triple digits during that awful time in her life, she never regretted the money or hours spent in long-distance conversation. Damita's calm encouragement had prevented Elise from falling apart, from caving in, and from taking Junior and leaving Blake. Damita might be the only person, besides Blake, whose advice Elise dared seek out and follow.

With twenty minutes until the start of the community meeting, Elise continued toward Damita's house, a thread of apprehension beginning to tighten her stomach. Facing the public with the sketchy information she had managed to pull together this morning was going to be tricky. There were always sticky issues to complicate matters when a big company like ScanTron had some explaining to do. That was to be expected. But she wished she'd been able to get her hands on a detailed description of the contents of the warehouses. Anything to help make her case. But Al had been outright rude in his denial of her request for inventory logs, citing competition and security as his reasons—reasons that Elise doubted would carry much weight with the rebellious crowd she was about to face.

What could she tell the residents of Flatwoods that they hadn't already heard? And then there was Carlos, who more than likely would be at the meeting, microphone in hand. Suddenly she felt overwhelmed, skittish about facing the people, and she wondered if, perhaps, Al had been right. Maybe Farren had made a serious mistake by giving her this assignment.

Moving deeper into the neighborhood, she saw a scattering of residents nosing around. One man was standing in the street, scrutinizing the charred remains of his house, scratching his head. A few were at the curbs and in driveways trying to wipe away the thick coating of yellow goo that had settled over their cars, their lawn furniture, and anything that had been left outside. Others were picking through the ruins, looking for pieces of prized possessions. A lost dog wandered through a blackened vegetable garden that looked as if it had suffered an atomic blast. The trees facing Baymark Road, which created the only barrier between Flatwoods and the ScanTron complex, stood like black sticks of charcoal rising from the earth.

Elise drove to the end of Baymark and turned right, entering Thornhill Road. She stopped at the end of the street where a yellow wooden barricade erected by the fire department had been set up to keep curiosity seekers from getting too close to the now smoldering area. Fire trucks were still pulling away from the site, leaving two heavily protected sentries standing guard over the rubble.

When Elise got out, the stench of burned wood, seared wire, and melted plastic hit her in the face, making her cough. Covering her nose with one hand, she ducked under the barricade, crossed the street, and headed toward a redbrick bungalow in the middle of the block.

This area of Flatwoods had been spared the fire, though a layer of ash and soot covered every surface. From the curb, Damita's house looked intact but unoccupied. Several newspapers were on the porch and the curtains were drawn. Damita must not be at home, because if she had been there, the shades would be up and Benji would be sunning himself on the front window sill, licking his angora coat. Elise mounted the steps and picked up the newspapers. She pulled back the flimsy screen door and knocked loudly several times but got no response.

After trying to see inside the house through a slit in the curtains, Elise stepped off the porch and took the side path around to the back door. Automatically, she leaned down when she came to the low-hanging limbs of the leafy maple tree where she and Damita had played dolls and practiced the cuss words they learned from listening to the rowdy Thompson boys who had lived next door.

At the soot-covered hedges along the back porch, she paused, remembering when she and Damita had helped a stray cat give birth to a litter of kittens at that very spot. They had hidden the mother and the kittens in the old toolshed, transforming it into a cozy little playhouse. The dilapidated structure leaned precariously to one side, its slatted door hanging by rusty hinges.

Elise took a deep breath, distressed by the sight of the scorched debris that had drifted all over Damita's backyard. She saw several places along the rear door where bricks had cracked or fallen out, and several panes of glass were held in place with strips of masking tape. The outside of the place might be in bad repair, but she knew the interior reflected Damita's zest for cleanliness and her cheerful nature with its yellow ruffled curtains and watercolor landscapes of various scenes along the Tide County coastline.

Elise rapped on the back door. No one answered. Standing on tiptoe in front of an ivy-draped window, she peered past the masking tape, surprised to see the furniture covered with sheets and all three of Damita's cats standing in the middle of the kitchen staring forlornly at her!

Elise stepped back, perplexed. Damita wouldn't go away and leave her precious cats alone, not if she could possibly help it. Elise's mother had even taken care of them once or twice when Damita had come into Houston for a visit. She rarely ventured so far from home that she'd have to be away from Ben, Benji, and Benny overnight. Something must be wrong.

Quickly circling toward the front of the house, Elise's mind clicked off possibilities. Perhaps Damita had been evacuated so quickly she'd been forced to leave her pets behind. Maybe she was still at one of the Red Cross shelters, which did not accept animals. But judging from the looks of her side of the neighborhood, there was no reason to stay away now.

Rummaging in her purse, Elise found a pen and notepad and was about to scribble a note to stick on Damita's front door when she saw a man crossing the damp, matted grass between his house and his neighbor's. He hurried over, waving vigorously.

"Hello," Elise said. The man looked like a displaced farmer. He wore bib overalls and a white cotton T-shirt, and held a sun-faded canvas hat in one hand. In the other he held a small brass key.

"Good morning," he said. "You looking for Damita?"

"Yes," Elise replied, introducing herself as a longtime friend.

The man eagerly shook her hand. "Glad to meet you. I'm Mose Greer. Live next door."

"Do you know where Damita is? At a shelter, maybe?" Elise prompted, eyeing the man closely.

"Oh no," Mose replied quickly. "She missed the fire completely. I'm supposing she's still over in League City. Told Ethel, my wife, she'd be gone only for a day, but it's been three days now and we haven't heard a word. Was hoping you might of come with some news."

Elise stared at the man, puzzled. To her knowledge, Damita had no relatives or friends in League City, a typical oil refining town about fifteen miles down the interstate. Plus, when she'd talked to her last week, she hadn't mentioned going away for any length of time.

"News?" Elise repeated. "Sorry, I don't know anything. Why is Damita in League City?"

Mose set his work gloves and hat on the wide porch railing, unable to meet Elise's eyes. "Ethel said . . . ," he began, pausing as if unsure of what to say or how to say it.

Elise waited, nervous about the worried expression on Mose's face.

"Well, she asked Ethel not to tell anybody, but we've been pretty worried. . . ."

"Tell what?" Elise interrupted, beginning to panic.

"Well, Damita told my wife that she had to go over to the League City Hospital for some kind of tests. Said she'd be only be gone for the day, probably be back before dark. But that was three days ago. She left Ethel a key to go in and check on the cats . . . was ninety-eight degrees yesterday, and we were beginning to get a bit worried. We don't mind caring for the cats; they're fine during the day, but I tell you, they carry on at night. I hear 'em crying all night long."

"A test?" Elise asked, her voice hoarse. "What kind? Why?"

"Now that, we don't know," Mose said.

"Did you call the hospital?" Elise was so upset she could hardly get the words out.

"Oh, yes. But you know how they are. Won't tell us a thing on the phone. I was just saying to Ethel, maybe we ought to drive over and find out what's happened."

Elise hurriedly stuffed the pad and pen back into her purse. "Damita didn't mention to me that she was sick."

"Well," Mose said, drawing out his response, "She had been looking a little tired. Ethel says she's too thin. Maybe it's just a checkup, something to do with her job."

Elise doubted that. Damita had been a secretary at Saturn Chemical for close to fifteen years, and it was doubtful that the company would send an employee all the way to League City for a routine physical exam. It must be something more serious.

"Tell your wife that I'll go over to League City immediately after the meeting at the community center and see what I can find out."

"Good."

Elise nodded at Mose Greer, stepping down from the porch. He walked with her across the patchy lawn.

"So," Mose said, cocking his head to one side. "You gonna be at the meeting?"

"Yes," she replied confidently, then hesitated, not ready to reveal who she was.

"Well, we've got a fight on our hands. That company"—he pointed across the road to the burned-out warehouses—"has ruined Flatwoods. When they set up over there, everything changed around here. Taxes shot sky-high, folks started moving away. A lot of the old people are losing their homes. I just knew it'd come to no good. But did anybody listen to me? No. Look at this place." A hard glint flashed in his dark eyes as he surveyed the neighborhood. Raising a hand, he blocked the sun from his eyes. "A mess. A big mess that we gotta clean up."

Elise nodded sympathetically, realizing, for the first time, that there were an inordinate number of FOR SALE signs stuck in front yards on Thornhill Road.

Mose checked his watch, then went on. "Well, it's about time to get over to the meeting. You'll have your chance soon enough, young lady, to let that company know what you think of them. We can't sit by and let them get away with what they've done." He sniffed, then said, "I didn't know you lived round here. Never seen you before."

Elise shook her head, backing slightly away. "My parents live in town," she offered, hoping the tremor in her voice would go away. He'd learn soon enough who she was. "I'm from around here, but I don't live in Flatwoods anymore."

Stopping, Elise searched the row of smoke-damaged houses lining the road across from the complex, then lifted a hand to point. "I was born in that house over there. The one with the hole in its roof."

Mose Greer narrowed his eyes almost closed as he looked from the house to Elise, then back across the neighborhood. "That so?"

When he opened his mouth to say something else, Elise hurried to intercept his question. "Yes. That's my old house." Then, waving good-bye, she walked quickly down the street, relieved that she had parked far enough away from Damita's house to prevent Mose Greer from seeing the bold blue letters emblazoned on the side of her company car.

CHAPTER 8

T
he people of Flatwoods were against the construction of those warehouses from the beginning," Yusef Kirk stated in rich, resonant tones, immediately commanding everyone's attention. He grabbed the freestanding microphone that was rocking back and forth on its wide flat base after having been shaken in anger by the previous speaker. With slender brown fingers, Yusef steadied the mike, pulling the top of it higher, leveling it with his mouth. "I was asked to come here and represent these frightened residents, and I agreed to speak for them in hopes that at least one of you might care enough to tell them the truth. They've told *you* the truth." He stretched his tall frame upright, falling silent as he assessed the panel, waiting for someone to speak.

Dr. Boyd glared. Justin Snyder of the EPA drew another doodle on a piece of paper. The fire marshal and the county judge both glanced quickly at Elise, who looked away just as their eyes connected with hers.

Focusing on the stack of insurance forms Al Patterson had insisted she bring along, her thoughts locked on Al's selfish refusal to come to the meeting. He'd been rude about not wanting to be there and had even rejected Darrell Grimes's offer to stand in for him as a representative of management. Now Elise was left to deal with not only the angry residents but also the technical details of explaining the company's policy on filing damage claims, an area that was totally beyond the scope of her job.

A mental weariness overcame her as she realized how much of an obstacle Al Patterson was becoming, but she forced her thoughts to stick with the discussion, listening cautiously to Yusef's continuing tirade.

Tossing his head to one side, Yusef flung several of the pencil-size dreadlocks that brushed his mahogany cheeks from his face, then went on. "They've been woefully wronged, but has anyone taken their concerns seriously?" His smoky brown eyes narrowed, then widened, as his gaze darted over the faces of the people sitting at the wood-grained folding table on the small stage at the front of the room. "No!" he told them. "And these folks deserve better! They should have been given as much information as possible about the potential health risks posed by the placement of the ScanTron facility so close to their homes." He assessed each representative keenly. "And they should have been warned that the value of their homes would suddenly decrease. Why has this happened, they ask. And I tell them for no reason other than the poisoning of the environment."

Elise sat up a little straighter, Mose Greer's words coming back, and she began to see why so much property was for sale in Flatwoods.

"And who is buying these properties?" Yusef lifted his shoulders in exaggerated question. "No one. The houses stand vacant. Deteriorating. Becoming eyesores and health hazards within the community."

An audible murmur of agreement rumbled through the crowd.

Kirk stared at Elise. "We have listened to your explanations and unfounded assurances with patience—a strained patience to be sure —but now it's time to get down to business."

Elise tensed when the Channel 3 television crew turned their bright lights on her, then panned the rest of the panel. Channel 3 was the only station to carry the meeting live. Elise assumed it would also be aired during the evening news, and she was surprised, though relieved, that Carlos was not there.

Just as well, she thought, realizing that the first round of questions from the press had gone badly. She must have come off looking like an ill-prepared high school student trying to con a teacher. Her words had rung empty even in her own ears and she had groped to support her statements about safety. Had she sounded convincing? Probably not.

If Al had given her the data she needed, she might have been better able to make a case for ScanTron. If he had been agreeable to showing up, his presence might have helped temper Yusef's cutting remarks, or at least strengthened the appearance of ScanTron's concern for public health, the image of the company, and for the job she had to do.

Elise was beginning to wonder about Al. If he was such a dedicated employee, why didn't he want to talk to the people who lived outside his company's door? Why couldn't he trust her with the inventory logs? And what could possibly be motivating him to ignore the storm of protest that was quickly gathering momentum?

Emotionally drained by the heated exchanges that had been going on for nearly an hour, Elise rubbed her shoulders while Yusef Kirk's pointed questions to the county judge began to fill the room. She frowned. Yusef was going after the judge like a dog determined to dig up a long-buried bone.

"Why did you grant ScanTron a building permit to construct its warehouse complex so near a residential area?" Yusef asked Judge Rectir.

Elise's spirits sank at the sight of the judge shifting uncomfortably on his hard metal chair. With a cough, he cleared his throat. "There was no reason to deny the permit," he replied in his calm, noncommital tone.

"If ScanTron had wanted to build its facility adjacent to Seabreeze Estates, where I believe you live, Judge Rectir, would you have granted the permit?"

A loud guffaw broke out from the crowd, followed immediately by a few muffled giggles. The outburst momentarily broke the tension but did not sit well with the now embarrassed judge, whose face turned angry.

"Well?" Yusef pressed.

Tapping a pencil on the table, the politician answered in a cool, businesslike manner. "That's a moot point, young man. But if you would like to have a crash course on county construction codes, feel free to drop by my office. I will personally go over each of the regulations with you." With that the judge folded his arms and pressed his lips together. He was finished answering questions.

Elise silently congratulated Judge Rectir for avoiding Yusef's trap. Without entering into the debate that the activist-lawyer had obviously anticipated, the judge had easily made his point. But Elise had to admit Yusef was sharp. His brash mannerisms annoyed her, his cockiness grated on her nerves, and his appearance—what could she say? Braided hair and Kente cloth ties certainly set him apart, out of place among the plain folks of the small refining community. She wondered how many of them knew that Kirk was just as slick as any East Coast lawyer and definitely looked out for himself.

Elise had read about Yusef Kirk in an in-depth newspaper story during the salt dome protest last year. Born in Florida, educated at Berkeley, he was used to winning. He had traveled to Africa, the Caribbean, and South America several times to represent people in isolated villages where environmental racism was openly practiced, taking on several industrial giants doing business there.

But he was also just as comfortable in the boardrooms and Wall Street offices of his high-powered, big-city clients—wealthy investors and developers who depended on Yusef's expertise to keep their projects within EPA and local regulatory guidelines, paying him well for his advice and representation. Yusef Kirk's reputation as a lawyer who could garner respect, instill trust, and organize a group of people with a mission was internationally known.

A disconcerting blend of anger, pride, and respect stirred Elise. She could not help but be impressed with Yusef's clear, concise way of making a point or with his extensive knowledge of environmental law. Though his provocative tactics were sometimes ruthlessly blunt, his charismatic approach usually produced the results he wanted.

Under other circumstances Elise would have congratulated the outspoken residents of Flatwoods on their choice of representation, but not today. It could not be more obvious—Yusef Kirk was out to nail the Tide County Emergency Clinic, the county judge, and especially ScanTron Security International. Without any conclusive results from the EPA tests or the state investigators, whom Yusef had called in, not much would be resolved today, but at least everyone with a complaint had been given the opportunity to let off steam at the microphone.

Elise let her eyes wander over the crowd. The racial and cultural makeup of Flatwoods had certainly changed, she observed. It was no longer an all-black community: there were also Asians, Hispanics, and a scattering of whites glaring back at her. Sitting in the audience, concern on their faces, were her parents' neighbors, Janet and Vick Poston. Behind them sat Julius Tarrant, the man she'd spoken to yesterday morning, and beside him was Mose Greer, staring at her with contempt in his eyes.

What are my chances of getting any of them to trust me? she wondered, while at the back of her mind, as it had been all afternoon, was Damita's mysterious visit to the hospital. Checking her watch, Elise worried. A quarter to two. If Yusef Kirk would just get on with it and wrap up his preaching, she might be able to get to the hospital before afternoon visiting hours were over.

Turning her attention back to the discussion, she was distracted by the unexpected appearance of her father at the rear of the room. He stood in the doorway looking around for a few seconds, then slipped into a chair without acknowledging her. Elise watched him sit rigidly, back straight, paying careful attention to what Yusef was saying.

Damn, Elise cursed silently, wishing her father had not come. As the minutes ticked by she grew more uneasy. Wasn't she under enough pressure and scrutiny without having to worry that her father might be the one to put her on the spot? As much as she loved him, right then she just wished he would disappear.

Yusef tilted his head in a thoughtful pose as if summing up what he was about to say, then angled himself so that the people in the audience and those on the panel could see his striking profile.

"Ladies and gentlemen," he began, "I truly hate to say this but it appears to me that what we have here in Tide County is a conspiracy. A terrible conspiracy against the poor, disadvantaged, hardworking residents of Flatwoods. This is a case of environmental racism if I've ever seen one, and believe me, I've seen many. These people have been taken advantage of by the medical, industrial, and political power brokers who are only concerned with themselves."

The county judge shot to his feet. "Watch it, Kirk. You have no basis for such allegations."

Yusef continued as if the judge had not spoken. "Such a conspiracy takes many forms, one of which is the hasty diagnosis of potentially life-threatening health conditions that ought to be taken more seriously. What we need is the truth."

"I have told the truth here," Dr. Boyd called out, "and if people are still experiencing symptoms of irritation, they should consult their doctors or come to the clinic, but I don't expect any long-term health problems."

"How can you be so sure?" Fred Camden called out from where he sat. Rising to his feet, he waited for an answer.

Elise flinched, almost putting a hand to her mouth as she tried to catch her father's eye. He avoided looking at her, but everyone else in the room glanced from him to her, then back to Fred.

"What about the ongoing quality of our lives?" Fred asked, holding on to the back of the chair in front of him as he tilted his upper body forward. "There was another fire this morning. Will there be a third flare-up tomorrow? The next day? When is this going to end? And why is there no security at the site? I drove by on my way here. The guards posted by the fire department are gone. None of this makes any sense."

The fire marshal coughed, then pressed his paunchy body closer to the microphone, clearly annoyed. "Undetected hot spots are not unusual in this type of fire," he said. "In some places, the debris may be six, seven feet deep. The crust of cool metal and plastic that formed yesterday must have cracked, allowing oxygen to seep beneath the rubble and hit molten metal and other materials that were still hot. A flare-up occurred, but it was quickly extinguished. The personnel assigned to the site have pulled away because everything now is under control." He leaned back, daring anyone to challenge his remarks.

"But what if it happens again?" Fred Camden asked. "Can anyone assure us that we aren't being exposed to poisonous fumes? Who knows what may be inside those warehouses that hasn't even burned yet." He finally looked at his daughter, giving her an apologetic half smile. "Most of you know that I now live in town, but I still call Flatwoods home. It's where my heart will always be. You also know that Elise Jeffries is my daughter. I love and trust her deeply. But" —he swung to his left, focusing on Kirk—"she speaks from a different perspective. She *has* to say what her company tells her to say, and rely on whatever data they provide. I understand that. And I know that she has given you all the information she can. She's not at fault. It's the company. Not her!"

The silence in the room was oppressive, and all eyes were riveted on Elise. Fred let a burst of air escape from his lungs and shook his head wearily, visually pleading with Elise to forgive him. Then he sat back down.

Mortified, Elise wanted to crawl under the table and hide. How could her father have embarrassed her so? He was taking up for her as if she were a child being bullied on the school playground. She could hold her own in the face of complaints, insults, and the demands made on her by her boss and the public. That was her job! She didn't need her father's help.

The fire marshal broke the stunned silence. "The firemen who worked this fire put their lives on the line for all of you. And they did an excellent job. As far as flare-ups are concerned, I will make sure sufficient manpower and equipment remain at the site until such dangerous conditions have passed."

Several people nodded vigorously. A few groaned, as if they didn't believe a word of what he'd said.

Yusef Kirk began pacing back and forth in front of the residents as if he were contemplating closing arguments in a court case. Stopping abruptly, he stared at Elise, then said in a deep, resonant voice, "Why won't ScanTron level with us, Ms. Jeffries? Why can't the company responsible for all this grief tell the people of Flatwoods what was stored right across the street from them?" He paused, glancing over his shoulder at the restless audience, then turned to face Elise again. "Why?" he shouted, causing several people to jump.

Elise licked dry lips, swallowed, then opened her mouth to speak, but the impatient activist answered for her, enhancing the drama with raised, flailing arms.

"Because," he said, "according to Ms. Jeffries, ScanTron Security International has industry secrets to protect." He chuckled, a smirk on his lips. "In reality, she refuses to tell us the truth because she represents a company that has no conscience. Is she alarmed? Upset? No!" He began pacing again. "She is only a mouthpiece with no sense of compassion."

"I take exception to that remark, Mr. Kirk." The words flew from her mouth. "Once the results of the soil, air, and water samples are in, ScanTron will be at liberty to discuss the repercussions in detail. Until then, I refuse to speculate on the matters brought up here today."

Elise held her breath, feeling as if she were sitting in a witness chair waiting for the jury to decide her fate. What in the world was happening? The poor souls of Flatwoods must think her heartless and cold. Damn Yusef Kirk. Damn Al Patterson. And as she tried to blink away the glare of the spotlight, along with the tears now gathering in her eyes, she also cursed her father for making her look like a fool.

Damn it, she had followed her boss's instructions and tried to calm the situation to buy some time, but under the circumstances she now wished she'd gone over Al's head and talked to Farren about getting her hands on the facility's inventory logs. Well, she'd done the best she could, she concluded, a knot of worry weighing heavily in her chest.

Yusef did not back down. "Ms. Jeffries, now that I know you are a former resident of Tide County and that you used to live in Flatwoods, I am even more disappointed." His matter-of-fact tone cut through Elise. "I would think that you owe your people more than the half-truths presented here."

His remark brought a chill to Elise's arms and forced a lump of fear to swell in her throat that, fortunately, prevented her from making a disastrous, nasty reply.

"Unlike you," Yusef continued, "the faithful residents of Tide County still have to breathe the air, drink the water, and eat the vegetables grown on their property. *They* cannot and will not run away." With a dramatic toss of his head, he flung his dreadlocks from his face, searing Elise with a contemptuous glare. "You are toying with people's lives, Ms. Jeffries, and none of us find such behavior amusing."

The outburst slammed Elise in the face, burning her with its ring of truth. Somehow, she managed to summon up the necessary resolve to match Yusef Kirk's unflinching stare with a steely one of her own.

"I'm sorry you misinterpreted my remarks, Mr. Kirk," Elise replied, her voice surprisingly strong considering the weakened state of her emotional control. "I thought I made it clear that because of security reasons, ScanTron is not at liberty to turn its inventory logs over to *you*. As the investigation proceeds, I'm sure we will make such records available to the *proper* authorities, if such a measure is warranted. All regulatory health and safety measures required by law were followed during the construction and warehousing of ScanTron's components. Absolutely nothing burned except metals, plastics, paper. Nothing at all that the EPA considers toxic in itself."

Yusef rolled his shoulders back, squaring himself in front of Elise. "Toxic in itself? What kind of double-talk are you throwing at us now?" His words exploded in the room.

Beneath the table, Elise's leg began to shake and she pressed one foot to the floor to keep the quaking from taking her over. "I consider your remarks insulting, Mr. Kirk. Be careful what you say, or you might just wind up defending yourself in a slander suit. I am not giving you double-talk, and I *assure* you, I am not toying with anyone's life. Your accusations are most unprofessional and disturbing. A decent person would apologize." The words erased the smug expression on Yusef Kirk's face.

He stepped away from the microphone, shrugging nonchalantly, but did not offer an apology. Elise could tell he was taken aback.

She relaxed. Her leg stopped shaking and her confidence surged. Well! She'd got his attention. The brash Mr. Kirk could be silenced after all, she mused, congratulating herself as she turned her attention to a man who quickly replaced Yusef at the microphone.

"I'm Mr. Jacobs. Me and my wife, Rose, have lived in Flatwoods going on twenty years. I took Rose to the clinic yesterday for a checkup because she said her eyes were burning real bad. The doctor checked her over and gave her some eye drops. Said she'd be fine. No sooner we got back home than Rose started coughing something terrible; then a red rash spread all over her face and arms. Called nine-one-one. Rose is in the hospital in League City right now. Don't know quite yet what's wrong with her, but it's serious. Last night she could hardly talk." Mr. Jacobs wiped tears from his eye with the back of his hand. Unable to go on, he sank down into his chair.

Yusef immediately stepped back to the mike.

"Listen to him, people! How can the Tide County Clinic, the only medical treatment facility readily available to you, treat you so shabbily? Why weren't Mrs. Jacobs's complaints taken more seriously? Why?" he repeated like a preacher stirring up his congregation. "I'll tell you why. Because the doctors and nurses over there don't want to be bothered."

"Mr. Kirk," Dr. Boyd broke in. "We are only a clinic, not a hospital. There is only so much we can do."

"Right," Yusef granted, "but if Mrs. Jacobs needed additional tests, why wasn't she immediately referred to the League City Hospital? Is that out of your realm of treatment, Doctor?"

"Absolutely not," Dr. Boyd replied. "If Mrs. Jacobs was given a clean bill of health, her condition must have deteriorated after she left the clinic. But without additional staff it's hard to—"

"So," Yusef interrupted, "if I understand you correctly, your medical staff is only able to provide cursory, superficial examinations when the people need complete physical examinations and in-depth diagnosis. Is that it?"

Dr. Boyd shot to his feet, jerking the lapels of his white jacket to compose himself. "No," he stated firmly. "Any patient who needed to be referred to a larger hospital, even the medical center in Houston, was so referred. If you'd like to come into the clinic, *my* records are open for your inspection." Turning to Mr. Jacobs, he said, "I am extremely sorry about your wife, but I am relieved to know that she is getting proper care."

In a surprise movement, Yusef approached the table and stood directly in front of Elise. "Ms. Jeffries," he began. "Wouldn't it be a grand gesture on the part of ScanTron Security to assist with the funding of additional medical personnel at the clinic so that the people of this county—some of whom you have known since childhood —will get the care they deserve?"

Stunned that he would so boldly put her on the spot while the television cameras were rolling, Elise could only stare at Yusef, unable to respond. But the silence that gripped her and made her mute was not only because she had no words to toss back but because of the way Yusef Kirk's fiery eyes were riveted on her—as if he were reading her soul.

CHAPTER 9

A black crow squawked from its perch in the red-pepper tree, splitting the oppressive silence that had settled over the countryside like thermal insulation. Startled, Carlos jumped, turned to face the bird, then looked back at his car, which he'd parked in the shade of a towering mesquite tree by the side of the dusty country road.

The testy crow squawked again, continuing with its annoying caw until Carlos reached a sagging gate, where he fumbled with a rusted latch and forced it to spring open. Quickly, he passed through the dodge-post fence and strode toward a timber shanty that sat in the middle of a grove of china trees. Swirling puffs of yellow-brown dust stirred like powder at his feet.

Shading his eyes against the blinding sunlight, Carlos peered across the yard. On the front porch, a woman sat on a stool, her head bent over a white enamel pan, her hands moving in a rhythmic flutter as she shelled crowder peas into a pot. She didn't look up until Carlos had crossed the clearing and called out to her.

"*Hola*," he said, surprised to see how young the woman was when she finally tilted her face toward him, though her expression had no life and her mouth was a thin unhappy line.

"*Busco El General,*" Carlos called out, advancing to a stop at the foot of three rotted steps.

Without a word, the woman inclined her head in respectful acknowledgment, got up, opened the screen door, and went inside.

A scrawny dog with patches of mange on its back emerged from under the porch floor, sniffed Carlos's shoes, then scampered away into the woods behind the isolated cabin.

Carlos mopped sweat from his face with a handkerchief, then pulled his boldly printed shirt away from his body, fanning his neck as he waited. He was glad he'd picked up a change of clothes in Victoria before checking into the motel last night. He wondered just how hot it was and how much hotter it was going to get, because it was only ten o'clock in the morning.

Within seconds, a frail man with snow white hair and a slight bend to his body appeared in the doorway. He assessed Carlos from beneath lowered lids, then gave a slight bow of recognition.

Carlos's heart began to pound. It was him, all right. El General. And he didn't look a day older than when Carlos had interviewed him six years ago.

"*¿Me recuerda?*" he asked, hoping the old man's memory hadn't completely failed.

"*Sí, sí,*" came his reply, a wide smile exposing a few remaining teeth. "*La televisión. Entre. Entre,*" he said in a stronger voice than Carlos had anticipated. The man held the screen door open for his visitor. "Welcome, *mi amigo.* Welcome."

When Carlos stepped inside, a rush of cool air swirled at him from three large table fans positioned around the room. He wiped his face again, then glanced around, letting his eyes adjust to the dimness. When the old man motioned for him to take a seat on the frayed cane-bottomed bench next to the sofa, Carlos grinned and accepted the invitation, glad to see that time had been kind to Guillermo Venustio.

Making hospital visits was not something Elise liked to do. When she was a girl, her mother used to drag her along as she made Saturday-morning house calls on many of the elderly and homebound in their neighborhood. Myra Camden never showed up without a smile on her face, a basket of food on her arm, and a cheerful stream of buoyant conversation.

Elise usually didn't mind tagging along, and would stand aside as her mother worked her magic, chatting casually on all types of subjects—the weather, a new recipe, a recent news program, or the latest gossip about the Newtons, Flatwoods's notorious couple that had married and divorced each other an unheard of three different times. When Myra finished her visit and was ready to leave, more often than not, the person she had been visiting would beg her to stay a little longer, and sometimes Myra and Elise would not get home until it was dark.

But Elise was not comfortable around sick people and always felt awkward in hospital rooms, unable to decide if she should talk about the person's illness, avoid it, try to act as if everything was normal, or openly express her concern or sorrow. She was even worse when it came to wakes and funerals, which she avoided at all costs.

As she walked down a corridor in the League City Hospital, she purposefully kept her eyes straight ahead, not glancing into the open doors along the hallway. To her, there was nothing more depressing than the sight of sick people lying in their hospital beds staring at the TV or gazing into space as they waited for their next meal or visitor or some interruption to help make the hours slip by.

When she came to Damita's closed door, Elise took a deep breath, hesitant to go in. Perhaps Damita didn't want to see her, Elise thought, fingers curled around the cool door handle. Maybe she should have stayed away, letting Damita call and tell her what was wrong when she was ready to talk. Frustrated by the mixed feelings that swept through her, Elise paused to think about what might be going on.

Damita was the dearest friend she had, close to being a sister, yet she hadn't felt inclined to discuss whatever was wrong. What was compelling her to act so strangely? Suddenly, Elise's annoyance with Damita overshadowed her worry, and she knocked softly, entering when a weak voice said, "Come in."

The first thing Elise noticed were the dark circles under Damita's eyes and how sallow her beautiful tawny complexion had become. Her face was drawn and thin, her jet-black eyes were dull, and her russet-colored hair, which was usually perfectly coifed, lay plastered to the sides of her head.

Without a word of greeting, Elise went straight to the bed and enveloped her friend in her arms. As Elise held Damita closely, she could feel the bones in her shoulders pressing against her hands and she shuddered to feel the weight loss her friend had obviously suffered. Blinking away tears, Elise could almost feel the pain Damita must be in, or have been in, for God only knew how long.

"Well," Damita said, falling back on her pillows when Elise turned her loose. "You tracked me down."

"Damn right I did, mystery lady," Elise said rather sternly, yet smiling. "What's all this about? Huh? Going off without telling me you were sick."

"I'm not sick," Damita replied. "Just having a checkup."

Elise sank down onto the bed and picked up Damita's hand, rubbing it softly between hers. "Come on. What kind of tests take three days to run?" She tossed her purse onto a chair, tucked one foot beneath her hips, then leveled hard eyes on her frail friend. "Don't even try to act like nothing is wrong. I can see it in your face. You're not well, are you?" She fussed with the top sheet, smoothing out some wrinkles before folding it down over the blanket.

"You shouldn't have come," Damita said in a tired voice.

"Yes, I should have." Elise tossed back. "And don't you say another word about it." Nervously, Elise fluffed up an extra pillow, then moved to place it behind Damita, who managed to lean forward so that Elise could put it behind her. When her hospital gown fell open in the front, Damita jerked back, clutching the fabric, trying to close the gown across her chest.

"What's this?" Elise looked at the great swath of gauze and elastic bandage covering Damita's chest. "Oh. No," was all she could say.

Again, Damita tried to pull the gown fully closed over the bulky white wrapping, but gave up, giving Elise a look of resignation. "You got me." She nodded. "Yes, I'm afraid it's true."

Elise gently slipped the pillow behind Damita's head, then firmly grasped both of her hands. "When did you have the operation?"

"Day before yesterday," Damita said softly, then added, "It wasn't so bad."

"When did you find out?"

"You know, it was strange. Three days after I went to the clinic for my regular checkup, Dr. Boyd called to tell me he wanted to have my mammogram done over again. Routine, he said. Nothing to worry about, but I had a feeling something was wrong. After the second X ray, he sent me directly here, only gave me an hour to pack and get the cats squared away before I had to check in. The surgery was done the next morning." She lowered her head to look at the wide surgical bandage inside her gown. "Both breasts," she murmured, her eyes quickly filling with tears, which she wiped away with a tissue Elise pulled from the box on the bedside table. She raised her eyes slowly, hesitantly. "It all happened so fast, Elise. I would have called . . ."

"Shh," Elise whispered, stroking Damita's arm. "I know you would have. I'm just glad I found out about this now."

"How? Who called you?"

"Nobody," she replied, explaining why she had returned to Flatwoods and what Mose Greer, Damita's neighbor, had told her.

"I saw the fire on TV last night, but I didn't see you. Sorry."

"Probably just as well," Elise said, filling Damita in on her run-in with Mr. Tarrant and her dicey exchange with Carlos Rico.

"So, you're already facing the lions for ScanTron, huh?" Damita grinned, throwing off the wan expression that had been on her face. Her beautiful smile lit up the room, and with a rather unsteady hand she tried to smooth her matted hair. "God, that's great. After all you've been through, Elise, you can prove yourself now."

A shadow slipped over Elise's features as she got up off the bed and flopped into a nearby chair. "We'll see," was all she could manage.

"What's wrong? You don't like it?" Damita asked.

"There's a lot about this particular assignment I don't like," Elise offered, going on to tell Damita about Al Patterson, Yusef Kirk, and the remark her father had made at the meeting.

Damita chuckled, her smile stronger, momentarily lifting Elise's spirits. "Well," she began. "Your dad is going to have his say. You know he was only trying to make you feel better."

"Ha! I wanted to die. Right there! Can you imagine how that must have looked and sounded on live TV?"

"Any reaction from your boss?"

"Not yet, but I'm sure I'll hear from him soon enough."

Sinking back onto her pillow, Damita chuckled. "The media spokesperson for an international company has her dad making excuses for the way she's doing her job."

"Oh, girl, it was humiliating."

"You'll be okay, Elise." Damita turned her head toward the vase of pink roses and baby's breath her coworkers at Saturn had sent.

Elise wanted to level with Damita about how scared and disappointed she was, but couldn't. Now was definitely not the time to burden Damita with *her* problems. Rising, Elise headed toward the adjoining bathroom.

"Where's your comb? Your brush? Hot rollers . . . something to get your hair together, girlfriend." Turning at the doorway, she gave Damita one of those "Chile, comb your hair" looks, then burst into laughter.

Damita giggled, holding on to her bandaged chest as she struggled to keep from breaking into uncontrollable laughter. "Over there, in my bag. And please. Don't make me laugh, it hurts. Anyway, I can imagine what I look like."

"No, honey, you can't," Elise replied, returning to the side of the bed with comb, brush, and curling iron in hand.

During the long drive home, Elise tried to corral her thoughts into an optimistic vein, but her concern about Damita kept sabotaging her efforts. Though her doctor seemed optimistic about Damita's prognosis, believing they'd removed all of the cancerous tissue, she would still need a series of radiation treatments and chemotherapy before she could be considered in a safe zone.

At least her spirits were high, Elise thought, unable to keep from chuckling again when recalling Damita's joke about her upcoming breast reconstruction surgery, which would occur when she was stronger. She had told Elise she was trying to decide if she should put in a request for a size double-D cup since she'd always wanted a more impressive bosom. Elise had howled with laughter and a little mock envy, warning Damita she'd better not emerge from surgery looking like a candidate for Ms. Black Texas.

The first lights along the freeway blinked on as she cruised north toward the hazy purple skyline of Houston. It was dominated by the steel-and-glass skyscrapers of downtown, shaded by an emerging sunset. Though it was already past seven, it was still rather light, and Elise worried that Blake might allow Junior to stay outside too long. That's what usually happened when she was late getting home and Blake got caught up in tinkering with his motorcycle. When he was in the garage trying to overhaul an engine or detail a fender, he always lost track of time.

When she came to her exit, she quickly cut off the interstate but was caught behind a slow-moving truck until she managed to turn right and head home. It had been an emotionally exhausting day, and all she wanted to do was stretch out in the recliner in the den and stare into space, emptying her mind of everything, at least until tomorrow morning.

When she pulled onto her block, there was Junior, riding his bike down the middle of the street. She honked her horn and waited until he pedaled over to the curb. Then she turned into the driveway and rolled down the window. Leaning across the passenger seat, she scolded her son. "What is wrong with you? You know better than to ride in the middle of the street."

He lowered his eyes, a contrite look on his face.

Elise didn't let him off so easily. Though the area was quiet and she knew all of their neighbors, she wished Blake would be a little more watchful. "It's way too late for you to be out here, anyway."

Junior looked at Elise, his lower lip turned down in a pout. "Dad said I could ride my bike. He's in the backyard. I wasn't that far away. I've been right here on the sidewalk all the time, but I crossed over to see Jimmy's lizard."

With a resigned sigh, Elise nodded, not happy to see that Junior was wearing the dreadfully faded Dallas Cowboys T-shirt that she had threatened to throw away at least four times. "All right. Go on. Put your bike in the garage and get washed up for dinner."

When she had been working as a temp, her workday had started at nine o'clock, giving her plenty of time to fix breakfast and supervise Junior's choice of clothing, and she was always home before six. That wouldn't be possible now. At the back of Elise's mind was the uneasy realization that the comfortable routine she had established with her family was rapidly beginning to unravel.

Well, it couldn't be helped. If giving up time with her family was part of the deal, so be it. Blake would just have to be a little more attentive. After all, she mused, he was the one counting the days until this job became permanent.

Elise parked the car and left the garage with Junior holding her hand. When they entered the backyard, they were hit by loud music coming from the transistor radio Blake had propped up against the side of the house. He was on his knees beneath the big Harley cruiser that he had rolled into the center of the yard.

"Hi!" Elise called out over the music. Junior ran over and squatted down to watch his father finish tightening a bolt on the dash of the cycle.

"You're home!" Blake reached over and turned the radio off, then half stood to peck Elise on the cheek. "Just want to get this new panel in place before I quit."

"So I see," Elise said dryly, shooing Junior inside to wash up. When he had disappeared into the house, she assessed the mess Blake had made. A can of oil had tipped over, spilling its contents into her rosemary bed, and there were flakes of rust and drops of paint on her prized basil and parsley plants. Looking down at him sprawled on the lawn, she started to chastise him but kept silent, ashamed to feel so annoyed.

Blake was a good father, a faithful husband, a great lover, and—thank God—he could cook. But sometimes he looked and acted more like the carefree college student he'd been when she met him than like the responsible CPA, father, and husband that he was. Lately, his obsession with riding and restoring his old Harley was driving her crazy. Though she tried to be understanding, there were times when she wished he'd let go of those dreams that, she knew, he'd never be able to recapture.

She struggled to keep her voice light as she brought up the subject of their son's supervision. "Don't you think it's too late for Junior to be wandering the neighborhood?"

Blake's head snapped up. "Wandering the neighborhood? He was supposed to stay on the sidewalk in front of the house."

"Oh, he was out there all right, but not on the sidewalk. He was riding his bike down the middle of the street."

Blake frowned. "He was?"

"Yes!" Elise shot back, the accumulated stress from her day suddenly taking its toll. "With your head buried under that thing and music blasting, how can you possibly be aware of where he is or what he's doing?"

Blake dropped the wrench he was holding and stood. "Whoa. I'm sorry. I got—"

"Caught up with that toy you call an investment," she finished. "You might try putting our son's welfare above your hobby, Blake. Just think what could have happened."

Now Blake's eyes crinkled in stunned surprise. "This is not a hobby and you know it. Once I get this restored it will be worth a bundle."

"Yeah," Elise mumbled.

Blake flinched. "Where's this coming from? What's eating you?"

"Nothing."

"Don't give me that. And for your information, I asked Jimmy's mom to keep her eye on Junior. Lorna was working in her flower beds. Jimmy caught a lizard. I knew where he was, what was happening. Give me some credit. Please!" He angrily jerked the motorcycle around and rolled it back into the garage.

Elise waited in silence until he came back, tensing as Blake began snatching up his tools. "It scared me to see him in the street, that's all, and I didn't see Lorna in her yard."

Blake slammed his tools into his toolbox. "She's right down the street, Elise. What are you trying to say? That I can't control Junior? Well, I hate to disappoint you, but he *does* listen to me. You're not the only one who can discipline him."

Elise opened her mouth to hurl some equally hurtful remark at Blake but stopped, not wanting the exchange to escalate any higher. She *hadn't* seen Lorna outside, but then she hadn't really looked either. "I'm sorry," she said, feeling contrite. "I'm just worried." But with a lift of her chin, she quickly added, "And you know I don't like him wearing that awful T-shirt to school. Why'd you let him talk you into that?"

Blake wiped his hands on a dirty mechanic's rag, then tossed it into his tool chest. "Hey. I'm doing good to get any clothes on his back, as slow as he moves in the morning." Without waiting for Elise's reply, he left her standing in the middle of the patio and went to the hose at the side of the house and started washing his hands.

The sound of water splashing onto the grass and the yells of kids riding dirt bikes along the trail behind their house filled the strained silence. Blake returned and broke it with a direct question, his tone almost accusatory. "It's not Junior, or me, that's bothering you, is it?" He was drying his hands on a clean paper towel that he jettisoned across the patio into a nearby trash can. "Something happened today. What was it?"

Elise sat down on one of the white wrought iron chairs at the glass-topped table. Blake sat down across from her. As the summer light faded from the sky, she told Blake about the community meeting and her father's remark, and was unable to keep from breaking into tears when she described Damita's condition.

Blake got up and went to stand behind Elise. He began massaging her shoulders with firm fingers. "Well, I have to confess. I missed the five o'clock news, so no, I didn't see the report. Who cares what this guy Kirk thinks? Don't worry about him. I know you did fine. I'm glad you didn't waver in your allegiance to ScanTron. That was a very smart move because that's what counts. You can't afford to let a half-baked environmentalist make you lose focus of what's important."

Elise tried to summon up a positive response but couldn't. It was easy for Blake to say such things. He hadn't been in the hot seat, been embarrassed and accused of lying on live TV. Sometimes she wondered if he really understood how difficult her job could be.

Blake was saying, "That's terrible about Damita. Jesus, I know how close you two are, but try to stay positive. If the doctors say they got all the cancer, she'll probably be back to work and back to her old self within a matter of weeks."

"Let's hope so," Elise replied, wiping her eyes, squeezing Blake's hands. "It's just that she's so young—she's *my* age!—and there was no warning."

He was her anchor, the center of her life, and at times like this she treasured their ability to discuss whatever was on each other's mind. From the day they married, they had never gone to bed angry and now she knew exactly why. Blake wouldn't allow it. He was always the one to open up first or apologize—sometimes even when she was the one at fault—and he never failed to find a way to get her to talk. She not could fool him. His desire to listen calmed her and helped her release whatever was grating between them in order to work it out and move past the problem. She hated that she'd jumped on him so hastily, and was thinking about how to phrase her apology when Blake interrupted her thoughts.

"I have some news that ought to cheer you up."

Elise turned in her seat, gazing up at Blake, loving the way the evening shadows played over the sharp ridges of his cheekbones. At times, he looked more Indian than African-American with his ruddy complexion, high-planed face, and coal black hair that he kept cut short. But it was when he took off his shirt that his Indian heritage most pleased her. He had a completely hairless chest. Smooth, muscled, and bronze, exactly what she liked. She impulsively reached up and ran her hand down the center of his torso, feeling his hard, flat stomach beneath his flimsy cotton T-shirt that had a black X on the front.

"What's the good news?" she asked in a voice filled with love. "Is Century giving out raises? Christmas bonuses in July?"

"God, no," Blake groaned. "It's better than that. I went to Nations Bank and visited with a loan officer on my lunch hour today. She went over my projections with a fine-toothed comb. She said I have a viable business plan and ought to have no difficultly getting a start-up loan approved."

Elise gave Blake a skeptical, one-sided smile but was startled when he frowned.

Mildly annoyed, he asked, "What's the matter? Don't you think that's good news?"

"I, I guess so," she replied vaguely, too tired to deal with that touchy subject. When a flicker of disappointment crossed Blake's face, Elise's heart beat faster in sympathy. He hated his job, she loved hers, though at times—like today—she wondered why. But when Blake got all heated up and began talking seriously about his plans to leave Century Trust, her sense of practicality kicked in. Maybe things would work out, but she was afraid of moving too fast. "You didn't do anything rash did you, like sign any papers, commit yourself?" she had to ask.

Blake stepped back, letting Elise's hand fall away, returning to his seat. He calmly observed her in the dim light radiating through the kitchen curtains. "No," he said matter-of-factly. "I can't do a thing unless you agree to cosign the note. Your salary will have a major impact on the bank's decision. It has to be taken into consideration. You know that."

"Yeah," Elise breathed heavily, getting up. "I guess it will." She started toward the house, but Blake stopped her with a touch on her arm.

"I brought the papers home. Let's go over them after dinner. Okay?" When Elise tilted her head as if thinking about his request, he pressed on. "It's time to move forward, Elise. I'm in a dead-end situation at Century and you know it! You will sign the papers, won't you?" His words were tight with impatience.

Elise rubbed the side of her cheek, irritated that the mosquito buzzing around the patio light had already bitten her. "Okay, we'll talk about it later. Let's eat." She circled an arm around Blake's waist as they entered the house. She sniffed, then looked up at him. "I smell your famous spaghetti sauce."

"Just for you," he said huskily, nuzzling the side of her neck.

"I'm famished."

"Good. You, go relax. I'll call you when dinner is ready." He brushed his lips over hers, then straightened up, but Elise slipped one hand behind Blake's neck and urged his lips back to hers. She kissed him with meaning, urgency, and commitment, trying to let him know she was sorry for the way she'd spoken to him.

After entering her bedroom, Elise threw her briefcase on the floor, kicked off her shoes, and flopped across the bed. Watching a muted TV, she rubbed the sole of her foot and tried to solve the puzzle on *Wheel of Fortune* but gave up and just stared at the screen.

Did Blake really understand the risks involved and how much pressure she was going to be under once they committed to being hundreds of thousands of dollars in debt? She began to tremble. He was so damn focused on leaving Century Trust, and it was evident she was going to have to go along with him. She'd never be able to live with herself, or with him for that matter, if she intentionally kept him from trying, but unless she got better support from Al Patterson or somebody with clout at ScanTron Security, there might not be any income for her to list on a loan application, and no motorcycle dealership in Blake's future.

CHAPTER 10

After the meeting in Flatwoods Elise was swamped, and by the end of the week, the routine aspects of her job had become monumental tasks due to Al Patterson's blatant refusal to cooperate. He chose to ignore her, rather than interfere with her work, sending messages and directives through Pete Tremont, using his assistant manager as a convenient buffer.

Al was consumed with holding on to the confidence of important accounts that had deserted the company after the fire. Elise understood the bottom-line aspects of doing business but resented being left to struggle alone. She tried hard to balance what she wanted to say to the people of Flatwoods with what ScanTron expected of her, but it was difficult in light of the fact that she had no corporate data that might help her wage a better fight.

Four days after the second flare-up, the fire remained front-page news. The *Houston Chronicle* and the *Leader*, a local four-page weekly that was tossed on lawns of Tide County residents, hadn't let go of the incident. Though the sentiment concerning ScanTron's culpability remained vague and inconclusive, Elise could read between the lines—the reporters constantly alluded to the question of what had been in the ScanTron warehouses and why the company was so reluctant to reveal it. Unfortunately, it was a question Elise, too, had silently begun to ask.

Yusef Kirk was everywhere—on TV talk shows, radio call-in programs, at City Hall and County Court. Blazing with passionate conviction, he was clearly the media's darling, and viewed by the public as more of a savior than a lawyer, a man devoted to bringing out the truth. He made the news every day.

Elise was trying to counter Yusef's press by pitching stories to the media about the people who were healthy, safe, and thankful to have been spared major damage. She scored a coup when the community cable channel agreed to showcase some residents returning to their homes. The two-part report featured determined citizens replanting gardens, patching badly scorched roofs, cleaning up their property, and talking in hopeful terms about the future.

Elise knew that a skillfully positioned campaign of positive images, backed by hard facts, might help erase the ugly pictures of loss and devastation that the press exploited. She worried that Yusef Kirk's critical remarks and outrageous predictions, which had spread like wildfire through the coastal community, had tainted the minds of the locals so badly she'd never get them to believe a word she said.

When Elise approached John Farren about the possibility of ScanTron making a donation to the clinic, with lots of press and community members present, he'd said he thought it was an excellent idea and promised to present the strategy to the board of directors. He had been hopeful but had warned Elise that some board members might see such a move as an admission of guilt.

Elise in turn warned Farren to take Yusef Kirk seriously because Al Patterson certainly wasn't. She was still uneasy over the challenge she'd seen in Yusef's eyes. She'd seen it close up and couldn't get it out of her mind. He meant business, and she double-checked the wording on each piece sent out, cautious not to give him any ammunition with which to undermine the little progress she was making. Dealing with the public and the press was tedious, exhausting, and frustrating, yet she couldn't deny that she loved her job. If it was the last thing she did, she'd prove Yusef wrong about ScanTron and herself, with or without Al Patterson's support.

Exactly one week after the fire, Justin Snyder of the EPA appeared unannounced at the ScanTron offices and asked to speak with Al. Elise watched as the man in jeans and muddy boots with a pager clipped to his wide belt entered Al's office and closed the door. The two men remained closeted for fifteen minutes; then the door burst open and Al bellowed for Elise to get inside.

Startled, she jumped to her feet, grabbed a pad and pen from her desk, and headed for Al's office, leaving the wording of a press release in midsentence and her coworkers staring after her with eyebrows raised.

Elise greeted Justin in a professional manner, shaking his hand as he crinkled his mustached lips in a half smile of recognition and tugged on the end of his pointed goatee. Looking more like an oil field roustabout than the respected environmental scientist he was, Elise knew that Justin Snyder's relaxed attitude disguised a fierce commitment to his profession.

"I think you'd better hear what Mr. Snyder has to say," Al told Elise, who sat on a red plastic chair beside his desk, hands clamped together in her lap.

"We've got to handle this carefully. Understand?" Al said, a hint of conspiracy in his ice blue eyes.

Elise nodded at Al, then turned to face the boyish-looking EPA representative who was busy unzipping a brown leather notebook.

Justin Snyder pulled out a densely printed computer page and held it up. "The test results of air samples taken at the site of the fire just came in." With his head tilted to one side, he fixed Elise, then Al, with a serious look. "We found traces of benzene and arsenic in the samples."

"Arsenic? Benzene?" Elise repeated, horrified. "How much?"

"Fairly low levels," Justin replied. "The amount detected is not considered dangerous."

"But once this hits the papers, I have a feeling the public is going to panic," Elise said.

Justin lifted his hands, making a gesture of uncertainty.

Hunching over his desk, Al said curtly, "Let's talk plain, here, Snyder. I take it those chemicals are classified as carcinogens?"

"Most assuredly," Justin said. "But a single exposure would not be considered significant. You'd have to live with these levels a fairly long time for them to have a damaging effect."

Elise cautiously relaxed.

"No one's going to be interested in how long it takes for toxins to do damage," Al said.

"That's right," Elise agreed, weighing the reality of the report against the mood in the town. "What they're going to be interested in is how and why such chemicals were present in the first place."

Al said nothing, sitting with his bottom lip turned down, closely watching Justin.

"Oh, I agree with you Ms. Jeffries," Justin replied.

"How much exposure is considered dangerous?" Elise asked, determined to get some hard facts from someone.

"Oh, years. Maybe a lifetime," Justin replied quickly, lifting a shoulder. "Remember, these results are preliminary. The data on soil tests are still incomplete, and although the water supply at the site is in a closed system, it could have been affected, too."

Elise groaned, propping her chin on tented fingers. "Bottom line? Based on what you know now?"

With a glance toward Al, Justin answered, "Those exposed to the fire might experience discomfort, but they are not facing serious health risks."

"Can I quote you?" Elise asked.

"Sure, but you'd better emphasize that people must continue to be cautious. They should destroy any garden vegetables that were exposed to smoke, and if the water tastes odd, give us a call. No reason to take any unnecessary chances. We'll be conducting more extensive tests, so let's hope nothing else turns up."

Al went to stand by the glass window in his office that faced the common work area shared by the rest of his management team. He frowned to see Pete Tremont staring at him. Al spun around and focused on Justin. "There's more. Right?"

Waiting, Elise pressed her pen to her notepad so hard the tip broke through the top page.

A shadow of concern touched Justin's plain features as he slowly nodded, then said, "Yes." He put the computer printout in his notebook, zipped it shut, then sat back in his chair, propping one foot on his knee as if ready to get down to business.

"Finding traces of benzene and arsenic here is not that uncommon," he began. "With so many chemical and crude oil refineries concentrated in this area, it's almost expected, but I'm puzzled. The substances *are* hazardous, I guarantee, but not deadly in these quantities. There's something missing here."

"What?" Elise asked.

"As I said, these toxins are usually associated with petrochemical refining," Snyder hedged.

"And?" Al pressed.

Justin paused, then asked his own question. "Did ScanTron warehouse large amounts of crude oil or unrefined gas on its property?"

"Absolutely not," Al quickly replied, moving forward to tower over Justin.

The EPA official remained seated, yet met Al eye to eye. "Well, what light can you shed on these test results?" He tapped his leather notebook. "The chemicals had to come from somewhere—if not ScanTron, where?"

Elise stiffened as Al returned to his desk and slammed his thick body back into his upholstered chair, making a dull thud. He began swiveling from side to side, his eyes darting from Justin to her, then to the glass window that overlooked the common office.

"Crude oil? Unrefined gas?" He gave an exhaustive sigh, then tentatively said, "Could be Global. Yeah. Better check with Sam Hawkins. See what he has to say."

"Global Oil?" Justin said, puzzled. "Their refinery is four miles from your facility. That's a stretch, Patterson. I don't see the connection."

"Oh, there's a connection," Al replied smoothly. "It's right under our feet."

Involuntarily, Elise glanced down at the floor, and when she lifted her gaze, Al was staring directly at her. Shifting in her chair, she was suddenly uncomfortable. "A pipeline?" she guessed.

"Well, well. Right on the mark." Al's voice was laced with sarcasm.

Justin thumped his foot to the floor. "Global's got a pipeline running under ScanTron?"

"Exactly," Al said. "When ScanTron was negotiating for the land where the warehouse complex was to be built, Global tried to outbid us but failed. Eventually, a compromise was reached—a long-term lease agreement, granting Global Oil a pipeline right-of-way. Twenty feet wide. It runs beneath the ScanTron facility. . . . It must be leaking," Al concluded. "And it's Global's responsibility to maintain it, not ours. There have been problems before, Snyder, but Sam Hawkins is too damn cheap to spend the money to properly maintain that pipeline. I knew something like this was going to happen one day— cause *us* big problems. Well, now it's happened."

"What is in the agreement about maintenance?" Elise asked.

"Damages that result from exposure to any product or by-product of the refinery that has leaked from the pipeline are Global's responsibility, not ours." Suddenly Al grinned hugely, looking as if he had just won the lottery. "Better get on down the road and tell Sam what you found, Snyder. And tell him if he's planning to dig up any of ScanTron's property to repair his broken line to give me a call before he starts."

As soon as Justin Snyder left, Elise rose, anxious to get back to her work, but Al stopped her with a lifted finger.

"Wait a minute. I'd like to talk to you."

"Sure," Elise replied, easing back into her seat. "But when the EPA report hits the evening news, we'd better be ready."

"Right," Al said flatly. "Arsenic. Benzene. Words that initiate panic."

Elise nodded, realizing how god-awful deadly it sounded, but for the first time since beginning her assignment, she was glad to finally have some government data to offer the public, and perhaps a legitimate reason to shift the public's focus away from ScanTron over to Global Oil.

Al laced his fingers together, anchoring them behind his neck as an easy smile touched his lips. "Hell, this might be just what we need."

Caution kept Elise's tongue still.

"Now we've got the ammunition to get that goddamn militant off our ass."

"I take it you mean Yusef Kirk?"

"Hell, yes. Let him go after Global. Leave us the fuck alone."

Elise's brow creased in thought. "Well . . . maybe. But it hasn't been determined that Global's at fault."

Al made an exaggerated roll of his eyes, then sputtered at Elise. "Listen, you heard it straight from the EPA. Petrochemical refining produces arsenic, benzene. Toxins. And ScanTron sure ain't in the business of making gasoline. No way that's gonna be pinned on us. No fucking way."

A slow tightening began in the center of Elise's body as she recognized the beginning of another confrontation. "Al. We can't jump from theory to conclusion. Without an official determination, we're still in the hot seat, you know."

"Oh, no, we're not," Al muttered through tightly compressed lips. "Because you're gonna get us out of it."

Staring at Al, Elise calmly asked, "How?"

"By getting the news out. Fast. I want you to call all of your press contacts and drop a hint that Global's pipeline may be faulty."

Elise was horrified, and her silence let Al know how she felt.

"Hey. That's fair," he said. "And it's true. The pipeline *could* be leaking. You heard Snyder. And as for property damages . . . okay . . . we'll have to absorb most of those claims, but you better believe Global's going to pick up the medical tab."

"I can't circulate unverified information!" Elise set her notepad down firmly on the edge of Al's desk. "ScanTron could find itself in the middle of a lawsuit if it turns out the pipeline is intact."

A look of impatience came over Al's face as he waited for Elise to finish. "Rather skittish, aren't you? Haven't you learned by now how to play this game? That mess with Trinity still got you spooked?"

Elise pulled her shoulders back. "What does that mean? You don't know anything about that situation, and what I'm talking about now has nothing to do with my past. This is about telling the truth."

"The truth! For chrissake, the EPA has the proof! Benzene. Arsenic. What more do you need?"

"A statement from Global would be nice," Elise managed coolly, not about to raise her voice again. "The last thing I want is to set ScanTron up for more trouble than we've already got. Sorry, Al, I need more to go on before I start making any calls."

Slowly, Al rubbed his clean-shaven chin with the dime-size stone in his gold pinky ring. "You'd better wise up, Elise. You are paid well to protect *and* create our company's image, and so far, I can't say you're earning your salary. It would be a real shame if Farren knew you'd passed up an excellent opportunity to deflect negative press by refusing to make a few off-the-record calls."

Elise kept quiet, but her insides churned. How dare he twist the situation to make her look as if she were shirking her responsibilities when all she was trying to do was keep the company honest!

"I want you to sic Yusef Kirk on Global," he said firmly. "Get the heat off of us, Ms. Jeffries. Do your job."

Drawing in a long breath to steady her nerves, Elise nodded. There was no point in trying to press the issue. Resigned, she left Al's office.

The remainder of the morning became a miserable blur as Elise drafted and redrafted a statement, trying to word it in a way that would pull ScanTron from the spotlight without making a direct charge against Global. In a moment of panic, she called Donald Munser, the Global Oil refinery's spokesperson, to ask for the company's official position on the EPA report, but wound up talking to his voice mail.

Two hours after she left her message, the telephone rang. Snatching it up, she balanced it between her ear and her shoulder, continuing with her typing.

"Elise Jeffries," she said, praying it was Munser.

"Yusef Kirk," a deep rich voice came back.

"Oh," she said involuntarily, a little too loud. She stopped banging the keys on Darrell's computer to listen, more surprised than apprehensive to hear from the lawyer. "What can I do for you?" Her voice was stiff, like the cardboard placards his followers carried on the picket line outside the clinic.

"I just received a fax of the EPA report on the air samples taken at the ScanTron fire," he said.

Elise was curious. "Really? Who sent it?"

There was a shuffling of papers, then the reply, "No name. Came from fax number 555-9080."

Elise murmured something, not recognizing the number. Maybe it had come from Justin Snyder's office. "And?" she prompted.

"Can you shed any light on the findings? Benzene. Arsenic. Rather scary, don't you think?"

Letting a short pause drift between them, Elise carefully calculated her reply. It would not be good to give him too much information . . . or too little. "Certainly the report gives cause for concern," she began. "But I've discussed it with Mr. Snyder and I fully understand that the results must be kept in perspective."

"In perspective? Can you explain what that means?" Kirk's tone was pointedly skeptical.

"As a mater of fact, I can," Elise replied, deciding to set Yusef straight. She told him about the pipeline right-of-way lease agreement between Global Oil and ScanTron, and Snyder's statement about the low levels and lack of risk involved.

"So, Ms. Jeffries, are you trying to say that your company is now absolved of all responsibility?"

"No, that's not what I'm saying," Elise quickly clarified. "But I caution you to proceed carefully, Mr. Kirk. This is a complicated situation. For all of us. It would be wrong to exaggerate the dangers and terrify the public."

"Well, what happened to the inventory logs?" Yusef replied. "Didn't you say that information would be given to the proper authorities? What about that promise, Ms. Jeffries?"

"These things take time," she replied, a sinking feeling creeping through her. It had become clear to her that neither Al nor Farren had any plans of ever making those records public, unless forced to do so by a court order. "I'm afraid I can't comment further on the issue," she said, wanting to slam down the phone and be as rude to him as he'd been with her, but her manners and better judgment prevailed. She kept listening, her hand wrapped tightly around the receiver.

"Well," Yusef replied. "I should not have expected any more of you, but I have to give you credit. You've certainly mastered the art of double-talk, though I am disappointed. I thought, perhaps, since our first meeting, you'd been able to rethink your position."

"I'm doing my job," Elise replied tightly.

"So I gather," Yusef said in a bitter retort. "I don't see how you sleep at night, Ms. Jeffries, knowing how deceitful your company has been to the people of this county." Then the line clicked off.

When she hung up the phone, she was shaking, but a vision of Yusef Kirk and his throng of picketers marching in front of Global Oil's tall gates immediately flashed into her mind and calmed her.

Maybe Al was right. She didn't need this grief, and things would be a lot less stressful if Global were found responsible for the medical problems suffered by the residents. Though tempted to call Yusef Kirk back and personally cuss him out for being so rude to her, she forced the conversation out of her mind and plunged back into her work.

Shortly after one o'clock, just when Elise was about to break for lunch, the buzz of the fax machine interrupted her. Swiveling around in her chair, she got up and crossed to the machine. The single page coming through was on Global Oil's letterhead.

There will be a Press Conference at 2:00 P.M. today in the press room, first floor, Global Oil Headquarters, 13500 North Coastal Highway. Topic: Results of the EPA's tests taken after the recent warehouse fire.

All right, she thought, grabbing the fax. Things were beginning to shake loose sooner than she'd anticipated. Elise checked her watch, anxious to see Yusef's face when Global admitted its part in the crisis. She couldn't wait.

Pretty short notice, she thought, yanking open her bottom desk drawer, snatching up her purse. It was ten after one, but she had enough time to grab a bite to eat and still make the meeting on time. For the past three days, she'd stayed at her desk and worked straight through lunch, but not today. Clicking off her computer, she headed out the door.

CHAPTER 11

That press room is going to be jammed, Elise thought, pulling her sunglasses over her eyes to shield them from the punishing south Texas sun. Driving along the coastal highway, she looked out across Galveston Bay to the thin blue line on the horizon where its waters slid into the Gulf of Mexico. The blue-green bay shimmered in the sunlight, reflecting silvery shadows of seagulls that were soaring and swooping above the mirrored surface. She let her thoughts drift along with the birds' movement, unable to do much else.

Her best friend was seriously ill. Her parents were frightened. Her husband needed her. No one else seemed to trust or believe her. An aching weariness settled deep in Elise's limbs, and she slumped in her seat, holding tightly to the steering wheel as she sped away from town.

A whirlwind of anger and fear was swirling through the county like sand tossed about in a storm. Elise could sense matters spinning out of control, and the concerns about her role could no longer be suppressed.

Maybe I ought to pull out of this assignment, she thought, silently cursing the possibility that Al's resistance to having her in the role of media spokesperson might be warranted after all.

How *could* she be loyal to her own professional values and still do the job ScanTron had hired her to do? And what about the residents of Flatwoods? Had she really been as open and honest with them as she could have been? And would she ever stop feeling guilty, as if she were walking a tightrope wire without a balancing pole? She didn't know the answers yet, but knew she had to find a way to hold on to her job as well as her self-esteem, if such a thing were possible.

The hollow pull of disappointment began, nearly bringing on tears, but she drew in a deep breath, determined not to lose faith. She had to get her career back on track, move toward financial security, and she'd cried too much and prayed too hard for this job to think of walking away. Running scared would prove nothing, and the challenge of taking on Yusef Kirk was suddenly somewhat appealing.

He could call her a mouthpiece and a traitor if he wanted to, but she knew who she was, and it wasn't the cold, calculating witch he had tried to make her out to be. She was a concerned homegirl with a personal stake in what went on in Tide County, and she would never intentionally dodge the truth. If anybody was guilty, it seemed like Al Patterson, and she wanted to find out why.

Elise cut off the two-lane highway and entered a sandy road that led to a shabby eatery called the Crab Shack. She set aside her troubles as she neared the small restaurant that had been serving soft-shell crabs and seafood gumbo at the same spot for close to forty years, and nothing much had changed about the place since she and Damita used to go there as teenagers to hang out with the boys after school—except the addition of a big electronic outdoor menu.

In front of her was an open-bed truck filled with rowdy boys in swim trunks jostling each other around. Sitting behind them, she let her mind turn, once again, to Al. What was his problem? Some dark, messy underhanded dealings he was trying to protect, or was she letting her imagination go unchecked? Did she dare challenge him and become a target for his nasty temper, or should she turn to John Farren for advice? As much as she was tempted to take her concerns over Al's head, Elise knew that would not be a professional approach. Better not chance violating the chain of command, she reminded herself, at least not unless she was ready to accept the consequences, which might be resuming her place in the unemployment line.

"God," Elise groaned lowly. "I sure as hell didn't bargain for this." As she pulled closer to the drive-through window, a disturbing thought began to unwind. What was it she was most worried about? Was it the company or her job that she was consumed with protecting? Or perhaps, was it her marriage?

Blake. He was her friend, her lover, her world. Without him Elise felt her life would be nothing but a hollow imitation of happiness, though recently, she had begun to feel caged, cornered, completely alone. Blake deserved her financial and emotional support, but his dream of leaving Century was rapidly becoming her nightmare. How much longer could she pretend to be as excited as he was about the changes he envisioned for their future?

She'd told Blake how delicate the situation between her and Al and the people of Flatwoods was becoming, but he blanked out, not seeming to take her seriously. His advice was to go along with the program, keep from getting Al upset, and not put any wrinkles in ScanTron's plans for her career. To get through this assignment without getting fired.

Blake had been testy and irritable for the past few days, infuriating Elise. She'd begun snapping and bristling back at him whenever the topic of his rapidly evolving business venture came up.

If only Damita didn't have such serious troubles of her own, Elise thought, wishing she could dump her problems on her best friend's doorstep as she'd always done in the past.

By the time Elise had crawled to the head of the line and a teenager's voice came over the black box asking for her order, her stomach was so upset, she drove away with just a cold drink, no longer interested in eating.

In the parking lot at Global Oil, she sternly shook off her worries and got out of the car. Once inside the building, Elise greeted the receptionist and showed her ScanTron ID. A uniformed security guard personally escorted her and a knot of other people into the press room, where she found a crush of reporters, cameramen, local businesspeople, and a large contingent of Flatwoods residents, Yusef Kirk moving among them. He was absorbed in animated conversation and didn't see her arrive.

Some of the people looked familiar, and Elise summoned up a polite smile of greeting but was hurt when few smiled back. After picking up a copy of the EPA test results from a stack on a small table, she turned away and threaded through the crowd toward a seat at the front of the spacious auditorium, purposefully avoiding eye contact with anyone.

Dropping her handbag to the floor, Elise slid into a chair, bent down, and pulled out a notepad and pen. When she looked up she gasped—Carlos Rico was sitting next to her. Immediately, she rose to leave, but he touched her arm.

"Elise. Hey. Don't go."

As she glared at him, all the hurt he'd caused surged back. Their eyes remained locked for only a second, yet she burned with a soul-filling anger. She jerked her gaze free, unsettled by what she'd seen: a suave Latin smile that belied the competitive gleam in his hard green eyes.

Elise chastised herself for allowing him to get under her skin again. His incongruous charm had once seduced her into trusting him, but she'd paid a high price for allowing friendship to cloud her professional judgment.

She turned back to face him. "I think it would be best—"

"No, it wouldn't," he interrupted, firming his hold on her arm. "Please stay. I'd like to talk to you."

It was the confrontation Elise had both prayed for and feared. Before their exchange on the morning of the fire, she had spoken to Carlos only once since his on-air betrayal, and that had been with her attorney present. But as long as she was working for ScanTron, and he for Channel 3, there would be no way to avoid him. She mustn't allow him to think he had any effect on her.

"Talk about what?" Elise asked coldly, hoping to convey her low opinion of him. "I thought you said everything in Judge Quarle's courtroom, remember?"

Carlos glanced nervously around the room, then back to Elise. "That whole mess was a big mistake. It kind of boomeranged on me. Really. I never should have aired what you told me. It was stupid."

"Vicious," she shot back, glad to see his face drain pale. "You have no idea what it cost me, Carlos, and I'm not talking cash." She pulled away. He tightened his grip. "You bastard. *You* are the one who should have been fired." She thrust her words at him, forgetting to conceal her emotion.

Quickly, Carlos let go of her arm, flinching, pressing a hand to his chest as if he'd been run through with a knife.

"Stop the dramatics, please. It's not funny."

"I know, I was just trying to lighten things up."

"That's your problem, Carlos. You're too damn light! You go around with nothing on your mind except getting the sensational story, raising the ratings and your market share. Don't you ever think about anybody but yourself—about the pain that you cause others?"

"Of course I do." His tone was no longer flippant. "And I admit that what I did to you was wrong." His on-camera, high-wattage smile started to dim. "But you don't know the pressure I was under. The show's ratings were slipping. I needed something."

"And I was it," Elise finished, quietly assessing Carlos's uneasiness. For the first time since she'd met him, he looked truly contrite, and it pleased her to see him squirm. But she wasn't interested in hearing another word of rationalization. It was too late for apologies as far as she was concerned. "Forget it, Carlos. I don't want to hear your sob story. You know, if you had talked to me like this two years ago, before I faced you in court, perhaps I would have believed you." She swallowed to gird herself to say what had festered far too long. "I trusted you. We used to be friends, colleagues, but you treated me like trash. On the air! You set out to destroy me, and now you want to talk? I don't think so." Grabbing her purse, she got up, moved three rows back, and dropped into a seat beside a woman in a blue halter-top dress.

Elise crossed her legs, glowering at Carlos, who swiveled around to see where she'd gone. He slumped down in his seat when her icy stare forced him into retreat. She gritted her teeth in silent triumph, glad to see Carlos Rico looking more like a little boy who'd had his toys taken away than like the smooth-talking reporter who charmed his viewers with his wit and style and damnable good looks.

The sound of a man speaking into the bank of microphones on a table at the front of the room got her attention. He cleared his throat and waited for the noise in the room to die down. Elise leaned forward in her seat. Out of the corner of her eye she saw Yusef Kirk hurry toward the front of the room. He didn't take a seat but stood, arms crossed on his chest, next to the side exit door.

Ready to pounce, Elise thought, turning her attention back to the man who had just introduced himself as Donald Munser, spokesperson for Global Oil.

"Thank you for coming on such short notice. We at Global Oil are always concerned with what is happening in the county. As your corporate neighbor, we owe you our support during this difficult time. The EPA report, a copy of which all of you should have now, indicated that low levels of benzene and arsenic were present in the air on the day of the fire. This is disconcerting, but not alarming. This type of discovery happens in our area from time to time and Global has initiated an extensive testing and evaluation program to assess all of its equipment and processing procedures. If the toxins found by the EPA did come from our pipeline or any component of our refinery, we will accept full responsibility for damages and move promptly to rectify the situation, including honoring all medical claims."

A murmur of disbelief rumbled through the crowd.

A reporter stood and waved her handheld mike. "Didn't a similar situation occur once before? Back in eighty-eight? Seven people died as a result of a pipeline leak."

A man in the back of the room shouted. "Yes! My son was one of them."

The TV cameras swung his way.

"We've been down this road before," the man yelled, anger trembling in his voice. "You big companies talk a good game, but we're not buying it anymore! We can't live like this!"

Loud voices offering support broke out, but Donald Munser sat calmly, unemotionally surveying the crowd until they settled down. "I cannot promise that our refinery will never have problems; accidents do happen. But I can promise you that we have followed, and continue to follow, every OSHA regulation required of us. We take every possible precaution to minimize the chance of such unfortunate occurrences. And since we do not yet know exactly what caused the release of benzene and arsenic into the air, I beg you to be patient as we work toward getting to the truth."

"You know what happened! You just don't want to tell us," someone shouted. "You're working out the spin."

"That is not true," Munser countered calmly. "But I can tell you that the amounts found are extremely low and not life-threatening. I urge you not to panic. If there is any evidence that Global's pipeline is faulty, immediate repairs will be initiated."

Elise watched Yusef closely. He was grimly shaking his head as if he'd heard it all before. But for some reason he did not speak out.

Reporters jumped into the discussion with detailed questions about Global's safety records, previous toxic accidents, and probing inquiries about hazardous materials. Elise tuned them out, slipping out of her seat, as she hurried to her car.

The heat was on Global now, and she was anxious to get to the library and dig out news stories of Global's history that she could use as fodder for her diversion campaign. Again, her thoughts turned to Al, and she struggled not to panic. The man's theories were beginning to make sense, and with Global's admission to prior toxic leaks she had exactly what she needed to do the job ScanTron expected of her, yet she wondered why it provided her absolutely no sense of triumph.

Justin Snyder squeezed between two stacks of boxes, his cellular phone pressed to his ear. As he listened, he threaded through the maze of shelving that filled his cluttered storage room. Lifting lids from boxes, reading faded labels, he impatiently tossed thick folders aside, troubled furrows of worry lining his forehead.

"Yes," he said to his caller. "Don't worry. I've got the data. It's been ten years since I've seen it, but I know it's down here somewhere." He shoved a crate aside with his elbow, tipped open its lid, then moved on. "Zephron, huh? Jesus, Bill. You know how deadly that stuff is?" Nodding at his caller's reply, Justin kicked a metal trunk aside and crouched down to pick up a slim black folder. "Got it!" he shouted, blowing dust off the cover. "I'll call you back in twenty minutes."

When Elise exited the small Tide County Library she had copies of every story about all of the refineries in the area that had ever had an accident. Global had had the most problems and negative press, but it was also the largest refinery operating in the county. One thing she'd have to admit, the company always told the public the truth and never shied away from accepting responsibility. That was encouraging but didn't prove they were not at fault this time.

When she reached her car, she fumbled in her purse, groping for her keys, then realized she must have laid them on the counter while paying for the copies. Turning to go back in, she stopped when a Channel 3 news van pulled into the parking lot. Curious, she waited beside her car until Carlos got out, but was not surprised when he immediately strode toward her.

"Doing your homework?" he asked lightly, adjusting his reflective Ray-Bans over his eyes. The sun caught the deep sheen on his jet black hair and radiated off in a burst of light.

"You got that right," she quipped, patting the manila folder under her arm, retreating a few steps when Carlos moved closer.

She winced at the smell of his familiar cologne that triggered memories of a time when she had actually enjoyed talking to him, being with him, working with him. He used to be fun, interesting, one of the reporters the staff at the hospital looked forward to seeing when there was reason to interact with the press. Whether setting up lights and mikes or giving an update on a famous patient or the statistics following a tragic accident, Elise had always felt at ease around Carlos.

She used to laugh at his Latino familiarity, the way he consciously and boldly flirted with all of the female doctors and nurses who crossed his path, and she good-naturedly refused to play the wagers game over whom the handsome reporter would target the next time he visited the nurses' station. Though it was only fantasy chitchat to liven up the day, Elise had been mildly piqued that her name had never come up.

"Find what you were looking for?" he asked.

"Yes. And it's very interesting reading."

"I'll bet," Carlos said, tapping his fingers on the trunk of her car. "Any chance of sharing what you've got there? Save me a lot of time."

An incredulous expression spread over Elise's features and she backed farther away, gripping her folder. "You've got to be kidding."

"Why? You used to help me out, remember?"

Elise rolled her eyes, a slow breath escaping through her clenched teeth. "Oh, yes. I do."

Carlos shifted his weight, his head tilted to the side in the chatty, nonchalant pose she'd seen him take in interviews many times. "Okay," he said. "Forget I asked. It's public information. I can find it."

"Correct," Elise replied, wishing she could jump into her car and burn rubber in his face. When she didn't move, he must have thought she wanted to talk, because he took up his plea where she'd interrupted him only an hour ago.

"We ought to be able to work together, Elise. Come on. I'd like to help."

"Help? What makes you think I need your help, or anybody else's for that matter?"

Carlos slowly removed his sunglasses, riveting her with liquid emerald eyes and an astonishingly knowing gaze. "Because Global's not at fault."

"How do you know?"

"You forget. I'm the best investigative reporter in the state. You once told me so yourself, didn't you?"

She froze, hating the truth of his words, wanting to slap his face, but too curious to stop him.

"Elise, I know the spot you're in. And believe me, you're not going to get through this without help from somebody." He eased his glasses back over his eyes. "So. Why not let it be me?"

If she'd been able to leave, she would have, but since she was trapped, she decided to listen. "Give me one good reason why I should even talk to you, let alone let you get involved in my work."

Entwining his fingers together, he half closed his eyes. "Because I owe you," he said hoarsely, chest rising beneath his hand-tailored suit from the effort it took to say the words.

Elise's pulse thundered as blood rushed through her veins and a plummeting sensation overtook her. He was right, she thought. He damn sure owed her, but did she trust him enough to let him pay off his debt?

"I have what I need to do my job," she said, turning away, starting back to the library to get her keys. She felt him watching her, but kept her back straight and her shoulders square, not about to weaken in front of him.

"Elise," Carlos called after her.

She kept right on walking.

"I think I know the name of the man who crashed the ScanTron gates."

She stopped and whirled around.

"And that's not all," Carlos told her in a breathless voice as he hurried closer. "I have a pretty good idea why he did it, *and* the only connection to an irrefutable source."

"Then tell the authorities what you know," she challenged.

"Not right now," Carlos hedged. "But soon. There are still a few details I've got to check out."

"Please!" Elise dismissed his ploy. "Don't play with me, Carlos. I've got better things to do than stand out here in the heat while your imagination runs wild."

"Watch," he challenged. "I'll break this case before the county sheriff has time to run his data through the INS computers. Wait. You'll see," Carlos promised, falling into step beside Elise.

She clamped her jaws firmly shut, making no protest as he accompanied her up the flight of marble steps. But when he bowed in exaggeration and pulled the heavy glass door open for her, she pierced him with a knifelike stare.

"Good luck, Carlos," she said dryly, heading to the counter to retrieve her keys.

CHAPTER 12

Blake drew in his chin and pressed his spine flush against the back of the chair that Mrs. Williams had indicated, with a wave of her hand, that he take. As the efficient loan officer looked over his papers, he fidgeted with the Century ballpoint pen clutched between his damp fingers.

He hoped he looked the image of a budding entrepreneur about to take charge of his future, prepared to take on the responsibility of the two hundred thousand dollars he was asking for, and not like the genuinely frightened soul he was right then.

When Elise had distractedly scribbled her name beside the red X on the bottoms of all four forms, he should have been elated, but instead, he'd felt lukewarm about her blessing. The weekend had been tense, her lack of confidence in his venture all too clear. The way she'd hurried off to work today without a word of good luck had caused a tidal wave of fear to rise.

All day he had fiddled with his files or stared sullenly at his computer screen, alternately confirming, then second-guessing his decision. What if the dealership failed? What if he discovered that he was no good at being the boss and should have stayed exactly where he had been for thirteen years—behind a desk manipulating insurance rates and annuity premiums?

Elise's attitude was not helpful. He knew she hated motorcycles, and it had all started the day he'd taken her for a drive in the country during her senior year at college.

They had been heading out to Mount Bonell on the west side of Austin. She'd been a good sport, holding on tight, laughing in the wind. Then, she'd burned her leg on the exhaust pipe and they'd had to make a detour to the hospital emergency room. The burn had been serious, leaving a scar that remained on the inside of her right ankle.

From that day on, Elise never sat on a motorcycle behind him, though Blake had modified his bike to ensure such a thing could never happen again. He wanted her with him on his big Harley cruiser with her hands around his waist, the wind blowing through her hair, but she adamantly refused his invitations and he didn't know how to erase the trauma of the past.

It *was* scary to dwell on the move he was making, but Blake had made up his mind to go forward, with or without Elise's blessing. After years of taking orders from incompetent managers, who never seemed to bore of talking interest rates and crunching numbers, Blake had to take the plunge. If he didn't make a change now, he'd wind up spending the best years of his life unhappy and become a bitter, grouchy old man with no hope, no drive, no joy. Besides, Paul was counting on him to come through and he would not let his brother down.

But the more Blake worried, the more it became clear that meeting with the loan officer at Nations Bank wasn't the only bothersome matter occupying his mind. Still stunned over Elise's revelation that Carlos Rico had apologized to her, Blake was obsessed with wondering why. Why was Carlos taunting Elise with information that he obviously didn't yet have? And what in the world had possessed Elise to even listen to that bastard?

A maddening jealousy heated Blake's face at the thought of Carlos Rico talking to Elise. With a shudder, Blake tried to shake off the uneasiness. According to Elise, their conversation had been strictly professional, but Blake still didn't like it. Rico was a ladies' man, a dangerous flirt, the kind of man who expected payment, in some form, for any favors he granted. Giving unsolicited advice and tips on how to handle a difficult media assignment was not typical of Carlos Rico, Blake was certain of that.

Blake had spent Saturday and Sunday thrusting such preposterous ideas from his mind, reprimanding himself for even letting such insecurities come to the surface. Though the television reporter was extremely handsome and popular and, as Blake knew, recently divorced, surely he was no threat to Blake's marriage. Besides, Elise hated Carlos. So why this sudden and unexplainable desire to listen to what the man had to say? Elise ought to put her energy into supporting her husband's dreams instead of worrying about solving a mystery that should be left to the police.

Blake hated obsessing, but could not help himself. Worried that Elise was growing more distant and difficult each day, he rarely talked to her anymore. He understood the pressure she was under at work, though she swore he didn't, and Blake, who wasn't thrilled about going into debt, could also understand Elise's reservations. She had never been as stressed-out and nervous as she was now. She was wound as tight as a spring inside a clock.

"Everything looks to be in order," Mrs. Williams told Blake, shaking him from the brink of depression. She opened her desk drawer and took out a business card. Handing it to him, she said, "I'll submit your papers to the loan committee this afternoon. You'll be hearing from me by the end of the week."

Blake nodded, unsure if he should thank the woman now or wait until he heard whether or not the loan had been approved.

Mrs. Williams slipped the sheaf of papers into a white folder, stood, and extended her hand.

"Thank you," Blake said, taking her cool, dry fingers. "I'll be anxiously awaiting your call."

She gave him a bland smile with no words of encouragement, then escorted him to the door.

On the drive home, Blake impulsively stopped at Richards liquor

Store and paid twenty-five dollars for a bottle of champagne. When he got home, he started to put it in the back of the refrigerator, to have ready when Mrs. Williams's call of approval came through, but changed his mind and undid the wire top, hastily uncorking the dark green bottle.

Hell, he thought, taking a fluted glass out of the cabinet. *The papers are filed. I'm on my way out of Century. That's worth celebrating.*

Justin Snyder waited until all four of the agents involved in the ScanTron–Global Oil fire investigation had settled into their seats before he opened the oversize brown envelope and removed its contents for the second time that day. The puzzled expressions on the faces of his staff let him know he had their attention.

"Anybody here know what Zephron is?" he asked as if he were still lecturing rookies in forensics as he'd done for the Houston Police Department for twenty-one years. Retiring from HPD to join the EPA had been an easy transition for him.

Brad Lowe, who had the most years with the agency, immediately raised a pointed finger. "Deadly, that's what it is," he said, grinning at the twitter of laughter that came from his coworkers.

Justin nodded slowly, letting his staff in on the fact that what they were about to discuss was not a laughing matter.

"Brad. I believe you were in on the initial testing the first time Zephron surfaced in the States."

"Yep," Brad said in his easygoing Louisiana drawl, scratching the perpetual stubble on his beet-red face. "In the Permian Basin. Ten years ago."

"Right." Justin took over. "Listen up, you guys, 'cause we've got a serious situation on our hands." He picked up one of the sheets of paper he'd taken from the envelope, glanced at it, then said, "Zephron is created when contaminated oil is heated at an extremely high temperature. The resultant bacterium is a highly controlled toxin that has only been found once in the United States—outside a government research lab. That was in the Permian Basin, a freaky combination of man tampering with nature that got out of hand."

"Wiped out a town," Brad offered. "In less than a day. God it was awful going in there."

Justin assessed his team with thoughtful eyes. "I'm alarmed and puzzled about what we've got here. Zephron is nearly impossible to create. The first batch of man-made Zephron was achieved by a scientist in Paris in the sixties. Since then the deadly toxin has been used in chemical warfare in the Middle East. The damage is done when the bacteria-laced oil burns, creating a deadly vapor. It can occur during fires, explosions, from cooking oils, and even fuel. It's an effective method to breach security."

The lone woman on the team spoke up. "So where is it?"

"Zephron has been detected in the soil samples taken at the ScanTron fire site," Justin replied. He paused for their reaction, which was an audible gasp. "Anybody got any ideas why something so exotic and deadly would be showing up in Tide County, Texas? Or why ScanTron Security or Global Oil, or anybody else around here for that matter, might be storing it on their property?"

When no one answered, Justin handed the report to Brad. "Each of you read this report. Carefully. Understand what we're dealing with, okay? When you've finished, I have orders to destroy the findings. As of right now we're under a gag order." He held up a hand to hush the protests. "Orders from Washington, not from me. Don't discuss these findings with anyone. Got that? No one. If this leaks, I'll find out the source. It's classified until further notice."

The hulking shadow sitting at the patio table frightened Elise as she stepped out of the garage. She shrank back into the doorway to see who was there, then relaxed when she saw it was just Blake. He was slumped down, staring at three votive candles that were flickering dots of light on the table. Shadows rippled over the concrete floor when he lifted his champagne glass to his lips, then held it in her direction, urging her to join him. "Come on over," he slurred.

"What are you doing?" Elise asked.

"Getting drunk, I guess," Blake said thickly, then chuckled. "I hadn't set out to, I promise. Guess it just kind of crept up on me."

Elise put her briefcase on the ground and sat down opposite Blake, wondering what had brought on this midweek binge, since he rarely drank more than two beers at a time. "Where's Junior?" she asked.

"In bed."

"So early?"

"Early?" Blake checked his watch. "Nine-thirty is not so early for a five-year-old boy."

Elise bristled. Blake was right. It was late, but she'd hoped Junior might still be up.

"You could have called." Blake tossed out his accusation while sloshing more champagne into his glass.

"I couldn't," Elise replied, taking the bottle from Blake, emptying the remaining bubbly onto the grass. "I was just too busy."

Rubbing a hand over his short hair, Blake gave her an exasperated grunt, twisting in his seat to focus on her. "Hey, I was busy, too. By the time Lorna dropped off Junior from soccer practice, I had to get dinner together, bathe him, then finish that competitive analysis for Tharp—he wants it on his desk first thing in the morning, and I couldn't stay at the office to do it. I have to pick up our son on time, remember?"

Elise glared.

"So," Blake went on, "I brought *my* work home."

"Sorry," Elise offered.

"Sorry! That's all you can say?" Blake pounded the table, making the votive candles sputter and give off a burst of light. "Damn it!" he shouted. "Is it too much to expect a phone call from my wife to at least let me know she's alive?"

Elise watched the flames dance over the mirrored top of the clear glass table. "Don't get so dramatic, Blake. Of course I'm alive."

"Oh? Well, how would I know you weren't in some accident or that you'd been car-jacked at some isolated intersection? Those things do happen in Houston, you know."

She shrugged.

"Jesus, Elise. I never thought you'd start acting like this. I want you to succeed at ScanTron, but you're letting that company take over your life."

"No, I'm not," she replied tightly. "There's no reason for you to go off the deep end. Okay, I should have called, but I thought I'd get home earlier. Time got away from me, that's all," Elise finished, too tired to go into more details of her day.

"Must have been really enjoying yourself."

With a frown, Elise snapped back. "Enjoying myself? Get real." She rubbed the back of her neck, tilting her head until she was looking straight up into the blue-black sky. "A staff meeting is hardly fun." She looked down at the glass in Blake's hand, then added, "I obviously didn't have as good a time as you. I'm surprised that you'd be out here drinking. Alone."

"Why not?" Blake bellowed. "You didn't care enough to come home and join me."

Alarmed by the anger in Blake's voice, Elise began to explain. "Farren called an emergency meeting. It ran later than anyone expected. A big problem with the Dallas office. Nothing I'm directly involved in, but he wanted me there so I would be able to handle the questions that might be coming our way from a few reporters who've been hanging around."

Blake finished the last of his drink, then pushed the glass to the center of the table.

Realizing how futile it was to justify herself, Elise got up from the table. "I'm going in. I'm whipped."

"Did you talk to your friend Carlos today?" Blake's voice shot from the darkness.

Elise sat back down, stunned. "Carlos Rico?"

"Is there any other Carlos in your life?"

Annoyed, she slumped back in her chair, legs stretched out, focusing on her navy pumps. "So, that's what made you decide to down a whole bottle of champagne? Carlos Rico?" She grabbed Blake's arm, then burst into laughter. "Good Lord, Blake. Give me some credit! He's the last person on earth I'd want to spend time with. What's gotten into you?"

Blake glanced to the side, then sniffed dismissively. "Too much champagne I guess."

"You're right about that." She wanted to shake him, she was so upset, but when she saw the embarrassment on his features, she said in a soft tone, "Come on inside, you big baby. I'll make some coffee." Elise pushed up from the table and started toward the house.

Blake stood, rather unsteadily, then lurched forward and grabbed Elise around the waist, pulling her to him. He pressed her hips against the kitchen door as he smothered her with his presence. His breath was sweet and hot on her face. "I don't want any coffee." He kissed her at the base of her throat. "I want you. I want you back."

Startled by his closeness and his urgent plea, Elise whispered, "Back? That's crazy. What are you talking about?"

"Back like you used to be," he muttered.

Elise lowered her head to his chest, allowing her full weight to rest against him, letting the ordeal of her day drain from her shoulders. Nuzzling against him, she murmured, "Honey, I know I dashed out of here this morning in a pretty sour mood. Is that what this is about?"

He didn't answer.

"And," she continued, "I've been hell to live with lately, I know, but it's going to get better. It is. Tomorrow, I'll be home by six, no matter what. And *I'll* cook dinner."

"No, you won't," Blake broke in, "we'll go out. All three of us, okay?"

"That'd be great," she said, already feeling less tired and less guilty than she had all day. Rushing out of the house the way she had that morning had been selfish and uncalled for. "I should have told you this morning how proud I am of you, Blake. And I *am* glad you put in for the loan." She tilted her face up to his, gazing at him in the moonlight. "How'd it go at the bank?"

Blake simply shrugged.

"Come on. How's it look?" she prodded.

He kissed her lightly before he answered. "Good. Real good."

Leaning back, she looked at him with unspoken understanding, then whispered, "That's great." Touching him lightly, she ran her palm along the side of his face, then pressed her body closer, flicking her tongue gently over his bottom lip, sinking into the wellspring of security she found in his arms. "You could have saved the champagne until later. Celebrated with me," she teased, running her hands slowly up and down his back.

"There will be another call for champagne. Soon, I predict."

A faint chuckle of agreement escaped Elise's throat and a flash of optimism flared, extinguishing her childish annoyance.

Gently, he eased her from his arms and started toward the door. When Elise turned to follow, he said huskily, "Wait here, I'll be right back."

Within seconds Blake reappeared at the door holding the blue-and-gray tartan plaid blanket they used for picnics at the beach. Wordlessly, he crossed the moon-splashed yard and stopped beneath a towering magnolia hung with creamy, fragrant blooms.

Elise grinned, shaking her head at his deep masculine laugh that beckoned her into his arms. She went to him without hesitation, her blood racing, her knees weak with desire. When he moaned, folding her into his arms as he gently stroked her hair, she held him fast, completely aware of how lucky she was. Closing her eyes, Elise pushed their disagreement to a distant place and greeted her husband with a long, deep kiss.

Clinging to him, she felt oddly buoyant, as if she were being transported from her ordinary suburban backyard to an enchanted silvery haven where the mundane problems they'd been grappling with all week could not reach or hurt them anymore.

Sinking onto the blanket, they descended to their knees, lips still locked in hungry devotion. The feel of Blake's mouth was like velvet, his taste like sweet sugared honey, and they gripped each other with a fierce tenderness that silently celebrated the strength of their marriage. There was no need to speak, to explain, or to ask for a thing. Their love had been tested, severely, and survived.

With a throaty murmur, Elise dipped low, then slipped onto her back. Blake crouched above her, assessing her in a lovingly pensive gaze, then lowered himself alongside her. Tugging at his shirt, Elise eased it over his head, then kissed the smooth plane of his chest, his tight ruddy nipples, and the soft swell of his biceps, stirred by the iron-hard flesh beneath her tongue.

Blake pressed her tightly to his body, moaning as Elise traced her kiss down his stomach—low to his belt line, where she lingered to taste the warm glow of his growing need for her. Her desire for him boiled hot in her veins, scorching her heart, her mind, her lips.

Blake smoothed his hand beneath Elise's skirt, halting only to let her kick off her low-heeled pumps before slipping her silky panty hose down her trembling legs. When she grasped his zipper with practiced fingers, he tilted toward her, rubbing the warm flesh of his cheek against hers as she maneuvered his jeans from his hips.

Elise's hand lingered on his thigh for only a moment; then she spread her fingers in an expansive fan that slid upward in a maddeningly gentle caress against his hard, smooth shaft. Sheltered by the leafy canopy of night-blackened magnolia leaves, she arched her neck, thrust her chin toward the stars, and let him strip away the sheer barrier of her blouse and lacy bra.

The sudden, urgent clasp of his lips on her warm breast startled her with sweet expectation, and she murmured his name into the humid, ebony night while he traced the point of her breast with his tongue and his fingers traced the length of her spine.

With a movement that seemed almost choreographed, they shifted to accept each other, stifling their moans of pleasure as they gave themselves over to the exquisite joy of making love again.

CHAPTER 13

The front-page story in the *Houston Chronicle* a week later was downright depressing. Shaken with disappointment, Elise crushed the newspaper to her lap, then zapped the TV back to life, paying little attention to the antics of a dysfunctional couple arguing violently on *Jerry Springer*. Unable to concentrate on the program, she began to pace the floor, going from the round oak table to the pantry on the far side of the kitchen and back—twice—before stopping to think about the ramifications of the report.

"No problems found!" she muttered, unable to believe that ten days after initiating its probe, Global Oil's "smart pig" had found no corrosion, faulty welds, or other defects that might have caused a leak in its underground pipeline. She wondered why in the world the inspection device would be named after swine.

Elise smoothed out the paper and stared at the quarter-page article again. The finely printed columns blurred before her eyes as she tried to comprehend the history of the giant refinery and the corrosion safeguards built into its miles of underground pipeline. The description of the technical equipment that helped carry Global's crude and refined products to their destinations was impressive. The analysis of the suspected problem with the line had been thorough, and the regulators had been satisfied that Global's pipeline was in tip-top shape.

The story also included an update on the county residents. Seven people remained hospitalized and thirteen were outpatients, still under a doctor's care, but one hundred thirty-two angry souls had already retained lawyers and were poised to file lawsuits against ScanTron, Global, or both. One woman was suing the Tide County Clinic, charging misdiagnosis and deliberate neglect based on racial bias.

Yusef Kirk was quoted at length, charging that both companies were guilty of conspiring against the community and were committing blatant environmental racism. And imbedded in the article was a statement from Donald Munser, expressing Global's regret about the incident, emphasizing his company's deep concern for its neighbors and its ongoing preventive programs.

"Precisely what I would have said," Elise thought, putting herself in Munser's place, wishing she were in her office and not at home hovering over a sick little boy.

Of all days for Junior to get sick, just when Global's report hit the paper. Her brows drew together in concern. Junior had awakened in the middle of the night, complaining of bad stomach cramps. This morning, when she'd taken his temperature, it had been normal, but she'd decided to keep him home.

Though Blake had implied that Junior's sudden illness might be a ploy to get his mother's attention, Elise didn't care if that were true. She'd been working long hours, and now she had as good a reason as any to stay at home with her son. Though Al was more than likely chewing nails about her absence from the office, she refused to let it get to her. Maybe it wasn't a good time to take off, but Blake had had an early staff meeting he absolutely could not miss, and if Al had a problem with her decision, he could take it up with her tomorrow.

It felt good to distance herself from the immediate pressure of being in the office and dealing with the crisis situation that didn't seem to be easing at all. During the time it had taken Global to check out its pipeline and other sections of its huge processing complex, she had been a jittery bundle of nerves, embarrassed to admit even to herself that she secretly hoped the pipeline would turn out to be the source of the illness plaguing Flatwoods. The fire department hadn't ruled out arson, and the county sheriff was still mum about the identity and motivation of the truck driver. The investigation remained open, still very much a mystery, and Elise was beginning to feel that she was back to square one.

Mulling over the impact the news story might have on those who claimed that ScanTron was responsible, Elise turned her thoughts to Carlos's unexpected invitation to help. Her first impulse was to give him a call and explore the possibility of accepting his offer, but how could she, really? The last thing Elise wanted was to place herself in a position to be used—again—but if Carlos *could* access information that had somehow eluded the authorities, why shouldn't she listen to him?

At first she'd thought he might be boasting in order to impress her, but now she was beginning to think that he might actually have a line on the truth. Trying to think like the television newsman, Elise pondered Carlos's motives. If he did have something that might help her bolster ScanTron's image, where had it come from, and what was he going to do with it? Certainly he had not dug it up just for her.

Intrigued by Carlos's interest in the incident, she wondered what kind of television program he might be planning and where he would point the finger of blame. An exposé on the explosion at ScanTron could be a horror story waiting to happen. It made Elise uneasy to think of the damage Carlos could do if he pulled it off.

It was Carlos's job to inform, expose, and initiate debate, and he did it well. It certainly had nothing to do with her. She had not been hired by ScanTron to play detective or investigative reporter, so why should she get tangled up with anything Carlos set out to accomplish? She knew she was curious enough to take Carlos's tempting bait, despite the friction it could cause in her marriage. She shook her head, unable to believe that Blake had actually been jealous of the man she despised with every fiber of her soul.

The passion she and Blake had shared under the stars had helped heal the terrible rift they had allowed to threaten their marriage. Curved warmly against Blake's sleek, hard chest, she had promised him she would slow down, pay more attention to the needs of her family. She wanted to normalize their life and banish the under-current of strain that had been simmering for weeks, but lately, when-ever the telephone rang, Junior flinched, Blake stared at her, and she was almost afraid to answer. She could sense Junior's anxiety that at any moment he expected to see his mother grab her briefcase and dash off.

No more, Elise vowed, sick to death of running up and down the interstate, of returning home to find her son already asleep, and of eating cold leftovers alone. Blake had apologized for his selfish re-action and had become much less vocal about his displeasure with her long hours, but she had begun to see that their home life was deteriorating into a series of quick hellos and abrupt good-byes.

The approval of the loan had brought more tension than joy. Going into debt for close to a quarter of a million dollars was scary, and Elise had turned cold with fear when Blake had called her with the news. She'd listened to his bubbling report with dread, her blood pumping like ice water in a rush to her head, but she had accepted this giant leap into their future and vowed to stop second-guessing the project.

Blake was in heaven, happily and furiously reviewing his plans, spending long hours at the site with Paul. He was also counting the days until he would be free of Century, and in the wake of his nonstop chattering and excited calculations about the growth he envisioned for Texas Rider, it was hard for Elise not to be swept up in her husband's childlike sense of anticipation.

Going to the kitchen counter, Elise poured her third cup of coffee that morning, pondering her predicament. Today's story would keep ScanTron in the spotlight, and she'd better get busy plotting her strategy to counter the impact of Global's report, or she might be staying at home permanently.

Elise grabbed the phone and began to dial, relieved when Darrell Grimes answered. For some reason, and maybe it was because he treated her more like a friend than a coworker, she trusted the chemist and believed he would tell her the truth.

"Yeah, he's real ticked off that you stayed home," Darrell told Elise, confirming her suspicion that Al was bad-mouthing her all over the office.

"Well, he'll get over it," she said, trying to act as if she didn't care what Al said or thought about her. Listening closely as Darrell filled her in on the morning's events, Elise's courage began to shrivel.

"Whatever Justin Snyder is onto must be big," she replied after hearing about an early morning impromptu visit paid to the office by the EPA.

"Snyder had a search warrant," Darrell confided.

"A search warrant? Why?"

"That's a good question. It was a federal warrant, and he refused to tell anybody what he was looking for. Took each one of us into Al's office and gave us the third degree."

"What kinds of questions did he ask?"

"Things about chemicals used on the complex, from routine cleaning supplies to research materials. He wanted to know if we had contracts with any Middle Eastern countries, and what kinds of security devices we marketed overseas. It was like the Spanish Inquisition. Of course, we cooperated, but Al had told Snyder that most of the information he wanted would have to come from headquarters. I didn't like the way Snyder went about it. He talked to us real rough, made me feel like some kind of criminal. I finally told him I wasn't saying another word without consulting my attorney. That's when he told me I could go."

Elise stiffened. She had never heard Darrell sound so dismayed.

"Snyder had his staffer round up the records of the accounts that had escaped the fire. He went through those line by line, then left."

"Did he take any files?"

"No. I guess he didn't find what he was looking for. I do know he's over at Global doing the same thing."

"How do you know that?"

"I've got sources in this county, too," Darrell hedged, adding, "and some good contacts in Washington, D.C."

"At the EPA?" she prompted.

"Mm-hm. And I think I'll make a few calls, see what I can find out." Darrell had been speaking in a low voice. Suddenly he assumed a tight, more professional demeanor. "Thanks for calling. I've got to go."

Someone must have been listening, or watching. "I'll call you later this afternoon," Elise told him, praying he'd be able to pry some information from his contacts in the capitol.

Without saying good-bye, Darrell hung up.

Elise replaced the receiver but remained sitting with her hand on it, thinking. Something pretty serious must be going on. When Justin Snyder had come to ScanTron with news about the presence of arsenic and benzene, he'd said those test results were only preliminary. The complete analysis of the soil and water samples must have finally come in.

What a day for me to be out of the office, she thought, restlessly beginning to pace again. How could she sit still with so much going on?

The ringing telephone made her jump, and Elise took a deep breath before picking up, certain it would be Al asking her if she planned to come in tomorrow. When she answered, Elise was pleasantly surprised to hear Damita's voice.

"You're finally getting out?"

"Yeah," Damita said flatly, not sounding pleased.

"Excuse me? You don't sound happy about returning to your cozy little bungalow."

"That's because I've been ordered not to drive myself home, though I'm perfectly prepared and capable of doing so."

"Whoa! You're not ready for that, and you know it."

"Well, my car is here. It's been sitting in the parking lot for nearly two weeks. If I don't get out of here today, I'm going to scream. Really, Elise, I just might start acting a real fool."

"Hold on, girl. This can be handled."

"Yeah, but my doctor refuses to sign the release until I tell him who is going to pick me up."

"Gosh," Elise said. "Damita, I'd be there in a heartbeat, but Junior is sick." The phone was silent as Elise thrashed around in her mind for an option. "What about your neighbors? The Greers?" she offered.

"Already called. No answer." Damita paused, then asked tentatively. "What about your dad or mom? I hate to ask, but . . ."

"Damita, don't say that. I'm sure they'd be glad to come, but they're in Galveston. Mom called last night and told me they were going to get an early start and probably stay all day."

A sigh of resignation slipped over the line. "Well, looks like I'm stuck for a while."

The disappointment in Damita's voice hurt Elise and she knew she couldn't let her friend down. "Listen. Get packed, get dressed. Tell your doctor to get the papers ready. I can bundle Junior into the backseat of my car and be there in forty minutes."

"Are you sure?" Damita hedged.

"Absolutely. It's time you got yourself home because I need your help, girlfriend. You won't believe what's happening."

Elise hung up and went down the hall to Junior's room and peeked in. He was sound asleep and after the medication she'd given him, he'd likely sleep all morning. As much as she wanted to, she just couldn't wake him up.

Pulling the door closed, Elise went into her room and pulled on a pair of slacks and a white tailored shirt, then hurried toward the front of the house and looked out her big bay window.

Lorna's car was in the driveway, as Elise knew it would be. Each Monday Lorna stayed home to do paperwork and review the books of her fast-growing chain of beauty salons. Maybe she wouldn't mind doing her books over here, Elise thought. If she could stay with Junior for just two hours, it would be enough time for her to pick up Damita at the League City Hospital, drop her at home, and get back before rush-hour traffic clogged the interstate. Elise picked up the phone and speed-dialed her neighbor's number.

"I wouldn't put it through too quick," Al Patterson growled into the phone. "If she thinks she can stay home every time that kid of hers eats too much candy and pukes, she'd better get with the program. I don't think she's gonna work out, Farren. Too emotional. Too cautious. We need somebody we can really depend on, no matter what comes up."

Those were not the words the president of ScanTron Security International had hoped he'd hear from Elise Jeffries's on-site manager. He'd taken a chance hiring Elise, in light of the incident at Trinity Hospital, but she'd impressed him as a competent, professional, and experienced media representative, a rare combination he'd been hoping to find. And she was the first African-American woman to ever fill the slot.

"Is this her first time taking off?" Farren asked.

"Yeah, but you know how that goes," Al said. "Let 'em get away with it once, and watch, pretty soon there's a pattern. I can't be bothered, Farren. I'd hold off on making her permanent. Give it a little more time."

Farren scratched his chin thoughtfully. "I don't have a lot of time. The position must be filled by September first, and that's only six weeks away. I don't want to start the recruitment process all over when I have a perfectly capable candidate already on the job."

"Suit yourself," Al said gruffly, clearly miffed that his opinion seemed to carry little weight. "But I don't think she's got the right attitude. I warned you. Her connection to Flatwoods is not sitting well with most of the people down here. We'd be better off with someone who has no personal interest in the incident."

"I've thought about that, Al, but for some reason I believe Elise Jeffries will be able to swing public opinion to our favor. I'd like to give her the chance, at least. Face it, we've got a lot going against us. I'm sure you've read the paper. Global is out of the hot seat, and we're back in, it seems."

"You better believe it," Al agreed. "And putting Elise Jeffries on TV to speak for us might backfire, Farren. You know it could."

There was no immediate response from Farren. Then he said, pacing his words, "Al, thanks for being so frank. I appreciate your input and understand your concerns. I'll be back in touch tomorrow."

"Sure," Al said curtly, hanging up.

Farren clicked off, too, then picked up a thick manila folder. Flipping through Elise's personnel file, he turned Al's assessment over in his mind but quickly pushed the manager's warnings aside. After the Tide County case was off the front page, Elise would be working in the main office, more closely with him. She and Al Patterson would have little contact. Farren wasn't about to make a decision on Elise's future without thinking about the ramifications, and so far it appeared that Elise Jeffries would do fine in the long run. That's what counted.

There was a bold solidness about Elise that Farren found impressive. She had been through a difficult ordeal and emerged intact. He liked her fighting spirit, her never-give-up attitude, and the optimistic way she carried herself without being pompous about it. She was loyal, professional, and levelheaded.

Setting aside Al's reservations, Farren leafed through the papers in Elise's personnel folder, rereading the generous reference given her by Trinity Hospital despite the unfortunate incident with the Baby Kitzmiller case. Her academic and professional training records were impressive, and she was a stable married woman. The only item missing was a printout of her Class A security clearance, which he knew she'd passed since Internal Investigations had already given him an oral okay.

Farren buzzed his secretary. When she came in, he lifted his eyes from the paper he was signing that would formalize his support of the board's recommendation that Elise Camden Jeffries be permanently appointed media relations officer of ScanTron Security International.

"Yes, Mr. Farren?" the brunette in the doorway asked.

Farren set the form aside. "Judy, would you please walk down to Internal and get that Class A clearance on Elise Jeffries? I hate to pull you away from your work, but I need it right away."

"No problem," Judy said, backing out the door.

CHAPTER 14

Animals didn't usually bother Elise. As a child she'd had two dogs, a parakeet, and a white rabbit that ate anything she fed it, but Damita's three cats were suddenly taxing her patience. Elise was jittery, and alarmed by the fragile state of Damita's health.

Damita was stoically struggling to maintain a sense of optimism, but Elise could tell it was difficult for her. After straightening up the house, stocking the empty refrigerator, and picking up Damita's prescriptions for pain medication, Elise was feeling rather helpless and extremely apprehensive about leaving Damita alone. Wandering from room to room, she kept finding one more thing to take care of, stalling her departure.

Why Damita thought she'd be able to drive herself home and slip back into her normal, self-sufficient routine puzzled Elise. She also didn't understand the doctor's decision to release Damita, who did not appear strong enough to manage on her own.

The hollowed cheeks, the gaunt, corded neck, and the listless glaze in Damita's eyes worried Elise. Her friend had lost too much weight, too rapidly, and her thick ruddy hair had become thin in places, making Damita look prematurely old and tired. This was not the same woman Elise had visited in the hospital only a week before, and as hard as she tried to act as if her best friend hadn't changed, Elise suspected Damita could read her thoughts.

During the drive from the hospital, Elise had babbled on about the story in the paper and how much more difficult her job was becoming. She told Damita about the progress Blake was making with his motorcycle dealership, and bragged on the flush crop of basil in her newest patch of herbs. Anything to keep from discussing the obvious change in her friend.

But now that it was a quarter past three, it was time to head home. Elise knew she ought to go but couldn't bring herself to leave.

I'll stay until after she's eaten dinner, Elise decided, stirring the soup that was bubbling on the stove.

When Benji, the noisiest of the three cats, wouldn't calm down, Elise hissed back at him, trying to stop his nerve-wracking mews.

"Put him outside in the yard," Damita suggested, pulling a brown crocheted afghan over her legs. She was lying on the sofa, propped up with pillows, exhausted after the ordeal of settling back into her home.

Elise opened the back door to let Benji scamper out, then resumed stirring the vegetable soup she'd made, glad Lorna had agreed to stay with Junior until Blake got home from work.

"Soup's on," she called cheerfully from the kitchen, ladeling steaming vegetables into a bowl that she placed on a tray along with a sandwich. Damita was so horribly thin, it looked as if she hadn't had a decent meal for weeks.

With a flourish, Elise positioned the tray of food over her friend's lap, then handed her a small white pill and a glass of water, waiting until Damita had swallowed her pain medication before flopping down at the end of the sofa. "Now, eat every bite of that, you hear?"

Damita scowled, then smiled, inhaling the steam rising from the bowl. "This smells great." She took a taste and nodded. "Thanks, Elise. Really. I guess I got spoiled in the hospital. I didn't realize how tough it was going to be once I got home."

Blowing out a long, knowing breath, Elise nodded. "It'll get easier. Give it time." Elise patted Damita's leg, then smoothed the soft afghan in place. "If you want, I can stay over tonight," she began, genuinely afraid to leave Damita alone.

"No!" Damita said sharply. "You go on. I'll be fine. The Greers, next door, are back, and I can call them if I need anything."

"All right," Elise agreed, warily eyeing Damita, "but I'm calling Mom as soon as I get home and have her come check on you tomorrow morning. You two put your heads together and come up with some kind of a plan to have someone here several times a day. You hear? At least until you get stronger."

A weakened smile slipped over Damita's lips. "Aye, aye," she quipped, winking one eye.

"I'm serious. Okay?" Elise pressed.

Damita nodded, turning somber.

"Fine," Elise decided, tickling the underside of Damita's sock-clad foot.

With a twist, Damita shifted, turning her face away from her friend, but not before Elise saw the sudden sheen of tears that came into her eyes.

"Girl. Don't you start," she cautioned, swallowing hard to keep moisture from gathering in her own eyes. "You're going to get through this, and I'll be here to help."

With a clatter of metal on china, Damita set her spoon down on the plate beneath her bowl, inhaling so deeply that her flattened chest raised the fuzzy blanket. "Elise," she said calmly. "Things are not going to get better."

"Shut up, now. Don't talk like that." The words flew from Elise's mouth like sharp but loving slaps. "You're going to be fine."

"No, I'm not," Damita whispered, setting the tray on the floor, untangling the afghan from around her legs. With effort, she haltingly scooted down the sofa to be nearer to Elise. "I haven't been completely honest with you, and it was stupid to think I'd be able to fool you." She reached over, taking Elise's hand in hers. "My prognosis is not as optimistic as I've led you to believe. The truth is, my condition is terminal. I've got three, maybe six months to live."

"No," Elise whispered, tightening her grip on Damita's moist fingers. "That can't be true."

"I'm afraid it is."

Suddenly, the music on the Pepsi commercial on the TV seemed to be tunneling into the room from outer space. Nothing existed for Elise but the sound of Damita's labored breathing as she fielded another wave of pain.

Elise glared at Damita and shook her head in denial, not wanting to acknowledge what she'd heard. "I told you not to say that. *Don't* go talking like that. There're all kinds of alternative treatments. Natural diets, herbs, ways to stop the cancer from growing. There are new medications approved all the time. There's always hope, Damita. Don't think that doctor knows everything. I'll take you into Houston to see a specialist at the Medical Center. I read a story about a woman with—"

"Don't," Damita interrupted, squeezing Elise's hand in a fearful, uncertain way. "I haven't given up, but I won't try to fool myself, either." Blinking rapidly, she forced tears from her eyes. They tracked wetly over her muddy brown cheeks. With a moan, she confessed, "I can't make it go away, Elise. The truth of it swims around in my head twenty-four hours a day, even in my sleep. I have dreams. I . . . I . . . don't know what to—" With a loud sob, she broke down, crying openly into her palms, hunching her thin shoulders up to her ears.

For a split second, Elise was paralyzed; then the roar pounding in her ears eventually dissolved into a low whistle. Slowly lifting her arms, she gathered Damita to her breast, wrapping her friend's quaking body in a circle of love.

Their mutual trembling took over. Elise held on to Damita tightly, almost fiercely, as if she could absorb the pain that was threatening to engulf them both. For a long time they sat clasped in silence and friendship, unable and not needing to speak until the emotion subsided. Soon, Damita's pain medication kicked in and she drifted into an uneasy sleep. The creases on her brow lifted away.

It was six o'clock when Damita awoke, still on the sofa where Elise had remained holding vigil over her friend. Damita was glad Elise had not left, but urged her to go home to her family.

"I will," Elise promised, "after I help you change those bandages and you're all set for the night."

Once Damita had bathed and arranged for Ethel Greer to check on her in the morning, she walked to the front door with Elise. There they paused and gently hugged each other; then Elise pushed the screen door open.

"God, it's still hot out here," Elise grumbled. "Must be ninety tonight."

"Yeah," Damita agreed. "I'm praying my creaky air conditioner will hold up for the rest of the summer. Next year, I'm getting . . ." She stopped, realizing what she had said.

Overwhelmed by the cruel reality of what they were facing, Elise averted her eyes.

Damita broke the uncomfortable moment by moving past Elise to step out onto her porch. "You know, I used to spend a lot of time out here thinking, planning." She sat in her weathered wicker rocker and began tilting back and forth.

Elise eased down on the top porch step and stared across the road at the back lot of the ScanTron complex. "Just look at that mess. It will take a long time to clean that up and rebuild," she said, anxious to steer the conversation away from Damita's condition. The burned-out piles of concrete and steel towered in a twisted black mountain that was silhouetted against an orange-red sunset.

Damita slapped at a buzzing mosquito. "I hope they don't rebuild. Remember when that field was white as far as you could see in the summer—filled with Queen Anne's lace and daisies?"

"I sure do," Elise replied. "And it was a much prettier sight than you have right now." She glanced over her shoulder at Damita. "Why are so many houses for sale?"

"The property taxes out here have nearly doubled in the past five years. Lots of people can't manage the payments, so they have to sell out."

"So, who's buying?"

"Nobody." Damita's reply was sharp, resentful. "Most of those properties sit vacant; some have been on the market for years. I hate to see the neighborhood go down, but no one's buying. Especially not now. Nobody wants to live here. It's a joke." With a nod, Damita went on. "After the warehouses were built I used to sit out here and count the empty houses. I watched this neighborhood fall apart. Family by family. Broke my heart when some kids set fire to the Davis place."

"The house at the end of Thornhill Road?" Elise remarked. "I always thought that was the prettiest house in Flatwoods. I remember Bobby Davis. Boy he was weird. He used to scare us with dead lizards and water rats." Elise laughed under her breath.

"After high school, I heard he joined the army. Never saw him again, but his parents lived here until Mr. Davis retired from Saturn. Then the house was put up for sale. I don't know who bought it, but it was never occupied. It sat empty until some kids playing in it accidentally set it on fire. People may not like Yusef Kirk, but I'm glad he is drawing attention to what's going on around here. Now maybe somebody will get serious about lowering our taxes and cleaning up that ditch behind my house."

"What ditch?"

"You haven't seen it?"

"No," Elise replied.

"There's a low place, like a shallow gully that runs parallel to the road. I first noticed it after ScanTron started construction. Sometimes there's vapor and an awful, rotten kind of smell coming from that area."

"Have you complained to the city?"

"Sure. For what good it did. A work crew from ScanTron finally came out. They tested the water, then told us that the vapor was steam escaping from the warehouse waste control system and there was no reason to worry."

"You never told me this."

"Never thought about it much until—"

"Until what?" Elise prompted.

The porch floor squeaked as Damita rocked back and forth. "Until so many of us here on Thornhill Road got sick." A hollow pause stretched before them like a gaping black hole. "Now it's my time."

"There are others who are ill?"

"Mm-hm. Jenni-Lou Watts, three doors down. Mastectomy. Right after Christmas last year. Then the Robins twins. Remember those old ladies who used to dress alike?"

"God, it's been years."

"Well, they're still around. But one's got stomach cancer, the other has problems with her lungs. I'm not sure what's wrong, but she's really sick and she doesn't smoke. I used to see her walking that yapping poodle of hers, but come to think of it, I haven't seen her all summer."

Shaken by what she'd just been told, Elise pressed the back of one hand to her mouth, thinking. Was something toxic lurking under Flatwoods? Could ScanTron unknowingly be harming, even killing its neighbors?

"Would your neighbors talk to me about their illness?" Elise impulsively asked.

"I don't see why not," Damita replied, "seeing as how you're with ScanTron. You may be the only one in a position who cares enough to help."

On the way back to Houston, Elise could hardly keep her mind on the traffic as the image of Damita's frightened eyes and shrunken body blinded her to the lights of oncoming cars.

Did she dare gather information from Damita's neighbors? Raise false suspicions? Perhaps jeopardize her job? The prospect was terrifying, but Elise knew she had to do something.

"If I find out that Damita's condition is in any way related to ScanTron Security, I'm going to resign," she vowed, pulling into her garage.

She zapped the overhead door into action and got out. But then she started across the shadowed patio and saw Blake standing in the doorway waiting for her, and she knew her vow had been impulsively made and she'd never forgive herself if she shattered Blake's dream. Again.

CHAPTER 15

The sight of dirty dishes stacked on the countertops, pots without lids on the stove, and the smell of broiled fish greeted Elise when she entered the house. Tossing her purse onto the bar stool, she grimaced at the mess, then went into the den, where Blake and Junior were huddled in front of the computer engrossed in an intense game of Minesweeper.

"Hello!" she said, forcing gaiety into her voice, moving to stand behind the two men in her life. She rubbed Junior's hair, relieved to see him out of bed, laughing and jostling with his father. "Feeling better?"

He looked up and nodded. "Yep. Good as new. Lorna gave me ice cream and I didn't even throw it up."

"Fine," she said, glad his spate of illness had passed. She *had* to get back into the office tomorrow.

Blake broke away from the game and gave Elise a long, firm kiss, his flickering tongue issuing a seductive invitation.

Catching her breath as his lips broke from hers, she tilted her head and smiled. Heat rippled through her stomach and down her thighs as she silently responded to his conspiratorial wink.

Since the approval of the loan he seemed a decade younger, brash with a confidence she hadn't seen for years. The day after signing the final papers from the bank, Blake had given Elise a shocking-red satin teddy from Victoria's Secret and a pair of fluffy low-heeled pom-pom slippers that matched. She'd laughed her head off when she opened the box, but later that evening, lying in his arms, she'd whispered soft words of thanks. Elise liked this teasing, sexy side of Blake, who now held her gaze fast with his.

"I see you guys already ate dinner," she said, loosening the top button on her shirt as she headed toward the stairs.

"Right," Blake replied, leaving Junior in front of the computer to follow her up to their bedroom. He quietly shut the door.

"How's Damita?" he asked, his playful mood gone. He sat on the edge of the bed while Elise changed into a comfortable pair of tie-dyed shorts and a white T-shirt. Then he stretched out his arms as she came toward him.

"Not well," Elise said, sinking down beside Blake, curling her head into the warm spot on his shoulder. She stared at the floor, trying to find the strength to tell Blake not only about Damita but about the other sick women on Thornhill Road.

When tears bordered her eyes, Blake held her tighter, kissing the top of her head. When her anguish turned into racking sobs, he enveloped her in his protective embrace, letting her cry against his chest.

"She's so frightened," Elise said at last, her voice a raw whisper. Wiping her eyes, she raised her chin, catching his glance. She silently pleaded with him to understand her pain. "She's so thin. All eyes, no cheeks. It's horrible. She looks like some starving little kitten that's been abandoned." A fresh round of sobs overtook her, and she clung to Blake until it passed, clutching his shirt with an iron-hard grip.

"Is there anything she needs? Anything we can do?" he asked.

"She shouldn't be alone," Elise started, inhaling deeply, trying to pull herself together. "I'm going to call Mom and ask her to help out. I suggested she come back home with me . . . just until she got stronger," Elise started, pausing to gauge Blake's reaction. "But she insisted she wanted to stay in her own house."

"I can understand that," Blake replied.

"And there's a drainage ditch or some kind of gully behind the fence that could be toxic," Elise said, describing the situation.

"It's probably nothing."

"Oh, I don't know," Elise hedged. "I'm going to do some checking. I promised Damita I'd talk to some of her neighbors and see what I can find out. Sounds rather suspicious to me."

Blake eased Elise's arms from around his shoulders, leaning slightly away to assess her tear-streaked face. "Be careful. I'd stay out of it. Don't take on a problem that you can't solve."

Dabbing her eyes with a crumpled wad of tissue, Elise sniffed. "I didn't say I was going to solve anything, but I'd like to explore the possibility that there might be a connection between Damita's illness and the vapors in the ditch."

"Let the authorities do that. You are not an investigator. Poking around in places where you shouldn't could backfire, especially if ScanTron's waste system is in any way involved."

Elise stood, rubbing the side of her neck as she considered Blake's words of warning. "I know I don't *have* to do anything, but do you really expect me to forget about what Damita told me? Just because a work crew told her there was no reason to worry? Headquarters may not even be aware of what's happening."

"Three or four people getting sick doesn't make an epidemic, Elise. Coincidence, that's all." With a wave of his hand, Blake dismissed her concerns.

"Don't be glib," Elise warned.

"I'm not," Blake threw back icily. "But I don't want you playing detective . . . or tattletale."

"Excuse me?" She could not believe her ears. "I wouldn't call bringing a potential problem to my company's attention being a tattler. I'll bet John Farren would want to know about this, and he'd be grateful that the person bringing the problem to his attention is an alert employee rather than a nosy member of the press. This is the kind of information that is easily hyped and blown way out of proportion."

"Maybe," Blake reluctantly agreed, "but don't count on Farren being happy to hear that you think ScanTron is unknowingly killing residents of Flatwoods. The fire's caused him enough headaches, and whistle-blowers rarely wind up looking like heroes. If your company is going to be put under a microscope, let it be done by government regulators. Tell Damita to call the Texas Natural Resource Conservation Commission. They're listed in the phone book. It's their job to investigate, not yours."

Elise jerked back, shocked. She raised her hand as if to hit Blake, then lowered it and stood trembling, stunned by his coldhearted remark.

"How can you be so selfish?" she hissed. "Damita is dying! *Dying!* The least I could do is help find out why, and maybe save a few lives in the process."

Blake stood, inches from her face. "Wise up, Elise. Don't try to play big sister. Stay *out* of it. Your career is finally swinging into high gear, you're six weeks away from completing probation, and this kind of thing could blow it apart."

"Oh?" The word rode on a knowing whisper. "Is it my career or that two hundred fifty thousand dollars sitting in the bank that's got you so worried, Blake?" Tears threatened, stretching her voice thin and tight. "I can't believe keeping my salary coming in is more important than a deadly health hazard. It's all you care about, isn't it? Not Damita, not my parents, or anyone else in Tide County."

"That's low. Really low," Blake growled, turning away, going to the polished cherry dresser where he slammed his fist down hard. The Chinese porcelain lamp that Elise had scoured dozens of antique shops in Houston to find teetered on its base, then crashed to the floor. Neither made a move to right it.

"I am not saying I don't care," Blake shot back through clenched teeth, deliberately lowering his voice. "I'm just trying to make you see how dangerous it could be for you to get so damn personally involved in a situation that is potentially explosive. Don't close your eyes to what's at stake here." He massaged his knuckles, glaring. "Please, don't do anything stupid."

"Don't get personally involved?" Elise threw back incredulously. "I *am* personally involved, whether you like it or not." Swiping fresh tears from her cheeks, she yelled. *"And don't you dare call me stupid!"*

Blake struck the air with a closed fist, pacing toward the door. "I didn't call you stupid! But it's time you rethought your position, sweetheart, and it's also time to make some hard choices." A long pause followed. Blake pressed a palm to his forehead, collecting his temper.

Elise gulped down a swallow of air, as terrified by the harsh words they were slinging back and forth as by the angry scowl darkening Blake's face.

"Why can't you understand how I feel?" she asked. "Since starting this job I've managed to balance my allegiance to ScanTron with my duty to my people, my family . . . and that includes Damita. But I'm tired of pussyfooting around the issue, Blake. Something's got to give."

A glimmer of sympathy softened his frown, and he stepped closer, attempting to calm things down. "Believe me, I'd be worried and anxious to do something, too, if Paul's family or one of my friends were in the same situation. But there are times when you have to bite the bullet and think before you leap. Elise, think about what this could do to you. To us."

"Oh? So, you think this is one of those times when it's okay to put *my* needs first?" she said contemptuously.

"Yes, I do!" Blake yelled. "You have to be careful! Don't make a mistake that could cost *us* everything." He snatched his car keys off the tray on his dresser that held change, cuff links, and a silver-framed miniature of them on their wedding day. "Yes. I want you to think about *us* for a change because I'm not going down that financial hardship road again!" Fists clenched, he pushed past her. "You'd better not mess things up!"

With a jerk, Elise stumbled back, reeling as if he'd actually hit her. "You're going out?" she snapped when Blake gripped the doorknob.

"Yes. Paul and I have some figures to go over." His tone dropped low, and he almost sounded contrite. "You can reach me at his house if you need me."

Without a backward glance, he left, leaving the door partially open. Stunned, Elise stared after him until she heard the back door slam shut with a crack and the engine of his car roar to a start. Then she threw herself down on the bed, abandoning all control, and cried into her hard-balled fists until there were no more tears to be shed.

Carlos gave Sherry his most irresistible grin as soon as she appeared in the doorway of the spacious house he had once called home. Whenever he returned, he was pained anew by the reality of his loss. He loved the house, the landscaped acre and a half on which it sat, and the exclusive gated community where he'd had it built seven years ago. And as much as he'd wanted to fight for it during the divorce, he knew he'd done the right thing by signing it over to Sherry, along with a contract to fully maintain it until his boys were grown.

Though it was foolish of him to dream of ever living in the sprawling glass-and-stucco hacienda-style house again, Carlos quietly prayed that Sherry might fall in love with a man who would whisk her off somewhere and give her the kind of nine-to-five, traditional marriage that he, regretfully, had not been able to provide.

He stared at his ex-wife, who stood before him, mouth slightly agape in surprise, one hand atop the red-and-white-striped tube top that stretched across her generous bosom. She was wearing navy blue stirrup pants that clung to her curvaceous body like a spandex wet suit, and had white plastic earrings shaped like anchors dangling from both ears. Her hair was pulled up into a loosely tied bundle atop her head, making the former Miss San Antonio look more like a dark-haired Pebbles Flintstone than the ex–beauty queen she was.

Carlos stepped closer, his face level with Sherry's, and hooked her with that sheepish, little-boy expression that, in the past, had weakened her enough to believe anything he said. Tonight he was desperate and knew he'd better temper the irritation on her face and the sting of her tongue before telling her why he'd come over unannounced. "You look great."

"Thanks," she said, disinterested. "I doubt you came over to shower me with compliments."

"You never know," he cooed, unruffled.

"I should have guessed it was you. The boys are long asleep. I told you they're leaving for Camp Rancho early tomorrow morning. You coulda tried to get over earlier if you wanted to see them."

"Sorry, I forgot." He gave her an embarrassed shrug. "I'd like to have seen the boys before they take off, but really, I came to talk to you. Glad I caught you before you turned in."

Sherry checked her watch, then rolled her eyes. A smirk of doubt eased over her full red lips. "It's only eleven. You knew I'd be up. Cut the crap, Carlos. What do you want?"

Boldly, he moved across the threshold, slipping past Sherry to stand in the center of the softly lit entrance hall.

"Well! Come on in," she grumbled sarcastically, hands on her hips.

He looked up at the crystal chandelier above him and nodded. "I see you put in a new fixture. I liked the other one better."

"You don't live here anymore." She started to close the door behind Carlos, but he rushed to stop her, maneuvering to stand between her and the dark shadows outside.

Sherry let her hand fall away from the door, puzzled. "What's going on?" she asked.

"I need a tiny favor?" His sculpted lips curved slyly.

"Oh? A favor? Why didn't I guess? What is it this time?" Sherry groaned, exasperated. She'd been through this routine too many times.

"Yeah, well. Listen, I need to use the empty maid's room above the garage."

The tip of Sherry's nose wrinkled in disbelief. "You've got to be kidding. Why would I let you move in there? So you can spy on me? We're divorced, remember? You can't come around and mess with me anymore. I can have whomever I want over here, and if you don't like it, you can stay the hell away!"

Lifting a hand in caution, Carlos quickly said, "No, you've got it wrong. I'd never do that, Sherry. Be real."

"Then why do you want to move in?"

"Ah, it's not for me. A friend of mine needs—"

"Who?" she interrupted, brushing back a stray tendril of raven hair that had slipped out of her spiky ponytail.

"Well, he's not a friend, really. But he did know some of my father's people." Carlos failed to clarify.

"Shit, Carlos. Close the door. You're letting all the cold air out of the house."

Carlos did so, clucking his tongue to hear Sherry curse, but he knew better than to dare give her a lecture about a bad habit he could tell was getting worse. She had always been quick-tempered and blunt, traits he had grown to tolerate, and she could cut a man down to size with a few well-placed words from the tip of her punishing tongue. When they'd been married, he'd found her sharp wit and stinging retorts amusing; now he worried that his sons might start imitating their mother. He'd have to spend more time with them.

"Where is your friend?" Sherry asked.

"In the car waiting. I told him it'd be okay."

"You did what?" She pushed Carlos out of her way and peered into the darkened drive but could not see much more than a black shadow sitting in the front seat of Carlos's car. She turned around. "You've got a hell of a lot of nerve! Shit, no. He can't stay here. What's the matter with you—trying to pawn a stranger off on me?"

Holding his palms up, he attempted to calm Sherry down. "Don't get excited. He's not a stranger, and he's a harmless ninety-one-year-old man. Do you remember El General? The man from southern Mexico I profiled six years ago when I did that piece on the Lacandone Indians and the Guatemalan border wars?"

"Vaguely," Sherry admitted.

"Well, I'm doing a follow-up piece and I'm sure this man is the key to the story that's going to take my show out of the little leagues and set it up for national syndication. I can feel it! I want to tape an interview with him in the studio tomorrow morning, and I just got back from Refugio where I picked him up tonight."

"Tape him for what?"

"He's the key figure in the program. And I've got him. Hey, at ninety-one, he might not live until I get the rest of the players together. I've got to move fast."

"And?" Sherry wasn't going to make Carlos's task easy.

"And, I can't stick him in a hotel room," Carlos said sadly, squeezing sympathy from each word. "He's already frightened. He's not used to being in a big city like Houston. He's agreed to help me out. He trusts me. How can I dump him in a Motel Six and walk away? Could you?"

Sherry cursed under her breath. "So why bring him here? Take him to your place."

Carlos squinted, allowing a pitiful droop of his eyes to work on Sherry's emotions. "You know I live in a one-bedroom with barely enough room to do jumping jacks without touching the walls. And you've got more room here than you can even use. You could give me a break."

"Why should I?" Sherry shot back, used to Carlos's weedling ways.

"Because this man has a story that's gonna rock the city. What he's going to say will make Channel Three extend my contract. They'll want to tie me up for the next five years. But I wouldn't sign such a contract if it were offered. I'm holding out for syndication, you know?"

"God, you're dreaming," Sherry said, shaking her head.

"Believe it, baby," Carlos quipped, reaching out. He gently fingered a wispy curl that was hanging alongside Sherry's flushed cheek. Surprisingly, she didn't pull away. "This story is worth a twenty-five, maybe thirty percent increase in pay, and I know you want me to be successful in my work." He made a point of glancing around the house, letting Sherry silently calculate how much he paid to keep her and his kids in style. "Don't you?"

"One night?" Sherry hissed.

"Right. Just tonight. I'll pick him up at seven in the morning."

"What's his name? His real name?"

"Guillermo Venustio. But call him El General; he likes that."

Excitement glowed in Carlos's triumphant eyes, causing a deep red flush to stain his cheeks. "Would you mind fixing him breakfast in the morning?"

Sherry's eyes shot daggers at Carlos.

"Please? I could only get thirty minutes of studio time and I want him strong, ready to talk."

With a stiff nod and a resigned wave of her hands, she said, "All right. You win. Wait here. I'll get the key."

When Sherry turned away, heading into the kitchen, Carlos raced across the lawn to the passenger side of his car. He tapped on the window. Guillermo Venustio rolled it down. Carlos helped him out, patting the old man on his shoulder as they made their way up the drive and over the flagstone entryway. "It's all set, El General. This is my house. Where my kids live. You'll be fine. Just get a good night's sleep and I'll see you in the morning."

After turning his charge over to Sherry, Carlos left. On the drive across Houston to his one-bedroom apartment, an odd mixture of relief and trepidation filled him. Putting El General on the air was chancy, but if his hunch paid off, Carlos knew his future would be solid gold.

CHAPTER 16

As the elevator ascended toward the twenty-eighth floor, Elise's courage plummeted. With each stop it made to unload passengers, her decision to talk with John Farren seemed more and more irresponsible. If he labeled her a whistle-blower who was determined to embarrass and cause trouble for the company, she might find herself scratched from the ScanTron employee list before even moving into her headquarters office.

The crowd of people on the elevator began to thin, increasing Elise's anxiety. She was tempted to exit the mirrored cage and take the next elevator down to the lobby and flee back home. But as she watched the ScanTron headquarters employees hurry toward their workstations, she held her place, fidgeting nervously with the strap on her shoulder bag, unable to believe that the president of the company would resent her appeal. Surely he would see that the situation in Flatwoods could easily turn into more of a public relations nightmare than it already was.

Hiding behind large black lenses was not her style, but today her reflective sunglasses made her feel a little more secure, though few in the building would have recognized her. She'd been hired from the outside, rushed through orientation, then shuffled off to Tide County for her first assignment. Other than the management types and a few employees in the public affairs division, she'd met only a few of the headquarters staff and was certain that none of the people standing with her now had any idea who she was or what kind of mission she was on.

The elevator slid to a quiet stop at the twenty-second floor and all of the passengers exited except two secretaries, who continued chatting about the day's lunch plans, and three conservatively dressed men who were desperately trying to salvage a proposal that they'd obviously messed up the day before.

Impatience gnawed at Elise. She straightened her back. She had to follow through. This was where she wanted to be—in the guts of the company, sitting in Theresa White's pale beige office on the twenty-seventh floor and not stuck in a makeshift warehouse in Tide City with a boss who probably didn't even own a suit or a tie.

With a dry hand, Elise smoothed her gold-buttoned houndstooth jacket and tugged at the cuffs of her white silk shirt. It felt good to be dressed as a corporate sister for a change, and not in the casual skirts, plain short-sleeved blouses, and flat shoes she had adopted to fit in in Tide County.

When the secretaries and the two men got off on twenty-four, she was finally alone. Checking her image in the mirrored wall, she nodded. No dark circles under her eyes, no puffiness above her cheeks, though she didn't know why. After Blake's upsetting departure, she'd cried off and on all night, bolting awake when his car pulled into the driveway at two o'clock in the morning. They hadn't spoken when he slipped into bed or when he rose before her to dress in the darkened bedroom, then left early for work.

For the first time in their marriage they had neither kissed good night nor said good-bye, and Elise's heart was heavy. The argument may have temporarily clouded her feelings about Blake, but her mind was clear. She loved him and wanted to respect his wishes, but she could not live with herself if she did nothing with the information Damita had given her.

As hard as it was for her to admit it, Blake had been right on several points. It was not her job to investigate environmental matters concerning her company, nor was she paid to ferret out potential hazardous sites. But she did feel a responsibility to ScanTron and the residents in the area, and Damita Chapman was one of them.

Immediately upon rising, she'd called John Farren, who had quickly agreed to see her this morning. He was a fair, honest, reasonable man. Hadn't he proven that when he'd hired her when no one else had been willing to take the chance?

Elise got off the elevator and walked to a glass door at the end of the quiet hall. Farren's secretary greeted her with a smile, indicating that Elise should go right in.

The geometric tie and the bold gray-and-white plaid jacket would have looked terrible on anyone other than John Farren. A swarthy, handsome gray-templed man, he carried himself with a deliberate pride that was more impressive than arrogant. He wore well-tailored clothes in the latest cuts, and colors not usually seen in stuffy corporate offices. Elise had heard through the rumor mill that the CEO of ScanTron never wore the same designer suit twice and had his personal barber came to his office to groom him three times a week. On his lunch hour he was said to walk the treadmill in his private exercise suite on the thirtieth floor for exactly thirty minutes, then steam in the adjoining Finnish sauna for twenty more.

Elise took the chair John Farren indicated, exchanging professional pleasantries about the hot spell that had gripped Houston since the first of July. She nervously settled down.

After excusing himself to take a long-distance call, Farren finally turned his attention fully on Elise and asked her what he could do for her. She reviewed the situation in Flatwoods and suggested that another test be made on the contents of the drainage ditch.

"I hope I'm not being an alarmist," Elise said, drawing in a deep breath.

"No," Farren said, "I wouldn't call being concerned about people's health . . . and this company's health"—he smiled—"being alarmist."

"Good." Elise let herself relax. "Then you will have the area tested again?"

"Most assuredly, Elise. I appreciate your conscientious approach. If the press got ahold of this before us, it could turn into the kind of downward spiral as far as our image goes that could be difficult to pull out of. Then," he added lightly, "it would be up to you to hold the jackals back." He made a note on his open calendar. "I'll put someone on it today. You know, a strong offense is the best defense."

"I'm glad you see it that way," Elise replied, feeling as if a huge weight had been lifted from her shoulders. "When Al learned that I was born in Flatwoods, he said I was too personally involved to fairly represent the company. But I don't see it that way at all. The residents are beginning to trust me, and that's good for ScanTron."

Farren nodded. "I agree. I'm sure you know that Al and I spoke about your connection to the area. I told him to wait and see what developed."

"I appreciate that," Elise said. "I was afraid you might take me off the assignment."

When Farren said nothing, Elise decided to press on, ready to clear the air. There was too much on her mind and too much at stake for her not to know exactly where Farren stood on the subject of Al Patterson and his management style. "I suspect you've heard that Al and I haven't always agreed on the way to launch a public relations campaign."

"I have."

"We've managed to keep our disagreements civil and to get on with what has to be done, but I can tell you now that I seriously considered resigning."

Twirling his Mont Blanc pen between slim fingers, Farren studied his hands for a moment. "I'm sorry Al made you feel unwelcome. That's not the reception I would have wanted for you. I hope you know he does not represent the majority of our supervisors. His case is somewhat . . . ah . . . different."

"So I gather."

"Elise, you're a valuable asset to ScanTron and I want you to know that I fully support your approach to your work and I see a very bright future for you here."

"Thank you," Elise murmured, feeling much better.

"As for Al Patterson, he's been running his operation his way, without much supervision or interference, far too long," Farren said. "He'll fall in line, I'm sure. But, in the meantime, don't let him scare you into running off." Farren gave Elise a fatherly smile. "Come to me with your problems, Elise. My door is always open to you and all of the employees of this company."

When his phone buzzed again, he lifted a hand, excusing himself a third time, and Elise used the moment to uncross her legs, which she'd unknowingly tensed so hard, her foot had fallen asleep. Silently, she congratulated herself as she jiggled life back into her toes. She'd scored major points with Farren, and now knew, as she'd suspected, that Al's opinions didn't carry that much weight. He couldn't fire her, or even run her down in Farren's eyes. Thank God she wouldn't be at the Tide County site much longer.

Elise thought of Blake's outburst and smiled in relief. He had been totally off base. She had been right! But the revelation brought no sweep of satisfaction, only a despairing sense of loss. Their words had been harsh and hurtful and would not be easy to retract. If only he hadn't been so fixated on the importance of her holding on to her job, she thought, it might have been easier to talk about what was really going on. He wanted her support. She needed his. But the tension that had settled over the house lay like an unwelcome fog. She didn't like what was happening at all.

Farren hung up the phone, nodding vigorously. "It's a good thing you're here, Elise. That was a call I've been waiting for."

She lifted a brow in question.

"That was Hector Hillard, chairman of the board. Seems the board has voted to make a generous donation to the Tide County Clinic. I was hoping your excellent proposal would be approved. This is going to go a long way toward mending fences."

"I'm sure it will," Elise replied, feeling buoyed by yet another victory. "How much will the company be giving?"

"One hundred thousand," Farren said proudly. "The actual presentation is to be made live on *The Inside Story*, Carlos Rico's show, tomorrow evening. You need to be there at six-thirty sharp. You'll be on the program with Hector. He's not much of a public speaker, but he must be the one to actually hand over the check. It's already arranged, so call over to Channel Three and get the details. All right?"

Elise nodded numbly, unable to smile quite as enthusiastically as Farren, though a flutter of a challenge did rise at the thought of facing Carlos on camera again. This time, she would be the one in control.

Farren went on. "Today, I want you to stick around headquarters and draft Hector's remarks. Let's use this airtime on Rico's show wisely, you know?" He laughed, then added, "But you're the expert on that, aren't you?" He buzzed his secretary as he told Elise, "We've got to get you settled in over here. This is as good an opportunity as any. I think Al can handle the situation in Tide County for a while, at least until something breaks."

After instructing his secretary to help Elise get settled into Theresa White's vacant office, Farren turned back to Elise. "You're doing a good job, and I may as well tell you now that I've signed off on the board recommendation to make the position a permanent appointment."

"Oh?" Her eyes went wide in surprise. "That's wonderful news. Thank you," was all she could manage. Gratitude and relief rushed through her. "Mr. Farren," she boldly added, "you won't be sorry. I am so looking forward to serving this company and I promise to do the best I can to protect and maintain ScanTron's positive public image."

"I'm sure you will, Elise. Bringing that potentially dangerous matter in Flatwoods to my attention assures me that you understand how things must be done. We've got to stay on top of the details. It's easy to let things slip."

Elise nodded, smiling. Her instincts hadn't failed. She'd been able to do what she'd promised her father. Compromise her values? Not likely. And John Farren was on her side.

Farren picked up her personnel folder and opened it. "There is only one thing I need clarified."

"Yes?"

"Have you ever been arrested?"

The words struck her like a blunt heavy club. She stared at him stupidly, blankly.

"Ever?" he stressed the word.

Elise began to shake, and she searched her mind for a plausible explanation for his question, but finding nothing, she slowly shook her head no.

Farren's face creased into a pensive frown. "Think back, Elise. Way back."

Suddenly, the memory of her and Damita's rebellious childhood shoplifting spree in the five-and-dime store careened toward her like a blazing comet.

"Nineteen seventy-one," she murmured, her breath trapped in her chest. "The East Shore Variety Store in Beaumont."

With a slow nod, Farren agreed. "You were twelve years old. The police held you until your parents picked you up. You had to sweep the floors and stock shelves for the next three Saturdays in restitution, right?"

"God. I'd forgotten about that." She almost smiled, but the serious look on Farren's face stopped her. Palpitations hammered under her houndstooth jacket and her palms grew slick with sweat. "Damita was my best friend. The one I told you about who is ill." When Farren remained stonily silent, she plunged ahead. "Damita stole a packet of red plastic hair barrettes, I took a cheap four-leaf-clover bracelet. We had run off together into town because our parents had threatened to ground us. I don't even remember why. It was a childish, impulsive thing to do." Tilting her head back, she focused on the ceiling tiles. "I didn't think I had a record."

"Technically, you don't. You were a minor. No one except a security firm like ScanTron would ever have been able to access sealed records."

"What does this mean?" she asked tentatively, almost afraid to hear his answer.

Farren leaned forward, elbows on his desk. "Our company's application for employment asks prospective employees to state whether or not they've ever been arrested. You checked No."

Elise struggled with what to say and how to say it. "I felt the incident happened so long ago, it was not important. I was a child."

"I understand, but if false information is discovered in any employee's application, it is grounds for immediate dismissal."

In a carefully controlled tone, she probed his puzzling remark. "But you said the position of media relations officer was mine . . . permanently. Are you saying I'm to be—"

Farren interrupted. "Let go? No, you are not going to be removed before you even get started. I don't plan to make this information known to anyone outside this room. I can understand why you'd omit the information, but I wanted you to know that I am bending company rules in order to make my recommendation." He sat back, looking content with his decision. "Now go on and get started on those remarks for Hector. I'd like to go over them with you before noon."

On stiff legs, Elise rose and made her way to the door. Turning back, she caught Farren in a self-satisfied smile. He winked. She let out a long deep breath, then slipped out the door, across the plush carpet to the water fountain in the hall.

Gulping down the cool water, she tried to calm herself. So, Farren was not so fatherly after all. He'd clearly wanted to scare her—to let her know that nothing was secret from him and he'd use the information if need be. It was emotional blackmail designed, no doubt, to insure her loyalty to ScanTron.

Determined not to panic, Elise dabbed water on her face, then pressed moist fingertips to her lips, refusing to let her imagination run wild, vowing to do the best damn job she could for ScanTron. The position was hers! She managed to smile her thanks when Judy came over and handed her a set of keys.

With a shaky finger, Elise punched the elevator button, then stepped inside when it arrived. As music played on the speakers, she found herself humming, her thoughts already wrenched from Farren's veiled threat. Descending in a soft whoosh, she thought about several paintings she could bring from home that might brighten up her new office.

At exactly 4:30 the next day, Blake picked Junior up at the day-care center and headed to Paul's house on the north side of town. Starting out before rush hour got in full swing, Blake was able to make it to his brother's house in record time.

When Paul's wife, Cathy, answered the door, she had Blake's niece anchored on her hip and a pot holder in one hand.

"Hello, Blake." She quickly cut her eyes away from his to look down at Junior. "Well, boy. Looks like you've grown two inches since I saw you. Been about a month, huh?"

Junior screwed up his mouth and glanced at his dad, unsure about how long it had been since he'd last visited his aunt.

Cathy bent down and hugged her nephew.

From the way she'd opened the door, yanking it back to glare at him, Blake could tell that Cathy knew about the fight he'd had with Elise, though he'd asked Paul not to tell her. A sharp-tongued sister who loved to quote television talk-show hosts, Montel Williams being her favorite, Cathy loved discussing the man troubles of her girl-friends. And he knew how cutting Cathy could be when she felt a sister had been wronged. As he watched her kiss Junior, Blake suspected that she had one of her preachy lectures waiting for him and he was in no mood to listen.

"Where's your momma?" Cathy asked Junior.

"Still at work," he answered, squirming from beneath his aunt's hand, which she'd allowed to rest on the top of his head. He darted past her into the hallway.

Cathy focused on Blake. "So. This new job is sure keeping Elise busy. You two need make time for each other. Don't let Elise get it into her head that she can make it fine on her own. You know that's what happens when a sister moves up as fast as she's going to at ScanTron. They get real independent. You gotta keep up."

"Please, Cathy. Don't start."

Cathy scowled. "I saw her on TV a few times." She motioned her brother-in-law inside. "She's lookin' good, Blake. Damn good.

Lost some of that weight she put on when she was sitting at home feeling sorry for herself, didn't she?" Before Blake could reply, she flew on. "Some brother's gonna have his eye on her. Be careful. You'd better stick close to home. Pay attention."

"Yeah," Blake muttered, thinking about Carlos Rico as he followed her through the small, neat house.

"Well, come on back; I just finished baking peanut butter cookies."

Junior hurried ahead of them, leaving Cathy alone with Blake.

"I hope you apologized to Elise," she started right in. "You had a lot of nerve jumping on her the same day she learns her best friend is dying. You ought to be ashamed, Blake." Clucking her tongue in dismay, she started to walk toward the kitchen.

"I don't want to talk about it," he said tightly, grabbing her arm. "Don't say anything about this in front of Junior."

With a sharp laugh, she grimaced. "Please. From what Paul said, I wouldn't be surprised if Junior already knows that you and Elise are fighting. He lives in the same house with you, doesn't he?"

"Please, Cathy. Just cool it, okay?" Blake replied, annoyed. He and Paul were close, as they'd been throughout their lives, and Blake should have known he wouldn't be able to keep his mouth shut with his wife.

Sweeping into the kitchen, Cathy changed the subject, speaking louder. "I hope you and Elise are planning on going to the beach with us next month. Your mom asked me to get a head count on how many are coming. Guess there's going to be quite a crowd."

"What's the date again?" Blake asked, wishing things at home were stable enough to make plans so far in advance. With Elise working such crazy hours, he doubted they'd be able to squeeze any time from their schedules to lie on the beach. Since his parents' purchase of their getaway house on Bolivar Island last year, he and Elise had only managed one visit.

"The week of the twenty-first, but I'm going down early on Friday to help Mother Jeffries open the house. Please try to make it. It's been too long since you and Elise got out and enjoyed yourselves. We missed you guys last year."

"A lot is going on, Cathy. I'm not sure what our schedules will be like by then. Elise has been—"

"Your mother has remodeled the beach house. It's beautiful. Elise would love it," Cathy cut in. "Talked to her just a few minutes ago."

"You didn't say . . . ?" Blake frowned.

Cathy waved her hand, dismissing Blake's concern that now his mother knew about the argument. "Don't worry. You're not going to get one of her 'you better listen to me, boy' sessions." She laughed as she placed the baby in her playpen.

Blake sighed in relief. He'd suffered through those heart-to-hearts too many times. His mother always said she was not interfering, only clarifying the issues, but the way she spoke to him, you'd think he was still twenty-one, not pushing forty and about to start his own business.

Blake loved his family dearly and valued their supportive interest in his life, but sometimes he felt crowded with so much free advice. During the Kitzmiller incident he'd thought he'd lose his mind with Cathy and Paul and his parents telling him what he ought to do. In the end, he and Elise had pulled through on their own, as they would now, if Cathy would stick to minding her own affairs.

"You know how Elise loves the beach," she continued. "Y'all better be there. Give that girl a break, Blake. She needs to see the family. Have some fun. Seems all the poor soul does is work." Cathy handed the baby a cracker, then took another tray of cookies from the oven.

Feeling soundly put in his place, Blake stood uneasily beside the kitchen table where Junior was already nibbling on a cookie. He glanced around the blue-and-white country-motif room, ready to make an escape.

Junior reached over and tugged on Blake's sleeve. "Can we go to the beach with Gramma?"

"Depends," Blake sullenly replied.

"On what?" Junior asked innocently.

"On whether or not your mom has to work." He patted Junior's hand. "We'll see."

Cathy handed Junior a glass of milk. "Your daddy ought to bring you and your mom over more often," she said, then added, "You look hungry. Want a sandwich?"

"Don't even ask," Blake laughed. "We came directly from day care. He'll eat anything you put on a plate."

"I'll bet he will," she said, opening the refrigerator door.

"We can't stay long," Blake said. "Just thought I'd check out the detail job Paul said he was going to put on that Honda scooter today. He out back?"

Jerking her head to the door, she replied, "Where else?"

Blake went to find his brother.

In the ovenlike garage Paul was squatted down beside a shiny black scooter applying a thin stripe of gold paint down the rear fender. He looked up when Blake came in. "Thought I heard your car." He continued to trace the thin gilt line down the curving metal. A more mature yet trimmer version of Blake, Paul had the same muscular, athletic build as his brother but stood at least three inches taller. "What's up?"

"Nothing. Just thought I'd swing by."

"Swing by?" Paul stood, stretching his back. "This is hardly on your way home." He knelt again to resume his work.

Blake shrugged, then picked up a screwdriver Paul had left on the floor and tossed it into his brother's toolbox. "Guess I just didn't feel like going home."

"Or facing Elise," Paul said, tapping the paintbrush to make a few flecks of gold at the tail end of the fender. "That ought to do it." He stood again, admiring his work.

"Looks good," Blake said.

Capping the small jar of gold paint, Paul stuck it on a shelf. "You two make up last night?"

"Naw. I got home late again and had to get out early this morning."

Paul began wiping his hands on a rag. "Two days. Not good, and not a very original excuse for letting things drag along. Sounds like you're avoiding her."

"That's not true."

"Then talk to her, my man. Don't let things get out of hand. Apologize. Tonight. Okay?"

"Yeah, I been thinking about what happened. It just mushroomed. When we went upstairs, the *last* thing on my mind was having a fight with Elise. She was really upset about Damita. I've been tense about this big debt we've taken on."

"I asked you if you guys were ready to deal with that, before we went to the bank, remember?" Paul slowly wiped the tip of the paintbrush on the rag, cautiously observing Blake. "Don't tell me this is not going to work. We've gone too far to back out now."

"Don't worry," Blake said. "We can handle it. I'm ready."

"But is Elise?"

"She'll come around. She's just under a lot of pressure." Blake ran a hand over his damp forehead. "I shouldn't have tried to reason with her the other night. My timing was awful. What I meant and what I said didn't exactly come off as I planned. I *want* her to do what she feels is right, but not do something foolish, you know what I mean?"

Paul nodded. "But you can't deny that she's got a point, and maybe a reason to follow through." Finished, he tossed the dirty paint cloth into a box beside the garage door. "Go easy on her, okay? She's got a lot to think about, and now is not a good time for either of you to get emotionally strung out."

Blake knew his brother spoke the truth. Neither he nor Elise could afford to become unraveled with so much facing them.

"Do something nice and romantic for her," Paul suggested, chuckling as he hurriedly backed up from the playful jabs Blake threw his way. "Hey. You know what I mean, and don't act like you don't. Swallow that damned pride of yours, turn on the charm, and turn down the lights and surprise the hell out of her. Tonight. You guys have been through worse and survived." Reaching into a nearby cooler, he took out a can of beer and tossed it to Blake. "And before you start romancing your wife, get a haircut, bro. You look like hell."

CHAPTER 17

Three years had passed since Elise had been in KPLT's elegantly appointed reception area, but as she entered the glass doors on Wednesday evening and crossed the mottled gray-and-white marble floor, she realized not much had changed. The same mural of Texas pioneers crossing golden, grassy plains was on the wall facing visitors, and Dorothy, the middle-aged receptionist who wore sister curls and bold African earrings, was sitting at the same semicircular desk, wearing the same cheerful smile that Elise remembered.

"Elise Jeffries!" Dorothy called out as she hung up the phone. "Good Lord. It's good to see you. *How* are you doing?"

Realizing she was going to be asked that question many times now that she had resurfaced in the media arena, Elise didn't flinch with her reply. "I'm fine. Glad I took some time to be at home with my son, but you know I'm back."

"Yeah. Working for ScanTron Security International now."

Elise nodded.

"Go girl. You're on your way." The respectful tilt of Dorothy's lips signaled her high opinion of the multinational company and her genuine happiness that Elise was working there. "Good for you. Staying busy with the fire and all, I'll bet."

"Mmm," Elise agreed, "busier than ever."

"What can I do for you?"

"I'm here for *The Inside Story*."

Surprise brightened Dorothy's pecan-colored face, and she made no effort to hide her thorough understanding of Elise's past. "You're brave, girl. I can't believe you'd let Carlos interview you after what he did."

In carefully controlled tones, Elise said, "Well, life goes on. I'm here to make a special presentation on Carlos's show. That's all."

Dorothy picked up a roster of expected station visitors, flipped through several pages, then raised her lashes. "So I see. With a Mr. Hector Hillard and Dr. Boyd of the Tide County Clinic?"

"That's us," Elise replied, getting nervous about being on the set of *The Inside Story*. While drafting Mr. Hillard's remarks and discussing them with Farren, she had purposefully kept her mind from dwelling on being interviewed by Carlos again, but Dorothy's candid remarks stung, reopening old wounds Elise had convinced herself had healed.

"Well, have a seat," Dorothy said. "You're right on time, but Carlos isn't here yet." She fluttered her fingers at the grouping of sofas, returning to her work when several buttons on her switchboard lit up.

Taking a seat in the cluster of richly upholstered chairs grouped around a big-screen TV, Elise stared dully at the sitcom that was on.

Lord, she prayed silently, *let this interview go off without a hitch and don't let Carlos start some mess that will make me lose it on TV.* All she wanted to do was give her "we're your corporate neighbor" pitch after Mr. Hillard presented the check, and go home. She wanted to see her son, talk to her husband—clear the air with Blake. Two days had passed since they'd had their fight, and things certainly couldn't stay at this standoff much longer.

Mentally rehearsing her remarks, Elise had tuned the noisy laughter on the TV sitcom out, and did not hear Hector Hillard and Dr.

Boyd approaching from behind. When the chairman of ScanTron's board tapped her on the shoulder, she jumped and whipped around.

"Mrs. Jeffries?"

"Yes?"

"I'm Hector Hillard."

"Nice to meet you," she said quickly, standing with an extended hand. Dr. Boyd came around, also greeting her with a handshake, then sat in the chair next to hers. They exchanged pleasantries, but before they could relax and get comfortable, Carlos rushed through the door and strode confidently toward his guests.

"Looks like everybody's here," he said with a dazzling smile. "Let's head on back to Studio C." With no particular greeting for Elise, he turned and started down the long, narrow hallway. Elise, Hector, and Dr. Boyd hurried to keep up with his energetic stride.

Once they were seated and fitted with mikes, the countdown started. Elise was glad the camera crew had been set up and waiting so they could go immediately into their segment. Sitting around making small talk was not what she wanted to do. Carlos had treated her, so far, with a great deal of professional courtesy with no snide or cagey remarks. In fact, he was acting downright civil. But she knew not to let down her guard, because once the cameras started rolling anything could happen.

But nothing extraordinary did. Carlos was obviously well-informed about the situation and asked probing, insightful questions. He patiently gave each of his guests sufficient time to reply, in contrast to his trademark method of leveling his guests with a barrage of questions, barely letting them catch their breath.

After an overview of the disaster and the current status of the situation, the check was presented. Dr. Boyd made his acceptance remarks. Elise followed him with her carefully scripted spiel about ScanTron's worldwide commitment to environmental safety; then Carlos posed a final question.

"Ms. Jeffries," Carlos said earnestly, leaning over, acting as if they were best friends sitting at her kitchen table, sharing coffee. "I cannot conclude this interview without letting you respond—that is, if you'd like to—to the charge of conspiracy made by the well-known environmental lawyer and activist Yusef Kirk. Why would he say there is a conspiracy against the people of Flatwoods? And is there anything you'd like to say in response, or to those who obviously believe his theory?"

Elise tendered Carlos a smile of gratitude, accepting the unexpected opportunity to get into a subject that was eating her up.

"I'm glad you asked that, Carlos. I can't tell you what Mr. Kirk is basing his theory on, but I assure you, ScanTron has nothing but the highest regard for Mr. Kirk's enthusiastic representation and qualifications to speak for the residents of Flatwoods. I implore anyone with a legitimate claim to *file* for damages if they have reasons to, but not to line the pockets of certain lawyers who often take advantage of those in unfortunate circumstances. My hope is that Mr. Kirk will do the right thing. And, if he is watching, he'll realize that neither ScanTron nor Global Oil would ever set out to do anyone deliberate harm."

"That's right," Dr. Boyd broke in. "And this donation from ScanTron will allow us to bring on two more doctors right away and upgrade our diagnostic equipment."

"And so," Carlos began, clearly surprised at the way his barbed question had been successfully fielded by Elise, "what started out as a disaster for ScanTron and the residents of Flatwoods may have turned into a win-win situation after all."

He shifted slightly to face his invisible audience. "I want to thank my guests and you, my audience, for being here with me tonight. Stay tuned. After these messages Urless Brown, our guest host on the second segment of *The Inside Story*, will bring you the inspirational tale of fifteen-year-old Yolanda Gonzales, whose struggle and determination got her out of the barrios of El Campo to win the crown of Miss Fiestas Bonitas de Tejas. We'll be right back."

The floor director counted down the last seconds of the show, and then the producer gave Carlos the all-clear signal. Elise consciously let herself go limp. She hardly remembered a word she'd said, but Hector Hillard congratulated her warmly and they all exited the set to allow the guest host and a pretty Hispanic girl in a blue silk dress with a sparkling crown atop her head settle in.

Hector Hillard and Dr. Boyd left together. Elise looked around to see where Carlos was, deciding to thank him for the airtime. The program had gone well, and professional courtesy dictated that she express her appreciation on behalf of her company. But Carlos was nowhere to be seen so she left, stepping cautiously over thick cables, nodding to the producer as she pushed through the heavy double doors and started down the brightly lit hallway.

There were pictures of Channel 3's on-air personalities hung in a horizontal line along the wall. When she stopped to look more closely at Carlos's cocky smile, a door opened beside her, making her jump. Glancing over, she saw Carlos watching her. She just stared, waiting as he approached.

"Good show," he said, lounging casually against the wall, one shoulder pressed beside his portrait. He crossed his arms on his chest and let the sensuous flames in his green eyes flicker at her.

Elise could tell that his debonair stance was a practiced move to get her attention, and against her wishes she found herself drawn in in the space of a heartbeat. Suddenly, her cool composure was gone, and she groped for a reply, wishing she'd left immediately as the other guests had.

"My sentiments, exactly. I think it went well," she managed, wondering why her voice was so rough. Clearing her throat, she continued. "On behalf of ScanTron, I'd like to thank you for arranging this presentation on your show."

"No problem," Carlos replied, a bemused smile tugging his lips. "I had no doubt you'd do fine."

Elise struggled to maintain her corporate demeanor, but the way he was looking at her made her skin warm and her mouth grow dry. Running a finger under the collar of her severely tailored shirt, she asked, "Can I get a copy of the tape? For our files?"

Again, he replied, "No problem," but didn't make a move. Still leaning against the wall, he carefully assessed Elise. "You can pick it up tomorrow."

"Well," she adjusted her purse strap nervously. "Send it to me at headquarters, along with an invoice. Whatever . . ."

"No cost. Not for you," he stated matter-of-factly, then added, "As I said, Elise. I *owe* you."

"Let's not talk about *that*," she cut him off. Going on his show at her boss's request was one thing. Getting involved in a conversation to rehash the past was quite another, and she wanted no part of whatever he had on his mind. "Let's leave it alone, Carlos. Please." She brushed past him, starting toward the front of the building, anxious to get home. It was late. Blake and Junior ought to be back, and she wondered if Cathy, who was an excellent cook, had invited them to stay for dinner. For some reason the thought made her slightly jealous and a little sad.

"Why don't you want to talk to me?" Carlos called out after her. "What are you afraid of?"

Elise stopped and turned around, infuriated to see that he had made his remarks while maintaining his back to her. The way he was orchestrating the exchange burned her up, and she started to stalk off again but decided against it. Maybe it *was* time to clear the air. Maybe she needed to have this conversation with Carlos in order to get on with her life—a life finally recovered from the damage he had done.

Walking back to where he stood waiting, she jerked him by the shoulder, forcing him around to face her. "I'm not afraid of anything. Especially, not you. I just have nothing to say. I said it all in court."

Lifting his square jaw, Carlos disarmed her with a maddening display of superiority as he gazed down his nose at her. Elise cringed at his posturing. What the hell did he want?

"Perhaps you don't have anything to say," Carlos replied, "but *I* do. And," he lowered his face level with hers, "I'd really like you to listen. Your future with ScanTron could be at stake."

The rapid rise and fall of Elise's chest stopped. What could he possibly want to discuss? What did he know? About her? The fire? The sick people of Flatwoods? This was the second time he'd offered to help her; maybe she'd better hear him out.

"All right, tell me," she hissed, curiosity winning out over rising annoyance.

Relief softened Carlos's arrogant expression. "Not here," he said, reaching past her to open a door. "Come on, sit down. You won't be sorry. I promise."

A slow warning started drumming inside Elise's head, but she didn't let it stop her from following Carlos into his private office.

Blake drained the last of his beer with a gulp, then punched the remote and turned off the TV. Smiling, he nodded to himself. Elise had said the right things, in exactly the right tone, not smugly confident or coldly aloof, but in a down-to-earth manner that made her believable. He was proud of his wife's ability to hold her own under Carlos Rico's attempt to embarrass her. Blake grinned. Ending the interview with a strong rebuttal to Kirk's conspiracy charges had been a compelling move on Elise's part.

His heart swelled with pride, yet a twinge of shame surfaced as he recalled the message she'd left on his answering machine at work yesterday after her successful chat with her boss. She'd been right to grind it in, making him squirm for yelling at her. He'd been wrong and she'd been right. Taking a chance on talking to John Farren had been the wisest route.

As Blake replayed her words in his mind, shame shifted to envy. Elise was comfortable making the kinds of hard decisions that he would never have tackled at Century Trust. She'd been brave enough to act on her convictions and come through the experience intact, earning Farren's praise and the permanent title of National Media Spokesperson. She was on her way to the top, he could feel it, while he was about to give up the career he'd thought he would have until he retired.

Boy had he been wrong. He'd made a good living at Century and wasn't sorry for the years he'd given to the company, but it was simply time for a change. Resigning was going to be the riskiest thing he'd ever done. Job security was rare in any field these days. Nothing was guaranteed. Blake crushed the beer can in his fist. Not even with big corporations like ScanTron.

He had to patch things up, make Elise happy, and erase those tiny frown lines that were becoming permanent between her beautiful eyes. And he had to admit that he wanted to experience the joy of loving her again.

Tonight he'd tell her how sorry he was for losing his temper and for not trusting her judgment as he should have. Could the damage he'd done with his thoughtless outburst be repaired with only a humble apology? Maybe Paul was right. Maybe he'd better do something special to create a romantic mood if he expected her to forgive him. And she would forgive him, he knew, because neither of them wanted to let their thoughtless, stupid remarks mar the progress they'd made in the past year. They'd survived enough heartache to last them a lifetime, and now that things were finally moving forward, they could not chance a setback.

He slumped lower on the sofa, still mad at himself, then checked the brass clock over the big-screen TV. Elise should be home within the next thirty minutes, and he wanted to try, again, to let her know how much he loved and supported her. Getting up, he went into the kitchen and took two steaks out of the freezer and stuck a bottle of wine in the cooler. A nice candlelight dinner, ready when she walked through the door, might help set the stage for him to show her how deeply sorry he was.

From their twin recliners in their comfortable den, Fred and Myra Camden had watched the interview, too. When Myra glanced over at Fred and made a thumbs-up gesture, he inclined his head in agreement.

"She did a good job, didn't she?" he admitted. "Looked great. Really had control of that Rico guy this time."

"Yes, indeed," Myra said. "I'm proud of her. I know it wasn't easy sitting down with him like that. It took a lot of courage, I'm sure."

"I guess she's still mad at me for what I said about her at the community meeting," Fred commented. "But I can't say I'm sorry I spoke up."

"Oh, honey. She's not mad at you. You caught her off guard, that's all." Myra tried to appease her husband's bruised pride. "The only reason Elise hasn't been by for a visit lately is because she's so busy—and you know she's worried about Damita." Myra got up from her chair and went to the phone. "I think I'll call Damita now and see how she's reacting to the new medication the doctor prescribed. I hope she saw Elise on TV."

From her bed, Damita stared at the television, unable to focus on the pretty Yolanda Gonzales, who was telling the hostess how winning the beauty pageant had changed her life. Damita's eyelids closed dully; then she blinked herself awake and reached for a glass of cold water. The medication was kicking in early, yet she didn't want to go to sleep. She'd been spending her days and nights in bed lately, sleeping entirely too much. That wasn't like her at all.

The pain had been fairly tolerable when she first came home from the hospital, but with each passing day it was getting more impossible to bear. Though weak and listless, she was managing to care for herself with little assistance, but she had to take her time. Moving slowly, she cooked her meals, bathed, and dressed, stopping to rest when exhaustion literally swept her off her feet.

At first, her neighbors had crowded into her home with covered dishes and offers of sympathy. Now they pretty much left her alone with her cats and her rambling, troubled thoughts.

Damita was no longer frightened about facing up to the truth of her condition, and accepted each day as the blessing it was without wondering what might happen tomorrow. The only thing she wanted was to get to the truth. Some nights, it was the pain of not knowing what was lying beneath her house and rising in the shallow gully that edged the community that scared her more than the pain that gripped her as she lay in her bed.

When the phone lying atop the bedspread shrilled, she immediately snatched it up, grinning sleepily upon hearing Myra Camden's soothing voice.

"Yes, I saw her," Damita told Myra, listening as the older woman praised her daughter. "I agree, Mrs. Camden. Elise was prepared, poised, and made perfect sense. But . . . I hate to sound negative. . . ."

"Oh?" The line went quiet as Myra waited to hear Damita's complaint.

"More doctors and a lot of sophisticated equipment at the Tide County Clinic are not going to solve a thing."

"What will?" Myra asked.

Damita sat up higher in bed. "Well, calling off Yusef Kirk is not the answer either. Why can't Elise see that, Mrs. Camden? She knows what needs to be done. I told her what I suspected. We need to stop what's *causing* all the sickness and death in this town."

CHAPTER 18

I hope you're not in a hurry," Carlos said, resting a hip atop a low file cabinet. Like a model posing for the camera, he righted his broad shoulders, straightened his red silk tie, then rested both hands on one slightly raised knee, fastening emerald green eyes on Elise.

Battling the sense of indignation that suddenly rose, Elise simply stared at him, waiting for him to talk. He was the one who wanted to have this discussion, so let him start, she thought. When he continued to stare at her, she finally spoke. "You know I have a family waiting for me at home, and it is pretty late. What do you want?"

"There's a videotape I want you to see. Thirty-three minutes." He paused, eagerness flickering across his face.

More curious than irritated, she gave him an easy lift of her hand. "Okay. Roll it."

"Great," Carlos said, rising. He crouched down in front of the gray metal cabinet, unlocked it, and took out a square black case.

"What's on it?" Elise asked, definitely interested.

"Someone you might remember." He slipped the tape into the VCR, pressed a button, then moved toward the doorway, where he rotated the dimmer switch to darken his office. Standing behind Elise, he waited until an image of an old man sitting on the set of *The Inside Story* emerged on the screen; then he pressed the pause button on the remote control. "Recognize him?"

"El General," Elise replied, puzzled. "Ventio, or something like that."

"Guillermo Venustio," Carlos corrected. "I thought you might remember him."

"Oh, yes. I was in the audience when you won the ACE Award four years ago for the exposé you did on him. As a young man he led a peasant uprising in Guatemala against the vicious Vargas regime that was in power in the 1930s. A Lacandone Indian, isn't he?"

"The oldest living member of that tribe and a survivor of the infamous Lacandone guerrilla army," Carlos said.

"Wasn't there something about him claiming to be a direct, pure-blooded descendant of the last ruler of the Mayas?"

"Very good," Carlos said. "Yes, El General claims ancestry to Canek, the last warrior-king who ruled the Mayas. Canek had settled his people in northern Guatemala about the time of Cortés's arrival, and centuries later, in El General's time, the Lacandone were still there. When the Vargas regime tried to force the Lacandone under Guatemalan rule, it met with great resistance. The Lacandone uprising failed, forcing Venustio and his men to flee for their lives and hide in the mountains of southern Mexico, where many remain today."

"Didn't El General immigrate to the States, though, to live like a hermit somewhere in south Texas?"

"Yes. Refugio," Carlos supplied. "That's where I found him. He has never given up hope of establishing an independent Lacandone state, and not surprisingly, the dispute with Guatemala went on for generations, in fits and starts of guerrilla activity in isolated pockets along the Mexico-Guatemala border."

"Why'd you go looking for El General?"

"Because contrary to what's been reported, the elderly rebel was not the last living link to the legendary ruler, Canek. Seems the old man had a grandson he never told anybody about."

"Had? Is he dead?"

"Precisely. He died five weeks ago—in a fiery crash. His truck exploded." Carlos paced his words, teasing Elise.

"The ScanTron accident?"

"You got it."

Elise took her eyes off the screen, turned in her seat, and studied Carlos's somber face. "Why him?"

Carlos's natural tan flushed red with excitement as he went to his desk and sat down. "Interesting, isn't it?" He swiveled side to side in the rich leather chair.

Elise leaned forward, tapping her fingernails on the thick vellum paper wedged into the leather blotter on Carlos's desk. "Come on. What's going on?" she asked, giving him her full attention. Carlos could be so damn cagey at times, but she knew he wasn't bluffing, and he would not be giving her this much time and information unless he was onto something big.

"Watch. You'll see." Carlos pressed play, turning up the volume so that Elise could understand the frail man's heavily accented English.

The interview began. At first they talked chattily, like old friends, and when the older man was feeling at ease before the camera, Carlos zapped him with a question.

"Who was the man who crashed the ScanTron Security gates a few weeks ago?"

"My grandson, Zenoyo Venustio." El General's voice was clear and strong.

"Are you positive it was your grandson?" Carlos asked El General.

"Yes, I am positive. I went to the morgue. I identified him. It was Zenoyo. The last of the Venustios. The last."

Shocked, Elise pressed back in her seat, mouth slightly open. When had that happened? she wondered. No information had come from the sheriff's department that the body had ever been positively

ID'd. She clamped her jaw shut, holding her tongue, too intrigued by the tape to interrupt.

"What do you think happened on that dark, lonely road?" Carlos gently guided the man into his theory.

"Zenoyo was murdered. The Vargas got to him. I knew they would; that's why I never told a soul that I had any family still living. The Vargas reach far, and their hands are strong like iron. I had hoped to protect my last living flesh."

"Are you saying Zenoyo was assassinated?"

"God only knows."

"The fire department said nothing about evidence of explosives or foul play at the site of the crash."

El General simply shrugged, his mouth curling down in caution. "There are many ways to kill a man, or make him wish so much he was dead, that he turns his own hand against himself."

"Oh? A suicide mission?"

A muffled cry slipped from El General's wrinkled lips as pain filled his deep brown eyes. With a sigh, he looked down. "Yes. I believe the Vargas made him take his own life."

Knowing he'd hit the right button, Carlos uncrossed his legs and hunched closer, hands between his knees. "A guard at ScanTron, who witnessed the whole thing, said the driver deliberately aimed his truck at the gates and didn't try to escape when it caught on fire. You believe that?"

With a jerk of his shoulder, El General replied, "Yes. I think maybe it happened like that, but it was the Vargas who killed him, I am certain. My grandson simply helped them along."

Frowning at the double-talk, Carlos pressed on. "Why do you believe, after all these years, that the Vargas family would want your grandson dead? Forgive me, but why him and not you?"

The weary sadness that had claimed El General's face momentarily dissipated as a glimmer of pride illuminated his features. "Because Zenoyo was young, strong. Ready to fight again. He had gathered men, women, arms, and ammunition and fled to a secret place in the mountains. He was living there with all who claimed Lacandone blood. They worshiped him. This time we

would have our own state. A place for us. Not Mexico. Not Guatemala. Only Lacandone." El General turned away from the steady red
light on the camera and peered anxiously from side to side as if expecting the Vargas to fly at him from the darkened edges of the
studio.

"If your grandson, Zenoyo, was such a fighter, why would he take
his own life?"

"Rosalía," El General whispered, blinking away a sudden sheen
of tears. "She was gone. The baby growing inside her, gone, too. So,
you see, Zenoyo had no more inspiration. No reason to go on. He
had crossed into the States and come to me the day before he died,
talking of Rosalía, of giving up the fight. I tried to make him see that
he had to go back, to continue the fight. Many were counting on
him. But he had lost the pulse of life. I know now, he was already
dead when he came to my home in Refugio."

"Rosalía was his wife?"

El General answered with a slow nod. "So young and beautiful,
she was."

"How did Rosalía die?"

"Oh, the mountain sickness took her . . . as it has been taking
two, three men a month in the mountain camp. Zenoyo believed the
Vargas were poisoning his people. He was certain that's what was
happening. The Vargas are crafty, evil men. And they are everywhere.
Even here in Houston, no descendant of a Lacandone is safe."

A look of doubt touched Carlos's face, but he managed to maintain his on-air presence, sticking with the old man's theory. "So, when
Rosalía died, I take it Zenoyo was not only sad but angry."

"Yes. But no more a fighter. He was lost."

"So you think he came to Texas, believing he'd find the Vargas
who killed his wife?"

The old man shrugged.

"To seek revenge?"

Again, he only shrugged.

Carlos studied the old man's creased, weathered face, as if unsure he was going to make it through the interview. Knowing he
could not ease up now, Carlos pressed on. "I was told that Ze-

noyo was looking for a brother who supposedly worked at ScanTron."

"No!" El General shot back, showing real anger for the first time. "That is not true. He had no brother. He was alone in the world, except for me." El General threw trembling liver-spotted hands over his eyes. Carlos sat back, visibly alarmed.

Elise remained glued to the screen, watching Carlos's dismay at the way his guest was starting to unravel. She could almost hear him silently cursing, afraid he might have got all he would from the fragile, heartsick man.

When El General regained his composure, he spoke. "My grandson had no brother. *That* I know. He was looking for the Vargas and . . . Rosalía." Sobs once again shook the man's frail body like a twig rattled in a strong coastal wind.

When Carlos gave the cameraman a choppy wave, Elise heard the floor director call out, "Cut. Stop tape."

In a gentle voice, Carlos told his guest, "Thank you so much for talking to me, El General. I know how difficult this has been."

The VCR went fuzzy with white snow as blank tape whirred in the machine. Carlos sat silently, letting several long seconds pass before zapping it off. After raising the lights, he returned to his chair but said nothing.

A slow mix of confusion and sadness roiled inside Elise as she pondered what she'd just seen. It was compelling footage, fraught with intrigue, but what did it really mean?

"Well?" Carlos prompted, rocking impatiently, anticipation glowing on his high, flushed cheeks.

"Well, what?" Elise asked. "Guatemala? Mexico? Guerrilla Indians fighting a military dictatorship? What does this have to do with me? With ScanTron?" She was ready for some answers and was getting antsy. Carlos had better make it good.

"You don't get it?"

Elise chose to interpret the tone of his remark as surprise and not a put-down. "No."

"Someplace between what El General said and what he is afraid of lies the truth," Carlos said. "If I can put the two together correctly, I think I'll find out why Zenoyo really caused the explosion."

"That's a leap, Carlos. A giant leap. What you have on tape is an old man who is deeply upset, and he's trying to make sense of his grandson's death. Are you saying that Zenoyo wanted to sabotage ScanTron in order to somehow get to Vargas? Where are you headed with this?"

Elise's skepticism didn't seem to phase Carlos. "I've done some checking," he said. "The Vargas family is still feared by the Lacandone who live along the Guatemalan border. They are terrified of the vicious regime and refute the Vargases' claim that the land they occupy belongs to them."

"So?" she prompted, equally as blunt. "You can put this together? Make it make sense for ScanTron, the authorities?"

"I could do it. I have sources, Elise. I speak the language. I can get to the Vargas family and the Lacandone to find out if Zenoyo Venustio really took his life in a fiery explosion or was indirectly murdered."

"Go ahead," Elise said, suddenly tired of Carlos's imagination for intrigue. "You don't need me, that's for sure."

"Oh, but I do," Carlos said. "There's a connection between ScanTron and the Venustio family, and I'm going to find it. Zenoyo Venustio rammed the gates of your company for a reason, and apparently was ready to die. Rosalía had been poisoned by the Vargases. According to Yusef Kirk, the people of Flatwoods are being poisoned, too. How? Why? There's a link somewhere, believe me."

"What do you want from me?"

"Information about that Global Oil pipeline easement that runs beneath ScanTron's property."

"It isn't leaking, remember?" Elise said.

"I don't care what the official reports say. I want building records and permits."

"Go to the county. What you want ought to be there."

"Too superficial. I want company records. The earliest plans. Before the land was developed and the plans had been modified to conform with the county's requirements."

"Sorry," Elise replied. "I doubt I could get my hands on them. The EPA confiscated what hadn't been destroyed in the fire. Headquarters' files would be difficult to access. No, you'll have to find another way in."

Carlos's persuasive smile didn't flag. "*You're* my way in, Elise, and you know it. I need blueprints, contracts, agreements, names. I want to know why ScanTron Security International decided to build its research and warehouse complex in Tide County, Texas. Of all places, why there? And why so near to Flatwoods? Who are your company's clients? And what kinds of security are you providing to your Latin American clients? And, most of all, I want to know what's underneath that tangled mass of burned-out steel and concrete."

Steadying herself, Elise smoothed her hair nervously. Hell, she'd like those answers, too, but the lump resting tightly at the base of her throat warned her not to let Carlos know.

The tragic fate Damita was facing, the conspiracy charges leveled by Yusef Kirk, and the fear that pulsed through the people of Flatwoods swirled through her head, making her dizzy. Sensing danger, she backed away.

"I can't help you, Carlos. You're asking me to be a corporate spy. A traitor! I'm not about to jeopardize my job. Especially not for you!"

"You won't be doing this for me," Carlos said smoothly, the edge in his voice totally melted. He shifted back, away from the light radiating from the tall lamp behind his desk, putting his face in half shadow. "Isn't your best friend dying of cancer?" he said soothingly. "Aren't you worried about your mother and father, who live only a few miles from the crash site? I know about the ditch that runs along the back of Flatwoods. Aren't those reasons enough to help me get at the truth? It's obvious the authorities aren't taking this case seriously."

A low blow, she thought, irritation flaring, but how could she counter him without sounding like a hardhearted bitch? Sure, she was worried about Damita and her parents, but she'd done her part by going to see Farren, following the corporate chain of command.

"My boss is aware of the situation," she replied. "And he promised to initiate a complete investigation. He was actually pleased that I brought the matter to his attention." She dropped the information casually, giving Carlos something to chew on.

"Do you really think he'll follow through?" Carlos picked right up. "Be real. All he's going to do is get a cleanup crew out there to dump a load of topsoil into that gully. John Farren's no fool. He told you exactly what he knew you wanted to hear. What did you expect?"

Elise tensed, unsure if she was impressed or frightened by the thoroughness of Carlos's research. Blake's words of caution came rushing back. "Sorry," she said. "No insider trading, Carlos. I've got too much to lose."

Shadows cast by the tall floor lamp washed Carlos's face an unhealthy gray, making him look older, menacing, and hungry for the story only she could help him get.

"You have to do it, Elise." His voice rumbled across the desk.

She pressed her knees together, determined to resist.

"You're not the type to sit back and watch the people you love be hurt," he continued. "That much I do know about you. You have to admit there are a hell of a lot of unasked and unanswered questions buried in that rubble. No ruling from the fire department nearly five weeks after the fire? The sheriff didn't release the identity of the truck driver to the press or the public, even though El General made a positive ID. Why? Huh? And there is still no reasonable explanation for the presence of benzene and arsenic in the air. Face it! For some reason this case has been written off as an unfortunate accident involving a drunken illegal. Not worth investigating further."

Though his argument was beginning to make sense, Elise refused to acquiesce. "Why are you so fixated on this story? There are sexier things you could use for your résumé. Isn't that what you want, Carlos? Another ACE Award from the Press Club to add to your trophy wall?" Her eyes swept the neatly framed plaques, citations, and photos of him with celebrities and politicians that crammed one wall from ceiling to floor.

"Maybe," he admitted calmly. "Sure. I like winning, and I like high ratings, but that's not why I'm hooked on this story. I want to help you get to the truth. Don't you owe that to the people in Flatwoods? Isn't that what you'd like to see happen?"

Unable to reply, she glared at him, furious at how he was manipulating her. "But why do *you* want to help *me*?"

"I tried to tell you at the Global press conference, and at the library, but you wouldn't listen. Now you're on my turf; you've got to hear me out." The genuine tremor in his voice was uncharacteristically poignant.

Elise waited, enjoying his uneasiness.

"I owe you. What I did to you was wrong, and I'd like to make it up." He thumbed a brass button on his navy blazer. "Maybe we can start on a fresh page. . . . I like you, Elise. I've always liked the way you operate. We had some fun times working the Winter Ball, but we also shared some pretty tense moments during hospital crises. Working with you was always pleasant, and I never planned to deliberately harm you. It was blind ambition, and ever since, I've had a hard time liking myself."

"Oh? I'm really sorry about that." Her words rang with sarcasm. She should have known there was a self-serving measure hidden somewhere.

"Sound stupid?" he ventured.

At first, Elise grimaced her affirmation, but a hint of a smile broke the frown. "You need help liking yourself? Please, run that line on somebody else." Rising, Elise began brushing at the wrinkles lining the front of her wilted linen skirt. "I've got to go."

"Wait. I'm serious. I feel awful about using your off-the-record remarks to punch up my ratings, and if I can, I want to help you solve this mystery, maybe even save some lives. I . . . I'm asking you to forgive me."

She struggled over what to say. "I'll think about it," she finally replied, a bit shaken.

Carlos jumped up, thrusting both hands into his pants pockets, pulling back his jacket and exposing the *CR* monogrammed in satiny letters on the pocket of his shirt. "I understand how angry you've been," he said. "But . . . accept my apology, Elise. Please. I'd really like to bury what happened. Wouldn't you?"

He seemed sincere, but Elise still wanted to punish him, to hurt him as much as he'd hurt her, but what good would that do? She might need his help to learn more about what was threatening her friends and family, so maybe she'd better lighten up. But if she forgave Carlos, Blake was going to pitch a fit. Perhaps he never needed to know.

"I'd like to be able to work with you," she admitted, "and not worry about what I say. It's impossible to be honest and open if I'm concerned that my words might come back to haunt me." There. She'd let him know in a very kind way that she still didn't trust him and probably never would.

Breath whooshed from Carlos' lungs. "I deserved that. But believe me, I learned my lesson, Elise. I'd never do that again."

"I can't say I'll forgive you," she started, "but if you want me to, I'm willing to listen. Just don't expect me to play spy. I won't."

"Can't ask for more than that, I guess." He stuck out his hand. "Thanks for staying and watching the tape, and for hearing me out. Elise, I think this thing is bigger than anybody suspects."

"I do, too," she told him, a shiver racing up her arms. She took his hand in hers, closing the wound that had pulsed between them since the day he betrayed her on the air.

Heading home, adrenaline pumped through Elise. She was gripped by shame and dizzy with curiosity.

What might the two of them accomplish? Could his television-star status open doors and bring the results that, it was obvious, the public officials couldn't deliver? Her heartbeat skittered as she braked for a red light and the car behind her blasted its horn.

As she waited at the intersection, a torrent of thoughts tumbled around in her head, spiraling her back to reality. What was she doing, thinking of joining forces with Carlos? How could she have agreed to listen to him? He'd stuck it to her once; he'd do it again. And what about her promise to Farren? Didn't she owe ScanTron total loyalty? Her boss's words of confidence and thinly veiled threat should she forget what she owed him pounded in her brain as she stared blankly at the traffic whizzing by.

When the light changed, Elise forced herself to relax, to let her mind drift, a technique that usually helped unravel a knotty issue.

Now, however, her mind continued to tick. Carlos was good at his job, connected, and had the top-rated investigative news show in the state. If she had to work with him to bring the mysterious case into the spotlight, so be it. Maybe that would spur the authorities into action.

But what were they looking for? she worried, absently making a right turn without blinking her turn signal. How could a lovesick man with a vendetta, a near-forgotten guerrilla uprising in a remote part of Mexico, and a charred security complex have anything in common? And the talk about poisons? It was all very strange, yet for some reason, Elise believed that she and Carlos might be able to pull the fragments together.

"All right," she murmured, stepping down hard on the accelerator. "Carlos, you're the hotshot investigator. Let's see what you can do."

It felt good to know that someone besides herself was interested in solving the mystery of the crash, but finding a legitimate way to help Carlos and not get fired in the process nagged at her as she sped toward home.

Still too upset with Blake to do more than be civil for the sake of peace in the household, she knew better than to tell him of her meeting with Carlos. Maybe later, when things were less tense, she decided, turning onto her street.

CHAPTER 19

On Fridays, John Farren always left the building early, and today was no exception. After poking his head into Elise's office to see how she was settling in, he chatted with her for a few moments, then headed toward the River Oaks Country Club to meet his wife for lunch.

After he'd left, Elise thought about her boss as she resumed unpacking the few personal items she'd brought from home to brighten up her new surroundings. With pride, he'd told her that he'd had this standing luncheon appointment with his wife for the past ten years and had never missed the noon hour date, let alone arrived late.

Sheepishly, he'd admitted that he still looked forward to that surprising sensation of falling in love all over again each time he entered the elegant dining room to find her sitting at their regular table, perusing the menu or chatting with the maître d'. Obviously, John and Ruth Farren were young at heart and still in love after more than thirty years together, and worked hard to keep the magic alive.

What a romantic couple, Elise thought, aching for the rocky period in her marriage to smooth out. She was tired of the tension in her family and wanted desperately to banish the emotional chaos that was tearing her and Blake apart.

A smile tilted Elise's lips as she recalled Blake's attempt last night to apologize for shouting and stalking out on her. She had to give the guy credit—he was definitely no slouch in the romance department.

Blake had greeted her with words of praise for her television appearance, a great dinner, chilled wine, and a down-on-one-knee, hands-folded plea for her to forgive his childish behavior.

Touched by the effort he had gone to, as well as the sincerity in his voice, she'd wrapped her arms around his solid shoulders, placed her lips gently over his, and tried to slip into the comforting oblivion that making love to him always brought.

The candlelight dinner and Junior's overnight visit to Blake's parents' home had provided what should have been a seductive mood, the perfect opportunity for them to make up, but her heart had not been in it. They had even slow danced on the patio to music from his portable radio, swaying back and forth in the moonlight. But something had interfered with her attempt to lose herself in Blake's embrace, and now she sighed, wondering if she'd simply been unable, or unwilling, to let him off the hook so easily.

Once they were in bed, they had lain spooned together quietly for a long time, neither talking. Elise had wanted to tell Blake about her conversation with Carlos, but knew that the subject would only dredge up bad memories and set him on edge again. Opting for peace, she'd kept the intriguingly curious temptation of Carlos's offer to herself.

When Blake finally spoke, it had been to remind her about the get-together planned at his parents' beach house in August. Elise had agreed that they ought to let Junior go, even if work prevented either of them from being there. After all, the boy hadn't had much of a summer vacation this year.

Blake had hugged Elise impatiently, burying his face against her breast, holding her tight for long moments at a time. She'd pressed her body close to his, absorbing the warmth he radiated, trying to fill the emptiness she had been carrying around for days. When Blake's hands had trailed lazily over her shoulders, then slipped the straps of her silk nightgown down, she'd helped him strip her soft negligee over her hips. Then, for some reason she still could not explain, she'd retreated emotionally, unable to go any further.

The sprinkling of kisses he rained over her neck and shoulders had been tantalizing in their distraction, but when she accepted the hard and searching press of his lips, her mind began spinning like a Ferris wheel with Damita's gaunt face and huge empty eyes tumbling around in her head. She had avoided Blake's questioning gaze by burying her face in the clean scent of his chest, horrified by her lack of response.

The touch of his fingers as he stroked her cheek, her hair, her neck had been calming but had done little to clear her congested mind. Even his swift, practiced tug, when he had urged her beneath him and gently parted her legs, had not been enough to pull her thoughts away from shaking Carlos's hand.

Blake whispered into her ears the naughty murmurings of desire that usually made her shudder and grow eager to have him buried deep inside her, but that night she hadn't caught fire. She gripped Blake tightly, terrified that she couldn't summon up the electric response he expected and she craved.

Their drive to satisfy one another eventually grew muddled and off-balance, though Blake's cooing words and languorous strokes did push her close to fulfillment. And each time she came close to reaching climax, her mind always spun back to the videotape, throwing her into frustration.

Was she betraying Blake by not telling him about her meeting with Carlos, or was she protecting her marriage from additional stress? Had she entwined herself in Blake's arms for some reason other than her love for him? When their bittersweet coupling failed for her, she'd been left feeling empty, disappointed, and raw inside.

Elise shoved a stack of empty boxes and two bulging plastic trash bags into the hallway for the cleaning people to take away, determined to stop worrying. Blake had been gentle and understanding when their lovemaking had fallen short, and had comforted her by telling her she must be overtired and still stressed from the TV interview, and all she needed was a good night's sleep.

Tonight I'll make it up to him, she vowed, thrusting her encounter with Carlos to the back of her mind.

With a yank, Elise pulled out and emptied another desk drawer of old pens, rusted paper clips, and brittle rubber bands. Theresa White might have been compulsively neat, but she had also been a bit of a hoarder. There were piles of useless junk left behind that Elise had to sort through and discard.

In the long credenza under the bank of windows that provided a spectacular view of Houston's glassy skyline were copies of *Media Monitor* dating back four years, manila envelopes—sealed and labeled in chronological order—of news clippings and photos taken at press conferences, and detailed reports of PR campaigns, accidents, celebrations—any event involving press, the public, and Theresa.

There were three-ring notebooks crammed with notes from staff meetings that were fascinating to Elise but held no company secrets, and Elise felt ashamed of the unconscious way she was digging for anything that might be useful to Carlos.

Theresa's files were filled with copious scribbling in the margins, providing in-depth character studies of the corporate players at the main office. All of John Farren's positive remarks on Theresa's PR maneuvers were highlighted in yellow, his criticisms in pink.

The afternoon passed quickly as Elise cleaned and rearranged the sunny office, aided by Betty, the pool secretary on her floor. Whenever Elise was not quite sure about the historical or future value of a box of papers, Betty, who'd been with ScanTron for twenty years, would help her decide.

When Elise was close to finished, she came across a battered accordion file. Beneath the string closure she read the dog-eared label —TIDE COUNTY PROJECT—and hesitated before opening it, momentarily stunned by the discovery. Calmly, she told Betty to head on home because she was going to work a little late.

When the secretary had departed her workstation, Elise pushed herself up from the floor, closed the door, then settled into her brand-new armchair and opened the file.

Most of the papers were routine press releases related to the announcement of the construction of the complex. There were names of the builders, contractors, and designers who had worked on the project, and letters related to the county, state, and federal entities whose standards and regulations had to be met.

There were yellowed copies of Farren's staff updates detailing the progress of the project, along with newspaper clippings of the short-lived protest staged by Tide County residents. The controversial decision to build the security research facility in their backyard had been made while Elise was in college in Dallas, and she'd somehow managed to miss most of the newspaper coverage. Now Elise read the stories with interest, vaguely recalling how infuriated her parents had been during that time.

As she worked her way through the file, she was pleased to see how Theresa had wisely countered the negative press with a series of stories detailing the economic impact ScanTron's arrival would have on the area—including impressive statistics on the number of new jobs the company would bring to the long-depressed town.

Crammed tightly into one bulging slot were three single-spaced pages. Elise pulled them out, squinting at the tiny print. It was a detailed memorandum from Al Patterson to John Farren, describing prospective clients he thought ScanTron ought to woo.

Elise scanned the pages, stopping when she came to Puro Corporation, Antigua, Guatemala—the only Central American company on the list. Did this company have a connection to El General's story, to his grandson? Who owned Puro Corporation and what kind of products or services did it provide, she wondered, letting her thoughts spin ahead unchecked. Fingering the paper, she remained uncertain of its importance. Maybe it was a long shot, but it might be precisely the connection she'd been hoping to find. She slipped the memo into her purse, then left the office and headed home.

As soon as the clerk at the Tide County courthouse handed Carlos the papers he'd requested, he put them into his legal-size briefcase.

"You doing a story on architects?" the clerk asked, dragging slim fingers through dirty blond hair.

Carlos chuckled. "Not really. Just digging up background information for a story I'm doing on variances in building codes and construction permits."

"Glad I could help," the clerk replied, fidgeting with a felt-tipped pen. He reached under the counter and pulled out a blank sheet of paper. "Uh, would you mind giving me your autograph? My wife just loves your show."

Smiling graciously, Carlos took the pen. "No problem. What's your wife's name?"

"Oh, make it to Diana . . . and Dan. That's me," he said, watching as Carlos scribbled a short message on the paper.

"Thanks."

"Sure," Carlos said, tucking the cardboard tube that was filled with county maps and charts under his arm. He nodded to Dan, then turned to leave, more than ready to get out of the stuffy little room where he'd been searching for records all morning.

Luck had been on his side—Dan, the morning clerk, had immediately recognized him and been willing to bend the rules to assist him. Requests like his usually had to be in writing and cleared by the county judge before being honored. Being a TV personality had helped, as it usually did, though he knew celebrity could sometimes swing the other way, putting people off, making them nervous. Carlos had come to believe that some people refused to cooperate with him just to be difficult or because they were jealous of his celebrity and were too small-minded to see that he was digging up stories that might help improve the quality of their lives.

It was time to get back to Houston before something went wrong. Carlos didn't want to press his luck. He had uncovered more than he'd expected to find, but remained disappointed that no blueprints of ScanTron's Tide County complex had even been filed. He couldn't wait to closet himself in his office to study the county building codes, the land surveys, grids, and charts that Dan had managed to unearth from the mountains of paper in the musty county files.

Whirling around, he was startled to find Yusef Kirk standing in the doorway watching him. The activist's shoulders were soldier straight, his face a taunting mix of inquiry and recognition.

"Excuse me," Carlos said, attempting to pass. Yusef shifted slightly, redistributing his weight in a subtle challenge. Carlos squinted his annoyance, holding his ground. "I'd like to pass. Do you mind?"

"You're Carlos Rico, aren't you? *The Inside Story*, right?" Yusef tossed a dreadlock from his cocoa-colored cheek, bestowing a grin on Carlos that obviously expressed pleasure at having unexpectedly encountered the well-known news reporter at work.

"Right." Carlos juggled his briefcase into his left hand, extended the other toward Yusef. "And I know who you are. Yusef Kirk." Within the space of a second, Carlos sized the man up. He had that "I want to be on your show because I know more than you" look smoldering behind hooded eyes.

The two men warily shook hands.

Slowly, Yusef stepped backward, drawing Carlos into the dim high-ceilinged foyer of the courthouse. "Why won't you let me on your program?" he asked pointedly, not angry, appearing genuinely perplexed.

"Let you?" Carlos repeated. He had no idea what the man was talking about, and was not about to engage in a confrontational conversation. The papers were burning a hole in his briefcase, and he didn't have time to deal with the suspicion clouding Yusef's face.

"I've uncovered information that I believe the public ought to have," Yusef said, "and I've got important things to say."

"Yes, I've heard some of them," Carlos replied, pacing his words. Though he had briefly considered interviewing the lawyer, the timing still wasn't right. Later, when more of the pieces of the story had come together, he'd consider talking with Yusef Kirk.

Yusef continued. "Yeah, I talked to your producer, Joe—somebody."

"Joe Wasserman," Carlos provided.

"Yeah, that's him. I left three messages before he called back. I told him I wanted an opportunity to tell the real inside story on what's happening out here, not the whitewashed, watered-down version that you let Ms. Jeffries and that man, Hillard, foist on the public last night."

Interested yet wary, Carlos replied, "I've heard and read about your charges of conspiracy, but do you have any proof to back them up?"

Yusef raised his chin, setting his dreadlocks swaying back and forth as he patted the thick folder of papers clutched in the crook of one arm. "What I've got here might just blow the conspiracy against the people in this little town wide open."

"What is it?"

Throwing back his head, Yusef guffawed. "Not so fast, my friend. It took considerable time and effort to get these papers. Surely you don't think I'd give them up so quickly."

Carlos shrugged. "Suit yourself," he said blithely, though curious. "If you change your mind, let me know."

"I will. Soon. I'm close to understanding why so many people have moved from this town, and why so many more stay despite the unhealthy conditions that exist."

"Close?"

"Yes. There is definitely a conspiracy against the people of Flatwoods. The question is, who's behind it?"

"You tell me," Carlos challenged.

"I will. In time, I will, believe me. I've worked enough of these kinds of cases to see right through the stalling tactics and double-talk that's going on down here. It's all part of a plan to confuse and dupe the unsuspecting public."

"That may be true," Carlos conceded, "but hunches don't fly on my program. I promise my viewers that I will inform, educate, and deliver the real inside story. I can't do that without hard facts." Carlos watched Yusef closely, letting his words seep in. "Call me when you are ready to reveal the facts of the conspiracy and only if you've got proof." Carlos liked the look of retreat that suddenly shadowed Yusef's dark face. "If there's a conspiracy, why would ScanTron give a big chunk of money to the county clinic?"

"Publicity. Diversion," Yusef tossed back. "An obvious ploy to overcome guilt."

"ScanTron's buying trust?"

"You'd better believe it, and using that Jeffries woman as their front." Yusef blew air through his lips, disgusted. "That's a sorry sister if I ever saw one."

Carlos was startled to hear Yusef's accusation, but he had to wonder—if that's what the activist thought of Elise, what must the people of her own hometown be calling her behind her back?

"You don't have a high opinion of Mrs. Jeffries, do you?" Carlos asked.

"Nope," Yusef said quickly, coldly. "How she can be a mouth-piece for a company that refuses to level with the people she grew up with is beyond my comprehension. I'm going to expose the un-derhanded dealings that have been systematically forcing old people from their homes, and I'll get those inventory records from ScanTron if I have to take the liars to court. Ms. Jeffries ought to think carefully about what she is doing. She could be charged as an accessory if this disgusting scandal reaches into the management of ScanTron."

"Is that so?" Carlos murmured, alarmed but not surprised by the legal tack Kirk was taking. Another lawsuit would devastate Elise, and Carlos resented the threat. *This slick bastard is not going to hurt Elise, or scoop my story*, he decided, realizing that Kirk was smart, focused, and a man whose views could add depth and credibility to an exposé on environmental issues. But Carlos doubted the lawyer had a clue about the international implications of the crash at the ScanTron gates. *That* was what Carlos was after, and that was what he knew would make this seemingly unimportant back-roads tragedy the most explosive story of the year.

"Well, Kirk," Carlos said, deciding to keep the communication channels open. "I'm always interested in a new angle on anything that affects the public." He took out his card and handed it to Yusef. "Here's the number to my direct line at the station, and my home phone. When you've got something hard to talk about, I'm interested. But make sure it's worth putting on the air." He lifted a wave to Yusef. "Gotta get back to Houston. But don't hesitate to call. I'll be looking forward to hearing from you."

As soon as he got into his office, Carlos decided he had to call Elise. He took his cellular phone out of his briefcase and called ScanTron headquarters.

"Elise Jeffries, please." He paced the room, his phone to his ear so no one at the television station could mistakenly pick up on his line.

Elise clicked on to take his call. "Hello?"

When she came on the line, he hesitated, unable to answer for a second. Her clear, oval tones had unexpectedly stirred him, entering his veins like liquid heat. He'd felt this way once before, long ago—the first time he heard her voice—before he learned she was happily married and not the least bit interested in his romantic overtures.

He'd laughed it off then, moving on to become her friendly colleague. Why was he so affected by her now? Had her faltering acceptance of his long-overdue apology rekindled the sparks he'd successfully suppressed so many years ago?

"Elise? Carlos. I need to talk to you." His throat narrowed tightly as he waited for her to speak.

"Carlos? Hold on, I've got the *Beaumont Leader* on the other line. Can you wait a minute?"

"Sure," he said, inhaling deeply, stunned by the reaction he was having. Truly, he'd thought he had this under control. Perhaps there was more to his peace offering than even *he* realized.

When he'd met Elise, her marriage had been on solid ground while his had been racing fast-forward toward divorce court. On many occasions, they had discussed and debated the phenomenon of a happy marriage, with Elise giving him tips from the perspective of a self-assured, blissfully married woman on how to keep Sherry from leaving. Clearly, her tips had not worked.

During that low period in his life, Carlos had asked for and valued Elise's advice, and as their friendship deepened, they'd interacted with a casual camaraderie that he'd never before experienced with a woman.

After his divorce, he had bumped into Elise at press conferences and meetings, and even partied with her at the Southwest Media Convention in Fort Lauderdale several years later. Always the consummate professional, Elise had been his friendly confidante, maintaining just the right balance of sincere interest and professional courtesy without compromising herself.

He had marveled at the way she had managed it, vowing never to jeopardize their friendship, her marriage, or her trust in him, but he'd failed miserably, hurting himself as well as Elise, when he'd been faced with low ratings and the threat of his show's cancellation.

Waiting for Elise to come back on the line, he walked to the window and looked out, attempting to focus on the wilting hedges of pale pink roses blistering in the sun, but saw nothing but his own reflection staring back.

"You sorry bastard," he riled lowly at the camera-pretty face he saw. "You'd never deserve a woman like Elise."

The man in the shiny glass was the stranger he'd created. All traces of Carlos's poverty-ridden childhood were gone—banished by his tailor, his personal trainer, a clever dentist, and the steady hands of a good plastic surgeon. He had transformed himself into an image he believed would ensure the longevity of his television career. He had the number one investigative news show in the state, legions of fans across the country, the jet-set life of an unencumbered bachelor, and a salary that still made him gasp in surprise each time he sat down with his CPA. Carlos had everything that should have made him deliriously happy—until he thought about Sherry, who treated him as a joke, and his children, who no longer put much store in his promises.

He was not looking forward to another evening at home with the laptop, the stacks of newspapers and magazines he devoured from cover to cover, and the whirring thump of the air-conditioning unit in his small but elegant one-bedroom apartment.

Elise was the lucky one, he realized. She'd managed to get it all and hold on to it, too, despite his disasterous betrayal. His heart shrank in admiration. "She's still sharp, still beautiful, but still very much married," he reminded his dim reflection.

Carlos relaxed, letting Elise's image swim into view, smiling as it emerged. He put a hand to his stomach and pressed hard, unsettled and a little angry over the steady throb of his racing pulse and the heat that rose in his belly.

CHAPTER 20

On Monday morning, Elise awoke feeling as tired as she had on Friday evening. Usually up and on her way to work before Blake or Junior finished their breakfast, this morning she had tapped the snooze button twice and still wasn't motivated to get out of bed.

She pulled the sheet up to her chin, listening to the water in the shower drum against her husband's back, thinking about Carlos's unexpected invitation to meet him at his apartment to look at some papers he'd unearthed at the county courthouse. She'd turned him down flat, almost before the words had come out of his mouth, but now she wondered if she'd made a mistake.

What did he want to show her? What was he up to? And what harm could there be in talking to him if it might shed some light on the issues facing her?

Snuggling deeper into her cocoon, she thought about Theresa White's file on the Tide County project. Clearly, the papers had been there for years, so she knew no one was looking for them. Tempted to share what she'd found with Carlos, she tried to rationalize why she should be helping the man she'd hated for the last three years.

The water in the shower stopped running. Elise sat up, poised to plunge into her day after what could only be described as a strained weekend.

On Saturday, she'd shopped with Lorna at the mall all afternoon, while Blake spent the day either talking on the phone to Paul about the dealership or tinkering with his Harley in the garage. In the evening she and Junior had watched *The Lion King* for the sixth time while Blake attended the last class in his summer course on tax-sheltered annuities—required for all Century CPAs.

Though the session had ended at ten o'clock, he'd been late getting home, and now Elise felt ashamed that she'd pretended to be asleep when she'd heard his key in the lock.

On Sunday Blake had taken Junior to the Thrill and Wreck Show at the Astrodome, returning to bury himself in his business proposal for the remainder of the evening. She'd curled up with a book. For a week now, they had not had a normal conversation, and the tension that kept them politely avoiding each other had not abated at all. Elise had no idea how to make the week looming ahead any better.

What was wrong? Why was she avoiding Blake? He had apologized profusely, romantically, and she believed he was sincere. Was she afraid of what might come up if they sat down and had a real discussion? How could things possibly get back on track once she revealed her inclination to trust, once again, the reporter she'd vowed to destroy? There was no way Blake was going to buy that.

Standing, Elise shook off her weariness, determined to make more of an effort to be honest and open with Blake, but as soon as he came into the bedroom, she slipped past him, closeting herself in the steamy bathroom. It was too early to get into a deep discussion about anything, she told herself. Tonight, she'd sit down and level with him.

When Blake had dressed and gone to wake Junior, Elise had wrapped herself in a white terry robe, come out of the bathroom, and pushed her hair from her face. She was reaching for her lingerie when the ringing telephone stopped her.

"Probably Farren," she grumbled, grabbing the phone on the bedside table.

When her mother's taut voice greeted her, Elise knew immediately that something was wrong.

"What is it?" Elise asked.

"It's Damita," Myra Camden said. "She called me about five this morning, delirious and incoherent. Fred and I rushed right over. We're at the hospital with her now."

"Oh, my God. What did the doctor say?"

Myra blew her nose, then cleared her throat. "He can't promise anything, but he was honest and frank. Damita's condition is serious, and she's failing pretty fast."

The tight band that had been around her heart since learning of Damita's terminal condition drew even tighter, squeezing Elise's fears to the surface. Her pulse raced. Damita had said three, maybe six months, and Elise had convinced herself she probably had a year. Surely this was only a setback. A change of medication, new treatments, something would pull her through. She had to make it, damn it! She just couldn't up and die, not like this.

"I'm on my way," Elise told Myra, reaching for the black-and-white pantsuit hanging on her closet door.

The early morning rush hour traffic turned the forty-minute trip into an hour-and-a-half crawl southward down the interstate. Once at League City Hospital, Elise walked on wooden legs behind the nurse who escorted her to the section where Damita lay fighting for her life.

As soon as they rounded a corner and emerged into a sunny yellow wing, Elise saw her mother rise from her seat in the small waiting area and hurry forward.

Myra embraced her daughter, holding on as if she feared Elise might dissolve in her arms. Fred came up behind his wife, stretching his arms around the two women, squeezing Elise's shoulder.

Elise broke away first, frightened to see the reddened rims of her mother's swollen eyes and the grim set to her father's jaw.

"I'm so glad you got here," Myra said, pressing her cheek to Elise's quivering lips.

"How is she?" Elise asked.

"Conscious, but groggy with medication," Myra said. "She's asked for you several times. I told her I'd called and you were on your way." Nodding at the nurse, Myra asked, "Can my daughter go in? She's Miss Chapman's best friend."

"Certainly," the nurse replied, touching Elise on the elbow. "Come with me. I know she's anxious to see you."

Elise waited in the hallway while the nurse slipped inside Damita's room. In the few seconds she was alone, Elise pulled in a deep breath, searching for control, terrified that the tension that had propelled her here would break loose, giving way to the flood of tears she could feel pressing behind her lids. This was the nightmare that had plagued her dreams for weeks, and it was hard for Elise to accept the reality of the moment.

"Be strong, be strong," she chanted under her breath, clenching, then opening a fisted hand. "Damita's going to pull out of this and surprise everyone."

"You may go in," the nurse said as soon as she emerged. "But make it short, okay?"

Elise nodded, chewing her lip as she pushed the door open.

"Well, hello." She briskly crossed to the side of the bed where Damita was lying on her side, head propped up on several pillows. A slant of sunshine lay like a golden ribbon across the foot of the bed, and a spray of white flowers was standing in a brass vase on the bedside table.

Damita smiled weakly, the kind of smile that tore at Elise's heart and warned her not to expect too much.

"Hi. You made it," Damita whispered, licking parched lips, exhaling softly. "Musta flown down that freeway, girl."

Elise chuckled, glad Damita's sense of humor was still intact. "You know I did." Perching on the edge of the chair beside the bed, she reached over to stroke Damita's hand. "Anything I can get you? Water?"

Damita shook her head.

Elise stared at her friend, at a loss. What should or shouldn't she say? This had to be some terrible mistake that would be cleared up at any moment. Elise felt heat rise on her face, panic stirring inside, and her heart constricting.

What was she going to do without Damita? Who would she call late at night to discuss the things that she couldn't tell Blake? How could the void left by the loss of a thirty-six-year friendship ever be filled? With what? Elise clutched the arm of the chair, thinking back to the day she'd brought Damita home from the hospital.

She'd been optimistic then, hopeful that Damita would be back to work and her old self after a few days of decent rest. Now she saw that her friend's battle was about to come to an end. Even when Damita had confessed that her time was short, Elise had stoically refused to believe the prognosis. Only twenty-one days after leaving this same ward, Damita was back, too weak to even brush her teeth.

A silent wail rose from deep in Elise's gut. She swallowed hard, blocking the words of comfort she'd rehearsed in the car. A huge black void lay before her and she feared starting any conversation that might propel her headlong into it. How could she bring up the trite, inconsequential news of her life? What could she possibly talk about that would make any sense at all? It was impossible to say a word.

Damita solved the dilemma. "Just talk to me, Elise. About anything. I don't care what you say; I just want to hear your voice."

"All right." Elise sniffed, openly wiping her eyes with a tissue. "Let's see. . . ."

Damita shifted to better see Elise, extending a hand, fluttering her fingers. "Tell me everything. What's happening with you? Blake? And . . . the J-O-B, because I don't want to talk about me. I've had enough of consultations with doctors, radiologists, and nurses. I've heard enough stories from cancer patients who like to despair over what's happened to them. Feeling sorry does no good, you know. Looking forward, if only to the next ten minutes, is the only way I know to deal with this." She grinned slightly, then fell quiet for a moment. "But," she began, "if this is my destiny, there's nothing I can do about it, so enough about me. Boring stuff, I assure you."

Elise forced a smile, lacing her fingers through Damita's. "Okay, if that's what you want, but things around my place have been pretty routine. In fact, nothing exciting's going on."

Scowling, Damita clucked her tongue. "Don't give me that nothin's goin' on, stuff, Elise. I saw you on the Rico show. How could you go through that after what he did?"

Glad to see an angry flush rise on Damita's cheeks, Elise gave up a throaty laugh. "Hold on. Okay. Okay. I'll tell you everything."

Elise brought Damita up to date, even about the mysterious El General and Carlos's theory about an international connection to the crash. She confessed that she had not completely forgiven Blake after their argument, and of course she told Damita about Carlos Rico's tender confession and request for her forgiveness.

"Did you forgive him?"

Elise slumped. "I guess so, because I keep thinking about working with him."

"Oh, is that so?"

"Yes. But not like you think," Elise clarified. "It's crazy. I try to discount him every chance I can, but dag, he's starting to make sense. Listen to this. He called me at the office on Friday. Wanted me to meet him at his apartment to discuss some papers he got from the county clerk's office. At his apartment! Can you believe it?"

"Mmm," Damita murmured knowingly.

"Of course, I turned him down." Elise's gaze flitted from Damita to the huge spray of flowers, then back. "He must be out of his mind."

"Girl, sounds like that man's got *you* on his mind and he wants more than a discussion about the ScanTron fire." Damita half rose on an elbow, a playful curve to her lips. She started to say more, but a flash of pain forced her back to her pillows.

Scooting closer, Elise whispered, "You know, you may be right. He was polite, kind of uptight when he called. Definitely not his usual suave self, and he had the nerve to sound disappointed when I turned him down. I'm so damn curious, I don't know what to do."

"Meet him."

"You think so?"

"Yes," Damita murmured. "Go to his place. See what he's got to say."

The words settled over Elise, falling into place like the pieces of a jigsaw puzzle, but the picture was wrong. "Blake would be furious. Carlos goes after what he wants. That's his job, girl, and you'd better believe he'll do anything to get his story. I don't dare underestimate that man."

Unable to comment, Damita shrank back into her pain.

Elise lunged forward, but Damita waved her hand weakly, shaking her head. "It passes pretty fast. Guess I'm kind of used to it."

Determined to distract Damita from her pain, Elise rushed on. "I know I've got to be cautious about all of this intrigue and far-fetched conspiracy, and I don't want to get tangled up in something that could turn out to be dangerous. If El General's granddaughter-in-law was killed by a vicious Central American family with a grudge to settle, I'm not sure I want anything to do with exposing them or their presence in the States." Elise stopped talking long enough to take a tissue from the box on the nightstand and dab at the sheen of perspiration on Damita's feverish brow.

Lying still, Damita said nothing, and the lull in the conversation terrified Elise. If she didn't keep talking, she'd surely break apart, and once she started crying, she knew it would never stop. Plunging ahead, she said, "It *was* strange."

"What?"

"Talking to Carlos. Like old times, when I worked for Trinity. He and I used to be pretty good friends."

"So you gonna go meet him?"

"You really think I should?"

"Damn straight," Damita whispered. "Help Carlos get the goods on who's connected to the fire. If anybody can do it, it's Rico."

After a moment, Elise said, "Now I kind of wish I hadn't been so rude to him."

"See? It's not too late. Work with him, Elise. Please." Damita coughed, an awful, hollow sound that filled the room. "Carlos Rico cares. Maybe he has a self-serving motive, maybe not, but at this stage, who cares? Better hope he can get to the truth before that spotlight-grabbing Yusef Kirk does."

Elise took in Damita's observation, impressed. "Yes, and I believe Carlos could do it. But maybe there's nothing more to all of this than a drunken illegal who ran off the road."

"There's more," Damita challenged. "So, help him, okay?"

"I want to, but not until I discuss it with Blake."

Looking pleased, Damita turned fully onto her back and stared at the ceiling. A fresh wave of pain rode over her, making her wince and shut her eyes. She stiffened as the raw tremor passed.

Alarmed, Elise stood, leaning over Damita. "Hold on to me," she said, gripping Damita's hands, holding fast as the pain tore through her friend's emaciated body. She wished she could absorb the impact for her.

Once released from the brutal jolt, Damita went limp. "Don't take too long, Elise," she begged. "Help Rico save Flatwoods. Blake will understand. He'll be proud of you for taking a stand. Someone's got to do it. I would if I could."

"I know," Elise said, standing by silently, unable to say more. Her heart told her to follow Damita's urging, but Blake's angry face loomed large. He would be devastated if she trusted Carlos Rico and wound up losing her job. *Lord,* she thought, raising her chin, *this is not going to be easy.*

When Elise looked down, she saw Damita's eyelids flutter as they feathered up and down for several seconds. Her face grew slack, her eyes dulled, and the sheets across her chest rose and fell with her uneven gasps for air. Lolling her head from side to side, Damita struggled to focus on Elise.

"Please, do what you can," Damita whispered in an urgent burst of energy. "That's all I ask."

Throwing off a slight shudder, Elise watched helplessly as life quietly drained from Damita's pinched face. Grasping Damita's hand, Elise said in a clear, strong voice, "For you, I'll do it."

Damita blinked lazily. "Thanks, girl. I love you."

Stroking Damita's thin cheek with the backs of her fingers, Elise stood watch, suddenly calmed by the commitment she'd just made. It was the least she could do for her best friend, whose death might be caused by something she could help expose and eliminate, preventing others from suffering like this.

The two women, who had been born on the same day at this hospital thirty-six years ago, remained silent while time stood still, absorbing the comfort of simply being together.

When Elise realized that Damita's flesh was no longer pulsing with the vibrancy of life, she drew back her hand and pressed it to her heart.

Damita was gone. Swiftly, silently she had crossed over.

Refusing to panic, Elise savored her last moments with Damita, touching her lips with a trembling finger, running a nervous hand over her permanently shuttered eyes, smoothing tousled brown hair that was sticking to her clammy brow. Elise smiled as the wiry curls sprang back into place.

"Don't worry. I'll fix it for you, girlfriend," Elise murmured, twining a lock around her forefinger, memorizing the familiar ruddy coil.

God, how many times had she fixed Damita's hair? She grinned, remembering the old-lady bun she'd pinned at the back of her best friend's head when they'd played dress-up in her mother's fancy clothes. For the senior prom it had been shiny sister-girl curl, and a conservative page boy for her first job interview.

The tears that Elise had willed into submission broke lose, flooding her cheeks, purging her sorrow. Gladly, freely, she let them flow.

When her sobs had subsided, she rang for the nurse. Elise wiped her eyes, leaned down, and kissed Damita's still-warm cheek.

"I'll give it my best shot," she said, placing a palm to her chest in promise.

CHAPTER 21

During the days following Damita's death, Elise moved in a melancholy fog. Lonesome, sad, and restless, she forced herself to focus on the precious memories of the happy times she and Damita had shared, instead of dwelling on her absence. Since Damita had left no surviving family members to assist with funeral arrangements, it fell to Elise, so she decided to have Damita laid to rest in the Tide County Cemetery next to her parents.

The short funeral service was held on Wednesday afternoon, and immediately afterward, Damita's single-page will was read. Elise was shocked to learn that she was the beneficiary of a fifty-thousand-dollar life insurance policy and the new owner of Damita's mortgage-free bungalow in Flatwoods. The news was startling but pleasantly comforting, and Elise told Blake that she wanted to fix up the house and keep it. Why, she wasn't quite sure, because she knew she'd never live in Flatwoods again or dwell in the house that held so many memories.

Drawn together by the tragedy of Damita's death, Elise and Blake pushed their problems aside to take care of closing down the house.

They fell into an awkward truce, neither willing to plunge into the dangerous waters surrounding their marriage. With her promise to Damita still fresh in her heart, Elise had already made up her mind, and braced herself for the confrontation with Blake that she knew was on its way.

On the Saturday morning after Damita's burial, Elise and Blake went to Flatwoods, ready to work. After finding homes for the cats, they cleaned out closets and dressers, sorted and packed Damita's belongings. They donated most of the furnishings to a local homeless shelter. The only item Elise chose to keep was the wicker rocker on the porch where Damita had loved to sit.

On Sunday afternoon, Elise returned to the house alone, since Blake and Junior had decided to go fishing with Paul. She wandered the empty rooms restlessly, searching for signs of Damita's presence, desperate to talk with her friend. Of course, she found reminders wherever she looked, and they prompted Elise to voice her troubles to the musty old walls instead. As she paced the scarred wooden floor in the living room, Elise formulated a plan. She picked up a clipboard filled with clean paper, opened the front door, and went out onto the porch. She looked up and down the street, then across the road, as disheartened by the number of FOR SALE signs stuck in yards as by the charred silhouette of the homes and warehouses that faced Baymark Road.

Pulling her sunglasses over her eyes, adjusting her wide straw hat, she decided to head to the house where the Robins twins lived first, praying they would not slam their door in her face or sic their high-strung poodle on her. It had been years since she'd spoken to the elderly ladies, and if they were still as hermitlike and skittery as they'd been when Elise was a young girl playing around the neighborhood, she doubted she'd get much cooperation from them.

Proceeding along the street, she was saddened by the number of empty houses scattered throughout the neighborhood. If something didn't turn this trend around soon, Flatwoods could easily become a ghost town. Out of curiosity, she began writing down the names of the different real estate companies, wondering how much the asking price was for some of the abandoned property in Flatwoods. Maybe she'd call a few of the agencies and act as if she were in the market, just to see what they'd say.

Mildred and Mary Robins opened the door of their square brick house together. They were frail, light-skinned ladies in floral-print dresses, retired nurses who had never married and had always been reclusive. Surprisingly, they had come to Damita's funeral but hadn't spoken to Elise or her parents. They must have known about Elise's connection with ScanTron, because they had been tight-lipped and aloof, sitting in the back of the church, staring at her throughout the service. At the burial site in the cemetery, Elise had caught them again openly assessing her and had ventured a half smile that had not been returned. Now she wondered if they had been trying to get her attention. Maybe they wanted to reach out and confide in her but were afraid to do so in public. Recalling their expressions, Elise believed they had not been angry, but simply shy, as if they expected Elise to make the first move, giving them an excuse to talk. In her state of grief, Elise had not felt up to initiating a conversation.

But now, sitting on the twins' plastic-covered French provincial sofa sipping mint tea, she told the ladies that she had inherited Damita's house. She should not have been surprised to learn that they already knew, as did all of Flatwoods, Elise supposed.

"I understand you have not been well," Elise said to Mildred, the one with her gray hair pin-curled around her forehead.

"No. I've been poorly for some time. My problems began two months after the warehouses were finished," Mildred said. "When the smell from that ditch began making me nauseous, I called them. But nothing's been done. I swear you could taste the odor in your throat. For weeks, I had headaches and no appetite at all. Then I went to the doctor and he began running tests."

"Oh, yes," Mary broke in, "she's had a terrible time. Just terrible. Then my lungs started bothering me. Emphysema, I was told. And I had no problems breathing before that smell settled over us. Isn't that right, Mildred?"

"Oh yes. Some days it's so bad we have to leave. I take Mary out of here so she can breathe. We drive over to Webster or Kemah just to escape the smell."

"That's the truth," Mary said.

Mildred continued with the story of her ordeal with stomach cancer; then Mary described her bouts with emphysema, coughing as she struggled to speak, finally giving up to hook herself up to the portable oxygen tank that was always at her side. Mildred filled in what Mary left out, the two often talking over one another once Mary recovered. Mildred fussed over her sister in loving concern, anxious about each new coughing spell.

Elise made notes on her clipboard, not really sure what she was after, but distressed enough to try to find out. One thing was clear to her by the time she rose to leave: the sisters' health problems were not isolated cases. Mildred and Mary told Elise of numerous others in the neighborhood who had fallen sick, many who no longer lived in Flatwoods. The Robins twins had addresses and phone numbers of several of their old friends who had been forced to move into nursing homes or in with relatives after losing their property for non-payment of taxes.

"You call Betty Dickson over at Four Oaks Nursing Home," Mildred urged Elise. "She had a double mastectomy, just like Damita, but she survived it, God only knows how. She's sixty-four years old and lived sixty-three of them two blocks down from us." Mildred went to the window and pulled back her lace curtains, pointing to the left. "She lived in that house on the corner of Thornhill and Baymark. Come here. You can see it."

Elise came up behind Mildred and looked over her shoulder.

"The one with nothing left but the redbrick chimney," Mildred said.

Mary struggled to add, "And her only daughter, Clara, who lived with her, is in and out of the hospital all the time. The doctors can't even find out what's wrong."

"Yes," Mildred sighed, "whatever has got a hold of us is about to wipe out this community, but nobody will listen to us old folks."

Elise frowned as she turned from the window and went back to the sofa, her heart heavy with concern. "Oh, I believe you," she said. "And I promised Damita I'd do what I could to get to the bottom of this." She picked up her purse and flipped through the pages on her clipboard. "Thanks so much for talking to me."

"You selling the house?" Mildred asked as she walked with Elise to the door.

"No, at least not right away. I want to think things through. Maybe spend some time in my old neighborhood."

"We'd be glad to have you," Mary said, then chuckled. "Wouldn't do any good to put the place up for sale anyway. As you can see, nobody's buying around here."

For the remainder of the afternoon, Elise walked the streets, reintroducing herself to her old neighbors, meeting those she didn't know. She was surprised and pleased that most didn't hold the fact that she worked for ScanTron against her. Actually, they were grateful that she was willing to listen to what was on their minds, and hoped she'd take their information back to her company.

By the time Elise got back to the bungalow, she was dripping with perspiration and dying of thirst, and had heard enough testimonials to be well and truly alarmed. There were too many sick people in Flatwoods, and most of them lived in houses that faced or backed up to the shallow gully filled with a sluggish brown stream of water.

On Monday Elise ended her short period of mourning and returned to work at headquarters. She was hurrying to finish a media report that would update Farren on the Tide County incident while trying to keep her mind from wandering back to the disturbing conversations she'd had the day before. The buzz on her telephone interrupted her progress.

"Hello," she said in a strong voice, clearing away all evidence of her mental rambling.

"Good morning." Carlos Rico's silky voice slid over the wire.

"Carlos?" Elise asked, disturbed by her eager reaction.

"Yes," he replied. "Hope I didn't interrupt anything."

"Ah . . . no," she stammered, fingertips to her cheek. "What can I do for you?"

"I heard about your friend's death. I'm sorry."

"Thanks," she murmured, then added, "but I'm sure that's not the only reason you called."

"No. I have something to show you and a favor to ask."

"Oh?" she replied warily. Impulsively, she reached over and tipped the door to her office partially closed. Shouldering the phone against her ear, she asked, "What do you want?" A spiral of panic coiled through Elise as she recalled her promise to Damita. How could she not join forces with Rico after gathering the information she had managed to pull together yesterday? She'd been dreading the moment when she'd have to make a decision. Apparently it had arrived.

"I was able to get my hands on some information from the county clerk's office that I think you'll find interesting. I'd like to go over it with you."

"Well, I suppose . . . ," she began, then stopped, deciding to set some ground rules before going any further. "I don't want any trouble, Carlos. I admit, I'm interested in finding out more about what's going on, and it would make sense for me to work with you, but I'm warning you, you'd better play fair."

"Oh, I will. I promise. Just calm down, okay? I only want you to check some papers out."

"What are they?"

"I'd rather not discuss them over the phone. In person, privately. All right?"

"I don't know. I'm going to be pretty tied up today. Yusef Kirk's agitation caught the attention of the feds, and the ATF started its investigation today. I've got to get down to the Tide County site ASAP." She held her breath, waiting.

"If you want, I can meet you there, after you're finished."

"No," Elise said, not wanting anyone to see them together. "That would not be a good idea."

"Meet me, then," he urged.

Her throat tightened. "Where?"

"My place." The line was silent for a moment. Then he clarified, "That really would be best."

"Maybe, but . . . ," Elise stalled.

"But you're afraid to be alone with me?"

"Certainly not," she tossed back. "I'm sure I can resist your alluring personality long enough to go over some papers. Where do you live?"

"City West on Hermann Drive. Apartment 1023. You know where that is?"

"Yes, I do," Elise replied, not surprised to learn that Carlos was living in one of the most expensive high-rises in the city. "What time?"

"Six-thirty, okay?"

"Fine," she said. "I'll see you then."

As soon as Elise parked her car across from the burned-out ScanTron complex, Al Patterson came toward her. He looked agitated, anxious to talk.

She rolled down the window and through her sunglasses observed the men in yellow rubber suits who were climbing around in the rubble.

"You didn't have to come down, you know," Al said.

Elise tried to concentrate on what he was saying. She got out of the car and greeted him.

He stared at her blankly, obviously irritated by her presence, then lit another cigarette from the butt of the one in his hand.

Elise glanced around. There was a scattering of half-smoked cigarettes lying on the ground, and it looked as if Al had been hanging around for some time. She was surprised that he would leave his air-conditioned office to stand around in the sun while the crew from the Bureau of Alcohol, Tobacco, and Firearms sifted through the mountain of debris that used to be his responsibility.

"The EPA, the TNRCC, the fire department, and now we got ATF guys on our case. Jesus!" Al swore. "This is crazy! That guy Kirk's to blame for all this commotion. We got half the federal government digging around over there, and they act like they're gonna be here for a while." Al glared across the road. "That's all we need.

The goddamn United States government teaming up with the locals on this."

Elise was surprised by the bitter edge to his voice. "Why not?" she asked. "The more agencies involved, the more likely we are to get this investigation over with. A lot of people are anxiously awaiting a definitive report from someone."

Al grunted, working his jaw. "Just costing the taxpayers a lot of money, for nothing."

"But these men are good; they'll produce results. I understand some of them worked the World Trade Center explosion."

"Yeah," Al concurred, "but coming down here is just gonna keep the press zeroed in on us." He kicked at a beer can with the toe of his boot, scowling as it rattled into a ditch. "All this attention. We don't need it. It's time this investigating got over with so we can level this pile of crap and get on with rebuilding, maybe expand. Hell . . ." Al stopped himself. "All I want is to be left alone."

"I don't think that's going to happen."

"See that ATF guy standing by the main gate?" Al jabbed the humid summer air with a stubby index finger. "He's the leader of the unit. You'll be coordinating press statements with him, but if the subject of Global Oil's pipeline easement comes up, don't try to discuss it. Refer those questions to me."

Elise stepped directly in front of Al, realizing why he'd been hanging around. "You don't want me to discuss the pipeline right-of-way? Why?"

"Because you don't know enough about it to speak for the company. Okay?"

"No, I'm sorry. That's not okay. I've been brought up to speed by headquarters and I think I can handle that subject just fine. I do the talking for the company, Al. It's my job, remember? And it's what Farren wants." When Al reddened in indignation, she reminded him, "I'm permanent now."

"So I heard," Al begrudgingly muttered. "But not till September first. You'd better do as I say. If you don't, Hector Hillard and the rest of the board might be interested in reading a police file on a naughty little girl who robbed a store and lied about it, then went on to become head of this company's PR team. Interesting reading, I would suspect."

Elise's jaw dropped, and she rocked back a half step, steadying herself against the side of her car. "It wasn't robbery," she protested.

"Stealing? Does that sound better?"

"How do you know about that?"

"I'm sure you can guess, Elise. It was the East Shore Variety Store in Beaumont, wasn't it?"

She stiffened, unable to believe Al would sink so low. "Don't you dare threaten me. Farren knows all about that and has already signed off on my promotion. I don't think he'd take too kindly to your interference with his decision."

"All I have to do is pick up the phone, and your short career with ScanTron Security is finished, Ms. Jeffries. *Finito.*"

"Don't try it."

Al Patterson's beefy red face beamed satisfaction, initiating a curl of fear inside Elise. "Ha!" he laughed. "Farren can play guardian angel if he wants to, but it's the board of directors that pulls the strings."

"What are you trying to do, Al?"

"I'm just calling it as I see it."

"But what are you so damned afraid of? I'm not a threat to you. As soon as the ATF crew is finished, I'll be back in Houston, out of your hair."

"Listen. I've been running things fine down here for a long time, and there was no need for you to drive all the way out here just because the ATF is on the scene."

"Farren asked me to. Having the feds involved is new media fodder."

"Well, I'm asking you to stay out of areas you know nothing about."

"I can't do that."

"I'd try, if I were you. Don't get the crazy idea that you're indispensable to this operation. How long have you been on with ScanTron? Three weeks?"

"Five and a half to be exact," Elise said tersely, feeling her pulse gathering speed.

"So, Farren likes you. Fine. But it's going to take a whole lot more than his blessing for you to survive with this company." Al tilted his head, assessing her down the length of his nose. "Don't fool yourself, Elise. This is a big operation. You may think you know enough about this company to represent it, but I assure you, you don't."

Elise stared icily at him, not doubting for a second that he'd carry out his threat—if she were stupid enough to force his hand. So, Farren must have told Al about her childhood record. That was disappointing. His breach of confidence made her wonder who else knew and how closely she was being watched.

Al turned away and she watched him duck beneath the yellow-ribbon barrier, then, raising her voice, called after him, "If that's the way you want to handle things, fine."

Pushing herself off the side of the car, she followed Al in long strides, stopping when the leader of the ATF crew approached.

"I'm Elise Jeffries, spokesperson for ScanTron," she introduced herself to the man in the yellow rubber suit.

"Roger York, ATF," the man replied.

"Anything I can help you with?" she asked, ignoring the contemptuous expression on Al's face.

"Looks like we've got our work cut out for us here," he said. "We could use a blueprint of the complex and floor plans of each warehouse in order to move through this mess with any hope of being successful."

"I'll see what I can do," she volunteered, anxious to see such plans herself.

Al coughed, giving Elise a skeptical glance. "Those records were kept there, in the admin building safe." He pointed to the twisted mass of charred steel and scorched concrete that used to house his office. "They're all burned up."

"What about your headquarters in Houston?" York asked.

"Nothing there. At least nothing of importance." Al glanced uneasily at Elise. "All papers related to the construction and layout of this complex were stored here, in the company records warehouse. Everything's gone."

Al's comment piqued Elise's curiosity, and she shifted to the side, distancing herself from him when York headed back to his crew.

Lifting her gaze, she searched the blackened pile that was spread out behind the gates, realizing that somewhere in there lay the answers to the questions that had plagued her since the day she returned to Flatwoods.

Could the ATF, the fire department, or the EPA piece the mystery together? Did they care enough to try? Or, against her better judgment, was she going to have to place her trust in Carlos Rico to fulfill her promise to Damita?

Shading her eyes from the scorching noonday sun, Elise checked her watch, disturbed at how anxious she was for the day to be over so she could keep her appointment with Carlos. What was he up to? What had he found? And would he play fair this time?

The first news van to arrive on the scene turned onto the road. Taking a deep breath, Elise gathered her thoughts, forcing her own agenda to the back of her mind, clicking into her spokesperson mindset. It was going to be a very long afternoon.

CHAPTER 22

W hat did headquarters say?" Carlos asked as soon as Elise
replaced the slim receiver of his custom-made telephone
into its cradle.

"Farren agreed with Al. All blueprints of the Tide County complex were in the administration building or the records warehouse,
now buried under tons of debris."

Carlos glanced at the papers he had spread over his kitchen table.
"Seems strange to me. These papers I got from the Tide County
Courthouse are helpful, but they are just drawings, sketches, not the
actual plans I expected."

"Well, they do give us some details about the major sewage, water, and electrical installations at the complex."

"Oh, sure. And I suppose these lines," he tapped the complicated
grid of county property, "indicate pipelines." Carlos traced his finger
over the paper, then turned it over and examined the back. "There
is no date here, but all of these charts were pulled from documents
registered and filed with the county in January 1981, only a month
after construction started on the warehouses."

Elise sat back in her chair, letting her eyes wander over Carlos's apartment as she tried to put it all together. It was certainly convenient that the blueprints had been destroyed, and she could not get over how edgy Al had been. She had spent most of the afternoon fielding questions from the reporters who showed up to cover the ATF's arrival. Al had paced and prowled outside the gates, keeping a close eye on her, actually listening in on her conversations with the media, the investigators, and especially the curious onlookers from Flatwoods who wandered across the road to find out what was going on. He'd been a pain in the butt all day, acting as if he feared the inspectors would actually come across something that might be worth giving up to the press. He'd stuck around until four o'clock, then finally left her on her own.

Elise focused on a squat Aztec warrior, part of Carlos's impressive collection of pre-Columbian statuary that was displayed throughout his apartment. There were clusters of clay figures on tabletops, tall freestanding carvings that reminded her of totem poles, and colorful fiber wall hangings done in nubbly, natural cloth. His pride in his Mexican heritage was clear.

Carlos broke into her thoughts. "This large drawing of the Global Refinery indicates that a single pipeline runs from the center of Global, directly through the middle of town, then under Scan-Tron's property." He traced his index finger over a thin white line. "The pipeline ends at the plant where hydrodesulfurization occurs."

"Don't get too technical, now," Elise cautioned, trying to follow him.

"That's where high levels of sulfur are extracted from the crude."

"Oh. So, it looks normal? As it should?"

"Seems like it," Carlos said, then added, "as far as Global's pipeline is concerned. But see this second line here? I think it's a section of pipeline, too, and it's heading eastward. Toward Flatwoods."

"Yes, I see what you mean."

Carlos shoved the light gray paper aside to pull another scroll from beneath it. "Now, check the area where ScanTron built its complex." He straightened up, allowing room for her to get a closer look. "Interesting, isn't it?"

Using a magnifying glass, Elise leaned over to examine the county record. "Yes. This thing looks like it branches into two sections at the point that it passes off ScanTron's property."

"Exactly." Carlos agreed.

"If it's a pipeline, it doesn't appear to connect to anything on the Global plant."

"Right! And that's probably because ScanTron put it there, not Global." Carlos motioned for her to look again.

Elise edged closer, anxious to see and understand exactly what he'd found. Carlos's leg accidentally pressed against hers while she bent to examine the paper again. With a start, she moved aside, but not before she caught a glimmer of a smile flit over his lips.

"Don't worry. I don't bite," he told her.

"I know," she said, keeping her eyes to the table, hoping she hadn't made a big mistake by meeting him at his apartment.

It had seemed perfectly sensible not to examine the papers in his office or hers. Any public place was off-limits, and she wasn't afraid of Carlos. He was a flirt, and a tempting one at that, but certainly not dangerous. Since her arrival at his lovely apartment overlooking Hermann Park, he'd been straightforward and courteous. Just as she'd expected.

But now, as she sneaked a peek at his striking profile, she wondered if that brush against her leg might have been deliberate after all. Biting her bottom lip, she thought about the position she'd voluntarily put herself in.

"I'm convinced that it's a second, secret, pipeline and not a part of the Global easement," Carlos continued.

Elise pulled back from the plans and picked up the folder of papers Carlos had gotten from the courthouse. "Did you find a listing of the contents of the pipeline? Was an inspection rider filed?"

"None on record," he replied, going to the refrigerator to take out a soda. "Want one?" he asked, holding up a can, flashing her a disarming grin. "Not much else to offer. As you can see, I eat out a lot."

"Sure, I'll take a Coke," Elise replied, shaking off her impression that Carlos had made another pass. He was simply being nice, very much the gentleman in fact, and Elise realized that it was as natural for him to be flirtatious as it was for her to be reserved.

When Carlos's ex-wife, Sherry, had slapped him with divorce papers, Elise had been the one he'd turned to to discuss strategies to get her back. During happy hour at Take Five, where press people regularly gathered, he'd admitted to a series of romantic capers, keeping his confession low and conspiratorial to prevent his colleagues from hearing. He had been desperate to reconcile with Sherry, though everyone who knew Carlos doubted he'd ever get her back. Apparently he had been completely oblivious to the damage he was doing to his marriage, relying on a hit TV show, a fat paycheck, and a minimansion in the suburbs to keep Sherry content.

As Carlos handed her a can of Coke, Elise actually began to feel sorry for him. He was attractive, brilliant even, but obviously alone, and hardly knew his way around his kitchen. When he opened several cabinet doors, trying to find a glass, she saw how barren they were.

"That's okay, I don't need a glass," she said, tilting the can to her lips. The soda was cold, bubbly, and strong. Just what she needed to jolt away the wayward thoughts rolling around her mind. Giving herself a mental shake, she swallowed. "So what do we really have?"

Carlos crossed the room and leaned against a stool that fronted a small bar on the other side of the kitchen. He studied the adobe-colored tile on his floor. "We have a standard pipeline that runs from Global's refinery through the ScanTron acreage, then cuts south toward the Gulf where it delivers crude to tankers and barges at the coast. That's what should be there. Then, we have a second pipeline that is not connected to Global's that seems to run out from under the warehouse complex and along the fault line behind Flatwoods— where the shallow gully lies."

"And we don't know what it carries, or what purpose it serves, as far as the county is concerned."

"No, we don't. And there's nothing on file to prove it carries anything." Carlos downed the last of his Coke, then thumped the empty can on his gleaming black marble-topped bar. "But you can believe it's not empty. We've got to find out what it carries and why."

"According to Damita, ScanTron said the vapors were coming from their waste disposal system."

"Nope. I don't think so. Come here." He went back to the table and stabbed the paper again. "This is the county sewage plan."

Elise followed, peering at the map, still uneasy standing so close to him.

"The ScanTron waste disposal system is here, on the other side of the complex," he said. "Almost two and a half miles from Flatwoods. I don't see a connection."

"If there is no inspection rider filed with the county as far as that second section of pipe is concerned, does that mean that the content inspection was never done, or somebody didn't file the paperwork?"

"Or took the paperwork out of the files?" he prompted. "Good questions. Ones we need the answers to." Carlos rubbed his chin.

"I'm beginning to believe there is only one way to get the answers we want," Elise offered.

"What's that?"

"Run our own tests," she proposed.

"Test the water and soil in the gully?"

"Why not? Obviously the EPA hasn't disclosed its findings, and even though the ATF and TNRCC are conducting independent tests, they might not be released for months, maybe years."

"It could be an expensive proposition, if you use a private company to conduct the tests."

"I know," she hedged, a plan beginning to form in her mind. "I spent yesterday walking the streets of Flatwoods," she said, going on to tell Carlos about her interviews with the Robins twins and others in her old neighborhood. "Maybe I've set myself up, but I promised those people I'd do whatever I could to help find some answers. They're counting on me, Carlos, and if I have to spend every dime of the fifty thousand dollars Damita left me to stop the deterioration of Flatwoods, I will. Especially since I am now a property owner myself."

"I'd hate to see you tear off on a wild goose chase for nothing, waste your inheritance," Carlos warned.

"I know, but there are a lot of fearful, suspicious people in that community, and don't forget a charge of conspiracy that's been leveled by an attorney who is probably going to make a killing on this tragedy. And Al, our slightly paranoid plant manager."

Carlos laughed.

Elise shook her head. "It's not funny, really. I just buried my best friend. Thirty-six years old, and she's gone." Elise's eyes filled with tears that spilled down her cheeks, and when she spoke again, her voice was hoarse. "Maybe I'm chasing the wind, but I don't care. I'm convinced there's something deadly in that area, and for some reason, the suspicions of the residents of Flatwoods are not being taken seriously. Why, Carlos? Why do you think that is?"

Elise's emotion stirred Carlos. Turning, he took out his handkerchief, offering it to her. When she didn't take it, he gently reached out and wiped away the tracks of tears on her face. Elise held still as his thumb lightly brushed her skin.

"I don't know what's going on," he said soothingly. "But we'll find out."

Elise nodded as she put her hand over Carlos's and squeezed it, then took the handkerchief from him. She wiped her eyes, balling the small white square into a knot as she thought of the memorandum from Al Patterson she'd discovered while cleaning out Theresa White's office. She had held back telling Carlos about it, unsure of how deeply involved she was willing to get. But she had no one else to trust. Blake certainly didn't have the contacts, or the motivation, to help her track down what she needed. It was time to go all the way.

"Have you ever heard of the Puro Corporation?"

"Puro? No, why?" Carlos asked.

"I found something of interest last week, but I'm not sure what it means."

Carlos waited while Elise went to get the three-page memo from her briefcase.

"Antigua, Guatemala," she said, offering Carlos the pages. "I found this memo in my office credenza, so it obviously was not considered a document worth keeping in a safe." She spoke with confidence but felt like a traitor.

He quickly read through the names in the memo. "Interesting. Puro is the only Central American company on the list."

"So, you ever heard of it?"

"Nope, but I can check it out real fast."

"I did some checking on the ScanTron computer client listing. Puro didn't come up."

"If it's a legitimate corporation, I'll get to the source. Peeling away the multilayered paperwork of complicated mergers is my area of expertise."

"Expensive?"

"Yes, but don't worry. This one's on me."

"Good," she murmured, then asked, "Is this crazy? All this digging and searching for answers."

"I follow hunches and gut feelings all the time. I'm always winding myself into dead ends, then worming my way out. I've come to trust my basic instincts."

"If this stuff backfires, I could lose my job."

"I thought you said John Farren was glad to have you on the case in Tide County."

"Well, yes, but you've got to understand . . ." She hesitated, unsure of how to phrase it, remembering Al's threat. "Farren is the president of the company, and he's supportive, but he still has to answer to the board of directors."

Carlos shrugged. "True, but we've just begun, and frankly Elise, I think you're going to be pleasantly surprised at how easy it's going to be to get to the real story behind the ScanTron fire."

"*The Inside Story?*" she teased.

"Yeah. Exactly." He grinned, easing some of the tension.

"Well, that's easy for you to say. You don't have as much at stake as I do."

"Depends on how you look at it. Trust me."

The words stung like sharp arrows sprung from the past. "Trust you? Oh, sure . . . ," she breathed, starting to turn away.

Carlos snagged the cuff of her soft ivory blouse, halting her retreat. "Hold on. Don't be so edgy. I didn't ask you to play this game. You want to do it. I want to help. All we need is a plan. One that allows me, as an investigative reporter, to be the front man and ask the hard questions while you stay on the job—with eyes and ears alert to anything that might be helpful."

"So you do want me to spy."

"Well, you're in a better position than I am to observe the players in this little drama. Just listen, watch. You don't have to steal company secrets." He released her wrist.

Elise became uneasy. "Please, Carlos," she said. "This whole thing is getting pretty complicated. Risky, too."

Carlos pressed a palm to her lower back, urging her over to a bar stool.

"Sit down." He sat next to her. "We'll work it out."

With a wary glance, she sat stiffly, lowering her gaze to the slick ebony counter. Without realizing it, she began rubbing her wrist, upset by the burning sensation initiated by his touch.

What the hell is going on with me? she thought, groping for a reason to feel so unsettled. This was not a good sign, she silently chastised, feeling his eyes on her face, annoyed at the way he was studying her.

Pushing away from the bar, she stood. "Not now. Let me think about what you've shown me. Anyway, I've got to get going. I promised my son I'd take him to the mall." She strode from the kitchen, returning to the living room, where she picked up her purse and headed toward the foyer. Carlos followed, rolling up his papers.

"Take these." He thrust the roll at her.

She shied back as if they were poison.

"They're public records. Available to anyone. Nothing illegal here. Compare these plans with whatever you might come across at headquarters. That's not asking too much, is it?"

"Well, no," she answered, suddenly ashamed. "I think I can handle that." She picked up the empty cardboard tube and began stuffing the plans inside, but they jammed and spiraled out. Grimacing, she twisted the papers tighter and tried again.

Carlos placed his hand on hers. "Let me."

She pulled back quickly, as if he'd pricked her with a needle. Carlos laughed softly. "My, you sure are jittery, Elise."

She handed him the largest of the plans, watching as his well-manicured yet definitely masculine fingers deftly maneuvered the papers inside the protective shield.

"I'm glad we've been able to move past the bad feelings between us," he started, tapping the packing tube against one palm. "It means a lot to me. Really. I always liked talking with you, working with you."

"Is that so?" Elise replied coolly.

"Oh, yes. A conversation with you is very different from talking with any other woman I know." He handed her the package.

"I would hope so," Elise tossed back dryly, curious about where he was headed.

He stepped past her toward the door, then turned, locking eyes with her.

Elise tucked the tube under her arm, picked up her briefcase, shouldered her purse, and entered the white-tiled entry to plant herself directly in front of the door.

"Thanks for coming," he said. "This is going to pay off. For both of us. You'll see." Carlos never took his eyes from her face.

"I hope so. I agreed to come here only because I believe you are sincere about helping innocent people get some answers." Taking a deep breath, she continued with candor. "I hope you don't disappoint me, Carlos, because I can't afford to have you mess things up."

His expression remained cheerful in spite of the hurt she saw in his eyes. "Elise. Give me a break. Please. I told you I was sorry, and . . . I like you too much to mess things up again. Jesus! Is that what you've been thinking about me?"

"Who knows what's on your mind?" she quipped, determined to keep from weakening. "I just thought it would be best to clear that up right now, before you get the crazy notion that you are so irresistible that you can get me to do your dirty work to pump up your ratings and boost your career at my expense!"

"Damn! You think I'd do that."

"Yes."

"Oh? So now everything is quite clear," he replied.

Elise said nothing. For the first time since she'd entered his apartment, she thought he looked vulnerable, as if his television facade had finally slipped, letting the true Carlos Rico emerge. She felt ashamed. She'd really hurt his feelings, yet could hardly bring herself to utter the words she knew he wanted to hear. In a spurt of regret, she told him, "I didn't mean that Carlos. Not really."

Without making a reply, he took a long stride forward, closing the space between them. "I know you didn't," he said, suddenly too close, his mouth only inches from hers.

When he placed one hand beneath her chin, she flinched and flattened herself against the polished teak door, inadvertently drawing Carlos nearer.

His physical presence smothered her and his emerald eyes were hypnotic.

He kissed her softly, tentatively, yet fully on the lips, and for a split second, Elise just stood there, letting him play out his romantic overture, amazed at how smoothly he operated. Then she put her hands on his chest and pushed, but he slipped his palms to her waist and held her tighter, dissolving her feeble protest with the increased pressure of his mouth.

Elise squeezed her eyes shut, shuddering to feel the probe of his tongue against her tightly closed lips and the press of his thighs against hers. He felt too good to fight back. He tasted too good to get angry. Her defenses collapsed in a heartbeat. Unexpectedly, she relaxed and let his tongue dance lightly over hers.

Carlos swept his palms down her back to the swell of her hips, then slowly, teasingly, he lifted his mouth from hers—centimeter by centimeter, as if daring her to scream.

The encounter was over in seconds, but it might as well have lasted an eternity, for all the shame Elise felt when she looked into his eyes. When he extended an arm across her shoulder, anchoring it on the closed door behind her, she had to choose between bolting like a scared rabbit or holding her ground.

The position in which he had placed her was horrible. She was furious, yet a part of her longed to stay put, just to see how far he would go. But flirting with Carlos was flirting with danger, and she was not naive enough to think she could match him in that department. She ducked beneath his arm and went to stand, trembling, beside a leafy ficus plant that was set in a hammered copper pot in the corner of the entry. Glaring at him, she struggled to pull herself together.

"You shouldn't have done that." Her voice was not as strong as her resolve to keep her distance.

"I've wanted to do that for a long time," he admitted, his tone no longer as suave as earlier. "Don't hate me, please. I just . . ."

With an angry shake of her head, Elise pushed past him and grabbed the doorknob. "You just have no shame! Let me out of here, Carlos!" She yanked the door, then fumbled with the lock. "God only knows why I let you talk me into coming here."

"I'm sorry," Carlos said gently, sincerely. He reached past her to unlock the door.

Elise tensed.

Carlos held it open, freeing her to leave. "Believe me, Elise, I'm sorry I upset you, but I can't say I'm sorry I kissed you."

She stepped into the hallway. "You ought to."

"I'll call if I get any leads on the Puro Corporation," he said calmly, as if nothing at all had happened.

She bored him a seething stare, then let a long stream of air out of her lungs. What was she supposed to do now, call the whole thing off?

"Sure," she said tightly, unable to understand how Carlos Rico's mind operated. *He is so damn conceited. He must think I've been waiting all evening for him to grace me with a pass.*

"Let me know if there's anything I need to follow up on," Carlos offered in a normal, businesslike manner. He reached out and lightly touched Elise's lips with the tip of his little finger.

She jerked back. "Don't hold your breath," she said curtly, wiping her mouth with the back of her hand before turning to stalk away. She hurried down the carpeted corridor, conscious of his eyes on her back.

In the elevator, she finally exhaled, letting the tension that had gripped her release. Crossing the shadowy parking garage, she raged at herself for allowing him to get so close. She could have prevented the encounter. Behind the wheel of her car, she fought back tears.

Carlos Rico was nothing to her, nothing but a starstruck, egotistical, pretty-boy television personality with an oversize opinion of his romantic appeal.

She swiped her mouth again. What the hell had she been thinking of, going to his apartment? God, she'd been stupid to let him kiss her, but for some reason she was not completely surprised. She'd always suspected that Carlos was attracted to her. Maybe that was why she'd spoken to him off the record, and why she'd been so devastated by his betrayal.

Blake would go after Carlos like a mad dog if he ever found out what happened. She knew Carlos had been posturing, pushing her, testing her in an attempt to see if she could actually work with him. Well, she could and she would. As far as she was concerned, his trespass was already forgotten.

Racing across town, Elise tuned the radio to KLOL, assaulting her ears with hard-driving rock, but the strident twang of electric guitars and the jagged lyrics that blared from the speakers could not banish Carlos's kiss, which she replayed over and over in her mind.

CHAPTER 23

Blake held his breath as he left his boss's office. Gently, carefully, he pulled the heavy oak door closed behind him, then stood with his back against it, shaken with relief. He'd done it! He'd handed Tharp his formal letter of resignation, effective September 1, and had been brave enough to refuse the temptation of a bigger office and change of assignment—into legal, where he'd always wanted to be. The promotion had been dangled like a carrot in front of a jackass, but he'd been smart enough to turn it down. Tharp would do anything to keep from losing face, and having one of his senior accountants resign did not make him look good in the eyes of his peers.

Blake, simmering with resentment, understood all too well how Joseph Tharp liked to play the game favored by most of Century management: ignore talented people like Blake until they threatened to leave, then scramble to come up with an offer of appeasement. The last time one of the accountants in Blake's department had tendered a resignation, he had eventually backed down, accepting a change in assignment with a decent salary increase, instead of taking a position with Texas Equitable, Century's most aggressive competitor. All Blake wanted to do was leave the firm on good terms, without doing harm to his reputation or future prospects in the business.

Burning bridges, he knew, would not be a good idea. He was more than ready to strike out on his own, but who knew what could happen to upset his plans? Nothing Tharp could say or offer at that moment could make him change his mind, though the only concession Blake had agreed to was keeping the news of his impending departure from his colleagues until the end of the week. By then, the director of personnel would have pulled together his termination package.

By his calculations, he ought to receive five thousand dollars in sick pay, thirty-three hundred in unused vacation, and if Century Trust stock remained as strong as reported in the financial section of the *Chronicle* this morning, he planned to sell 25 percent of his shares and raise twenty-eight thousand more. That sum, along with Elise's unexpected inheritance from Damita—an unforeseen windfall that he had urged her to place in a mutual fund—would provide a cushion for them to fall back on while the dealership gained its footing. That fifty thousand, properly invested, could mean the difference between worrying about making ends meet or relaxing enough to enjoy their new business venture.

Blake felt like running through the building, pounding on desks, yelling his news to his colleagues. He was officially a short-timer, and ecstatic about it, but he wisely ducked into the men's room and stood in front of a mirrored wall, staring at his reflection as he calmed himself down.

Still, Blake's heart galloped with excitement. It was set. He and Paul had signed the lease on the vacant Toyota lot last week. The contractors they'd hired to renovate the property were already at work. This morning, when the news came that their franchise dealership application to Texas Rider had been approved, Blake knew it was time to make his move. Why wait and hem and haw around? The project was gaining momentum and had acquired a life of its own, pushing him, haunting him, making him sweat in fear and rejoice in expectation.

The business was going to succeed. It just had to. He'd waited too long, prayed too hard, and made too many sacrifices not to see it through. But there were so many details yet to attend to, and he could no longer handle them discreetly from his office phone or on his lunch hour. Paul had agreed to go to the site daily to oversee the renovations, and Blake had begun to feel isolated and out of the loop. He didn't like the idea of not pulling his weight.

No more, he thought, breaking into an expansive grin, pleased with himself. The money Damita left would come in handy, but the house—that was an entirely different matter. Elise's new status as a property owner had strengthened her ties to her hometown. Lately, all she talked about were property values, real estate agencies, and her desire to unravel the mysterious health crisis plaguing the residents.

Blake had made a big mistake suggesting she sell the house. She'd flown into a rage, accusing him of being too focused on money and not caring enough about her feelings or the lives of innocent people. Though she agreed that they'd never live in the house in Flatwoods, and had suggested they lease the place out, Blake wasn't too optimistic about finding a tenant for a coastal bungalow sitting in the middle of a block of charred houses. He sensed that the property was going to become another sore spot between him and Elise that they'd have to tiptoe around in order to keep peace.

Blake slumped against the wall, his ebullient mood slipping away. Things were tense at home. He didn't like it one bit but was torn about what to do. Should he leave her alone and watch silently while all that they'd struggled to achieve fell apart? Or stay on her case and widen the rift that threatened to crater their marriage? It was driving him crazy, but maybe when he was free of Century and able to devote himself entirely to the dealership, he'd have more time to spend with Elise to help her get over this crazy obsession with the fate of her hometown.

As media attention on the fire wound down, despite the fact that the public knew little more today than they had when the explosion rocked the county six weeks ago, Elise was permanently stationed in her office in Houston. Blake was glad that she was through running up and down the interstate, and hoped she could ease up, focus her attention on some new, exciting assignment.

Damn, he thought, wishing she were not so hardheaded. He loved her deeply, as much for her sharp intelligence as for her gentle personality, but sometimes she was too quick to dismiss him. Blake doubted that she even knew how humiliated he felt when she did that to him.

Blake straightened his tie, brushed a hand over his short black hair, then pushed open the swinging door and left the men's room. He walked back to his office with a leaden step, struggling to push his worries aside.

At his desk, he sank down into his chair until his spine was stretched out taut, then tilted his head back, hands behind his neck. The first thing he was going to do as soon as he got home was roll the Harley out of the garage and give it a good hand polish. The restoration was finished. It had turned out exactly as he'd envisioned. Now all he had to do was compose his ad for the paper, place it, and wait. He'd show Elise he knew the motorcycle market. He was going to get a nice piece of change for his restored, classic bike, and if he got his asking price, as he was sure he would, it would be his first real sale. The money was going straight into the business.

After the staff meeting Elise invited Darrell Grimes into her office, eager to show off her new spot at headquarters. Propping her chin on tented fingers, she focused on Darrell's sympathetic face, hoping she hadn't misjudged him, as she apparently had Carlos Rico.

Exactly one week had passed since Carlos kissed her, and she had not heard a word from him. A slow burn rose, flushing her face, whenever the memory surfaced. It was impossible to deny that she was more flattered than angry with Carlos for acting so impulsively, and felt no bitterness toward him. If she didn't believe that he truly wanted to help her, she'd never speak to him again. But something about that evening in his apartment kept Elise convinced that the kiss had been no more than a nervous reaction to the tension of the moment. It had meant nothing, and one thing was certain, it would not happen again.

Al Patterson had come into Houston for the meeting also but had barely acknowledged her when she'd passed him in the hallway on her way to the conference room. He was still ticked off at her for talking to the ATF crew leader despite his warning, though nothing, as far as she knew, had come of it. A week had passed since he'd threatened her, yet Farren had not summoned her into his office, nor had she heard from Hector Hillard. Apparently, she'd called Al's bluff.

After greeting him warmly in the hallway, forcing him to speak to her, she'd sailed down the corridor with a smile on her face. He'd squinted and mumbled a barely intelligible hello.

Neither Pete Tremont nor Garland Perkins had bothered to speak to her either, but she really hadn't expected them to. She was an outsider now, a main-office staffer, and Elise knew that Al's tight-knit team had little use for those who answered directly to John Farren. She didn't care what they said behind her back, as long as she had the title, the salary, and the spacious office to prove that she was an important part of ScanTron Security International. Al Patterson would have to get over it.

She gave herself a mental shake and turned her attention back to Darrell. She was glad he'd stopped by. Since moving back to headquarters, she missed their daily chats and was glad he'd come in for the quarterly company-wide staff meeting.

"I called three of the real estate agencies that have property listed for sale in Flatwoods, and was surprised by what I found," she said, resuming their conversation.

"Oh?" Darrell asked, taking a sip from his can of Dr. Pepper. The staff meeting had dragged on long after the sumptuous lunch Farren had provided for his employees, and most of them had headed back to their offices, relieved that it was over.

"Each FOR SALE sign in the neighborhood had a different logo and telephone number, but when I called, they all rang into the same office."

"Are you sure?" Darrell asked.

"The same woman answered each time," Elise replied. "I asked her if I'd called the right number, and she said yes, she was an answering service and had several real estate companies as clients."

Darrell nodded. "Makes sense." He took the notes Elise offered and looked them over. "Did you visit any of these agencies?"

"Oh, yes. Gulfway Realty, Rose Thompson Properties, and Suncrest. They are the ones that handled the most recent sales, and represent the majority of the properties now listed."

"What'd you find out from them?"

"That the property values in Tide County, especially Flatwoods, are much higher than I expected. I never thought I'd say this, but Yusef Kirk's belief that someone wants Flatwoods could be right on target. I also found out that one company, the Puro Corporation, snapped up quite a bit of land over a three-year period, then put it back on the market."

"Puro? Never heard of it. What kind of company is it?"

Elise's thoughts turned to Carlos, and she hoped he was moving forward on his promise to find out what he could about the mysterious corporation. "I don't know, but I have a friend checking on that. The only thing I was able to confirm is that Puro's charter is not registered with the state of Texas. I'd sure like to know who owns it."

"Probably some huge industrial conglomerate that plans to move into the area." Darrell's tone was matter-of-fact.

Elise, unable to buy the obvious explanation, shook her head. "Maybe, but why that particular tract of land when there is so much undeveloped acreage, with access to the coast, that is sitting empty and cleared, waiting to be developed?"

"Must be some technical reason," Darrell offered, handing Elise back her notepad. "Keep me posted, okay?"

"Sure," Elise replied, glad to have got Darrell's attention. At least he wanted to know more.

"So, are you on a new assignment yet?" Darrell changed the subject. "Or is Farren keeping you busy planning the annual stockholders' meeting?"

"A little of both." Elise thought about her job, which had many different facets, making each day a new adventure. But despite the love she had for her work, her love for Damita and the void left by her death still consumed her, preoccupying her to the point of distraction. "Farren wants me to go to Dallas on Monday." She checked her desk calendar, then sat back in her chair, glancing away. Next Monday was the twenty-first of August. Her and Blake's eleventh anniversary. She wondered if the strain between them would have eased enough by then to at least make an attempt at celebrating. Turning back to Darrell, she asked, "You know Judy Talor, don't you? Media relations director in the Dallas office?"

"Right."

"Well, she's in charge of security for some Latin American dignitaries who are on a tour of Texas. Tomás Aloyo, the Mexican minister of agriculture; Ben Turriba, his counterpart in Brazil; and the Argentine secretary of the interior—Abelo Ponto, I think is his name. They're coming to tour several ranches and observe groundbreaking technology in cattle breeding."

"Interesting. Expect a lot of press?"

"I think so. The department of tourism's really pumping this up. Seems Texas ranchers are on the cutting edge. Foreigners want to know how we manage to raise the best beef in the nation." Elise leaned forward, elbows on her desk. "I met Aloyo when I was with Trinity Hospital. He was there for a heart operation about four years ago. At the time he was only a midlevel member of the Mexican government. He's certainly moved up since then."

"You get all the exciting assignments," Darrell said, draining the last of his soda.

"I'm not sure I'd call it exciting. I'd rather stay right here, I have so much to do. But since I know Aloyo, Farren wants me to meet him at the airport . . . represent ScanTron."

"I guess so," Darrell said. "ScanTron's got several lucrative security contracts with Mexico."

"Right, we supply virtually all of their security checkpoint equipment for airports and most of the government buildings."

"Well, hobnobbing with foreign dignitaries sounds a lot more appealing than pushing papers around a desk in an abandoned JCPenney store while we wait to hear the fate of our facility."

Elise watched Darrell closely, sensing he was not too happy about the situation. "I don't see how you stand it," she said. "Couped up in that place with Al blowing hot air all day. He'd drive me nuts." She rolled her eyes. "I can't say I miss it."

"Yeah, some days it's tough. I miss the research. My lab. Working up new products for clients, and especially, the testing."

"Why don't you move up here into headquarters until the complex is either leveled or rebuilt? Use the facilities here."

"Al and I've discussed it, but as I'm sure you know, he's not keen on giving up much to the main office. I think he's afraid I'll jump ship and stay here, but I can promise you, I have no designs on a job in the city. Tide County suits me and my family just fine. I hope the fire department wraps it up soon, so things can start returning to normal."

A flicker of doubt shadowed Elise's face, but she kept quiet, wanting to move on. "There is something I'd like to run past you," she said.

With a tilt to his head, Darrell asked, "What?"

She sat up straighter, easing into her request. "I have a plan . . . *and* a favor to ask."

Darrell's mouth curved into an inquisitive half smile. "What's going on, Elise?"

"What did your contacts in D.C. find out about Justin Snyder's investigation?"

"Not much. Seems that Global Oil's finding of no fault with its pipeline kind of put a stop to the investigation. Nothing else was done, at least as far as I can determine."

"I thought so," Elise replied. "You're a chemist by profession, right?"

"A Ph.D. in chemistry from the University of Michigan."

"Can you run the same kinds of tests that the EPA ran at the Tide County site?"

"Air, water, soil?"

"Exactly," Elise replied, going on to tell Darrell about the shallow gully running through Flatwoods, the suspicions of the residents, and her conversation with John Farren.

Darrell listened patiently, then said, "Farren knows about this and told you he'd do something about it?"

"Yes, but that was weeks ago, and nothing's been done. I want to believe Farren will do something, but when?"

"Better wait it out."

"I can't. My best friend died and I have to find out if there is any connection between her death and the environmental conditions there."

"Well," Darrell hedged, "samples could be taken. Tests run. But it would be expensive. I'd have to pay for equipment and time in a private lab. Could be thousands of dollars, depending on what I'm looking for. Who'd foot that bill?"

"Me," Elise replied calmly. "My friend willed me her home and some money. I owe it to her to spend it on finding out what killed her."

"Whew!" Darrell's eyes grew wide. "You're serious, aren't you?"

"As a heart attack. I know it's asking a lot, but would you do it?"

Darrell sat back in his chair. "There's certainly no law preventing me from testing on your property. It is yours now, right?"

Elise nodded.

"Well, if that's what you want, I could do it."

"How long would it take to get results?"

"A few days . . . a week." He shrugged.

"I need the information as soon as possible."

"Fine. Tell me where your house is and I'll get over there this evening."

"Thanks, Darrell. I knew I could count on you."

Al Patterson raised his head from the water fountain, his back still turned to Elise's open door. He swallowed the cold water with a gulp, incensed over what he'd just overheard. Independent tests? Who did she think she was? And Grimes? What a fool.

Al wiped a drop of water from the side of his mouth, inhaling deeply as he stood in the hallway. He'd tolerated Grimes because he was good at his job and had come up with several innovative security devices that had kept the coastal facility on the cutting edge of the industry, making it the most respected branch of the entire operation. He'd even begun to kind of like the guy, despite his know-it-all attitude.

Now this. Just like *them*. They stuck together no matter what, which was why he didn't want too many of them at his complex. Trouble, that's what he knew would happen if the balance of his staff was disturbed. Well, Grimes's future with ScanTron was about to take a nosedive, Al decided. What a stupid ass, he thought, glancing into Elise's office, infuriated to see Darrell and Elise huddled conspiratorially over her desk. He'd be sorry he ever met Elise Jeffries. And that woman? *She has no idea what she's gotten herself into or the price she's gonna pay*, Al thought, moving down the deserted corridor.

CHAPTER 24

The headlights of an approaching car sliced the tar-black night, casting long white rays over a trash-littered section of broken pavement. The silvery light came closer, and Carlos calmly watched the twin beams in his rearview mirror until the car came to a stop behind his.

Leaving the headlights on, a man got out, slammed his car door, then walked directly to Carlos's driver's-side window. He stood close to the tinted window and tried to see inside.

Carlos pushed a button and the glass slid down. Looking up, an expression of relief came to his features as he recognized Raúl Torres, his longtime contact with the barrio. He sure as hell hadn't wanted to hang around this gang turf any longer than absolutely necessary, though there had been a time when he'd have felt both safe and proud to be sitting in the heart of Sonny Macha's territory, waiting to make a connection. But now that he was a TV celebrity and his face was so well-known, he had too much to lose to be taking chances like this.

The blare of an ambulance racing down a nearby street reminded him of how dangerous this part of Houston could be if you didn't know the lay of the land, the hand signals, and your way out of the crumbling Hispanic ghetto that wrapped the east side of the city.

"*Hola.*" Carlos greeted a youngish, well-groomed man in a shiny gray silk suit. A week after calling his longtime informant, Carlos was anxious to see what he'd found. "*¿Lo tienes?*"

"Shit, yeah, I got it," Raúl replied, reaching into the inside pocket of his jacket. He pulled out a packet of papers that he fanned in front of Carlos. "Two fifty, man. You got *that?*"

Without answering, Carlos thrust a wad of bills at Raúl, then took the packet of papers. "It's all here? No dead ends?"

"Naw. Took some diggin', man, but it's there. All the way to the beginning." Raúl sniffed, thumbing his nose. "You oughta put me on a retainer, show boy. All the jobs I've done for you . . . oughta be getting . . . what you call it? You know. When your name is listed at the end of a show?" He laughed uneasily under his breath.

"Credits?" Carlos supplied, realizing Raúl was serious.

"Yeah, man. Credits. Whatever you need, you know I can get it. Things seem to be going pretty good for you, homeboy. We work fine together, you know?"

Carlos laughed aloud, swatting at Raúl with the heavy packet. "Jesus, get out of here, Raúl."

Raúl pocketed the cash, then pushed up the sleeves of his shiny gray jacket. "Just thought I'd ask, man. You know, I'm getting pretty good at this, right?"

"Yeah. Right," Carlos said, starting the engine, flipping on the air conditioner. "I'll remember that when I get to Hollywood." Rolling up the window, Carlos sped off, leaving Raúl standing in the trash-littered street, grinning as he counted his money.

Carlos drove directly home, sat down at his cluttered desk and immediately tore open the packet of papers. Reading each page, he moved deeper and deeper into the paper trail of the firm handling most of the property in Flatwoods. What he found was a mix of multilayered corporations: Suncrest, which was a subsidiary of the Bordes Company, had controlling interest in Gulfway Realty.

Rose Thompson Properties was owned by Deetering Specialties, which had its headquarters at the same address as Bordes in El Paso, Texas. There was a company called Rifers Inc. that also listed its address as the same post office box as Deetering Specialties. On and on went the convoluted, masterful maze of hidden ownership.

Raúl sure earned his pay this time, Carlos thought, trying to find a connection between the numerous companies, the names of the owners, and Tide County, Texas.

Finally, Carlos knew he'd hit pay dirt. There it was, Puro Corporation, with offices in Antigua, San Salvador, and Mexico City. Zooming in on the tiny print, he read the names of the thirty-seven people on Puro's board of directors and was not surprised to see that twelve of them had the last name—Vargas.

Grabbing the phone, Carlos dialed Elise's home number. She had to know about this right away. If the Vargas family was snapping up property in Flatwoods, El General may not have been too far off base, because it certainly looked as if the descendants of the once vicious Guatemalan regime were establishing quite a foothold in Texas.

The question was, why? Why had Flatwoods been targeted, and why would El General's grandson crash his truck at the ScanTron gates? And the sickness plaguing the tiny community? Could the Vargases have also manipulated that to scare folks off their land?

Carlos's heart raced, and he loved the rapid thundering in his veins as much as the sense of challenge it brought. It was the hunt, the chase, and the putting it all together that kept him pushing harder, searching longer, delving deeper into the stories his audiences craved.

He could sense the links falling into place, and his mind began clicking through various scenarios. It was clear that what he needed immediately was information about the history of Flatwoods. What had been on that land before refinery workers, coastal laborers, and drifters built tar-paper shanties, then brick homes to settle the swampy plains? Perhaps Elise, whose family had lived in the area for several generations, could help him find the elusive connection.

"Who's calling?" Blake asked, folding his newspaper into a tube as he looked at the time on the VCR. From the corner of his eye he could see that it was past ten o'clock.

"Carlos Rico."

Blake felt a slow burn begin deep in his stomach. He'd thought he recognized the voice. It was one thing to have his wife involved with the guy in a professional way, quite another to have him calling her at home. On a Sunday evening, too. This was going too damn far.

"I think it would be best if you contacted Elise at her office," Blake said stiffly, intentionally sounding royally pissed off.

"Oh, sure," Carlos said lightly. "I'm sorry. I didn't mean to disturb her, but I promised to let her know as soon as I got my hands on some information. I know she's anxious to have it."

"I think it can wait until morning," Blake replied curtly. "Call her at ScanTron. Tomorrow." He hung up the phone. The nerve of the guy, calling up and acting like he and Elise were buddy-buddies. That prick had cost them plenty, and the last thing Blake wanted was any contact with him. What the hell was going on that couldn't wait until regular business hours?

Blake picked up the newspaper, shook it with a snap, and resumed reading the sports page.

Elise came into the den carrying a basket of warm laundry, flopped down on the sofa, and began folding Junior's clean clothes. Brushing a stray curl from her forehead with the back of one hand, she looked over at Blake, who had buried his face in the paper.

She was exhausted but had to get the laundry done tonight. Tomorrow, at eight in the morning, Blake was taking Junior down to his parents' beach house on Bolivar Island. Blake planned to stick around for lunch, then head back to Houston. He and Elise would go down on Friday when Paul and Cathy arrived. After checking what Junior had packed by himself, Elise quickly realized that unless her son took more changes of clothing, Blake's mother would spend a lot of time doing laundry. Elise wanted to get Junior's suitcase packed tonight because her flight to Dallas left at seven-thirty in the morning. It was going to be one hell of a busy day and she hoped Judy

Talor was prepared for the crush of press her Latin American dignitaries were going to generate.

Elise folded Junior's favorite, the faded Cowboys T-shirt, smoothing her hand over the warm soft cloth. "Who was on the phone?" she asked.

Blake crushed the newspaper to his lap, letting his irritation flare. "It was your new buddy." He cocked his head to one side, a sarcastic smile tilting his lips.

"Who?"

"Carlos Rico."

"Really? What did he want?"

"Said he had some information for you. I told him to call you at the office tomorrow."

"What?" Elise stopped folding Junior's Power Rangers beach towel and stared at Blake. "I wish you had let me know he was on the phone. I wanted to talk to him."

"So, he'll call tomorrow."

"You know I'll be in Dallas all day. The South American delegation, remember?"

Blake shrugged and didn't answer.

His nonchalant reaction infuriated her and she was not going to let him off so easily. "Damn it, Blake," she shot back. "Why'd you do that?"

He gave her a long, level stare. "Because he shouldn't be calling you at home. It didn't sound like an earthshaking emergency. Who the hell does that guy think he is? Just because he's on TV doesn't give him license to intrude on people's lives whenever the notion strikes him."

"That's the most bizarre thing I think you've ever said, Blake. It was just a phone call. What's eating you? You're ridiculous."

"Oh? Really? You're the one who's been complaining all day about being tired and about how much you've got to do before you go to bed. You didn't have time to talk to Mother when she called earlier to discuss our plans about going down for the weekend, so naturally, I assumed you were too busy to be bothered with Rico."

"I told you I'd call your mother tomorrow, after I see what my schedule at work is going to be like this week. Don't worry. I'll make sure I can get out of the office by noon on Friday so we can get an early start."

Blake started to pull the newspaper back to his face, then stopped. "Well, I just don't want him calling here. Okay?"

Elise rolled two socks together, jammed them into the plastic basket, then snatched up a pair of red shorts. "No, I don't think it's okay. Are you out of your mind? You can't screen my calls. I know what Carlos was calling about and it was important."

"I'll bet," Blake said cryptically, rattling the pages as he returned to the paper. "What's with this sudden coziness? Calls at home? Visits to his apartment? I thought he wanted to help you *professionally*. Seems like more than helping you is on his mind."

Her mouth flew open in shock. "That's crazy, Blake! Could you give me some credit, please?" She slammed a stack of underwear into the basket, her lips pressed into a hard line. "You should hear yourself. You sound like a bully spoiling for a fight."

"I don't deny I'd welcome a good excuse to take Carlos Rico on."

"Stop it," Elise almost shouted, the memory of Carlos's mouth over hers, his fingertips on her lips, suddenly making her weak. *Oh, God,* she thought, *if Blake knew he'd kissed me, no telling what he'd say or do.*

"What do you expect me to think?"

"Nothing!" she shot back, her hands fumbling nervously with the elastic-banded waist of Junior's shorts. "So, I'd appreciate it if you didn't interfere. For your information, I left a message for Carlos earlier, asking him to get back to me tonight, *at home*, no matter how late."

Blake glared. "How am *I* supposed to know about the special arrangements the two of you concoct? You never tell me what's going on with you anymore."

"That's not true, and you know it. I've been open with you, Blake. Contrary to your suspicions, I'm not holding anything back." Elise set her teeth firmly together, her guilt fueling her anger. "When I try to talk to you, you don't listen. Your mind is stuck on that damned motorcycle lot. All you want to talk about are showroom designs and surface lot inventory. Well, frankly, I've come to the conclusion that there are more important things in life!"

"Yeah? You sure didn't think that way a few years ago."

"That was before I was unemployed and depressed and about to lose my mind."

"All because of the damage your new buddy Rico did. He humiliated you. He stopped your career in its tracks. How can you even stand to be in the same room with that creep?"

"God, don't start with that!"

"Well, *excuse* me! I thought I was being helpful. You said you had a lot to do tonight and I didn't think you wanted to spend time talking on the phone. Obviously, I was mistaken."

"Obviously, you were, but that's not the point. I was waiting for that call. He might have come across something important."

"Then call him back!" Blake shouted. "I'm sure you must have his home number."

Elise wanted to shout, *Yes, I do have his home number and when I was in his apartment, he treated me with more respect and concern than you are showing right now,* but she kept her mouth shut, so furious she began to tremble.

When she finally spoke, her voice cracked with the strain of trying to be civil. "You don't have to yell at me," she said softly. "Yes, I am busy, and yes, I am tired. But that's no reason to treat me as if I can't make decisions for myself. If it had been Lorna on the phone, you'd have told me." She slammed Junior's shorts into the laundry basket. "Wouldn't you?"

Blake cut his eyes away, looking on the verge of exploding. "Okay. Yes! I would have. But Lorna is different. Carlos Rico? No way."

"You've no right to decide whom I talk to, or when," Elise snapped. "I can just imagine how rude you were."

"You're right. I *was* rude, but I think I've got every right to be rude and I hope he got the message. I don't like him, I never will, and I hate that you've got it into your head that you can trust him."

"I'm not going to discuss this anymore." Elise stood, laundry basket in her arms. "Why are you so damned determined to use this against me? Do you want to hurt me? I swear I don't understand you anymore. People make mistakes. You make mistakes. Others forgive. That's part and parcel of what I believe is called getting on with life!"

"Some things can't be forgiven," Blake mumbled, settling deeper into his recliner. "I hope you know that the only reason he's acting so nice is to use you again. Get real, Elise. He's not thinking of anyone but himself, and you're too damn blind to see it."

"Carlos is trying to make amends so why don't you get over it? I've forgiven him, and I don't regret it."

"You will," Blake said evenly. "Trust me, Elise, you will."

"That's it," Elise said, stomping out of the room. "I'm going to bed."

"Fine," Blake said, picking up the paper, shaking it noisily as Elise headed through the kitchen toward the stairs. Calling after her, he managed to get in a last word. "If you two are going to plot and conspire, do it on your company's time, not your family's."

"Great," Elise grumbled, trudging up the staircase, wishing Blake was the one going off for two weeks at the beach. She could use some peace and quiet. Forcing herself to count to ten, she managed to calm down, then yelled over the banister to Blake. "I put that book on Texas wildflowers that I promised your mother in Junior's suitcase. Be sure she gets it."

Blake grunted his response.

Elise slammed the bedroom door, set the basket of clean clothes on the floor, then shoved it across the room with a kick. Sinking onto the bed, she lay with her face buried in the crook of her arm.

The last thing she had wanted was another argument with Blake, especially after the blowout they'd had last night when he told her about tendering his resignation. She had been caught completely unaware of his decision and they'd argued for hours, going around and around about the pros and cons of his leaving Century so soon. She'd thrown in the towel around midnight, curling into a ball on the far side of their bed, determined not to say another word.

On September first, Blake would be unemployed. It hurt terribly to have been shut out of such an important turning point in their lives, but Blake hadn't seemed to understand how it upset her. He had held his ground, refusing her suggestion that he stay on with Century until the first of the year. That Blake could have taken such a major step without discussing it with her was frightening. Was he playing payback with her for visiting Carlos's apartment without asking his permission? If that was the case, it was certainly a childish thing to do, and beyond Elise's comprehension. Couldn't he see how important her mission was?

Blake had really ticked her off last night when he started defending Paul, who had had so many jobs she couldn't count them on both hands. Paul had never sought the kind of security that Blake had latched on to early in his career, and Elise was sure that it was Paul's influence that was pushing Blake into this childish venture. A motorcycle dealership! God! She still didn't get it. And as long as she lived she'd never get on another bike again.

Elise reached down and stroked the scar on her leg, remembering the pain she'd experienced when she'd been burned long ago. She'd been young and adventurous then, trying to be a good sport. She'd always gone along with whatever Blake wanted to do, but this time he'd gone too far and she was secretly terrified about what might happen.

Darrell Grimes wiped his hands on a towel, then removed the glass vials from their stainless-steel holder. He picked up a plastic syringe and drew some of the liquid from the tube and put it under the microscope. He was glad Elise trusted him enough to let him in on what she was doing, and was relieved that he'd been able to get clearance to use the equipment at the local university research lab.

He was alone in the light-splashed room, as he'd expected to be on a Sunday evening. He fit his eye to the lens of the microscope and examined the smear on the slide, knowing the culture ought to be complete. He'd been in the lab every evening for the past week and so far had found little of significance.

He was flooded with mixed emotions as he analyzed another water sample. After a few minutes, he drew back, disappointed. Nothing.

A part of him hoped he'd find nothing. But to justify the money Elise was spending, he unconsciously wanted to prove that conducting her own tests had been worth the expense. He'd hate to tell her she'd wasted her efforts.

Why hadn't he found anything conclusive yet? And if the land around Flatwoods was severely contaminated, why hadn't ScanTron or the EPA found evidence of something more toxic than the low levels of benzene and arsenic that Justin Snyder reported?

With a sigh, Darrell settled in among the gleaming stainless-steel tubes and sparkling glass containers, and slipped another slide under the probing eye of the telescopic lens, ready to get back to work.

CHAPTER 25

The moment Elise stepped into the VIP lounge at Dallas–Fort Worth Airport, she was glad she had volunteered to make the trip, even though it had come at a stressful time. She hadn't slept well after the fight with Blake and had been up at five o'clock to fix breakfast and see him and Junior off. She'd wanted to call Carlos this morning, but with all the rushing around to get ready and make it to the airport, there hadn't been time.

It had been obvious that Blake was still upset with her, though he'd tried to act civil in front of Junior, barely brushing his lips across her cheek when he'd told her good-bye and left. He hadn't even mentioned that today was their anniversary, and this time she sure as hell didn't remind him.

And she was still angry, too, not only over the way he'd spoken to her but over his adamant refusal to admit that his adolescent attitude was much more threatening to their marriage than her working with Carlos.

Elise hated the bickering and discord that squashed her attempts to act supportive and interested, because she did want to be optimistic about the venture. Though it might turn out to be a disaster, it could wind up being the best move they'd ever made. There was no turning back now.

The VIP lounge was crowded. Elise scanned the area for Judy Talor and saw the tall blond at the rear of the room talking to a knot of uniformed men. She was wearing a severely tailored black-and-white suit and three-inch patent leather spectators that made Elise shudder and look down at her own comfortable, sensible low-heeled shoes. When Judy caught Elise's eye, she gestured her over, then resumed her discussion with a man who appeared to be a member of the airport security staff.

Elise's flight had arrived only thirty minutes before the private jet carrying Aloyo, Turriba, and Ponto was scheduled to touch down. Security was tight, causing a delay in disembarking from her plane and passing through extra security checkpoints. Now she had little time to go over the dignitaries' schedule with Judy.

Elise gave Judy a firm handshake and was not surprised by the less than enthusiastic welcome she received. This was the second time she'd met Judy, who had been with ScanTron for seven or eight years. Rumor had it that Judy had believed Theresa White's job would be hers, and had been upset when Elise had been chosen to fill the coveted slot.

Well, Elise mused as Judy turned away from her to confer quickly with another security guard, she was here at John Farren's request, an emissary of goodwill from headquarters, and she'd be here all day whether Judy wanted her to stay or not.

Farren's suggestion that Elise greet Aloyo, since she'd gotten to know him during his hospital stay, was a personal touch he hoped would pay off, keeping ScanTron's contracts with Mexico in force in the face of great competition.

"What's already in place?" Elise asked.

Judy finished her discussion with the airport staffer and turned her attention on Elise. "Thank God that's settled," she said. "The stupid jerk." She swept her tousled golden hair off her neck. "He was trying to block us from meeting the group on the tarmac. Something about a group of Mexican nationals who've been protesting outside the passenger pickup area. Don't worry, it's all straightened out."

"Good. The last thing we need is an airport demonstration."

"Well, each man has a personal security guard accompanying him, and they'll ride in limos with bulletproof glass." She checked her clipboard. "There will be twelve people in the welcoming party." Judy ran a bright red nail down her list of names. "You'll stand between the mayor and a representative of Trenton Properties, the company that manages the Paradiso Ranch. It's the first stop on their schedule tomorrow. When Aloyo steps out of the plane, he'll come over to the receiving line first; the others will follow. They'll shake hands, maybe make a few personal remarks, but no meeting with the press." Judy's brisk tone made it clear that she was running the show. "That will be later this afternoon."

"At the Fairmont?"

"Of course," Judy shot back. "And, before you ask, yes. Aloyo's been informed that you now work for ScanTron, and he is pleased that you will be here to welcome him back to Texas."

"Fine," Elise replied, unsure why Judy's voice grated on her nerves.

"After everyone has finished with the greetings," Judy went on, "they'll be taken to the hotel. Late lunch. One o'clock at the Fortune Club."

"Beef's on the menu, I guess."

"Absolutely. This is our opportunity to shine," Judy said, smiling cynically. "Then, this evening, they'll attend a private showing of the Roving Texans art exhibit at the Dallas Museum, followed by a taped interview with Paul Whitten."

"Paul Whitten?" Elise was impressed that the award-winning anchor was going to do it himself. "Is he coming to the hotel to do it?"

"Right."

"I wish I could hang around for that, but I've got to get back to Houston right after the luncheon. Pressing matters at home," Elise said.

"Well, try to catch the interview tonight. It'll be fed to KPLT in Houston. Might make the six o'clock. Check it if you're home."

"I will," Elise said, making up her mind to get home early and be there when Blake got back from dropping Junior. She wanted to make up, put the argument behind them, and forget the hurtful things they'd said to each other. Why not start tonight?

I'll pick up a strawberry cheesecake and a great bottle of wine, she thought. Maybe she'd make chicken cacciatore and Italian antipasto, Blake's favorite. Pamper him a little. Make love. It had been a week since she'd been in his arms, and for them that was far too long. After all, it was their anniversary, even though he'd obviously forgotten. She usually had to start dropping hints a week before to remind him, but now she planned to sit back and wait to see if he would recall the day on his own. Probably not, she realized, wondering why she suddenly expected things to change.

As mad as he'd made her last night, she was even more miserable today. Whenever they allowed their disagreements to simmer, she was left on rocky ground. They had better find a way to pull things together, and with Junior away for two weeks, it was the opportune time to concentrate on getting their marriage back on track.

"I understand that Farren's been nervous about the renewal of the Mexican contracts," Judy said, interrupting Elise's mental wandering.

"At close to two million dollars wouldn't you be nervous?"

Judy smiled sweetly, knowingly, eyes riveted on the bank of floor-to-ceiling windows overlooking the runway. She had a perpetual expression of smug assurance on her face that annoyed Elise. She was beginning to feel relieved that she'd only have to work with Judy for one day.

When the much anticipated 747 touched down Judy announced brightly, "They're here."

Squaring her shoulders, Elise smoothed her pale blue skirt and tugged at the hem of its matching jacket, hoping she didn't look too wrinkled, but in ninety-plus-degree temperatures, it was hard to stay looking fresh.

Rubbing her hands together, she tried to relax, surprised at how nervous she was. Providing security for high-profile people was always nerve-racking, and definitely chancy. Anything could go wrong in the space of an instant. "Let's hope the curiosity seekers, nutcases, and fanatics stayed home," she told her colleague.

"That's why we've been hired, remember?" Judy quipped, then lowered her voice to a whisper. "Can you believe the Brazilians dumped an extra twenty-five thousand in ScanTron's coffers for to-day's *enhancement* of Turriba's private security?" Judy shook her head. "That included a background check on each member of the Fair-mont's staff, from front desk to the dishwashers in the kitchen and an inch-by-inch search of the hotel rooms to be sure nothing had been compromised."

"Compromised?" Elise remarked. "Like bugged?"

"I guess so," Judy said, lifting a brow. "Hey, he may be a little paranoid, but it's good business for ScanTron."

"That's true," Elise replied, following Judy out of the VIP lounge toward the exit stairs that would take them out to the plane.

Once the entourage arrived, Elise shook hands with each man, reintroducing herself to Tomás Aloyo, who was extremely pleased to see her again and to know that she was now head of media relations for ScanTron. Elise chatted with him for a moment, assuring him that he was in good hands, wishing him success on his tour of Texas.

When he smiled broadly, bowing slightly in appreciation, Elise knew the extra effort it had taken for her to be there had had exactly the effect John Farren had anticipated.

The men were whisked into limos to be driven to the Fairmont Hotel where three floors had been cleared and sealed off for them and their attendants. Elise caught a ride to the hotel with Judy, sud-denly ravenous and ready for lunch.

It was five-thirty when Elise's plane touched down in Houston and she was numb. Chatting with the VIPs, helping Judy coordinate the surprising number of reporters who had shown up, and double-checking security-related details had sapped her. She hurried off the plane, into the shuttle to her car, then slipped inside her Volvo and rested her head against the back of the seat.

Thank God that was over. The visit was starting out smoothly. She checked the clock on the dash, disappointed that she would miss the six o'clock news. Maybe Channel 51 would run it at ten, she thought, psyching herself up to fight rush hour traffic.

Too exhausted to even think about cooking, she ditched her plans for chicken cacciatore. They'd go out, she decided. Blake would be tired after the long round-trip drive to Galveston and the ferry ride over to Bolivar Island, and would probably not want to get dressed up and go out to a fancy place. A quiet dinner at The Bistro would be good, she thought. It was casual and not too far from the house. The perfect atmosphere for them to talk and actually communicate for a change.

As soon as she paid the parking fee and drove out of the airport garage, Elise picked up her car phone and dialed Carlos at the studio. "My husband said you called last night."

"Right. Sorry if my calling you at home caused any problems. I sensed that Blake was not happy to hear my voice."

"Don't worry about him. Your call didn't cause any problems," she lied, still astonished by Blake's jealous reaction. "He was just tired. Working too hard, and I had an early assignment in Dallas today. I'm on my way home right now. What's going on?"

"I got the scoop on Puro."

"Yeah? Tell me."

"It was buried under a slew of dummy companies and not easy to get to, but it was just as I thought. The controlling shares of Puro are held by people named Vargas."

"Interesting," Elise replied, fascinated at the way things were falling into place. Hooking up with Carlos had been a good idea after all.

"Right," Carlos agreed, "but that bit of information is not as interesting as a call I got this morning."

"From?"

"Yusef Kirk. He's on his way over here now. I don't know exactly what he's got, but he assures me it's hot enough to put on the air, and I promised him I'd give him airtime if and when he had something new and interesting to say that was backed by fact." Carlos paused, then asked, "Can you swing by here before heading home? Yusef was somewhat mysterious, but he told me he's gotten ahold of something he calls 'explosive.' Plus, he specifically asked me to invite you to sit in on our conversation."

"I think he has a flair for the dramatic," Elise said, grimacing as she made a left turn. As far as she was concerned, Kirk was flashy, pushy, and out to profit for himself. All she wanted to do was go home. "I don't think so, Carlos. I'm whipped."

"Well, Kirk said he is about to go public with information that will have a negative impact on property owners in Flatwoods. That includes you, and he thought you'd like to hear it first."

It took forty minutes for Elise to inch through clogged traffic and get from Intercontinental Airport to the KPLT studio on the Southwest Freeway. When she walked into Carlos's office, his eyes connected briefly with hers and she swallowed hard, hating the constriction that tightened around her heart. His soft beige suit and pale green tie enhanced the emerald hue of his eyes, and she floundered for a moment, fighting the memory of him standing in the doorway of his apartment, a quirky smile on his face as he'd brushed her lips with his fingertip. The heat of that moment flooded back in a dizzy, humiliating rush.

Yusef Kirk was already there, looking businesslike in a dark navy suit with matching vest that was set with pearl gray buttons. After greeting him and settling into a chair in front of Carlos's desk, she listened closely to what the attorney had to say.

"My contacts at the Tide County Administration Office have confirmed my suspicions." Kirk paused, glancing from Carlos to Elise, then down at the spiral notebook on his lap. "Plans are moving forward, quite rapidly, to have Flatwoods condemned."

"Condemned?" The word flew from Elise's mouth. There hadn't been sufficient fire damage for the county to take such dramatic action. Other than the devastation done to the houses on Thornhill Road that had been in the line of the fire, the remainder of the homes in the neighborhood had suffered little damage from water or smoke. "Are you talking about the entire community?" she asked, unable to envision such a disaster.

"Eventually," Yusef said. "Right now the plan is to condemn, then demolish the abandoned houses first." He smiled wryly at Elise. "And I understand you are now the owner of one of those empty houses."

"That's right, but it's not abandoned."

"Then you must be aware of the fact that close to thirty percent of the properties in Flatwoods are now unoccupied. Absentee landlords are not maintaining their properties, so the county considers the houses as safety and health hazards. The records show that all proper notices have been posted and the county has the legal right to move its bulldozer into the area."

Elise stared at Carlos. "Can this really happen?"

Carlos nodded. "I checked it out."

Yusef continued. "If fifty percent of the structures can be officially condemned, the rest of the residents will be offered cash settlements to move out. I've seen this happen before. People move out quickly once money starts floating around."

"The entire community would vanish," Elise said, stunned by what she'd just been told.

"And it will happen unless some kind of action is taken. Soon," Carlos warned.

"Good Lord," Elise groaned. "Who's behind this?"

"One guess," Carlos prompted.

"The Puro Corporation?" Elise replied.

"None other," Carlos said, explaining to Yusef who the Vargas family was and the information his contact had unearthed. "They control this huge conglomerate of different businesses."

"Exactly what kind of company is Puro?" Yusef asked.

"Oh, it has controlling interest in a variety of businesses. Real estate, restaurants, hotel food service, shopping centers. It took a great deal of investigation to link Puro to a dozen or so real estate companies." Carlos lifted a palm toward Elise. "As I told you earlier, the Vargas family is in control."

Elise's jaw tightened. "This is scary."

"Precisely."

"But why condemn Flatwoods?" She faced Yusef. "What do they plan to do with the land?"

"That's the kicker," Yusef replied. "I came upon a projected land use proposal that had been filed with the county years ago."

"By?" Elise prompted.

Yusef tipped his head directly at her, a slightly triumphant smile on his lips. "ScanTron Security International."

Elise gasped. "ScanTron?" She wanted to call him a liar but couldn't. He was clearly not making this up. "What's in this proposal?"

"It's a standard notice of first offering. It states that if the tract of land we know as Flatwoods should ever come onto the market as an entire block for sale, ScanTron gets first bid on the purchase."

"Who submitted this notice?"

"John Farren," Yusef said.

"Well," she said, then added in a halfhearted attempt to defend her employer, "sounds like good business forecasting to me. I doubt it has anything to do with Puro Corporation's plans." Nervously, she glanced at Carlos. "Farren told me the company might expand. I'm sure it's been under discussion for years."

"What happens next?" Carlos pressed Yusef, anxious to get to the heart of the matter.

"Tide County law provides a method by which the public can challenge the demolition of condemned property. If the residents can get five hundred signatures on a petition *and* demonstrate that the community is able to rehabilitate the area, an injunction could be ordered."

"That usually doesn't work unless someone is waiting in the wings with a lot of cash to bring the properties up to county building code standards," Carlos said.

"True," Yusef agreed, "and as you know the people of Flatwoods are modest folk, without the financial resources to take that route."

Elise sat tensely, absorbing Yusef's prediction, trying to put it into perspective. There was nothing strange about a company wanting to expand. But did ScanTron have any connection to Puro? Could the company she worked for be a part of the conspiracy that obviously *did* exist?

"Carlos," she said. "Were there any names on the board of directors of Puro that were local? Even familiar?"

"No, I'm way ahead of you on that. No names I could connect to ScanTron, and I checked the list carefully."

Turning to Yusef, Elise asked, "Is it too late to do anything? How can we slow the process down?"

Yusef grinned, apparently glad to be in a position to orchestrate the solution. "It's not too late, but we must move fast. For the homes that are already condemned, we can petition the court for an injunction to halt the demolition . . . if someone agrees to post a good faith bond."

"How much?" Elise asked.

"At least a couple of thousand dollars," Yusef supplied.

"I'll do it," she said impulsively.

"You sure?" Carlos asked.

Elise nodded, then added, "But keep my name out of it."

"An anonymous donation?" Yusef said, a half grin raising the corner of his mouth.

"Exactly," Elise replied.

Yusef's half smile turned into a grimace. "That's fine, but the bond won't mean much unless we can gather enough signatures on a petition to make a judge take notice and buy us some time."

"Would it work?" Elise asked.

"I think so, with an aggressive, visible demonstration that would attract attention from outside the county. And if the media"—he paused to level a serious gaze on Carlos—"covers the residents' protest. Exposure like that could influence some wealthy developer to reach out and finance the salvation of the neighborhood. That's where you can really help, Mr. Rico. You touch quite a few people through your show. Will you put me on the air?"

"You got it," Carlos answered without hesitation.

"Thank you," Yusef said firmly, reaching to shake Carlos's hand. "Now. I have recruited some volunteers and we are going to start canvassing the area tonight, gathering signatures."

"I'll follow you with my camera crew," Carlos said.

"Good idea." Yusef arched a brow at Elise. "I hope you'll come along, too, Ms. Jeffries. You're a property owner. Your presence and voice in the matter would carry a lot of weight."

At the moment, Elise had no answer for Yusef. She stared blankly at him as her mind snapped back to Blake, to Junior, to the responsibility she had to her family. To her employer! Her blood raced at the thought that ScanTron might sanction the destruction of Flatwoods, yet she knew better than to go on record, or on TV for heaven's sake, in protest of her company's plans for expansion.

"I don't know about that," she hedged, rising to go to the window, turning her back on Yusef and Carlos, who, seeing her uneasiness, began discussing the focus of the television coverage.

Staring into the still-hot evening, Elise watched shimmering heat waves rise from the asphalt parking lot and the reflection of the setting sun on the brightly colored cars. She tried to corral her thoughts, never before having felt so torn. She really wanted to picket and protest and gather signatures alongside the people of her hometown. She wanted them to see her involvement and understand the depth of her commitment. Her parents would probably be out there knocking on doors, along with the old-timers who had been their neighbors. And if Damita were still alive, she would surely be there, too.

How can I stay out of this? Elise wondered, certain that joining the ranks of Yusef's volunteers would be an absolute death sentence as far as her career with ScanTron was concerned. She loved her job and wanted to keep it, and Blake was counting on her.

She balled her fingers into fists, anxious but unable to make a decision. The situation was far too complicated, and the timing was not right. The whole affair might blow up in her face. What she needed was time to think.

I won't act impulsively, she vowed, the sting of Blake's resignation still sharp. She'd been furious with him for what he did—no way would she do the same to him. She could level with Farren, put her worries on the table. By asking for his opinion, she might be able to maneuver him into telling her the truth. The last time she'd been unsure about what to do, taking it to Farren had helped immensely.

He was in her corner, he respected her opinion, and he understood her feelings of loyalty to Flatwoods. Surely he'd be able to help her again.

Turning back to face Yusef and Carlos, she said in a leaden voice, "Sorry. I'd better not get involved. Not yet, anyway. I'd like to discuss this with my boss and my husband."

Yusef laughed, shaking his head. "And I thought you were a sister who cared."

"Can't you see what a spot this puts me in?" she shot back, ticked off by his cutting put-down. She felt tangled in a web of demands and didn't need Yusef laying a guilt trip on her. She was doing a pretty good job by herself.

"I had even convinced myself that I'd misjudged you," Yusef said.

Elise wanted to slap his face. How dare he judge her in the first place?

Yusef stood, attaché case in his hand, haughty in his demeanor. "I'm truly sorry you are choosing not to join your people at a time when your involvement might be the key to helping them save their community."

"I'm not deserting my people! And who the hell are you to pass judgment on me?" Shaking, she withdrew, lowering her voice. "I need to be careful. Responsible. You seem to forget that some people might even consider me as part of the problem. I won't let you set me up. You want me to go out there and be crucified, don't you? You want to embarrass me? No way, Mr. Kirk."

"God, you're hopeless," Yusef said. "The only person who can embarrass you is you, Ms. Jeffries. Think about that." He went to the door and stood calmly assessing her, one hand on the knob. When he jerked his gaze from her and looked back at Carlos, he said matter-of-factly, "Meet me at the corner of Thornhill Road and Highway Eight at seven, and thanks for your interest in this tragic situation. It's people like *you*, Mr. Rico, who will truly make a difference. I appreciate your kind of support." Then he opened the door and left.

Elise was stunned. She felt like a traitor, the villainess in a tragic play, while Carlos was coming off looking like the hero. Snatching her purse from atop Carlos's desk, she gave him an angry stare, then hurried out the door, almost running to her car.

Damn it! What was she supposed to do? Sacrifice everything to make Yusef Kirk happy? Well, she'd wipe that sneer off his face. Somehow. She'd show the people of Flatwoods that she cared, and she'd do it without making a public spectacle of herself. But how? she worried, climbing into her company car.

Inching toward home in bumper-to-bumper traffic, Elise's spirits flagged. Then a thought came to her that nearly made her smile. Picking up the car phone, she telephoned Darrell Grimes.

CHAPTER 26

Darrell Grimes focused on the single tube of fluorescent light above his head, the only bright spot in the building. He rubbed the back of his neck, trying to relieve the knot of tension that had gathered between his shoulder blades. The sound of a cricket chirping somewhere in the cavernous catalog storefront creaked loudly, and Darrell lowered his eyes once more to the flat blank screen of his computer monitor.

He was alone. Pete, Bill, and Garland had left promptly at six, with Al following fifteen minutes later. With the excitement of the explosion now behind them, and most of their customers brought up to date, the workload Darrell shared with his coworkers was light enough to allow them to keep bankers' hours. It had never been like this before. In the past, when the staff was busy double-checking orders, preparing products for shipment, and finalizing new designs, Al's team never left the complex until seven-thirty or eight. There had been times when Darrell, so engrossed in a new system he was trying to perfect, would stay at his desk long into the night.

Darrell looked at the neat stack of papers on Bill Stokes's desk, and the lack of folders in Pete's in-box. He realized how much things had changed. Would ScanTron's coastal plant ever get back to normal? he wondered, drumming his fingers on the edge of his desk, impatient for something to show up on the screen.

Darrell had been pleased and excited when his contact in Washington had called earlier in the day; now he was just plain nervous. The background data and results of the EPA tests run at Flatwoods should have been downloaded into Darrell's computer an hour ago, at exactly seven o'clock central time. So far, nothing had been sent to him.

Darrell still could not believe what his contact had turned up. The local investigation by the EPA had discovered Zephron in the soil and water samples taken after the fire. Zephron, a pervasive, silent killer, had only been reported in the United States once—several years ago in a tiny west Texas town that had been literally wiped off the map by the lethal gas.

Darrell remembered that incident, had followed it closely, fascinated by the security-breaching implications in the story. Though the government had hushed up the discovery of Zephron in Texas, Darrell remained convinced that the unexplained appearance of the rare deadly gas had been a result of a bungled security test.

As soon as his contact revealed what Justin Snyder was onto, Darrell began researching Zephron. Earlier today he'd found information on the Internet describing the toxic gas, and learned that Zephron had been used recently as a chemical warfare agent by Middle Eastern terrorists.

The theory was that the victims, a Bedouin settlement deep in the Arabian Desert, had been exposed to Zephron when tainted barrels of cooking oil and lamp fuel had been brought into the town by an undercover trader. When the poisonous fumes had drifted from the stoves and lamps of those living in the remote desert camp, over half of the unsuspecting souls died in a twenty-four-hour period.

His on-line research with the *Chemical Journal* had also turned up grim photos of the victims of Zephron poisoning. Their bodies looked hauntingly alive, slumped over in their tents or lying on the ground in the open, frozen in time. The poisonous gas acted swiftly, catching its victims completely off guard, propelling them into death's embrace without pain, suffering, or fear. Darrell shook off the recollection and picked up the phone to call his wife.

"Marci?" he began.

"Don't tell me you're still at the office," Marci Grimes said, exasperated.

"Yeah, sorry, honey, but I'm almost done. The report I'm waiting for ought to be coming through in a few minutes. But I might not be home in time for us to make our reservation." He toyed with a shiny string of paper clips, bracing himself for her reply. It was the second time this week he'd canceled their plans to visit the new Italian restaurant at Stewart Beach, but he knew he could not leave until the information he was waiting for had been safely transferred into his computer.

"I'm starving, Darrell. Maybe we ought to forget about going out. Wait until the weekend."

"No," he said. "I won't be long, I promise." He focused on the screen, willing the data to fill it, knowing he didn't dare leave his desk until either the information had come through or he'd heard from his contact in Washington that it would not be downloaded tonight. Marci understood, she always did. She seldom complained, yet he didn't take her for granted, and had never allowed his dedication to his work to affect his commitments to her. But this was different. Elise was counting on him. In fact, he was so excited about the work he was doing, he had decided to waive the cost of his research and charge Elise only for the lab time and equipment he'd had to rent.

"Okay, I'll wait, but I'm on the verge of eating leftover spaghetti," Marci said. "Try to get finished as soon as you can. Don't you stay there all night like you did on Tuesday," Marci warned, then added, "Oh, Elise Jeffries called."

"When?"

"About forty-five minutes ago."

"Did she say what she wanted?"

"Not exactly. Said she'd met with that environmental lawyer, Yusef Kirk, and wanted to tell you what he's got going on. Said for you to call her tonight, no matter how late."

"That's my plan, as soon as this data comes in."

Elise put the jar of mustard back in the refrigerator, took her ham sandwich into the den, and pressed the channel tuner to 51, Houston's twenty-four-hour local news station. She found herself turning to 51 more and more often as her hours at work and erratic schedule prevented her from catching the news at six or even at ten.

She took a bite of her hastily prepared dinner, too tired and too angry to care what she ate, since Blake obviously didn't care enough about her to come home and make an attempt at celebrating their anniversary together. And to think, only a few hours ago, she'd been planning on cooking his favorite meal. What a foolish idea.

In the blur of repressed tears and the nudge of a lurking migraine, she replayed in her mind again the message he'd left on her answering machine.

"Decided to stay at the beach until the end of the week. You can catch a ride down with Cathy and Paul on Friday. Call me tonight when you get in."

"I don't think so," she mumbled, as mad about his impulsive decision not to return tonight as she was about his cavalier attitude toward her—and his job. "I guess I wouldn't be worried about hurrying home, either, if I only had a few weeks left on the job." If Blake preferred his parents' beach house to his own home, and their company to hers, he could stay there forever, for all she cared.

Swallowing the painful disappointment that lodged in her throat, she picked up her sandwich and took another bite. Grimacing, she grabbed her iced tea and gulped down half the glass.

She was pissed off, lonely, and discouraged. Eating a dry sandwich alone in front of the TV on her anniversary was not the way she had hoped to spend the evening. But it was clear that Blake didn't give a damn about her, their marriage, or the problems she was facing.

What had happened to the Blake she loved and trusted and had always been so sure of? How had the world they'd fought so hard to hold together become so twisted and selfish so quickly?

It seemed as if nothing went smoothly anymore. One of them was always either stalking around in stony silence or blowing up in frustration. How could they allow such petty selfishness to drive them apart? And who was at fault? she wondered, trying to think back to what she might have done to make things better. All Elise knew for certain was that Blake's decision to stay away was only going to make matters worse.

Rubbing her temples, Elise tried to think, but tears welled in her eyes and spilled over, shattering the fragile hold she had managed to maintain on her slippery emotions. It hurt too much to think about straightening out the mess they were in, and she silently cursed Blake for taking the coward's way out by simply staying away. He could have cared enough about her feelings to come home and make an attempt at resolving their problems.

Elise ran her fingers through her hair, lifting it from her neck, wishing Blake were sitting beside her now so she could tell him about her conversation with Yusef Kirk. The memory of his nasty remarks was giving her a headache, and she was beginning to regret her impulsive commitment of thousands of dollars for the bond. Well, it was her money, and the only way, it seemed, for her to make a contribution. She could spend her inheritance any way she pleased, but in the end, she knew she'd have to square the decision only with herself, no matter what anyone said.

"I just want my life back the way it used to be," she whispered, the memory of making love to Blake on the old beach blanket filling her with desire. The ache of missing him eased over her and she almost reached for the phone but stopped herself. He had made a choice and she wasn't going to beg him to come home. But how in the world, she wondered, could he possibly enjoy himself with their marriage edging close to disaster?

If Blake had been at home right then, she would have tempted him into the bedroom, where she'd relax in his arms as he massaged her shoulders, kissed her neck, and helped her banish the awful pounding that was roaring inside her head. They had fought before, but never like this, and the stress of it was making her sick.

She was miserable and wanted to be held, loved, and made to feel that their marriage wasn't lost. With so many complicated decisions to be made, more than ever, Elise needed to talk to someone who cared enough to listen.

Blake had deserted her for the company of his parents.

Lorna was busy working at one of her shops tonight.

And Damita. God, Elise thought, *I still can't believe she's gone.*

Panic struck, and she groped in her mind to find a way to fight off the flat, black cruelty of Damita's untimely death that threatened to crash down like a roaring tidal wave. It had been four weeks since the funeral and still Elise could hardly grasp the truth of her loss. The illness, the surgery, and the burial of her friend had been too quick, too unexpected, and too damned permanent.

Fear crowded Elise's heart, pushing aside her preoccupation with Blake's disappointing behavior. She would never have Damita to laugh with, cry with, or to complain to again, and the tragedy of it increased her emptiness. Blinking back her grief, Elise vowed not to drift into the melancholic self-pity that would settle over her like a damp, thick fog if she let it.

The situation with Yusef Kirk was a powder keg simmering with a short, lighted fuse. Talking to Farren, leveling with him, might be her only alternative. But no matter what he said, she knew in her heart that she wanted to support Yusef's campaign to keep Flatwoods from being razed, even if it meant testing her future with ScanTron. She had to take a stand, didn't she?

Shoving her plate away, Elise leaned back on the sofa, propping her feet on the bleached oak table. She wiped a rush of tears from her eyes. Why hadn't Blake come home? He could have met her halfway, shown her how important this day was to him. Staying at the beach for a week with Junior, leaving her to deal with her troubles alone, was an underhanded and mean thing to do.

"I wonder when he packed his clothes," she murmured, realizing that he must have planned all along to retreat from their problems. Pulling her feet off the table, she plunked them to the floor. "I hope he gets stung by jellyfish or gets a bad case of sunburn and has to stay in bed the whole week."

She reached for her sandwich, then stopped. Her appetite was gone. All she wanted was for Blake to walk through the door and put his arms around her and tell her she didn't have to do this alone. But he wasn't coming and he wouldn't help, so she'd better decide what to do.

Slumping back on the sofa, she stared glumly at the animated commercial that was flashing on the television screen, and when the telephone rang, it made her stomach tighten. She grabbed it, praying it might be Blake, but when Darrell Grimes's voice came to her, she cleared her mind of self-pitying thoughts to listen to what he had to say.

"The report just came in. Elise, this is serious."

"Tell me," she said, snatching a pad and pen.

"It's long, and complicated," Darrell replied. "You have a fax at home?"

"Yes. 555-9049."

"Good. I'm sending it now; then I'm getting out of here. Read it, carefully. I'll call you tomorrow from home."

The phone went dead in Elise's hand, but she hurried upstairs to stand beside the fax machine in Blake's study.

She read the pages as they slipped through, horrified by the graphic details of the Permian Basin incident. "The deadly gas is created when a mixture of low-grade crude oil and a bacterium called *cyphis bacillus* is burned at high temperatures for long periods of time. The bacteria-laced crude emits fumes that are extremely hazardous, depending on the duration of exposure and the intensity of the fire." Elise sank into Blake's leather wing chair, draping her legs over the arm, mesmerized by the report.

"Importation of the bacterium into the United States is controlled by the FDA. It has been known to occur naturally, and occasionally does, in remote jungles of South America and swampy forests of Southeast Asia where high humidity, rotting vegetation, and warm constant temperatures provide ideal circumstances for the bacterium to flourish."

Apparently the FDA had refused access to the highly toxic *cyphis bacillus* by an American construction company that requested a permit to import it from a Brazilian research lab. A Brazilian company had used Zephron to clear a tract of land in the Amazon Jungle of fer-de-lance and other deadly reptiles in preparation for the construction of a government research facility.

In the case of both the Bedouin and the Permian Basin incidents, where the landscapes were dry and parched, the authorities believed the poison had been man-made and deliberately introduced into the fuel oils used by unsuspecting victims. One theory was that terrorists had been testing the chemical in order to breach security at some other location in the Middle East, or perhaps the United States. There were no follow-up reports on that incident, and the file ended abruptly.

"Incredible," she murmured, rubbing her forehead, suddenly feeling warm. Zephron was deadly, illegal, and if in the wrong hands, could easily be used to destroy a nation, let alone a small town.

She propped her chin on balled fingers, methodically thinking things through. Had someone managed to concoct the hideous poison that might have caused the rash of illness now sweeping Flatwoods? Or had the conditions necessary for the creation of Zephron coalesced naturally in that area, seeping from the ground to burn in the recent conflagration? The EPA tests proved its existence, but how did it get there, and, most of all, why was no one told?

Slowly, Elise got out of the chair. This was big. Obviously big. *The government had better have a damn good reason for withholding this from the public,* she thought, going into her bedroom to put the fax into her briefcase. She wanted to call Darrell and talk but was too tired. Besides, what could they accomplish tonight? It could wait until tomorrow morning, she decided. And after talking to Darrell, the next call she planned to make was to Justin Snyder's office.

Returning downstairs, Elise began shutting off lights, preparing to retire, paying little attention to the voice of the anchorman on TV who was finishing up a story about the robbery of a local bank. But when he segued into the next segment of news, Judy Talor's frightened voice and pale face burst onto the screen. Elise stopped in the center of the den, fingertips to her mouth, eyes wide. Grabbing the remote, she pressed hard on the volume control button to hear what Judy was talking about.

"Was anyone hurt?" the reporter asked, thrusting the microphone toward Judy's trembling lips. She was windblown and disheveled. The jacket of the tailored black-and-white suit that Elise had admired earlier in the day was now smudged with dirt and hanging open, as if she'd been shoved around.

"No, thank God," Judy answered breathlessly, her eyes flitting from the reporter's face to the frantic crush of police, security guards, and anxious people milling around on the crowded sidewalk. "It was chaos. Pure chaos. I was knocked to the floor in the panic, but the security guards got to me and pulled me out before the bomb exploded."

"I understand they located the source of the device."

"Yes." Judy exhaled deeply, pulling herself together. She wiped her cheeks with shaking fingers, attempting to repair her appearance, but only spread the dirt, making streaks on her face. "The bomb squad found the metal case it had been in. Some kind of insulated box. They took it away."

"Who brought the bomb into the press conference?"

"A woman," Judy replied. "She bypassed the security at the door by posing as a hotel staffer and got into the press room by using the serving passage. I understand she told the kitchen staff that she was attached to Minister Aloyo's group, so they let her through." Judy frowned. "We can thank the ScanTron security team for getting suspicious. You see, they had done background checks on all of the hotel staff before the ministers arrived, and didn't remember seeing her. So they detected something fishy about her when she came in, and immediately cleared the room."

"It was a small explosion, wasn't it?"

"Yes, but at close range it could have done quite a bit of damage. Like those letter bombs. The Unabomber, you know? That woman was serious. Dead set on hurting Minister Aloyo."

The reporter blinked rapidly several times, then asked, "What more can you tell us about the suspect?"

"She strode into the room, went straight to Minister Aloyo, and put the box on the table in front of him. Then she spat and started cursing, shouting. I don't speak Spanish, so I don't know exactly what she said, but a member of our security staff said the woman was raving about Aloyo being responsible for several deaths in her family. She accused the minister of being responsible for poisoning her sister and her brother-in-law."

"Where was this supposed to have happened?"

"I don't know. But when she came in, the minister had just begun to talk about the progress he feels his government is making with farmers in a remote part of Mexico along the Guatemalan border. That's when she stormed in." Judy shook her mane of tangled blond hair, then smoothed it into place. "It's under investigation now."

The reporter unrolled a piece of paper he'd been holding in one hand. "I understand a group of Mexican nationalists were marching outside the hotel during the press conference." He showed the paper to Judy, then angled it toward the camera. "Several flyers like this were found on the sidewalk and strewn around in the lobby. What do you think they mean?"

Elise froze. On the leaflet was a big black circle, and in the middle of it was a red-and-green parrot with a long colorful tail. Beneath it were the words *Su aceite mata*. Elise dropped to her knees in front of the TV and stared.

"I don't know what that is," Judy said tightly, shuddering. "It was awful in there, I'm just so relieved and grateful that our security team responded quickly. A real tragedy was avoided here tonight."

"Will Minister Aloyo continue with his scheduled tour of Texas?"

"Yes, as far as I know, he will. He is fine, and he's cooperating with the authorities, right now. He will leave tomorrow morning, as scheduled, to visit the Paradiso Ranch."

The reporter pulled away from Judy and looked into the camera. "So, for viewers joining us late, a distraught woman interrupted the press conference of several Latin American dignitaries with a bomb threat here at the Fairmont Hotel. The bomb exploded after the room was evacuated, and no one was seriously injured. The woman, whose identity is still unknown, is in police custody at the Dallas

County jail. The Mexican foreign minister, Tomás Aloyo, is unharmed, as are his colleagues on this tour of Texas. I'm Paul Whitten, KJJD, reporting live from the Fairmont Hotel in Dallas.''

Elise placed a hand to her chest, stunned. A wave of apprehension gripped her as the image of the brilliantly feathered parrot hung in her mind. Her Spanish was not great, but she knew enough to translate the words on that leaflet: *Your oil kills.* She also knew that she'd seen that black oval with the bird in the center before, and it hadn't been on a piece of paper. She jumped up from the couch and headed into the garage.

The sound of Elise's ringing telephone was lost to the thump and crash of books and papers spilling onto the floor as she emptied the heavy old box. Pulled from beneath the clutter of Blake's camping gear, gardening tools, and stacks of *National Geographic* magazines, the crate was battered and scarred but still intact. It had sat unopened since she and Blake had moved into the house, though she'd always meant to bring it inside, sort the contents, and decide what was worth holding on to and what could be tossed, but she'd never had the time to get to it. Now she was glad, because if her hunch was right, what she was looking for ought to be stuck between the stiff black pages of the photo album she slipped from beneath her high school yearbook.

Squatting on the floor beside Blake's precious Harley, Elise opened the book, carefully examining the faded photos that were pasted in her childhood album.

A dog-eared picture fluttered into her lap. It was small, brittle, and deeply creased. Elise smoothed out the wrinkles, then moved to stand under the single overhead light shining in the dark garage.

"I thought so," she murmured, scrutinizing the faces of four children standing together in the front yard of a house on the street where she had been born. There was Damita, huge brown eyes dominating her face, her ruddy hair flying loose. And there was Mary Ellen Shafer—hair neatly braided and tied with ribbons as it always had been, even when she set off for college. And finally, there was Danny Roker, Elise's first boyfriend, holding her hand, a devilish smile on his round face.

The scene took her back to those carefree summer days when she and her playmates had drifted through the dusty narrow streets of Flatwoods, going in and out of one another's houses, playing marbles, jacks, or jumping double Dutch. But it was not the nostalgic black-and-white photograph of childhood friends that most intrigued Elise, it was the tall metal barrel on the porch of the house in the background.

The round container stood about four feet high, with two welded seams through its middle. There was a large black oval painted on the front; inside was a parrot. Elise touched the symbol, recalling how vivid the colors of the exotic bird had been, remembering that the barrel had always been on Danny's front porch. His father, a shade tree mechanic, had stored his tools in it, and the day the photo had been taken, Danny's mother had emptied it, scoured it, and filled it with water to float apples for bobbing at Danny's seventh birthday party.

Where had the barrel come from? It must once have contained some type of oil, but how had it turned up in Flatwoods? Would her mother possibly know? Or any of the old-timers still living around Flatwoods? Elise shoved the photo into her shirt pocket, snapped off the light, and headed into the house. Tomorrow she'd show it to her mother and maybe the Robins twins.

CHAPTER 27

Elise tapped the red button on her telephone. She wanted to press it, buzz through to John Farren's private line, and ask him to squeeze her into his busy schedule, but she feared the consequences of making such a move. Pulling her hand away, she picked up the styrofoam cup on her desk and sipped. Staring into the dark brown liquid, she thought of all the reasons why she should level with her boss about what she now knew and all the reasons why she should keep her mouth shut.

Disappointed by Farren's lack of follow-through, Elise swiveled in her chair, making a half circle before getting up to pace the room. Should she confront him with Yusef Kirk's findings, express her frustration at his inability to get test results, or keep quiet and, quite possibly, keep her job? This could be the most important decision she'd ever make, and standing in the center of her office she pressed her hands to her stomach, calculating the risks.

With each step Elise took across her beige soft carpet, the more she missed Blake. He'd stuck by her during the Trinity Hospital disaster, the lawsuit, and all those horrible months while searching for a job. It didn't seem possible that he would desert her now, not when he knew how much was riding on the outcome. It was not right, him staying away, not when she needed him so much. Swallowing her pride, she reached over her desk and dialed the number to the beach house but hung up before anyone answered.

"I *can't* go running to him," she vowed in a rough whisper. "He was the one who made the decision to leave me to handle this. I'll show him I can manage alone."

The previous night had passed in a restless half sleep that had left her tired and edgy. Thirty minutes before her alarm had been set to buzz, she'd awakened on her own, opening her eyes to the disappointment of an empty pillow. She'd dreamed Blake had come home in the middle of the night, but as she quickly saw, his side of the bed remained untouched, the sheets as cool and unwelcome as the disturbing mew of the stray cat outside whose crying beneath her bedroom window had interrupted her fragmented dreams.

Once awake, she'd lain there thinking, discouraged about the future. Then, foolishly, she had padded barefoot down the wide upstairs hall to the guest room on the other side of the loft, hoping Blake might have settled in there during the night. Of course he hadn't, and the guest room had been as empty and still as the ache in her heart.

Elise threw off the pain of Blake's abandonment, took a deep breath, and returned to her desk. *There is no other way*, she finally decided, both dreading and anticipating the encounter. Tensing, she pressed the red button. Farren told her to come right up.

Before leaving her office she took a long hard look at herself in the mirror that hung behind her door, suddenly confident about her decision. What she was about to do was not just her only option, it was the right thing.

John Farren listened patiently as Elise told him, in halting starts and stops, about why she'd asked Darrel Grimes to test the water and soil on her property. She told him about the petition Yusef Kirk was going to circulate to stop the county from condemning Flatwoods, letting him know how sad she was to hear that the community where she had been born was on the verge of being wiped out. She did not tell him that she was posting the bond to delay a court order to start the destruction. But understanding that blocking the razing of Flatwoods might mean blocking ScanTron's expansion plans, she told him she had no choice. Elise also described Damita's last hours to her boss, and how she'd held her dying friend in her arms and promised to do what she could to keep others in Flatwoods from experiencing the same kind of horror.

Unashamed of the tears that rolled over her cheeks, she related to Farren how she had canvassed the neighborhood, gathering stories from frightened residents, many of whom had known her since birth. Another thing that Elise deliberately withheld from her boss was Carlos Rico's involvement, for at that moment, Carlos's interest in helping her did not seem an appropriate topic to discuss.

After baring her soul and asking for his guidance, Elise sat nervously, twisting her wedding band around and around on her finger. Farren, who didn't speak for several torturous minutes, sat calmly, eyes riveted on a crystal picture frame that held a photo of his wife. When he finally raised his gaze to Elise and leaned forward, she held her breath, easing back from him, fearing he might reach out and slap her. Braced for the worst, she waited for his order to pack up her desk and clear out.

It was terrifying to contemplate being fired again, and in the space of a few seconds, the humiliation and anger she'd suffered before rushed back in stark clarity, making her pulse begin to race. It was all she could do to keep from breaking down as she matched John Farren's steely gaze.

"You're an extraordinarily loyal person," Farren finally said, rubbing his thumb over the expensive leather trim on his desk blotter.

She focused on his hands. To Elise, he looked like one of those elegant, ruthless English detectives, about to grill his suspect until she broke down and confessed. In a quiet, proper tone, he added, "That's an admirable trait, loyalty. In professional and personal matters."

"Thank you," Elise muttered, unsure of what else to say. His cool, aloof tone frightened her more than the verbal dressing down she had expected. But Farren was not one to raise his voice. She'd sensed that the first time she met him, and that was probably why she had taken the chance of telling him what was on her mind. She wanted to please him, impress him, and gain his trust and respect, but if coming to his office had destroyed her chances, there was little to do about it now. Glumly, she sat like a stupid lump, silently praying he'd forgive her nearly subversive activities.

"Then you understand . . . ," she started.

"Oh, yes. I understand why you feel so torn and why you feared telling me about this earlier. But I want you to know that I am not angry. Not with you." He shoved aside the pile of papers he'd been signing when she came in and carefully placed his thin gold pen back into its ornate holder. "Unfortunately," he went on, "a company like ScanTron doesn't move quite as fast as one would hope. The work order for the tests I promised you has to go through internal channels. Even as CEO I have to respect the chain of command. The paperwork I have to deal with is inefficient, but I assure you the order for the testing is in the works."

"I didn't mean to imply that you had gone back on your word," Elise said, feeling absolutely awful that he was being so nice. She'd come into his office prepared to let him know how disappointed she was in him, and he was already apologizing to her. He was the CEO of a huge international corporation with a lot more on his mind than following up on her request that water be tested in a drainage ditch. "Perhaps I've been overanxious," she admitted.

"Perhaps," Farren agreed. "Elise, you know our business is security. All kinds of security. From small personal alarms to sophisticated systems for airports and high-tech government facilities. From bodyguards to complex internal investigations." He paused, then broke into a comforting smile, dissolving his stern expression. "From what you've said, I think I've hired you for the wrong position."

With a start, Elise jerked forward. "I don't want to leave ScanTron, Mr. Farren. I love my job. I love working here. I hated feeling guilty over what's been going on, and that's the reason I wanted to clear things up, before they got so complicated that you might misunderstand my motives."

"Oh, no," Farren laughed, eyes crinkling in amusement. "I'm not suggesting you be terminated; I was only implying that maybe you would be more valuable to ScanTron in our internal investigations section. You seem to have that curious nature that is prerequisite for our investigators. What you've told me this morning makes perfect sense, and I want you to stay with it. Keep looking for the answers, because ScanTron cannot afford to take this lightly, though Al Patterson may have led you to think otherwise."

"Keep on the trail of the presence of Zephron?" she clarified, unable to believe what she was hearing. "Don't you have professionals who can do this for the company?"

"Yes," he said. "You. And you have at your disposal anyone here at headquarters who might be able to help."

"I can't thank you enough," she said, unclenching her fingers that had been twisted together since she sat down.

"There may be things that you see, or hear, from the people that would mean nothing to an investigator sent to Flatwoods to gather information. And . . . I'd like to evaluate Al Patterson's performance. Your cooperation would be most helpful."

Heart racing, Elise asked. "You're concerned about the way Al Patterson manages the Tide County office?"

"Yes." Not blinking an eye, Farren explained. "He's been there a long time and I know his employees are loyal, but that is not always a plus. Al seems dedicated to the company, but not to the team. I'm afraid he's been operating outside the corporate guidelines far too long. I've let him do his own thing, so to speak, without much interference, but now I'm more convinced than ever that what I need at the coastal complex is a true team player. I hope Al has not had anything to do with the delay in the tests I ordered. If that turns out to be the case, he will not be with us much longer."

Hearing Farren's reservations about Al made Elise almost sag with relief. She had a lot she could tell Farren about how Al treated his employees, especially Darrell Grimes, but decided to wait. He was much too busy to sit and listen to her tales; besides, her mouth was as dry as a wad of cotton and she was suddenly ready to leave.

"As far as ScanTron's plans for expansion," Farren said, "the fire and explosion may have already settled that question. If the costs and time necessary to clear the burned-out warehouses off the property and make it suitable for rebuilding are prohibitive, we may abandon that site altogether and relocate the facility on land that we own twenty miles up the coast. Nearer to our Beaumont location. But if we clear the site and decide to acquire the land where Flatwoods is in order to expand, I assure you we will pay fair prices for the properties and assist those who need help in relocating. That's the hard truth of the way business is done."

"I think that's fair," Elise replied.

"Our corporate property analysts are studying our options now, so nothing will be settled for some time to come. But your speculation about our illegally forcing people out of their homes is not valid. However, if the place is dangerous and about to be condemned, that decision is entirely up to the county authorities."

"Yes, I see," Elise agreed. Realizing he'd given her all she needed, Elise stood. "I appreciate your taking the time to talk with me and explain what has been going on. It makes the situation understandable and my role in this more clear." She turned toward the door.

Farren lifted a hand, halting her departure. "As for the tests you independently commissioned to find out what might have caused your friend's illness and ultimate death," he paused, sighing, then shook his head. "We all should be lucky enough to have such a friend."

Elise smiled.

He mirrored her expression, eyes gentle, assessing her, then assumed a fatherly voice. "I want you on my team, but you have to settle some things with yourself, Elise. If you can't balance your allegiance to ScanTron with your concerns about the public at large, not just Flatwoods, you will never be of much value to this company, or any other, for that matter. You must resist the temptation of being drawn into taking sides. Don't allow yourself to be used as a pawn by those who definitely have their own agendas."

Farren's words pierced Elise with their edge of truth, drawing Blake's warning back to her mind. "You are right, because that's exactly what was happening."

John Farren continued. "I know. And if you cannot resolve this turmoil, you have to move on. Think about it, seriously, before you tell me what you want to do."

The bitter remarks she and Blake had hurled at each other returned to haunt Elise and she swallowed the truth in Farren's candid assessment. She should have listened to Blake after all. He had had every right to be worried. In response to Farren's expectant expression, she answered his unasked question. "I don't want to resign," she admitted, humiliated that she had lost sight of what she should have been doing to better serve the company.

"Good," Farren said. "I'd hate to lose you. You can have a long, successful career with ScanTron, but I need your full attention, regardless of the pressure you feel from those who are looking to you for answers to difficult questions. I know the feeling. I've been in your shoes. Sometimes you think you are letting people down, but believe me, Elise, you aren't."

Elise felt a rush of gratitude. "Thanks for being honest with me. You've been so kind, and I appreciate the opportunity to prove to you that you didn't make a mistake by hiring me." Elise unclenched her balled fist and extended her hand across Farren's desk. "I will work on what you've suggested," she promised. "But I do want to ask another question," she added, unable to ignore what had been burning in her mind since yesterday evening.

"What?"

"Why hasn't the EPA leveled with us? With the public? Justin Snyder must know about the presence of Zephron. If he'd been open with that information, it would have been helpful."

Farren shifted in his chair. "I'm not a chemist or an environmentalist, Elise. I have the headache of running this company from behind this desk and trying to keep the shareholders happy. But I'm not so far removed from the day-to-day operations of ScanTron to be unaware of any remotely hazardous materials that may have been stored or manufactured at the Tide County complex. I have to be absolutely certain about things as serious as that, and I assure you that the chemical Zephron did not originate with us, though preliminary indications may make it appear that way. As for Justin Snyder's decision to withhold the test results, I'm curious, too. I think I'll give Mr. Snyder a call and have a little chat."

When Elise returned to her office, all she wanted to do was lock the door, put her head on her desk, and savor the sense of reprieve she felt. But when she found Carlos sitting in the chair in front of her desk, waiting, she knew her troubles were far from over.

She closed the door and crossed the room, slipping into her chair as she greeted him. "Did you get my message about Darrell's fax?" she asked.

"Yes, and I saw the TV coverage of the bombing at the Fairmont."

"Wasn't that awful?"

"Could've been worse," Carlos said, scooting forward, obviously excited. "The leaflet the reporter held up to the camera was what interested me."

"Me, too. I've seen that black oval with the parrot inside it before, a long time ago, on a large metal can that belonged to a neighbor."

"The bird is a quetzal, not a parrot."

"A what?" Elise asked.

"A quetzal, an exotic South American bird. The color, the crest, the long tail feathers. The national symbol of Guatemala, *and*"—he shook an index finger, emphasizing his point—"the logo for a brand of fuel oil sold in Mexico called Tecal." He paused, then added in a low voice, "Tecal is owned by the Puro Corporation."

"Oh, great," Elise groaned. "Now I see where this is headed. The leaflet said 'Your oil kills,' right?" Elise asked, unsure of her high school Spanish.

"Right."

"Does that imply a connection between Tomás Aloyo and Puro?"

"That's something I plan to check out next. But this morning, I telephoned El General to verify something else."

"And?" Elise prompted.

"The Lacandone Indians in his grandson's mountain camp were

using Tecal in their stoves and lamps. . . . Zenoyo believed that the fumes from the oil poisoned his wife and that the fuel was deliberately sold to his followers by Puro."

"The Vargas family."

"Exactly. They control distribution of Tecal oil in Mexico and Central America. El General is convinced that the fumes from Tecal oil killed his granddaughter-in-law, Rosalía, and made many others in the camp so sick."

"And that's why his grandson crashed the ScanTron gates?"

"Right," Carlos said. "Zenoyo was angry, convinced that ScanTron was the source of the contaminated oil. The crash was a mission of revenge, and Darrell's fax adds credence to that theory, doesn't it?"

"But there's no evidence to connect ScanTron to producing, packaging, or exporting any petroleum-based products," Elise defended, going on to tell Carlos of Farren's assurances.

Carlos removed a folded sheet of paper from his briefcase. "Maybe it's going on and Farren doesn't know it."

"Impossible."

Circling Elise's desk, Carlos stood beside her. "Maybe not. Look at this." He spread the paper open on Elise's desk. "This is Tide County."

Elise frowned. The oddly marked map was no more than a network of lines separating large tracts of land with stars dotted across the landscape. "Are you sure?"

"Yes, this is what the area looked like before there was a single factory, refinery, or housing development. Before there was ever a community called Flatwoods."

"Where'd you get this?"

"Oh, I have my sources."

"Okay, so what am I supposed to be looking at?"

"An old survey map made by a man who planned to dig for oil. The stars are sites where Sammy Ostermin, an early wildcatter, thought there might be oil. He was a German immigrant, and in 1899 did find oil right there." Carlos stabbed the map with a finger, indicating the crossroads of Thornhill Road and Highway 8. "It wasn't much of a find, but he managed to pump a few barrels out of the ground. It soon dried up and he moved on to another spot. But after seven months of dry holes and shoving his rigging from place to place, he gave up, packed his gear, and shipped it east—up the coast to the Spindletop fields."

"Are you saying Ostermin believed pockets of oil were all over the area?"

"Yes, according to the records that he left behind. After he sold his leases to rice farmers and ranchers, who claimed the area and settled on it, all talk about oil in the area died. Soon after, Global Oil built its first refinery at the coast. Then housing for the workers began to fill the empty land. Other industries began to move into the area and in time no one remembered that the feisty German wildcatter had ever been there before them."

"Oil reserves under ScanTron? Under Flatwoods?"

"Or abandoned wells that were never really pumped," Carlos suggested.

Elise shook her head, skeptical. "I've never heard about any of this, and my mother's family has lived in the area since the early thirties."

"Well, you can thank my expensive but thorough informant for digging all of this up."

Elise studied the lines on the map that separated one tract of land from another. "What if oil is under ScanTron, and somehow it's become contaminated with that bacteria that would create Zephron? Isn't it possible that the intense heat from the fire and explosion could have created prime conditions to burn out the leaky old wells and produce the kinds of fumes capable of making people sick?" Elise grew excited as she put the data in Darrell's fax and Carlos's information together.

"Could be," Carlos agreed. "And if this contaminated oil got into the wrong hands, on the market, then into the deals of brokers . . ."

"Disastrous," Elise broke in.

"Deadly," Carlos echoed.

"Only one way to find out," Elise said, lifting a brow, considering the challenge. Farren's words of warning and fatherly advice churned in her mind. "Meet me at 2307 Thornhill Road at six-thirty tonight," she said, assessing Carlos's beautifully tailored Giorgio Sant Angelo suit and Picasso-patterned tie. "Better wear something suitable for exploring."

"Exploring?" He grinned. "Charred rubble, perhaps?"

"You got it."

"I'll be there."

CHAPTER 28

The dull tap of Al Patterson's pen as he thumped it on his scratched desktop continued for three full minutes. As he leaned back in his chair, feet propped on his desk, the methodical tapping helped keep his mind focused and his mouth shut as he listened to Farren's summary of his conversation with Elise. Al bit his tongue to keep from telling Farren that he was well aware of what Elise and Darrell Grimes had plotted together and that he had already made up his mind what action was needed. The two were traitors, he thought. Subversives. That's what he would call them, and if it were up to Al, he would have fired Elise after the first staff meeting they'd had in his office.

"That's outrageous, underhanded, and I wouldn't tolerate it," he told John Farren, yanking his feet off the desk, slamming them to the floor, and settling his thick body into a sitting position. "Listen, Farren, don't let that woman take matters into her own hands. She'll embarrass you. She'll ruin your reputation along with this company's if you allow her to undermine all the hard work I've put into creating a good working environment for the ScanTron employees down here. I guarantee, she's nothing but trouble."

"Let's not overreact," Farren quietly suggested.

"Hey, I thought you were the one worried about going by the book."

"I am."

"Well, let me warn you. If word of Elise Jeffries's subversive actions gets to the board, I'm telling you it's not gonna fly. Based on the lie she told on her application, you know she never should have been kept on. The board of directors will want her gone. Fast." He sniffed in disgust. "At least she oughta be taught a lesson."

"Hold on, Al," Farren cautioned. "No real harm's been done."

"Not yet."

"I agree that it's a rather delicate situation, but I want to see how she handles herself now that we've had a little chat."

"Chancy stuff," Al grumbled.

"Did the inspection crew I requisitioned ever show up down there to take those samples?"

Rolling back his hulking shoulders, Al hesitated, then said, "Nope. Never showed." Glancing up, he looked out the large window and saw Pete busy at his desk. He could see the work order still sitting there. "I'll get somebody to follow up on it."

"Good. I promised I'd push the paperwork through. Give it priority, okay?"

"If that's what you want."

"It is. We need to handle matters like this in a more timely manner."

"Following the chain of command just slows things down," Al said, triumphant. "See why I don't care too much for going by the book?"

Farren made no reply.

"If Elise Jeffries respected this company, she would have been willing to wait," Al went on.

"Oh, I don't know. She's a concerned citizen as well as an employee. Believe me, she's well aware of how sorry I am that the tests were never repeated. I was glad she brought her concerns to me."

"Jesus, Farren, I told you not to make that woman permanent, didn't I? She's going to stir up a lot of attention. She's not the type we want or need speaking for the company. Can't you see that now?"

"Oh, she'll do fine. I'm not worried. She's genuinely concerned about the people of Flatwoods. Nothing wrong with that. In fact, I applaud that trait in my staff, and I believe her loyalty to the company is solid. I did caution her about following those who play on her sympathies and have a hidden agenda."

"Yeah, like that bastard Yusef Kirk. He's really dangerous, Farren. A fanatic and a troublemaker, and it wouldn't surprise me if he blocks the county's plan to condemn the houses where we've been planning to expand. Things look bad."

Farren cleared his throat. "Al, I've been rethinking the expansion plans. That site may not be the best location after all. Let's wait and see how this turns out. And would you have a talk with Darrell Grimes? He has to work independently, but he needs to know that he came close to working at cross-purposes with the company in this matter. Give him a gentle reminder about the potential for conflict-of-interest issues in this situation, okay?"

"Sure, don't worry. I'll take care of him." Al looked through the plate glass window again, his icy stare now focused on Darrell, who was concentrating on entering data into his notebook computer.

After ending his conversation with Farren, Al buried himself in the pile of order forms Pete had put on his desk. It took an hour to track down the materials to fulfill an order for a company in New Jersey, but he'd managed, paying dollars for the same components his facility used to manufacture for pennies. But he was feeling rather triumphant about the deal when there was a tap at the side of his open door that brought him quickly back to reality.

Looking up, Al's mouth dropped open; then he scrambled to his feet as blood drained from his face. "What the hell are you doing here?" he said.

Smiling sweetly, a woman dressed in expensive black silk slipped into Al's office and closed the door firmly behind her. She pulled off her round sunglasses and her wide-brimmed straw hat, then shook out her mane of thick dark hair, letting it settle in a ripple of ebony waves on her small shoulders. Moving to a faded love seat opposite Al's desk, she sat and made herself comfortable.

"Come." She patted the space next to her. "Sit down with me, Mr. Patterson." Her thick Spanish accent was more alluring than annoying. "We need to talk."

Al did as he was told.

"I have been informed that one of your employees . . . a Ms. Jeffries, I believe, plans to do some exploring tonight."

"I, I don't know . . . ," Al stuttered. He wiped his brow and cheeks with a swipe of one hand.

The woman crossed her legs, making no move to pull down her skirt, which rose high on her suntanned thighs. Unconcerned about exposing her long, slender legs, she made a tsk, tsk sound, pursing her bright red lips. "I'd stop her if I were you."

Too shocked to reply, Al stared at the only member of the Vargas family he'd ever met in person. As lovely as Carmela Vargas was, he knew she was equally dangerous, and he was terrified to have her sitting beside him with such a determined set to her smooth, square jaw.

"Your relationship with my family has been a good one," Carmela went on. "You made a lot of money. Providing my father with what he needed to get those mountain rebels off our land was a smart move, but don't be stupid. Surely you will not allow this woman to destroy you, or to implicate my father in what's been going on. Not now. The timing is terrible, Mr. Patterson, and my father is most upset."

The sunset was, without a doubt, the most beautiful Blake had ever seen, but as he sat on the shady balcony of his parents' stilted house, gazing over the blue-green Gulf, the sight almost made him physically ill. Without Elise at his side, it meant nothing. All the seascape did was stir up memories of the many hours they'd sat on the beach holding hands, making plans for the future.

Blake lowered his eyes from the red-orange blush sweeping the turquoise horizon to watch Junior scampering along the hard-packed shore as waves lapped and sucked at his ankles. He was a good boy. A handsome child, with so many of his mother's traits. And when he bent down to pick up a shell, which he immediately ran to show his grandparents, Blake smiled. Junior was a free spirit, having a wonderful time, while his father was as sullen and unhappy as a grumpy old hermit who had been pulled from his protective shelter.

Blake shuddered, wishing the heaviness in his heart would ease. Taking off to the seashore to ponder his troubles had not been a good idea. He flinched to see his mother let go of his father's hand long enough to take the shell from Junior and congratulate him on his find. That his parents were so happy, strolling the shoreline hand in hand, hugging, stealing kisses, made Blake hurt even more. Seeing them so carefree and deeply engrossed in each other only increased the anguish that he'd been trying to disguise all day. His mother and father looked far younger and happier than he felt right then, and it was difficult to watch, so he turned away, feeling like the heel he knew he was.

But Blake also knew he was lucky. He had loving parents, a handsome son, a chance to be his own boss, and a wife he had treated shabbily by running away from their problems. He loved Elise more today than the day he proposed eleven years ago, and all he wanted at that moment was her arm around his waist, her head on his shoulder.

The memory of his jealous outburst was a shameful one, and he cringed to recall the words he'd hurled at Elise. What in the world had pushed him into overreacting like that? He'd been boorish and stupid, a real jerk—over Carlos's simple request to speak to his wife. Elise ought to be furious.

And running off to hide at the beach on the pretense of spending quality time with Junior? Leaving Elise alone on their anniversary? God, *that* had been a selfish, childish, impulsive thing to do. He'd never been a vindictive person. What was wrong with him now?

He had telephoned Elise last night, though she hadn't even bothered to pick up the phone. Or, he thought uneasily, had not been at home to answer. She was probably running around Houston with

Carlos or that radical lawyer, Yusef Kirk, trying to save the world instead of concentrating her energy on her husband and her son. Instantly, Blake was ashamed of himself for letting his imagination run wild.

Lowering his head into this hands, he sat glumly, sick of wallowing in the mess he had made of his marriage. Why was he so mad at her? What, after all, was really eating at him? He'd never been jealous of Elise before and he knew his behavior was as totally foreign to her as it was to him.

Elise was confident, committed, and capable, no matter how difficult the situation might be. She was a survivor, a go-getter, and he'd always admired that about her. She had triumphed over the Kitzmiller setback, the devastating lawsuit, and had even been able to forgive her traitor. And look where she was now. In a top spot with an international company, moving forward with her career.

He was proud of her, damn proud, so why didn't he feel happy? Lately, it seemed he couldn't get excited about anything, not even his fast-approaching entrance into the business world with a venture he knew would succeed.

But will it succeed? he worried, the insecurities he'd been trying to suppress for weeks beginning to surface again. Blake squeezed his fingers around his can of beer until the aluminum container buckled. He couldn't let his fears get the best of him now, and neither could he let Elise find out how absolutely terrified he was about failing, but withdrawing his resignation was out of the question.

He felt empty and numb. *All I can do is give it my best shot,* he decided, tossing the can into the green plastic recycling basket at the edge of the porch. Unable to sit still a minute longer, he was weary of feeling sorry for himself. He was wasting good time.

Facing the spectacular view of the Gulf alone was about as enjoyable as sleeping on the beach with mosquitoes buzzing him all night as he'd done with Junior and his friends last night. Well, they'd have to go it alone from now on, Blake decided, tugging on his blue canvas cap.

Taking the outside stairs that led to the beach two at a time, he ran across the hard wet sand and picked Junior up. Kissing his son

and parents good-bye, he promised to return as soon as he could—
and not without Elise.

The gasoline cans in the bed of Al's pickup truck clanked noisily as
he bumped over the unpaved road. The summer drought had turned
the deserted back road into a wavy path of cement-hard ridges of
cracked dirt that undulated like the side of an aluminum washboard.
The radio played softly, some catchy country tune, and Al hummed
along with the whining vocalist as he drove parallel to the chain-link
fence that enclosed the burned-out complex.

The headlights of the truck beamed long and yellow, dispersing
the newly fallen shadows of late summer dusk. A jackrabbit popped
out from beneath the fence and ran into the road, stopping to stare
in fright at Al, its red eyes glowing like fiery coals. Suddenly, it made
a beeline into the wall of thick bushy shrubs on the opposite side of
the road.

Al laughed aloud. The wide-eyed rabbit reminded him of Darrell
Grimes and the look he expected to see on the chemist's face tomorrow when Al ordered him to clean out his desk. Hunching closer
to the steering wheel, Al hugged it, satisfied with himself for deciding
to handle the matter swiftly and cleanly, without a lot of explanation
or discussion. He'd simply tell Grimes that Farren disapproved of his
unprofessional liaison with Elise Jeffries and that his conduct had
been unacceptable. Agreeing to run independent tests, the results of
which might prove embarrassing to ScanTron, had been unwise. Such
tactics could not be tolerated or excused. And if Darrell Grimes dared
to protest his firing, Al knew he could get Pete or Bill to verify that
Darrell had always been belligerent and difficult to work with from
the day he came to the coastal complex.

*I'll get rid of that pretentious prick tomorrow, but now it's your turn,
Ms. Jeffries*, Al thought, swinging to the right, rumbling to a stop
under a low-branching elm whose limbs created a curtain of privacy.
Jumping out, he went to the back of the truck. *Farren can't save you
this time*, he mused, lifting a heavy metal can.

CHAPTER 29

Elise drove onto the grassy strip that separated Damita's house from Mose Greer's bungalow and angled her car into the backyard so that it could not be seen from the street. She turned off the engine and looked around, hoping no one had seen her come onto the property, though she doubted any activity on the block missed the keen surveillance of the Robins twins. Elise wasn't exactly hiding, but she didn't feel like explaining to her neighbors why she would be in Flatwoods tonight, especially with Carlos Rico.

This had better work, she thought, sensing an ebb to the rush of adrenaline that had buoyed her courage all day. Fatigued by the blur of telephone conversations with Judy Talor and members of the local press, who had wanted ScanTron's reaction to the aborted assassination of the Mexican dignitary, she wished she were back home, curled on her sofa eating chocolate ice cream instead of preparing to break into the shattered remains of the eerie warehouse on the other side of the street.

If this hunch doesn't pan out, I'm through, Elise decided, not daring to press her luck any harder. With Blake gone and her future with ScanTron at risk, she knew it was time to finish playing detective and move on to another assignment. *This is about as far as I can go for you, girlfriend,* she whispered to Damita. *Enough is enough, okay?*

Glancing into the rearview mirror of her Volvo, she saw the lights from Carlos's car as he crept along the curb looking for her house number. She got out, walked to the front lawn, and waved, motioning for him to pull off the street and park in the yard behind her car.

"Let's go inside," she said as soon as he got out and crossed the grass toward her.

Unlocking the back door, they entered the near-dark kitchen. The long summer day was working to their advantage as there was still just enough light coming through the curtained windows for her to find what she was looking for.

From a table in the center of the room, Elise picked up a flashlight and turned it on. In the single beam she examined the jumble of cleaning supplies, rubber gloves, and the various handyman tools Blake had left in a cardboard box on the table.

"Do you know how to get inside the complex from the rear?" Carlos asked, taking a pair of pliers, a crowbar, and a wrench from the makeshift toolbox. He slipped them into the black nylon bag he had brought with him, adjusting it on his shoulder.

"Yes," Elise assured him. "We can follow the ditch at the back of the property. It runs parallel to the fencing behind the houses on this end of the road and will take us right up to the back lot. There's no gate, but we ought to be able to get over the ScanTron fence without too much trouble."

"Or through it," Carlos said, sticking some wire cutters into the hip pocket of his black khakis.

"Here," Elise offered, handing him a pair of canvas gloves, then shoving similar ones into her shirt pocket.

"Good. Let's get our bearings," he said, unfolding the county survey map he had brought along. He held it under Elise's flashlight. "You've been in the complex before, right?"

"Yes. I toured it shortly after I was hired."

"Where would the company records have been stored?"

"In the Administration Annex." Elise leaned closer, examining the markings Carlos had sketched on the map. "About here," she said, putting a finger to an area on the east side of the complex. "I remember the building, because that's where I was introduced to Darrell Grimes. He was inside filing reports in a huge walk-in vault that had drawers marked with metal tags. Al, who had been showing me around, said the vault contained invoices, work orders, and memos generated by headquarters that were related to all activities at his plant. I recall that he was not adverse to expressing his displeasure with Farren for requiring that all documents be kept for seven years, even though most of the same information was also stored on computer disks. Al really started in on Farren. I was shocked when he began complaining about how much he hated answering to the head office. I could tell that he resented being told what to do, and was an independent manager. That's when I also realized that Al had little respect for Farren's management style and he wasn't shy about admitting it."

Going to the corner of the kitchen, Carlos gently kicked at a pair of knee-high rubber boots. "Yours?" he asked.

"They were Damita's, but I did wear them a few times while Blake and I were clearing weeds from the yard. Good thing, too, because we found snakes, rat droppings, and fire ant beds all over this place. Pretty dangerous."

"Better put them on," Carlos advised, testing another flashlight. "No telling what we'll run into on the other side of that fence, and it's not going to be easy to get to the annex building."

"I know," Elise said, pulling on the boots. "The ATF crew used a bulldozer to make their way through the complex when they were doing their investigation, and a lot of the debris has been shoved into huge piles all over the place. Could be rough going, even once we get inside."

Elise walked to the front of the house, her big rubber boots making muffled thumps on Damita's thin carpet. She looked out the window. Across the road, the hulking mass of twisted steel that used to be ScanTron lay like an ominous mountain, a taunting dare, challenging her to try to unearth the secrets buried beneath it. Turning from the window, she nodded at Carlos, who was waiting for her at the open back door.

"Ready?" she asked, lifting her chin, giving Carlos her bravest smile.

"Yep. Let's go," he replied, stepping ahead of her through the door.

They walked briskly to the rear of the yard, slipped through a space where broken slats had rotted out, and headed down a sloping embankment to the murky gully that lay like an open wound in the empty field behind the backyards of the abandoned properties.

Squatting down, Carlos traced a beam of light onto the dull trickle of water, then stood and said, "God, this is awful. I'd be worried, too, if I had something as putrid and foul-smelling as this at my back door."

Elise nodded, bracing one hand against the fence to steady herself as she climbed back up to level ground. Facing south, they began walking, moving cautiously toward the plant by following the ditch as it snaked its way along the leaning, vine-covered fences that defined the route of Thornhill Road.

Dusk rapidly deepened into shades of night, and soon the gray shadows outlining the complex began to fade. As the definition of the hulking mass of steel dissolved against the near black sky, Elise nervously trained her flashlight to the ground, feeling apprehensive about her decision to enter the shattered facility. The pale yellow beam gave little comfort as she inched her way along the weed-choked path. She was trying to follow the shallow gully but it became thinner and thinner until it completely disappeared in a stand of brush.

Once the trail had run out, Elise raked the ground with her light, then shined it up and onto the chain-link fence surrounding the ScanTron property. It rose about seven feet from the ground and the bottom section had been threaded with barbed wire. Looking through the crisscross of metal links, Elise could see a soft indentation in the ground where the gully came to the end of its course.

"There it is! That's the origination point for the drainage ditch. See where it's all dark and soft."

"Yeah," Carlos said, going up to the fencing. He laced his gloved fingers through the small diamond-shaped openings and peered through the barrier at the sunken wet pool that spread out for close to twelve feet across in the dry brittle grass. He stepped back, gauging the height of the fence and the feasibility of trying to scale it, then took out his pliers, reached up, and began cutting and bending back broken links to create a large, jagged hole.

"I'll go through first," he told Elise, sticking one foot into the break that he'd created above the spiked barbed wire. He jammed the flashlight into his jacket pocket, hoisted himself up, and wiggled his body through. With a flat, muffled thud, he hit the ground, landing on the balls of his feet. Springing forward, he regained his balance, then glanced around, as if he feared someone might be watching. "Jesus, this place is creepy," he whispered, reaching up to take Elise's hand as she swung herself down beside him.

She fell to her knees, despite Carlos's hold, but refused his help getting up. "I'm okay," she whispered, brushing dust from her jeans, searching the darkness to get her bearings. "This way." She moved in front of Carlos, hurrying toward the marshy area on the east side of the complex, dodging a fallen utility pole.

The place looked like a bombed-out wasteland that had been leveled by an atomic blast, devoid of any life, with the exception of two huge oaks that seemed to create the boundaries of the low wet spot. The ancient trees resembled giant gnarled umbrellas—twin relics of a time when their precious shade would have sheltered herds of cattle grazing the coastal plain under the punishing Texas sun. They had obviously been spared during the original construction of the place. Beneath the trees there was a large patch of grass that had somehow managed to escape the flames.

Feeling rather satisfied to have made it inside without a hitch, Elise let out a long breath and relaxed, moving the light up, then back down to the discernible sink in the earth at her feet—the source of the foul-smelling stream that ran behind her house. She stomped the ground with her thick rubber boots and felt it give.

Carlos did the same, walking over the marshy edges, testing the damp earth that was surrounded by hard, crusty layers of burned ash and dust. The soil where they stood was damp and soft, three shades darker than the earth only five feet away.

"Sounds hollow under here," Elise whispered, stomping again. "What do you think?"

"I don't know. Let's check it out."

Using the crowbar he'd brought from the house, Carlos stuck it into the ground. It sank easily but proved nothing. He pulled it out, looked around, then picked up a long rusty pipe and pushed it into the same spot. It plunged smoothly down about three feet before the sound of metal striking metal confirmed their suspicions.

"Something's down there," Carlos said softly, removing the pipe. He stuck it in again and again, testing various spots within the soft dark area. The same tinny sound rang out. "There's a piece of metal buried here. Maybe a trapdoor or a cover of some kind."

"We can't dig to see what it is."

"No," he agreed, "but if you remember the county grid we looked at, this is about where that second pipeline would have been."

"The one with no connection to Global's easement?" Elise prompted.

"Possibly," Carlos replied. "What we need are blueprints of this place, the construction designs, and unless the annex is now a pile of dust, I'll bet those records are still in the vault. Intact."

"Over there." Elise pointed to a heavily damaged structure that used to be the Administration Annex. Steel posts and iron beams that had made up the infrastructure of the annex jutted out of the rubble like black fingers clawing the sky. The roof at its front had partially collapsed. The forlorn structure, with its metal sheeting peeled away and its windows turned into black gaping holes, had been stripped of its pride and purpose.

Elise and Carlos jogged across a pitch-black clearing and stopped at the remains of the annex. They began to pull away chunks of wood, splintered paneling, cracked Sheetrock, and what was left of the collapsed roof in order to get to the blown-out door that was hanging by charred hinges.

They stepped inside, hands to their noses. Elise began to cough as cinders blew up into her face.

"Whew! This is ghastly," she said into her palm, sniffing the burned odor that rushed at her.

Their footsteps crunched the grit and ash that lay three inches deep on the concrete floor.

Carlos flashed his light to the left, then the right, above his head, and back down to his feet. "You're sure this is the right building?"

"Positive," Elise mumbled, afraid to open her mouth. She could make out enough of the interior to feel certain that they were in the right place. Remembering the first time she'd come there, she turned immediately to her right and felt her way along the lone remaining center wall that she hoped would lead her to the room where the records vault ought to be.

Shoving a blackened computer monitor out of his way, Carlos followed, kicking aside the remains of a ruined oil painting, stacks of water-stained papers, and several soggy boxes of what might have been padded envelopes and manila folders. The crumbling, water-damaged Sheetrock wall gave way beneath Elise's hand, falling in chunks each time she and Carlos touched it as they groped along.

They inched deeper and deeper into the pitch-black building, easing toward the fireproof vault at the back of the annex, taking care not to disturb anything that looked vital to keeping the structure from collapsing.

When they reached the buckled door of the room that contained the records, Elise pointed excitedly, running her light over its warped metal frame. "This is it."

"Stand back," Carlos advised, wedging the crowbar into the side of the door. He pressed hard against the bar, then stopped and searched the debris for something heavier to use as leverage, settling on a piece of iron he pulled from beneath a cratered file cabinet. As he tapped the crowbar, urging the door to open, it creaked and groaned, resisting the pressure. Then suddenly it popped, forcing dust into Carlos's eyes.

Elise rushed forward, shining the light over Carlos's shoulder as he searched the rows of gray metal cabinets, some of which still had their contents labels intact. When he came to one marked CONSTRUCTION, he opened it and began yanking out thick folders.

"Tide County Complex!" Elise cried out, snatching the file from the drawer. "That's it!"

From his hiding place between two sheets of corrugated roofing that had been reduced to shreds by the explosion, Al had watched Elise and Carlos enter the remains of the Administration Annex. The outright resentment that he had felt for Elise since the first day he met her flashed through him, warming him more than the lazy humid breeze that stirred the heavy night air. Loathing brought a bitter taste to his mouth, and Al squinted past the tangle of downed telephone wires and seared cable that lay in piles before him, his eyes fixed on the spot where the stealthy intruders had disappeared.

Retreating farther into the shadowy recess, he bent his head backward and took a deep breath. A film of perspiration dampened his face and gathered in pools at the base of his neck. He wiped his slick, trembling palms together, then pulled a crumpled towel from beneath his short-sleeved shirt. Al blotted at the moisture on his cheeks, frowning, thinking about Elise and Carlos, anxious to follow them and stop their galling interference in matters that did not concern them. Squatting down, Al wrapped the soft towel around the neck of the gasoline can he had brought from the truck, tipped it slightly, and saturated the bulky rag.

"Nosy bastards," he grumbled, setting the gas-soaked cloth aside. He reached into his canvas bag and pulled out another rag. Grimacing, he sloshed the rancid-smelling liquid over it, spilling an equal amount onto the ground. He was unable to control the quaking that made his hands seem to have a life of their own, and he cursed under his breath as he went about his mission.

His thoughts remained centered on Elise. He had to get her out of his way. His plans had been moving along just fine before *she* showed up, flapping her lips, spying, digging around. All this talk about saving her hometown. Hogwash! She'd shown little interest in her birthplace for the past decade; why was she suddenly obsessed with doing what was right?

Al spat in disgust, his spittle sending up a puff of ashy dust as it hit the ground and dissolved. He should have been the one handling the media all along, and probably would have done a much better job than Elise. And as far as calming down the residents in the area went, what good had it done to bring in a local? Obviously Farren's plan hadn't worked. The people in the county were just as angry and disappointed and wary of ScanTron as they'd been on the night of the explosion.

Al swallowed his rage. If Farren had shown him the least bit of confidence, this situation might have been avoided. But no, that had never happened and he'd been dreaming to think that it would happen now. If Farren wanted to give his hand-holding support to Elise, fine. But he'd soon see he'd made a mistake. No one at the main office had ever cared about what Al had had to put up with at the isolated facility. All the board cared about was the money he generated and the worldwide recognition his operation brought. The fact that Elise had been kept on staff despite her criminal record was appalling. Who else would have been given such special treatment? And why this nobody Elise Jeffries? Was it because she was a woman? Because she was black? Or was it because Farren feared a discrimination lawsuit if he dared remove her from her position?

Damn government quotas were gonna ruin this country, Al silently cursed. That was the only thing that executives worried about these days. Who needed the goddamn politicians and government agencies interfering with a manager's right to hire and fire as he chose? They were always ramming some crazy theory down his throat.

"Farren thought I wouldn't make it down here when he assigned me to this godforsaken place," Al muttered, a frown of distress creasing his brow. "Well, I made it, all right. And I worked hard to create my niche in this business. No way is this snippy brown-skinned noser going to mess things up for me."

Al knew that his future was on the line, and he wasn't about to stand by and let Elise Jeffries do him in. His little venture had been rocking along just fine, and even the accident could have worked to his advantage. If Elise hadn't started poking around, the case of the ScanTron fire would have been closed by now, chalked up to a drunken illegal driving off the road. Al had to smile despite his apprehension.

"Ha!" he spat out, unable to resist a muffled laugh at the irony of it all. The crazy truck driver's suicide mission had provided the perfect cover to his lucrative but played-out deal with Tecal. He never could have dreamed up a better one himself. He'd squeezed every dollar he could from the Vargas deal and had been hoping for a way out of the dangerous liaison. It would have ended perfectly if Elise hadn't been sent to speak for him. Now he had Carmela Vargas on his tail.

He remembered the day he'd agreed to the deal. When the land was purchased for the plant, he'd had no idea that it was riddled with abandoned oil wells or that they contained anything other than pure old-fashioned crude. He wasn't a chemist. He'd never heard of Zephron. Not until Ramón Vargas, the chemist at Tecal, had filled him in on what was lying beneath his feet. The family had been illegally pumping the abandoned wells for years before they discovered the unusual, potentially profitable contamination. ScanTron's arrival did not set them back. Al had quickly moved on their offer.

Well, Al thought. What the Vargases did with the crude after he sold it to them had never been his concern. He wasn't about to start feeling guilty. People got hurt, sick, and even killed all the time when security measures were breached. It was a tough business. A good one for him, and all he had wanted was to walk away, a little richer, a lot smarter, and retire at his beach house on Padre Island.

But he guessed he was going to have to get his hands dirty after all. He had to stop that twit of a reporter and Farren's precious protégée because, obviously, no one else was going to do a thing.

"They're history," Al vowed, standing, picking up the gas can, creeping toward the inky hole where Elise and Carlos had disappeared. He walked on the toes of his boots, dripping a stream of smelly liquid as he advanced toward the shell of the building.

At the entry to the Administration Annex, Al tugged at the door, easing the buckled panel firmly back into place. He stuffed the gas-soaked rags around its base, then tossed a match on the pile of cloth, tearing away from the scene as soon as he saw blue-and-orange flames begin to flicker.

CHAPTER 30

Elise dropped to the floor beside Carlos, settling in among the memos, computer printouts, cost estimates, and architectural sketches he had dumped on the ground. Quickly scanning the contents of the thick folders, Elise grew despondent. There were no blueprints, no schematic drawings of underground installations, or anything to indicate what might be buried in the ground between the huge oak trees.

Together, Elise and Carlos sorted through the papers, tossing routine communications, construction bids, and work orders aside until they came to a folder crammed with slick trifold pamphlets advertising ScanTron's services. Elise fanned the brochures while Carlos held the flashlight on the papers. When she came to a stiff rectangular pamphlet with the familiar black oval and colorful quetzal on the front, she yanked it free.

"Look!" She dropped the ScanTron leaflets, letting them drift like petals to the floor. Clipped to the brochure were what appeared to be invoices that had been completed by hand in blue ink.

"What do you think?" she asked, opening the trifold brochure, handing the invoices to Carlos.

"Can't tell," he said, examining the pieces of paper.

Elise held the brochure closer to the light. "Tecal Oil," she read, then, realizing the rest was written in Spanish, offered it to Carlos. "Here. Translate this."

"Tecal. The finest, cleanest-burning fuel you can use," he read. "Inexpensive, reliable, and locally refined."

"Yeah," Elise muttered, "and deadly, too."

Carlos gave the brochure back to Elise and flipped through the stack of invoices, then made a whistling sound through his teeth. "Well, well. These are receipts and old invoices for the delivery of thousands of gallons of crude. Dated from the early eighties"—he shuffled the receipts—"up to a few months ago."

Elise lowered her head, pushing a fall of hair from her face. "Let me see." Her heart began to race. "These receipts are signed and approved by . . . oh, I should have guessed, Al Patterson." She shuddered, both disappointed and excited. "This could be exactly what we need. ScanTron *has* been trading in crude." She sensed that the hunt might be coming to an end. "The supplier listed is ScanTron International, Tide County, Texas."

"Oh, boy," Carlos gloated, revved by the connection. He flashed his light over the Tecal brochure more closely, turning it over several times. On the front of the card was the date 1982. It was a promotional piece, advertising Tecal with quotes from satisfied customers who gave testimonials on the company's superior products. Some said they used the oil in their home heating systems and business establishments. Others testified to its clean-burning quality and how convenient it was to use in propane stoves. On the back of the promotional piece was a black-and-white photograph of Tomás Aloyo, the current minister of agriculture of Mexico, who was, at that time, the president of Tecal Oil. He was standing beside a small tanker truck that had the quetzal symbol on its side.

"This look familiar?" Carlos asked, tapping the photo. The truck was parked between two huge spreading live oaks. There was a fat suction hose running from the back of the tanker into the ground.

Elise gripped Carlos's arm. "That's the back lot." She spun around, thinking. "That picture had to have been taken right here. On this complex."

"I agree. That's the low place near the fence, where we jumped over and stuck that pipe in the ground."

"The main pump is buried there."

"Right," Carlos agreed.

"But why would Farren deny that ScanTron was ever in the petroleum business? Why lie? If there was oil under his property, why not take advantage of it?"

"Maybe *Farren* wasn't in the business," Carlos suggested.

"You mean . . . this was Al Patterson's private venture?" Elise murmured, gathering up the records. "Working on his own? You think he was running this bootleg operation independently, under Farren's nose?"

"I sure do," Carlos said, standing, then reaching down to help Elise to her feet. He took the files from her and stuffed them under his jacket. "Being this far from the main office, Al was left to his own devices, and it's pretty clear he liked it that way. Now you know why."

Elise dusted off the seat of her jeans. "Do you think he knew the crude was contaminated? That innocent people were getting sick? Dying?"

Carlos shrugged. "Who knows?" Pointing his flashlight back in the direction of the entry, he shook his head. "Let's get out of here."

They groped their way back toward the front of the building.

"This is going to be one hell of a story," Carlos whispered. His mind was already engaged in churning up teaser copy. "International intrigue connected to a local company. Homegirl saves her birthplace by keeping her promise to a dying friend."

"Don't get too far ahead of yourself," Elise cautioned. "There's a lot still to be proven here."

"Maybe, but believe me, it's all going to pan out in time."

"How long do you think Patterson's little side operation was going on?" Elise asked. "Selling tainted fuel oil? I can't believe he knew what he was doing."

"He probably knew. He always struck me as a greedy, unethical son of a bitch."

Elise remained silent, grabbing the back of Carlos's jacket, pressing closer, feeling faint from the stunning discovery. ScanTron, whether Farren knew it or not, might have been responsible for several deaths and most likely a rash of illness.

"Yeah, stick close to me," Carlos said, glancing over his shoulder at Elise.

She opened her mouth to reply, but the taste of fresh smoke rushed in, taking her breath away. "Carlos! I smell smoke."

He stopped. "So do I. Wait here!" Leaving her, he raced ahead but stopped halfway up the corridor, turning back to yell, "There're flames up there. This place *is* on fire!"

"Carlos!" Elise shouted. "Come back!"

He rushed up to her and curved one arm over Elise's shoulder, squeezing it firmly, almost roughly, pushing her back from the tongues of red-orange flames raging at the building's entrance.

"What are we going to do?" she said, coughing, covering her nose with fisted fingers.

"There must be a rear exit." Carlos shouted, jerking her deeper into the building, retreating from the hissing flames.

"I think so, but it may have been blocked when the roof fell in," Elise worried, horrified to see a fresh burst of fire boil up from a pile of trash at the end of the corridor. The firemen who had combed the place for hot spots had created mountains of debris throughout the structure.

A loud crack vibrated the unstable building and a section of heavy steel framing fell from somewhere above their heads. It crashed to the ground, forcing a thick cloud of soot, ashes, and pulverized concrete to fly upward in a powdery arc.

Elise screamed, terrified as much by the smoke and fire as the stinging spray of stone and wood that struck her in the face. Bending over, she wrenched herself from Carlos's protective hold and started running toward the back of the building.

"Jesus!" Carlos shouted, following her, his flashlight trained on the cavernous space ahead. "There's got to be another way out!"

Elise untucked her shirt as she ran, yanking it from her jeans, pressing it to her nose. Blindly pressing forward, she stumbled over a jumble of downed electrical wiring, nearly falling.

Carlos grabbed her by the arm and held her fast. She clung to him, digging her fingers into his arm, waving the tail of her shirt in front of her face as she desperately fanned smoke from her eyes.

What is going to happen to us? she worried, frantically regaining her balance. Her mind was whirling like the dizzying layers of smoke that were rapidly engulfing the annex. The place had been stone cold when they'd entered; now it felt like a furnace. Elise smelled the gasoline and she knew the fire was not the result of a flare-up from smoldering embers. Someone wanted her and Carlos dead.

The smoke thickened. Yellow flames licked the deserted corridors.

Carlos tugged Elise's arm, and together they dodged heaps of scrap metal and dangerous wires until they came to what should have been the rear exit doors.

"No!" Elise shouted. An interior wall had collapsed in front of the doors, burying the exit under a mountain of broken concrete, splintered framing, and steel support beams. The blockade resembled the kind of barricade set up by street fighters during an urban rebellion. The tangle of debris was impenetrable, making escape totally impossible.

"We can't move that," Carlos said, swinging his flashlight from the top to the bottom of the barrier.

Elise plunged into the mess anyway, clawing at the rubble, managing to shove a roll of scorched carpet aside. The pile trembled, disintegrating, then tumbled down, nearly burying her, but Carlos yanked her to her feet. She scrambled back, screaming.

"Leave it!" Carlos yelled, pushing himself between her and the cascading debris. He reached back protectively, trying to shield her from the dangerous situation.

But Elise avoided his touch, darting around him to plunge, once again, into the dusty pile of rubble. "We've got to get through this. Carlos! We'll die in here if we don't!"

When she grabbed a heavy, upended conference table that had

been anchored in place by three metal file cabinets and began tugging, Carlos took her by the shoulders and shook her roughly, forcing her to turn around and look at him.

"Stop it!" he shouted, shaking her. "Elise! You can't get through that. You're wasting time."

"We *have* to," she sobbed, tears making thin tracks in the film of soot that smeared her face.

"We can't," Carlos shot back. "The roofing beams alone weigh a ton. Elise! Calm down."

Her eyes were glazed with fear, and for a moment she was frozen in Carlos's grip. Then she slumped, whimpering into her palms as she pressed her hands to her face, trying to gain control. Biting down hard on her bottom lip, she forced herself to focus on Carlos, barely able to see him through the thickening smoke. "Okay. Then what can we do?"

"First, stay calm. We have to think." He stroked her arms.

She glared at him, frantic to hear his plan.

"There's only one way out," Carlos said firmly, taking charge. "And that's the same way we came in. We've got to go back."

"No!" She shied away, horrified at the thought of racing through a wall of fire.

"There are broken windows at the front," he said, moving directly toward the blanket of flames.

"But they may be too small to get through."

"We have to try," he said, squeezing her arm more tightly. "Come on."

"Carlos. That's insane." Elise yanked free and refused to move into the terrifying curtain of black smoke.

"We've got to make a run for it," he yelled above the hiss and cackle of burning wood. He tugged Elise by the wrist, pulling her lips so close to his they were nearly touching hers as he spoke. "Elise! Listen to me! Look at me!" Shaking her, he tried to make her focus on his plan. "We're going to get out of here. Now!"

Petrified, she nodded numbly. But over his shoulder she could see that the flames had risen higher, and as they licked their way closer an eerie sharp hiss echoed through the hollow structure. The narrow corridor they'd groped their way along earlier was glowing deathly red.

Carlos stripped off his windbreaker and grabbed Elise, urging her to follow him to the far side of the building where several partial inside walls were still intact. "Up there!" He pointed to a small set of broken windows. "We can slip behind that wall over there and reach that window. Once you get through it, run like hell."

From where they stood, Elise could see a small, high window toward the front of the building that had been shattered during the explosion. It was chancy, though possibly their only route of escape.

"You make a beeline to that wall. Jump up on that overturned desk. You can fit through the opening," he ordered, tossing his jacket at her.

Numbed, she caught it and wadded it against her chest. When she hesitated, he shoved her roughly, propelling her forward. "Go!"

Elise stumbled forward, then froze and looked back, certain she would be running to her death.

"Elise! You've got to do it! Keep your face down! Look at the floor. And once outside, don't stop running until you get over the fence. Don't look back; I'll be right behind you. Run like hell 'cause if there is oil under this place, we could blow like fireworks on the Fourth of July."

Holding her breath, Elise bent low, covered her head with Carlos's jacket, and plunged into the flames.

Carlos stumbled backward, terrified for her. "Go! Go! Don't stop, Elise!"

She didn't stop—she didn't dare—and firming her hold on his jacket, she hugged it over her head and slipped behind the roaring wall of flames. Forcing her mind to go blank against the incredible heat, she jumped atop the rickety overturned desk and propelled her body through the broken window.

Once her feet hit the ground, Elise ran, not looking back, and she didn't slow down until she came to the hole in the fence where she and Carlos had entered.

Scrambling through the jagged opening, she lunged forward, falling onto the grassy slope that banked the side of the gully. She screamed as her body tumbled toward the murky water, and rolling, rolling down, she kept her eyes and mouth firmly shut, bracing herself to hit the gully and its toxic contents.

"Elise!"

She felt strong hands clasp her feet.

Someone stopped her fall.

"Elise!" The strong hands pulled her from the edge of the ditch.

She could not see who it was, but when Blake's familiar touch grazed her cheek, she broke into tears.

He turned her face toward his.

Opening her eyes, she gasped in relief and held him tight, unable to speak for the space of a second. Then the words tumbled out— raw with terror, husky with tears she had been too stunned to shed.

"Blake. Oh, Blake." She buried her face against his shirt. The familiar smell of him brought instant calm. "Thank God, you're here."

"I had to come," he murmured against her hair. "But what the devil are you doing down here? Why were you in there?"

Elise stiffened, unable to answer, then she pushed him aside and stared in disbelief at the hole in the fence. "Carlos." She grabbed the front of Blake's shirt, pulling herself upright. "Carlos is still in there. Blake! He didn't get out! Please, help him."

Puzzled, Blake gave a short gasp of surprise. "Carlos? Why was he—?"

"Oh, Blake," she cut him off. "There's a small window at the back of the building. Please, go!"

It took a moment for her plea to register, but when it did, he kissed her quickly, then let her go. Picking up Carlos's jacket, Blake wrapped it around his head, scaled the fence, dropped to the other side, and ran flat-out toward the blaze in the distance.

Elise slumped onto her back and stared at the bright stars overhead. Her heart was tight with worry, her mind aflame with fear.

"Come back to me. You've got to," she whispered.

The tower of fire that clawed and raged at the entrance to the annex building had heated the entire enclosure. Drenched with sweat, Blake stopped to watch the roiling flames and catch his breath as he gauged the danger of trying to go in. Looking up, he could see the small broken window where Elise must have escaped, but now it was funneling fire.

Racing closer, Blake shouted up at the building. "Rico! Where are you? Rico!"

The smoke thinned for a second and Blake saw a dark shadow move on the roof.

"Carlos! Down here. It's Blake Jeffries!"

Carlos managed to poke his head through the drifts of smoke, coughing as he yelled, "Can you get something up here?"

"Hold on," Blake shouted. The red glow from the fire cast an eerie light, and he frantically scanned the shadowed area for something to prop against the building to help get Carlos down.

A loud roar, then a crash split the air when another section of the roof caved in. Carlos screamed and raced farther away from the rapidly approaching wall of flames. "Hurry! This thing's gonna go!"

Without thinking about whether or not he could move it, Blake grasped the end of a rusted steel beam and shoved it toward the building. Crouching down, he managed to get it onto his shoulder, putting his sessions of weight lifting to the test. He stood, balancing the beam as he inched closer and closer until he could prop it against the wall. Once it was secure, he raced around to the back end of the support and began pushing as hard as he could. The beam slid upward. Carlos stepped to the edge and when the beam had been positioned about three feet from the top of the roof, Blake yelled, "You'll have to jump!"

Carlos hesitated, clearly frightened. But when the flames began licking closer, he filled his lungs with air and jumped. He managed to grab the rough piece of metal and steady himself before wrapping his legs around it. Hand over hand, like a kid on a set of monkey bars, he was able to make his way down, but when his feet hit the ground, he buckled and fell.

"Hurry," Blake said, helping Carlos to his feet, but the reporter could not stand.

"Shit, I busted my ankle!" he shouted, groaning with pain.

"Lean on me," Blake offered, slipping his arm around Carlos's waist.

Elise heard the two men stumbling over the hard-packed ground and felt the earth beneath her vibrate as they thumped down on the safe side of the fence. Lying there, she could hear the crackle and pop of the sizzling fire and the sounds of fire trucks screaming in the neighborhood. Elise closed her eyes, then squeezed them tightly.

"Well, it looks like we did it, girl," she whispered to Damita.

CHAPTER 31

I t was him! Yes, sir. It was *that* man." Mary Robins shook a finger at Al Patterson, who was struggling to free himself from Yusef Kirk's firm hold.

Managing to get free, Al sputtered in rage as he flailed his arms at Mary. "You don't know what you're talking about."

Yusef tried to recapture Al's hands, but he balled his fists and held them up in the lawyer's face. "Don't you dare touch me again! Get the hell out of my face, you bastard."

Yusef backed off but remained with his hands poised, ready to grab Al if he tried to flee.

"I was going for help," Al yelled at the crowd that had gathered around him as soon as Yusef pushed him from his car. "This man interrupted me. He threw me into his car and has the nerve to accuse me of setting that fire!" He narrowed bloodshot eyes at the onlookers. "I had nothing to do with that fire! Nothing." He turned away from Yusef to glare pointedly at the two old ladies who stood beside the county sheriff.

"You were running away," Mary Robins insisted.

"Sheriff Parks," Yusef broke in. "You'd better check the back of this man's truck. See if you don't find some evidence."

"The devil, he is," Muriel added.

Sheriff Parks let out a disgusted grunt, then spoke in a resigned tone to the deputy hanging back in the shadows. "Billy-Joe, go on and cuff him. Put him in the car, then check out the back of his truck."

After the deputy clamped the handcuffs on Al and led him away, Parks walked over to Yusef, his chin flattened against his neck until his nose dipped low and he was able to look over the top of his rectangular half-glasses. "What about you?" His voice was firm and full of authority.

"Me?" Yusef righted his stance, positioning himself like a sentry guard on duty. "What *about* me?" he asked, as if daring the sheriff to implicate him.

"How'd you come to be out here yourself, Mr. Kirk?" Now Parks jutted out his jaw, suspiciously assessing Yusef.

"I was taking the back road to the Robins's house. Mary had called and said she wanted to sign my petition. When I spotted Mr. Patterson crawling from under the fence, running real fast across the road, I stopped my car. I saw him throw a gas can in the back of his pickup. Then I saw the fire, so I jumped out and managed to detain him."

The sheriff, who everyone in the county knew was Al's longtime hunting buddy, grunted, scowling at Yusef, before he turned back to the Robins twins, who stood with their arms around each other, trembling. "You ladies sure about what you think you saw?"

Mildred waved a hand back and forth, irritated to have to tell her story again. "Not what we *think* we saw, Sheriff. We're certain we witnessed the dirty deeds that man was up to. It was like I said. Me and my sister were sitting on our front porch waiting for Mr. Kirk when we saw *him*. Yes, I'm certain. That man. He was sneaking around in that area between the fence and the first warehouse on the back lot. The street lamp at the end of our road was fixed just this week, so we had good light. Our house faces the back lot so we could see him as clear as day. He was carrying a container of some kind, and real quick, he disappeared into the shadows."

"Then we saw smoke," Mary said, moving away from Mildred. She folded her arms across her chest, taking up the story. "No doubt about it. We recognized him as soon as we saw him. He's the one who used to run that place like a military compound. He never let a soul through those gates who didn't work for the company. Nobody ever knew what was going on in there. For years he was right in our faces; we saw him, but he never saw us. Every soul in Flatwoods knows who he is. It was him in there all right. I'm positive."

The chilling wail of an ambulance blared its impending arrival, and the onlookers grew quiet. The scream became louder the closer it came, and Mary peered into the night, her worried eyes focused in the direction of the siren. The emergency vehicle rounded a corner and thundered toward them. She followed the flashing lights with her eyes until the ambulance braked to a stop in front of Damita's old house. Mary turned back to the officer. "Excuse me, Sheriff," she said. "Are you finished with us?"

"For now," he muttered, making another note on his pad. "But don't leave the area. I may need to ask you two a few more questions."

Mary nodded. Muriel screwed up her face, creating a mask of wrinkles. "We been livin' in the same house on this block for fifty-six years. No reason to go anyplace now."

"Come on," Mary urged, pulling her sister away.

Sheriff Parks took Yusef by the arm, guiding him toward the road. "I want you to show me exactly where you saw Mr. Patterson come out from under the fence."

The two men left. Mildred and Mary hurried down the street toward the ambulance, their house shoes slapping loudly on the sidewalk.

In front of the house she'd inherited from Damita, Elise was kneeling on the lawn beside a body that was partially covered with a blanket. She stood when Mildred and Mary arrived. "I'm glad you two were on your porch tonight."

"Oh, yes," Mary agreed, then asked, "You okay?"

"A few scratches and bruises, but I'm fine." Looking down at

Carlos, she added, "And he's going to come out of this okay. Right?"

Carlos nodded weakly, a wry smile lifting the corner of his mouth. "Thanks to Blake." He rolled his head to the side, giving Blake a thumbs-up just as the paramedics knelt at his side. One of them set his bag on the ground and began checking Carlos's vital signs. The other examined his leg.

"And you?" Mildred asked Blake, who had stepped aside to let the paramedics do their job.

"Miraculously, I'm okay," he said, tugging the blanket he had given Elise more tightly around her shoulders.

Elise snuggled closer to Blake, tilting her face up to his. He kissed her lightly on the lips and held her close.

Suddenly, there was a loud boom. The jolt that followed the explosion made everyone rock back a few steps. Mildred cried out in fright.

Across the road they watched as the annex crashed to the ground. There was a horrific shower of sparks and black smoke. The people on the street fell silent as they watched streams of water from the fire trucks pound the smoldering ruins into submission.

"I'm glad you guys called nine-one-one as soon as you saw smoke," Blake said.

With a shrug, Mary reminded him, "Living in this area, there's always some emergency. We've had our share of scares."

"Yes," Mary conceded. "We've about worn the number out. The emergency center ought to know us pretty well by now."

"Well, thank you," Elise offered. "You two are the real heroes."

Mildred smiled. "Thank God the fire department got here so fast. The night of the first big fire, we thought they'd never show up. If that fire tonight had spread like the first one, no telling what would have happened. We could have lost our house, you know?"

Elise inclined her head but didn't reply, silently giving thanks that the duration and intensity of the fire tonight had not been severe enough to ignite the oil beneath the complex.

"How's my neighbor?" Mose Greer asked, coming from the knot of curious onlookers milling around on Thornhill Road.

"No problems here," Elise replied.

"And the reporter?"

"He's going to survive," Blake said, watching as one of the para-medics attempted to place an oxygen mask over Carlos's nose.

He brusquely waved it aside and sat up, clutching the folder of papers he had rescued from the fire. "I want to hold on to these, Elise."

She nodded. "Sure."

Carlos gave her one of his picture-perfect smiles, then seriously scanned the crowd. "I'll be back on the air tomorrow. With the *real* inside story."

"Please, sir, lie down," the paramedic ordered, placing a hand on Carlos's chest.

He resisted, but the medic insisted, urging him onto his back. Flat on the stretcher, Carlos quipped, "Don't forget to watch. Seven o'clock."

Laughter rippled through the smoky night.

"We'll be sure to tune in," Blake said, touching Elise on the arm. "Ready to go home?"

Sweeping a hand over her tired face, she tucked a wisp of hair behind her ear. "Oh yes, am I ever." Waving at the twins and Mose Greer, she let Blake guide her toward his car.

He kissed the top of her head, ruffling her hair lightly with his fingers. "We should celebrate this victory of yours."

"Ours," she corrected as Blake bent to open the passenger door. "But I think we have something more important than surviving this escapade to celebrate."

Blake glanced at her over his shoulder, a knowing grin on his face. "You're right." He straightened up and kissed her hard, pulling her body flat against his. "Happy anniversary," he murmured, tracing a finger down her soot-smudged cheek.

EPILOGUE

July 19, Two Years Later

Myra Camden handed the hammer to Fred, who moved one rung higher on the old stepladder, then pounded the red-white-and-blue fabric into place. Standing back, Myra admired her husband's handiwork. A tiny frown flickered between her eyebrows as she tilted her head to one side.

"Move it a little more to the left, honey," she suggested, judging the depth of the swag in the patriotic bunting that he was draping across the gazebo entrance.

Though June 19 was not the same as the Fourth of July, it was a kind of independence day for many blacks in the South, as it represented the day that slaves in Texas learned they were free.

"How's that?" Fred asked.

"Great. Now hurry up and get down. There's Carlos Rico with his television crew."

Fred looked toward the road. "Hmm . . . My, my. That's some limo."

They stopped what they were doing to watch as John Farren and his wife got out of the dark-windowed stretch limousine.

"I hope this decoration is dramatic enough. I want the perfect backdrop for Mr. Farren's speech." Myra tugged a wrinkled piece of the festooned swag back into place. "This is going to be a Juneteenth celebration that folks in these parts will not soon forget and it's going to show up great on TV."

Fred grunted, then tacked one more nail into the colorful drape.

"What do you think, Junior?" Myra asked her grandson, who was sitting on the railing of the octagonal structure, licking an ice-cream cone.

"Looks fine to me," he mumbled, taking another lick. "When can we eat?"

Myra laughed, shaking her curls. She put out a hand to help Fred down from the ladder. "Not until your mom and dad get here." Rolling up the extra drape, she added, "And after the dedication speech." Stepping down from the gazebo, she straightened the lapels of her fringed denim jacket. "Why don't you go and ask Mary Robins for a piece of bread, then go down to the lake and feed the swans."

"Okay." Junior finished his cone with a final lick, got up, and sprinted off across the grass, waving to a friend.

"Beautiful, isn't it?" Myra said, looking out at the crowd that had gathered for the dedication of Damita Chapman Park. "Too bad Mildred Robins didn't live to see this day. She worked so hard on the project."

Fred put an arm around his wife. "Yes, it's a shame. But it sure turned out fine. Especially since we know what a mess this place used to be."

They gazed over the huge expanse of green grass that was sculpted with lush gardens. A rainbow of colors spilled from the many flower beds. There were pink and white roses, shockingly purple petunias, and orange-red bird-of-paradise plants decorating the acreage that once had been covered with layers of ash. Brick footpaths wound through the riot of flowers, circling a man-made lake where swans glided over the surface and peacocks strutted along the shore. Across the road, the houses of Flatwoods sparkled beneath their shiny new roofs and gleamed with bright coats of paint. Not one FOR SALE sign could be seen on Thornhill Road.

Fred finished folding the ladder and started toward the van that he had parked in the roadside lot. Myra hurried to catch up, linking her arm through his. They strolled together past the huge blue-and-yellow striped tent beneath which were long wooden tables covered with white cloths. Trays of barbecue, corn on the cob, potato salad, and pinto beans were waiting for the visitors, along with the requisite cold watermelon and red soda water.

Myra squinted against the blistering noon sun. "It's hard to believe that ScanTron managed to create this park in less than two years," she said.

"Yes, quite a transformation, isn't it?"

"Mmm," Myra murmured. "Damita would be so proud."

Fred gave Myra's hand a loving squeeze. "Oh yes, but not as proud as I am of the part our daughter played in bringing this day about. I'm sure John Farren never would have dreamed of donating this land to the Flatwoods Community Association, after the money he spent cleaning it up and draining out those old oil waste pits, if Elise had not worked so hard to convince him that it was the right thing to do."

"With all the trouble ScanTron had to face over Al Patterson's nefarious dealings, is it any wonder the board of directors voted for this?" Fred stopped at the rear hatch of his new red van, opened it, and pushed the ladder inside. "A good PR move for ScanTron," he finished.

"Darn right," Myra said, giving him a hand. "Elise has done us all proud. She's helped save this community for future generations, and it wasn't easy."

Fred slammed the hatch shut. "Better get the band up there in the gazebo. Get the music going." He pointed down the road. "Looks like the guest of honor has arrived."

Myra put a hand over her eyes, shading away the glare, searching the dusty road. "Oh my Lord," she whispered. "This I *can't* believe."

"I'm not surprised," Fred chuckled, grinning at the sight of Blake's big Harley roaring down the road, with Elise, helmeted and clad in a black leather vest, sitting behind her husband holding on for dear life.

When they came to a stop beside the van, Elise pulled off her helmet, shook out her hair, and raised a clenched fist at her parents. "We're here!"

Myra Camden laughed her reply, "Right on, honey. Right on." Then she blew a kiss to her daughter.

· A NOTE ON THE TYPE ·

The typeface used in this book is a version of Janson, a
seventeenth-century Dutch style revived by Merganthaler Lino-
type in 1937. Long attributed to one Anton Janson through a
mistake by the owners of the originals, the typeface was actually
designed by a Hungarian, Nicholas Kis (1650–1702), in his time
considered the finest punchcutter in Europe. Kis took religious
orders as a young man, gaining a reputation as a classical
scholar. As was the custom, he then traveled; because knowledge
of typography was sorely lacking in Hungary, Kis decided to go
to Holland, where he quickly mastered the trade. He soon had
offers from all over Europe—including one from Cosimo de
Medici—but kept to his original plan, returning to Hungary to
help promote learning. Unfortunately, his last years were embittered by the frustration of his ambitions caused by the political upheavals of the 1690s.

2 1511 00048 2470

RICHMOND PUBLIC LIBRARY